for the night

A Sun Series Bonus Story

The Sun Series
Book Five

rae lyse

rae lyse books llc

Cover Design

Stefan P.

Image Attribution

LanaStock via iStock

Editing

Jenine Corneal of @imajinconsulting

content note

This is a **slow burn** adult contemporary romance that contains mature themes and subjects that may be disturbing to some readers.

The Sun Series
(Interconnected Standalone Series)

Saving Sunflower (Dominic and Claudette)
The Endgame (Josiah and Jade)
Bunny (Desmond and Logan)
Thirty (Natasha and Andre)
For the Night (Anthony and Venus)

He who finds a wife finds a good thing and obtains favor from the Lord.

— Proverbs 18:22

one

. . .

IT WAS the second day of school and Toriana Nunez still wouldn't say her name.

She was so quiet she hadn't even told the bus driver she didn't live at the apartment complex they dropped her off at the day before. She liked to hum, though—*a lot.*

"Is that 'The Wheels on The Bus' I hear?" Venus asked, peeking up from her phone at her desk.

Tori stopped.

"Oh, don't mind me. I thought I heard you singing." Venus waved her hand out to quell any embarrassing butterflies that might've been withering around in her tiny stomach. "I must've been hearing things."

Tori kept scribbling her purple colored pencil against the Puss in Boots coloring sheet Venus had dug out of her overflowing supply closet while they waited.

She had a big bush of soft hair that her mama kept twirled in two-strand twists with colorful barrettes at the ends and she smiled all the time. On the first day of school, Venus figured out that when she danced from side to side at her desk, it meant she wanted to help pass out snacks at snack time. She knew to call her "Tori," because her mama had written it on all of her belongings in permanent marker.

"Go 'head. Keep singing." Venus flung her hand out again as her phone dinged with another Tinder notification. "I'm enjoying it."

She wasn't actually singing, but she hummed so good that Venus' imagination filled in the ebb and flow of the nursery rhyme with the lyrics. It was great background music while she read Morris' messages. He was her first Tinder match that didn't make her skin crawl or make her question her own attractiveness.

"WYD?" She sighed. "Is that the only acronym he knows?"

It was possible. He had the audacity to type those same three struggle letters and press send at least three times a day, even though her routine never really changed.

"Nothing… still at work. What about you?" She read out loud and typed.

Afterward, she drummed her fingers against the stack of construction paper on her desk while staring at her response and analyzing it for any sense of desperation.

She held her breath until the lone "nothin'" popped up.

"*Nothing?* Okay, maybe men in 2023 are less forward. We've been texting for two weeks now. Who texts for two weeks and doesn't ask a person out? I could be a man for all he knows," she rambled. "I guess I gotta take the initiative here. 'Dinner tomorrow?' That sounds real grown woman-ish. Right, Tori?"

Tori sucked up a wad of mucus, coughed out a tiny choke, and then went right back to humming.

Venus pressed her thumb over Morris' profile picture and slid the other against the screen to zoom in. If her daddy—Malachi was there, he'd point out the hat Morris wore—an Atlanta Braves fitted cap. He swore only dishonest men liked the Braves.

"Sorry, Daddy," she muttered, rolling her eyes at the lackluster "a'ight" Morris shot back.

It was her third week perusing the dating app, and she was no closer to finding a decent dude than she was when she downloaded it at the advice of the school counselor, Logan. All she had wanted was somebody to fill the lull, on those quiet Saturday nights, when she didn't know what to do with herself. Now she knew what Daddy meant when he told her not to take dating advice from her married friends, as a single woman, but somehow Logan had snuck her way through the cracks as soon as she sat next to her in summer orientation.

"Nobody is meeting men at the grocery store or gym anymore. Get with the times. It's all about online dating!" Logan had exclaimed on their second lunch date.

As if *she* would know—she'd only been married for two years.

Morris was decent. He was clean cut, had a job at Wells Fargo, entertained her unhinged rants about her new cat Pepper with one-word responses and Logan swore he had a big dick. She said men with big dicks liked the Braves. Her theory was just as silly as Daddy's and Venus didn't think she should've taken dating advice from either of them because Morris was so blunt it pained her to ask him questions, and she saw a picture of him wearing grey sweatpants the week before—she was still searching for that dick print.

Two solid knocks made her jump and drop her phone.

Paula, the attendance clerk, scratched at her braids and dropped her phone into the crook of her neck as she pushed open the door. "Her daddy on his way to get her. I finally found part of her original registration form in one of the dry boxes in the basement."

"I thought you said you found her *mama's* contact information? Didn't you offer to call her—"

She walked off before Venus could ask how far Tori's daddy was, his name, or if she'd have to coordinate after school pickups for every kid whose parents kept sending them to the wrong address.

Thanks to a mysterious irreparable leak in the school's basement, most of her students' files were waterlogged and illegible, so Tori's daddy wasn't the only parent she didn't know and Tori wasn't the only kid with a disability she was unprepared for. She was still trying to figure out how to help Destiny Jefferson memorize the layout of the classroom so she wouldn't run into anything with her white cane.

She blew out a pathetic raspberry and checked the time on her phone—4:45 p.m. School ended at 2:45 p.m. Pepper was probably clawing at the front door in agitation because he didn't understand that she worked now. They didn't have endless summer days to stare at each other in her empty apartment.

She pushed her mouth into her best "trust me" smile and sat up straight. "Tori?"

Tori looked up from Puss and stared right at the coffee stain on her white button down.

"Can you say your daddy's name?" Venus asked.

She blinked once and then opened her heart-shaped lips while Venus gripped the edge of her desk.

This had to be it.

This was the moment.

She'd be twenty dollars richer tomorrow because she convinced Tori her voice wasn't scary on the second day of school, despite Daddy thinking his janitor superpowers were superior to her teacher ones. She kept having to remind him that Tori wasn't a floor that needed polishing. She was a kindergartner who probably needed speech therapy.

Venus twisted her lips and balled them together while her knuckles turned white. She held her breath and waited for a rasp of softness to flow from Tori's voice box.

Tori's eyes crinkled around the edges as her cheeks lifted. Then her mouth opened so wide Venus knew a Darius, DeJuan, or *Kayden* would pour out because that's what she called every kid's daddy at Hill elementary—Kayden. They all had names that were too young for the big responsibilities they had. Most of them couldn't even look her in the eyes when she talked to them, but they had tiny people calling them "daddy." It was weird.

She prepared herself to fake gasp as Tori's mouth opened wider and her eyes closed.

"*AH-CHOO,*" Tori belted out a wet sneeze that drenched Puss' purple face.

Venus pursed her lips and blinked. "Bless you."

Tori swiped her nose with the back of her hand and forgot about Venus again, so the melody to "The Wheels on the Bus" eased from the back of her throat while she kicked her legs back and forth.

"Boy, Kayden must really love 'The Wheels on The Bus,' huh?"

Tori didn't fling her head up and accuse Venus of calling her daddy the wrong name like Venus would have at her age. She just kept humming and scribbling until Venus didn't have a choice but to hum, too.

She picked up her phone again and stared at the dinner invitation she extended to Morris.

He'd sent a restaurant suggestion as an Instagram link. He didn't ask what she thought about the place or tell her what he'd heard about it. It was as impersonal as all of their other conversations.

She sighed, torturing herself with another Tinder prowl and "Wheels on the Bus."

"The wheels on the bus go 'round and 'round, 'round and 'round, 'round and 'round. The wipers on the bus go swish, swish, swish... swish, swish, swish..." She sang and scrolled past more men Tinder kept suggesting would pull her out of her post-divorce funk—podcast hosts, covert Kevin Samuel worshippers, gym rats, "entrepreneurs," social media influencers.

She cringed and sang, "I sure hope Kayden teaches you a

brand new song, brand new song, brand new song. I *really* hope Kayden teaches you a brand new so—"

"Hmm, that ain't how they be singing it on Gracie's Corner," somebody drawled in a smoky voice. "Who is Kayden?"

She stopped herself from choking on the rest of the lyrics while she tried to digest the voice.

It was masculine, raspy and so ATL it made her head ache. It sounded nothing like a Kayden, but definitely belonged to one because they were the only guys that roamed around Hill Elementary besides Principal Bivins, the gym teacher, and the janitor. This dude didn't sound like any of them.

Ugh.

How long had he been standing there?

She flung her head up.

This Kayden had a baby face, but not in that odd overgrown twelve-year-old boy way. It was the type of face folks envied because he'd look youthful no matter how many scowls he threw their way. A smatter of light freckles sat in sexy little bunches at the top of his cheeks. Suddenly she understood what other women meant when they said they'd came across a man that was "90s type of fine."

Her phone tumbled out of her hand again and landed on her desk as Tori stopped humming. She sucked another wad of snot up her nose while her daddy stared at Venus with judgy, heavy red eyes.

The nerve.

He wasn't that damn fine.

"School ends at two forty-five," she shot back, pushing away from her desk.

She rounded it and crossed her arms to cover the coffee splatter they kept staring at.

"Well, I got off at three-thirty." He crossed the threshold of her classroom and a skunky sweet cloud followed him. "I told Ms. Paula when she called me earlier. She said it was straight. She said you would stay and wait."

She tried not to be judgy like him and Tori, but if Daddy was there, he'd ask what damn job this boy had that let him clock in smelling like reefer with his pants hanging off his ass. Yes, Daddy still thought they called weed "reefer," and no this boy's exposed boxer briefs weren't supposed to entice her.

"Of course she did." She rolled her eyes, mentally drafting her complaint to Principal Bivins. "Since she volunteered my time, did she explain to you why this after school pick up was necessary?"

He glided up to Tori and fingered the purple Puss in Boots she'd been coloring. He smiled and then reached out, swiping the snot from her nose. Afterward, he wiped his hand against his sweats, leaving a wet trail along his thigh. Venus frowned and glanced at the Kleenex box he had passed up.

"Ms. Lucille says y'all didn't update Tori's transportation forms. Admin told me she had to bring Tori to the bus barn until they could figure out how to get in touch with y'all. So I told them it was best we hold Tori back today until we could get this straightened out."

She kept saying "y'all" because she didn't even know who was involved in Tori's care at this point.

"A'ight," he replied, pulling Tori out of the desk and slinging her backpack over his shoulder.

There was something in the air at Hill elementary that made all the Kaydens tight-lipped. They avoided eye contact, refused to answer their phones, gave one-word answers when she showed concern about their kids, and they weren't even a week into the school year. This Kayden was no different.

Tori's stubby legs dangled down his lean body and curled around his waist like she was accustomed to riding his hip.

Venus dropped her arms and sighed.

"Do you need help with the forms? She can't sit at the bus barn every day with Ms. Lucille and I can't stay here every afternoon waiting for you to get off work. I need to get home too. I have an appointment I'm gonna be late for."

Tori thrusted her arms around his shoulders while Venus talked to herself and he stared at the stain on her blouse. He was so stoic she planned to ask Daddy what kind of weed would make somebody so unresponsive.

"And she's not talking," she blurted without thinking. "She won't even say her name. Does she have an IEP I should know about? Unfortunately, I don't have access to some of the kids' files because of the basement flood. They...they sent out a note about it, but I know folks are busy..."

Her voice trailed off, and Tori and her daddy stared at her face now.

She shifted her hip and scratched the back of her head while also mentally drafting an email to Logan because this was *clearly* an IEP situation. She'd had shy kids before, but never any as shy as Tori. It was only the second day of school, but Tori never even indicated she *wanted* to talk. She didn't grunt or even whisper to her classmates. She just smiled and hummed.

He bit down into his bottom lip, then swiped his tongue against it.

His teeth were shiny, and she hated she even noticed they were. They weren't covered with the type of grills she remembered being in when she was his age. It was some new age shit where the gold wrapped around his teeth's edges and made her stomach twist a little because it reminded her of how out of touch she was.

"She talk at home," he spat.

"Okay, but she needs to talk *here*. I understand this is a sensitive topic and I can loop Logan in so she can provide some recommendations on next steps, but I need you to understand that most students thrive when there's structure in the home. I can walk you to Paula's desk and we can complete the transportation forms together."

Now she was rambling and getting nowhere with a coffee stain on her t-shirt and a Kayden staring at her like she was the worst thing that happened to him that day.

"Do you understand?" she asked.

And she'd lost count of how many times she said "understand."

Tori shoved her thumb into her mouth and sucked while her almond eyes darted from Venus to her daddy.

He snorted and yanked his sweats up at the waist. "You always like this?"

"Huh?"

"Are...you...always...like...this?" he asked, as if she was the one with the comprehension problem.

"Am I always like what?"

His judgy eyes scraped along her body, narrowing at her beat up ballet flats and then that damn stain again. "So judgmental."

"Excuse me?"

Her? Judgmental?

She still used water in her cereal when she was out of milk and she had put her lights in her ex-husband's name when she moved to Atlanta.

"I think this is all a big misunderstanding. I'm no—"

"I filled out the transportation forms *twice*. I filled one out in the front office after I dropped her off on the first day at the front of *this* school, like all the rest of the parents. Then I brought another one before I went to work this morning. So you took it upon yourself to make her stay off the bus and inconvenience me because somebody can't do they job? Like I asked Ms. Paula when she called, how many times I have to tell y'all we moved or how many ways it gotta be communicated? But don't worry, I'll tell Principal Bivins y'all losing paperwork and you tryna insinuate there's something wrong with my daughter."

Thank God for Daddy and his silky brown skin, because the shame that covered her body was hotter than an August day back at home. If she was any lighter, she'd be beet red.

She opened her mouth and choked on nothing because she didn't have a rebuttal for once.

He didn't even give her time to practice the boundary setting and healthy confrontation tactics her therapist Michole spent so much time teaching her before he walked off with Tori.

"Come on… come watch me fill these forms out for the third time—since I'm such an unfit parent with no structure and all," he called out over his shoulder while Tori gave her a longing smile with her thumb hanging out of her mouth.

two

. . .

"SO YOU HATE Munch's new teacher?" Tash snickered, swiping her tongue against the white rolling paper from her chair on Anthony's apartment balcony.

"I ain't say all that. I said they hire anybody at that school. It's a circus, bruh," he replied, kicking his feet onto the balcony rails from his seat beside her.

Munch's teacher had purple hair. Not like a muted purple, but a bright violet that jumped off her curls and made him want to touch them. And she needed a bib... badly. She also looked at him like a part-time daddy, as if he hadn't stressed all summer about Munch starting big girl school.

Tash peeked at him from under her blonde curls and smiled bigger. If he didn't know her, he'd think she was making light of the situation, but White Runtz just made her stupid giggly like a white girl.

"You said 'they hire anybody' when I asked about her. That's shady as hell and would definitely imply that you possibly dislike her, *funny man*." She shoved her sock covered foot under her ass and squinted as she twisted their joint up with too much seriousness. "You acting like sis isn't qualified to teach just

because she has purple hair or that Logan isn't a whole counselor there."

"Implying and explicitly stating something is two different
things, *shawty*."

"Hmm. Maybe."

Tash rolled the joint back and forth between her fingers while
he peeked through the blinds behind her.

Inside, his best friend Dre' twirled his finger around the ends
of Munch's last twist while nodding his head to the *Gracie's
Corner* episode they'd watched at least a hundred times. Munch
sat in front of him in a chair with her eyes closed and a belly full
of McDonald's as his fingers danced across her head. Her twists
had looked good to Anthony, but as soon as they pushed inside
their apartment with Dre' and Tash on their heels, she ran into
their bathroom and grabbed the edge control. It was a habit she
learned from her mama DeeDee, who'd gotten her hair and
makeup done just to sweat it all off while giving birth to her.

"She's a diva..." she'd said when the nurse slung Munch's
pale wet body against her chest.

She really wasn't. DeeDee had just forced her to be one.

The flick from Tash's lighter made him turn back to her and
sigh. He inhaled the light August breeze while he waited for the
joint.

He didn't start smoking papers until Dre' got out of prison
and fell in love with Tash and her tomboyish ways. Now, they
shared a joint at least once a week when she wasn't jet setting
across the country to dance for celebrities or teaching hip-hop
classes at the rec center.

Sometimes he hated when she left. She was the only female
he fucked with who knew the difference between the Braves and
the Falcons and she didn't judge him when he got high and
ranted for hours about how fucked up it was that Dodge was
discontinuing the Hellcat. They even fucked the same girl once.

A cloud of smoke billowed out of her red nostrils as she
passed the joint to him. "Y'all should have a parent-teacher

conference. You can formally meet her this time, voice your concerns, explain the situation."

He sucked in his own hit. "The *situation?*"

"Yeah, with DeeDee."

"Hell nah. Them folks don't need to be in our business. Logan don't even know what's going on and it needs to stay that way."

It was too early in the school year to be running off at the mouth to nosey school staff—Logan included. It didn't matter who she was married to. He always told DeeDee to keep niggas on a need to know basis. The only thing Ms. Thibodeaux *needed* to know was that Munch had family that cared. DeeDee's name was right there underneath "mother" on her registration forms in the front office and his was underneath "father."

"You're being difficult. The lady doesn't mean any harm. She's a kindergarten teacher for God's sake."

"A judgmental unprofessional ass one."

She hiccuped between giggles and snatched the joint from between his fingers. "Sounds like it's more going on."

"What you mean?"

She smirked and batted her long lashes as Dre' pushed the patio door open, swiping a loosie from behind his ear.

"A'ight, I combed her hair and that after school nap hitting something vicious." He scooped Tash's tiny body from her chair and slid into it, plopping her onto his lap. "What y'all talkin' about?"

"Nuney wants to fuck Munch's new teacher," she blurted.

Dre' howled out a loud laugh. "Swear to God?"

Anthony tried to widen his heavy eyes, but White Runtz made him lethargic, so he settled for waving his hand to shoo away Tash's lame joke. "Mannn. Ain't nobody tryna fuck on that lady."

Not even if she wore all the weird ass things that made him hard—like stained button downs, beat up ballet flats, and brown eyes that had experienced more life than his twenty-four-year-old ones had.

His head fell back against the chair and he stared at the hazy, red sky as the sun set. "I mean, she do got a fat ass, though."

It was fat, round, and so wide that it filled out every part of her cheap, polyester pencil skirt that would've made DeeDee cringe. Tash howled out a laugh, as if he couldn't notice a fat ass in the midst of being disgruntled.

The truth was, Ms. Thibodeaux had all the "good pussy" qualities him and his other best friend Josiah obsessed over—wide hips, a natural stomach that rounded at the bottom, and brown skin that probably darkened to a nice hue when she sat in the sun for too long. Her boring teacher clothes covered the rest of the shit he loved. He just knew there was a gang of stretch marks covering her ass, waiting on some lucky nigga to trace them with his tongue. The most tempting part of her was her face, though. It was heart-shaped with delicate fairy-like features. She didn't even need makeup.

"Look at him over there in fantasy land." Tash slapped her knee like she could read his mind. "You're a menace, bro."

"Ain't that like a conflict of interest?" Dre' shook his head, stealing Tash's lighter from her lap. "You can't fuck on Munch's teacher."

Not even if she looked like she hadn't had dick in a minute?

The pent-up frustration was in her wrinkled pert nose as soon as she flew from behind her desk to tell him off. Even the way her eyes flashed across his briefs screamed, "in need of good dick!"

"I don't wanna fuck that lady, bro. On God—I don't."

"Yeah, hope not," Dre' mumbled, sucking in a gulp of nicotine. "Handle your business like a grown man. Business always comes first."

"Yeah... yeah... whatever." Tash rolled her eyes. "You should do it. It'll smooth things over."

"I'm too fucked up for you to be playing devil's advocate

right now. Didn't I tell you Nuneyland was closed until further notice?"

It was especially closed for women like Ms. Thibodeaux because not only was she in need of good dick—she needed a good man attached to that good dick. It was obvious. Her left ring finger was empty, and he noticed the way she'd emphasized "Ms" with a red underline on her whiteboard. Bitter ass women like her never survived him.

"What the fuck is a Nuneyland?" Dre' asked, taking another drag from his cigarette.

"This lame ass nigga named his dick." Tash tilted her head up, letting him steal a wet kiss from her lips.

She giggled between smacks while Anthony rolled his eyes.

"Come on, bruh. Y'all talk way too much," Dre' muttered, pulling her bottom lip into his mouth. "And why you ain't got a name for my dick, bae?"

"This is exactly why it's closed." Anthony shook his head, crossing his arms into an X. "Fuck I look like, locked down like y'all? Ain't no good ever came to me while I was in love."

Tash snickered, pulling her lips from Dre's. "Dude been baby mama free for two months and already singing 'Love TKO.'"

"The problem was the person you was in love with," Dre' said. "You need to be with somebody that don't lie for sport."

Tash reached over, dangling the joint above his lips as if she was apologizing for Dre's outburst. They'd all had plenty of rants about DeeDee. Dre's wasn't even the worst. His granny Lola always said DeeDee's superpower was her ability to piss off every person she came across.

He smiled at Tash's pink chipped nail polish and shrugged while snatching the joint from her fingers. "Who cares about love and relationships? Fuck these hoes. They all just headaches anyway..."

And there wasn't time for any of it—at least not anymore. Apparently, he had loose ends to tie up that stopped him from living up to his full potential as a parent—that's what his lawyer

Lynn said once. She was always saying backwards ass, pretentious shit like that while making him do things he'd never done —like work a job for "optics."

Every time he clocked in, he thought about his mama Carlotta and the rest of the population that would spend their lives working with nothing to show for it but past due bills and chronic depression.

The patio door creaked.

Munch poked her head through the crack with her arm stuck behind her back and a smile. She dragged her face against her shoulder, wiping the sleep out of her eyes.

"What you got, Munchy-Munch?" he asked, flicking their joint on the ground and stomping on it before she noticed it.

She took off toward him with his shoe bouncing at her side and then tackled his legs because naps always lit her with a fire that overwhelmed DeeDee.

He pulled her up, running his fingers along the sleek baby hair Dre' had somehow tackled. He always told him and Josiah that knowing how to lay edges was required for girl-dads, but Munch didn't trust Anthony with her hair. They always ended up arguing about it.

"Let me see," he said.

She grinned with DeeDee's eyes and fat baby cheeks that he missed kissing and flung the shoe up at him.

"It's purple!" Tash rasped. "Sweet!"

Anthony groaned, turning the shoe over in his hand.

It wasn't purple when he bought it. Now, the icy white leather had deep purple swirls scribbled onto it and the tongue had intense purple dots like she'd been trying to draw a leopard's spots. The incriminating evidence was all over her white shirt and little hands.

Dre' tsk'd, snuffing out his cigarette. "Better nip that in the bud… *Daddy*."

"So you hate Nuney?" Logan asked, with her face buried in her phone as she sat behind her desk.

"Nuney?" Venus frowned. "Who's Nuney?"

Logan twisted her lips to the side and brought her phone up to them. "Desmond, the damn fish are still alive. I fed them yesterday."

She smashed her blue fingernail onto the screen, rolling her eyes. "Nobody told him to buy a damn pond full of high maintenance fish in Japan and ship them here so I can take care of them while he cooks for some Japanese dignitary's eightieth birthday celebration. Do you know how time consuming those fish were? I've been sending voice notes all day. I am *not* a voice note type of bitch."

They were ten minutes into their thirty-minute lunch break and Venus still hadn't gotten any direction on how to handle Tori and her combative daddy because Logan didn't understand how multitasking worked in a marriage yet.

She was supposed to have shot Desmond a vague update about his fish while Googling the nearest koi fish supplier and reassuring Venus she'd communicate with Tori's daddy about the problem at hand. She'd learn.

Logan tossed the phone to the side and sucked in a deep breath with her eyes closed. She was so tiny that even the round throw pillow she had under her butt did her no favors. Venus still towered over her from across the desk.

"Okay." She blew out a breath. "You can't hate Munch's daddy. It's only the first week of school."

"So, I'm gathering 'Munch' is Tori's nickname and 'Nuney' is her daddy's nickname, and for the third time, I don't hate the boy."

"Shit, *I'd* hate that lil' nigga if he told me off like that, but that's neither here nor there." She waved her hand. "I'll keep the referral open and you can monitor her for a few more weeks. Or if you feel strongly about it maybe you can suggest a conference and get him to sign the consent and agree to an eval this week?

Look, he *really* likes communication and you're the experienced one here. If you're suspecting there's a problem, it most likely is."

"You don't say?"

There was so much to roll her eyes at, that Venus settled on a deep negro sigh.

"Nuney" was worse than "Kayden" and she still couldn't believe it was *really* possible to see a dick print through grey sweatpants, but alas Nuney's dick was wedged right against his hip while he stood in front of her being judgy. Then there was Logan, being vague about why Tori would even need an evaluation if she supposedly talked so much at home like her daddy claimed.

Venus rubbed her temples. "So, I'm gathering that you *really* know Nuney and please tell me his real name because I refuse to call him that."

"What's wrong with 'Nuney?' We been calling him that since he was six and stealing Takis out the Citgo. Shit, I hope you checked your pockets when he left yesterday."

Venus pursed her lips, making Logan hunch over with a loud cackle.

"Okay, Desmond mentors *Anthony's* younger brother, DeShaun. Anthony's a good dude—a little eccentric, but good."

Venus had surmised the eccentric part when he breezed into her classroom smelling like a pound mixed with some chick's Bombshell perfume and looking her up and down like she was the problem.

She rolled her eyes. "So it's a family affair? I'm sure *Anthony* will be happy to tell you his version of our run-in at the next family dinner."

Logan snickered, straightening her back and reaching across the desk to grab her hand. "You, my friend, need dick."

She squeezed it like Sister Toy used to do when she'd go up to the front of Daddy's church and beg for prayer for her and Trey's marriage.

"Is it that apparent?"

Logan folded her lips under her teeth and nodded. "I know we're new in this whole co-worker friendship thing, but the lack of penis is in the tension in your shoulders, beloved. Relax them."

Venus' shoulders fell in a pathetic slump while Logan eyed the purple splatter on her tan and pink polka dotted button down. This time Treshawn Bolds gulped a mouthful of grape juice during snack time and then projectile vomited onto her chest.

"How long has it been?" Logan asked.

"Since?"

"Since ... you know." She nodded toward Venus' black slacks. "Since you got fucked."

Fucked?

Venus swallowed to quell her dry throat. She looked around Logan's coat room sized office while she tried to calculate the days and hours since a man fell inside of her.

There was that day last fall when she ran into Trey at H-E-B and told him about her planned move to Georgia. He had scraped his eyes across her chest and then beckoned her to their bare house where they fucked one last time. That couldn't have been the last time. *Could it?*

"Shit." Logan gasped. "You can't even remember the day. This is worse than I thought."

"Please—don't. I remember it."

At least, she thought she did.

"Okay, well, was it even good?"

It was just as uneventful as all the other times had been after their marriage fell apart, but if she told Logan that, she'd really look pathetic.

"Let's not go there."

"Okay, I'll be the bad guy here—you don't want to stay out of the game for too long. Plenty of people get second chances at love."

"How did we go from sex to love? They're not always synonymous."

"But they can be." She winked.

"I'm not looking for love. I've had enough of that."

The word even tasted bitter when she said it.

"So, you're looking for dick?"

"It sounds so raunchy when you say it out loud."

"Well then, what other reason would you be dating without a purpose?"

"'Dating without a purpose?'" Venus tsk'd, tossing her head back. "Does it have to be this complicated?"

"Yes."

She held in the rest of her rant for Pepper.

Were there not other like-minded divorcees who missed the hardness of a man, but not the responsibility of keeping one? Logan made it sound so ... bad.

"If you must know, the Braves guy wants to take me to Vaughn's tomorrow night with no indication he's looking for love or sex. Well, he didn't exactly ask me. I asked him, which was probably a huge no-no, but I'm so rusty at this shit that nothing feels right," she rambled. "I looked at their Instagram. There was no grass covered walls or hookah and he still hasn't canceled. These are all good signs. I think?"

Logan dropped her hand like it was on fire and made the sign of the cross against her chest. "Thank you, God."

"Please don't involve God in this."

"We need his strength, Veeny."

"And please stop trying to make that nickname happen."

"Listen, a good man will change your new post-divorce life and he could be that guy. You'll stop drafting those emails to Principal Bivins, you'll get rid of that damn cat, and you'll greet Nuney with a smile at this parent-teacher conference you're going to coordinate."

A glob of spit trickled down the wrong side of her throat and she choked. "Excuse me?"

"I love you, but that cat has got to go."

"I'm not talking about Pepper. I am *not* coordinating a conference with him. He's combative as hell and the way my mouth is —nuh uh. Nope. I don't meet with problematic, delusional ass parents alone."

Logan reached out and gave her hand a stern, church pat this time. "You are going to set up this conference because I have a backlog of evals I need to schedule between this school and the five other ones I'm responsible for. I don't have time to play referee between y'all. You're going to draft a prayer better than Ciara's and ask God to sprinkle every bit of the good man you deserve in this Braves dude. Then you will go and call Nuney and I will go figure out which East Atlanta fiend can find me twenty koi fish before Desmond gets back from Japan."

Logan's tiny nose wrinkled as she spoke in a gruff voice that would only sound good in somebody's pulpit. She swiveled around in her chair, swiping a crayon from under her desk and ripping a piece of paper from a notebook next to her laptop.

Venus groaned.

Being Logan's new co-worker friend was so chaotic.

Why did she ever find Logan's tiny self, enticing during that summer orientation? It was her smile—that had to be it. It was big, bright, and always lurking because she hardly took anything seriously. Venus even saw the way it turned her husband Desmond into a useless mound of pudding before.

Logan stabbed the red crayon to the paper and looked up with wide eyes that made Venus shift in her seat.

"Tell me exactly what you want in a man. The law of manifestation says you must be specific. He doesn't have to be the next man you fall in love with, but we want him to at least be worth your while."

Her demi wispies fluttered as she looked at Venus like one of those faux relationship experts her and her cousin Ginny watched on those cheesy matchmaking reality shows. "Tell me what he'll look like, how he'll treat you, how much money he'll make, how big his dick is, if he eats pus—"

"Logan..."

"Sorry. Anyway, tell me, friend. What tickles your fancy in a man?"

Venus shifted again while Logan forced her to stare into her eyes. They were like little brown orbs searing into her soul and relishing in the sweat prickling her armpits.

"Well?" Logan urged, waving her hand. "You're divorced. I know you got a running list of all the shit you want in your next man."

The problem was—she didn't, because marriage had drained all of that curiosity out of her.

She was only familiar with how Trey looked—tall and sienna skinned with broad shoulders and little twists that sprouted out of his head.

For ten years, he was the only man she loved, and he treated her with just enough respect in public that folks didn't side-eye him when news of their separation spread. They side-eyed her instead and gossiped about her inability to keep a happy home. And his dick? Mediocre at best. She'd even bargained with God about it after promising Trey she didn't think of her ex flings anymore because he was all she would ever need.

"You don't know what you want, do you?" Logan whispered.

A tiny choke flew from the back of Venus' throat.

"It's okay. It's okay," Logan reassured her, like a good counselor would do. "This is what I'm here for. Fuck Ciara's prayer. We about to draft Venus' prayer."

It was all ridiculous—even Logan's shoulder shimmying. Besides, she had wasted enough of God's time praying about love.

"Okay, close your eyes," Logan sang.

Venus widened them instead.

"Close them. Trust me. I used to do this with my high school girls. I've helped manifest clear skin, Drake tickets, and periods. I even got my mini-me Keyshia into private school. We will manifest a fine ass man with a big ass dick that doesn't wanna fall in love. See—I'm speaking it into existence already. Easy, right?"

"Oh my God." Venus groaned, tossing her head back and looking at the ceiling. "I'm leaving my future dating life in the hands of a manifesting midget."

A wad of paper struck her in the chest.

"Hey!" she yelped, giggling.

"Close them!"

three

. . .

LOLA EYED ANTHONY up and down behind her glasses as he dragged a frowning Munch, her McDonald's, her backpack, and her booster seat toward the front porch.

She sat the book she'd been reading on her lap and raised her eyebrow at him. "You look like a penguin."

He glanced at his black button down, slacks, and white apron. "'Preciate it...I think."

"Mhmm. I mean a handsome penguin, but still." She shrugged and looked at Munch. "Well, well, well... you still hanging tough with Daddy, huh?"

Munch curled her arm around his leg and stuck her thumb in her mouth as if she wasn't just screaming her new McDonald's order at him from his backseat. She ate one sausage biscuit for breakfast now because McGriddles made her "tummy feel gross."

Every time DeeDee said "fuck him" and whisked her away, she came back with something new—an extra space where a tooth had been, a new word she'd learned, or a new skill he didn't get to teach her. DeeDee didn't even let him teach her how to ride the bike he bought her last Christmas and now she knew the word "shit" and how to use it in a sentence.

"Well, you can't lay up under me all night and not talk to me while he's at work," Lola added, raking her fingers through her silver hair. "'Cause I ain't gon' be in here talking to myself."

He pulled Munch by the shoulder and nudged her toward Lola. "Yeah, her teacher got on me about it already."

"What she say?"

"A lot of nothing."

Lola eyed him, smirking. "I'd like to think she said a lot of something if the baby ain't talking to folks."

"She talking."

"Yeah, to *you*. Talking to you is normal, but ignoring the rest of the world for two months isn't. Now she's started school and other people have noticed."

"Look, I asked her why she ain't talking to folks."

"And?" Lola asked.

"She said she just ain't want to."

She actually hadn't even said that. She'd just shrugged at him and went back to dancing to the *Gracie's Corner* episode she'd made him cast to the TV from his phone.

"What'd her teacher recommend?"

He rolled his eyes and shrugged. Lola kissed her teeth in a way that made Munch giggle around her thumb.

"You can't be difficult with the lady, Nuney."

"Why not? She difficult with me."

"I'm sure she's got Tori's best interest in mind. Look at the care she put into the babies' take home folders. She's experienced."

Lola would know. Her mama taught for thirty years before she retired, so she was impressed with any person who claimed to be a teacher. She was also impressed by the steak at the Golden Corral and his grandpa Larry, who sometimes took breaks from his wife to spend weekends with her, though.

"You judging her character off some rinky dink ten cent bedazzled Walmart folders? *I* could've made them."

Ms. Thibodeaux had also put her phone number at the very

back of the folder behind August and September's lunch menus in the smallest font at the bottom of a random coloring sheet most folks would've thrown away. She wasn't slick, and he wasn't googly-eyed like Lola.

"Listen, you talk to me after you've taught with the bare minimum in some of the most deplorable conditions with parents who don't give a damn about whether or not their babies can write their names. Everybody ain't like you."

"Here you go..."

"Don't sass me."

"Don't push me to put my kid in special ed classes because she going through a phase."

"It's not special ed." Lola threw her hands up. "Is this about that court date next month? I told you nothing good comes from stressing."

They peered at Munch, who had gotten distracted by an ant marching across a crack in the porch. She squatted to poke at it.

When Lola used words like "court date" it made him do desperate shit like squeeze the top handle of Munch's backpack. The closer that court date got, the clingier he got. There were some days he didn't even have the urge to send her to school. It happened that morning. He'd woken up with a nasty pang in his chest that wouldn't go away while they brushed their teeth.

"I just don't wanna get in my feelings and make a stupid decision based on what some worrisome teacher saying. She might grow out of it in a couple of months."

He left out the other shit that riddled his thoughts while he watched Munch brush around her loose tooth that morning—like the questions Judge Montgomery would ask if he let the school in him and DeeDee's business.

Lola shrugged. "If she grows out of it, then snatch her butt right back out of whatever special accommodation they recommend."

He eyed her. "Oh yeah, just like that, huh?"

"I get it. Nothing with Tori ever happens 'just like that,' but you have to do what's right."

"Do I really?"

Lola pursed her lips and glanced at Munch out of the corner of her eye. "Has her M-A-M-A called?"

"Come on now, she can spell 'mama.'"

Lola held her hands up. "My bad. I'm learning her all over again."

"But yeah..." He swallowed. "She called."

And he didn't answer.

He couldn't.

Lola shook her head knowingly while Munch popped up with her thumb still in her mouth and the ant marching along her forearm.

She held it out for him to look at.

He crouched down so they could study its black body together. "It's a garden ant—a worker one. He ain't gon' hurt you."

She grinned at him and that nasty pang came back when he got a glimpse of the space where her bottom tooth used to be.

The tooth fairy had come and gone, but she told him nobody had helped her wiggle the tooth out and nobody had asked how she felt afterward because DeeDee didn't slow down long enough to ask anybody about their feelings—not even him.

Munch pushed her arm against his and watched in awe as the ant marched from her skin to his. It stomped over her tiny footprints he got tattooed the week after she was born.

"Okay, Tori. You gotta eat that breakfast on the way to school." Lola sighed, pushing up and stuffing her book under her arm. "That bus coming this afternoon, right?"

"Yeah, I took care of it."

"Good. Carlotta needs her car again this afternoon and I ain't got no way up to no bus barn. They said it'll be two more daggone weeks before my alternator comes in."

"I told you, you could drive mi—"

"Hell no. I'll walk before I do that."

"Come on…"

"Don't 'come on' me. You just be ready to put that alternator in when it gets here."

He rolled his eyes up as she shuffled to the front door, leaving him and Munch to stare at each other while she locked it.

Munch side-eyed her jiggling the lock and then reached out to tug his hand with a frown. They had company, so she wouldn't complain out loud. Instead, it all materialized on her face.

"We can't stay home," he muttered, gulping and tugging her thumb out of her mouth. "I'll get in trouble, and we both know what happens when grown-ups get in trouble."

———

Kindergartners had big feelings about the happenings in their little lives.

Ciara Johnson thought it was unfair that Jaylen Long got appointed line leader for the day, Treshawn Bolds got frustrated during snack time because their magic rug didn't give him real superpowers, and Ada Guzman was having an existential crisis because she learned about Hell in children's church. Yet throughout all their kindergarten drama, Tori still wouldn't talk.

"They're like little squirmy worms." Logan frowned from her spot in Venus' doorway.

She wiggled her fingers at Tori, who smiled back at her and then went back to wriggling around in her spot on their magic rug.

"Tori, do you have to use the bathroom?" Venus asked from over her shoulder.

Tori looked down and plucked an obscure piece of lint from the rug because she was a jittery plucker, or like Daddy used to call Venus—a teeny tiny jitterbug.

"You know, I used to be that way at her age." Venus smiled at Tori's leopard bow tied around her puff.

It went perfectly with her black tights, and there was no way Anthony picked out any of it. Her mama must've had impeccable preschooler styling capabilities.

"Girl, you were mute too?" Logan asked.

Venus scowled at her and slapped her hand against her forehead. "Remind me why you left your high schoolers to come rescue kindergartners again?"

"To confront my childhood traumas and make everything come full circle. Duh."

"Oddly enough, I believe you."

"Also, this school hasn't had a counselor in three years because of the district shortage, so they sent the best person to the rescue—*hello*."

"Anybody ever tell you that you have a grandiose sense of self-importance?"

"Every single day. Desmond says it's sexy."

Venus rolled her eyes. "Anyway, what's up? You're interrupting our story time. We're reading 'I Have Ants in My Pants' and we're all learning how to keep our bottoms on our magnificent magic rug and our hands in our laps. Right, Tori?"

Tori gave her a big smile. It was the same one she wore when she hugged Venus as soon as she marched into their classroom after lunch. It made Venus warm.

Tori was what her old mentor Shelly used to call a, "velcro kid." She had warned Venus that velcro kids were the worst students a single teacher with no kids could have.

"I hope you leave your teacher voice at home tonight," Logan muttered. "No grown man wants to hear about magnificent rugs or kids having imaginary ants in their pants."

"Did you stop by to insult me, or did you need something?"

"I came bearing gifts."

Venus raised her eyebrows, trailing her eyes up and down Logan's short frame, searching for the "gifts."

Rae Lyse

"Dang, they're not on me right now. They're in the truck. I brought you all the good things you'll need for your date tonight." She squealed like a teenager.

"And what good things would I need? We're going to dinner, not Vegas."

"Um, based on our conversation from yesterday, you need these good things so Mr. Braves can take care of that problem you got."

Venus inched forward, walking her out of the classroom's doorway. "Okay, what'd you bring?"

"Clothes...and shoes."

"I don't need any clothes or shoes. I already have something to wear."

Logan glanced at her pink Nikes.

"Don't do me like that. I have a cute H&M bodycon that I can still fit—"

"And you'll have to blow the dust off of it first, right?"

She shrugged.

The last time she wore it was supposed to be a joyous occasion—a reconciliation dinner with Trey he didn't even bother showing up to because their marriage was beyond repair at that point.

"I can tell by your long expression that you need to burn it. Hit me up if you need the lighter fluid. In the meantime, meet me in the parking lot when you're finished with bus duty."

———

Sadly, Venus forgot to include hair in Logan's manifestation prayer, so the dim lighting in Vaughn's reflected off the highest point on Morris' head. It was the third red flag since he pulled into her building's parking garage an hour before the time they agreed on in a Honda Accord that looked nothing like the Beamer he said he drove.

"So..." She smiled over the menu while following the trick-

30

ling bead of sweat gliding down his head. "What do you do at Wells Fargo?"

"Oh! I'm a—a uh a personal banker."

He shifted in his seat and looked around at the tables near them.

Even his eyes looked different. They were beady, light brown and kept scraping across the tips of her breasts because the dress Logan dug from her trunk hugged her in all the wrong places.

"What do you do, though? I don't think I've ever known a banker. Do you set up investment portfolios? Provide financial advice? Do you count money all day?" she rambled like she did in class when Jaylen Long asked her why she wasn't married like his mama was.

She swallowed, hoping a waiter would notice the way her eyes kept fluttering to the entrance, but they were all engrossed with the white old-money couples around them.

"Yeah, a lil' bit of all that. I rap on the side, too." He adjusted the sleeves on his too tight button down.

"*Rap?*"

"Yeah, you know I got a homeboy with a studio in his garage. Look my SoundCloud up." He flung his finger out while she tried to make eye contact with the second waiter that breezed past them.

Were post-divorce dates supposed to produce sweat in strange places?

None of it felt liberating. It was just plain ole awkward and having her cleavage hiked up to her chin made it even worse.

"So...you eat here often?" she asked, clearing the hunk of phlegm from her throat.

"Nah, I actually don't." He frowned at the menu and she didn't know if he was frowning at the exorbitant prices or the intimidating dishes: Yakitori, Yellowtail Sashimi, and Chilean Sea Bass.

They were all a mouthful, and her palate wasn't sophisticated enough to dissect them.

"Well, what made you pick it?"

"I figured a bougie girl like you would appreciate a place like this."

She frowned. "Bougie?"

"Yeah, you know, it's like an eclectic bougie, though. Like on some Kelis meets Rihanna type shit."

He didn't even talk like a banker and now she'd gone from judgmental to bougie.

She held in a groan as another plain-faced waitress walked by, ignoring her best *"save me"* expression. This waitress even had the nerve to smile like she wasn't on a date with a hat-fishing SoundCloud rapper dressed in a Forever 21 button down.

She shifted in the wooden chair and tugged at her purse strap that dangled off its arm. If Logan wasn't wrangling koi fish from crackheads on the east side, she would definitely send her an angry text.

"Damn, where the fuck this waiter at?" he grumbled. "They done served all these white folks, but keep walking past us."

As if to prove his point, another pale, plain-faced staff member bounced past them with an empty smile and a Y2K hairstyle.

"Uh... ma'am." Venus waved her arm in desperation.

The girl stopped and hiked her eyebrow up. "How can I help you?"

"Can you please tell us who our waite—"

"Server?" she replied, tilting her head and giving uncomfortable eye contact. "We're a gender neutral establishment and my pronouns are they and them."

Venus blew out a breath as quietly as she could while Morris stared at them with his phone plastered in front of his face like he was expecting a showdown between her and *them*.

"Okay, our server. Who's our server?"

Their eyes danced across her big hair and then stopped at

Logan's dress that she busted out of. "I'm not sure, but I can find out. Cute hair, by the way."

She chirped the last bit and then bounced off. Venus choked on the whiff of pachouli wind she left in her wake.

"How much you wanna bet they gon' send the only nigga they have up in here to give us some half assed service?" Morris complained. "Racist ass establishment. I should've known it was gon' be some shit when they ain't have no free parking."

The desperation was in her legs now. She needed out—immediately. Trey was a cheapskate, but he had *never* complained about twelve dollar valet parking.

She tugged her purse strap again and slid the purse into her lap while Morris sucked his teeth at another waiter that bounced by.

She eyed every corner of the restaurant, searching for the closest exit she could waddle to. "Uh, can you excuse me? I'm gonna run to the ladies ro—"

"How y'all doing tonight?"

Weed. Strawberry scent. Deep lazy Atlanta drawl.

Now, sweat pooled in the center of her smooshed thighs and she couldn't look away from the side entrance to the restaurant because it had to be a mistake that Vaughn's would hire a Kayden to pronounce fancy dishes and serve expensive wine he wasn't even old enough to drink.

She gulped and stared at Morris' gaudy paisley printed tie until a tattoo covered finger planted a wine glass in front of it.

"What's up, my boy?" he asked Morris.

"Shit... chillin'."

There were ten steps from their table to that door. She could slip Logan's narrow heels off and make a run for it. She could make i—

"How you feeling tonight, Ms. Thibodeaux?"

Ms. Thibodeaux?

She had to stop calling him Kayden now that he had thrown out her name in such a civilized way. Really, it was more than civilized. It came out slow and sensual, like he only existed to cater to her every need despite their ruminating beef.

All she heard was the "hmph" Paula had let out as he swaggered out of the front office, asking Tori about her second day of school as if he didn't threaten to end her with one email to Principal Bivins.

She tore her eyes off the door.

Less than forty-eight hours ago he was calling her everything short of a Karen and now he talked in a slow, casual drawl.

She glanced up at him and choked out, "I'm... I'm good, Anthony."

"Good."

An amused expression settled on his face like he knew she planned to make a run for it and he wanted in on her crazy ass escape plan.

She could strangle Logan because the entire evening started with her "innocent" Tinder suggestion.

"Oh shit. Y'all know each other?" Morris laughed, pointing between them.

Her eyes grew, but Anthony's red ones stayed in droopy splits. They raked her décolletage like he was familiar with it and then glided past the table to Logan's heels where they lingered too long.

"Huh? No! I mean yeah...uh I...I teach his daughter," she stammered. "I'm a kindergarten teacher, remember?"

Morris wrinkled his eyebrows. "You sure? I coulda swore you told me you was a secretary at—"

"This your first time dining with us?" Anthony asked her, blinking, and talking over Morris' goofy ass question.

He tugged out a wrinkle on the white tablecloth.

Afterward, his fingers brushed the area next to her elbow. They were long and the same hazelnut tone as his face. His skin was sun-kissed. It had the same toasty brown color as Daddy's banana bread and she was obsessing over his appearance again.

Her elbow tingled as if he touched it and she *really* needed out, because Logan's teasing questions about what she wanted in a man had her eye-fucking a juvenile.

She blinked back up at him while sliding her elbow off the table.

He should've looked out of place in Vaughn's, but he didn't. Instead, he was astute, with relaxed shoulders while he adjusted the cutlery in front of her. The tattoos that snuck from under his shirt's collar even looked like they belonged in the stuffy restaurant.

"So listen," Morris started, cutting his eyes and leaning forward toward Anthony. "Y'all ain't got no weekday specials? I was just over at Mystique the other night and they had lamb chops—two for twelve *and* hookah."

She grimaced.

The first crack in Anthony's astute demeanor came in his droopy eyes. This time they dragged across her mouth and she saw the wheels turning in his head and his thoughts forming. He wanted her to explain herself, and she really fucking wanted to.

He smirked, tugging the cocktail menu she'd been reading from in front of her. "Unfortunately, we don't have weekday specials or hookah."

It was embarrassing, and a little fucked up how the changes in the inflection of his voice made her body tingle with warmth. It volleyed between kinda poised and just straight *him*.

"Man, what kinda shit is that?" Morris hissed. "They been hyping this place up on the 'gram and you telling me they been paying a hundred dollars a plate for shit they can't even pronounce?"

Anthony blinked again like he couldn't wait to run home and tell Tori that Ms. Thibodeaux was so desperate she ended up with the biggest catfish Nev couldn't even explain.

Anthony swiped his tongue out and bit into his bottom lip as they listened to Morris' rant.

Now, sweat puddled at the back of her knees.

She had never even sweat there before!

Anthony eyed the ticking Rolex on Morris' wrist. "Shouldn't be no thang for you. You look like a big stepper. I know you can afford it."

"On God, I swear I am." Morris laughed, thrusting his hand out for Anthony to take, but Anthony was already bored with him.

It was in the second sweep he gave her sweaty body while Morris recovered from the embarrassing blunder and swiped his baldhead because Anthony didn't slap his hand.

She didn't even understand what they were talking about, and Anthony's droopy red eyes told her not to even worry about that shit.

"What kind of wine you like, Ms. Thibodeaux?" he asked.

She swallowed the cheap wine she almost blurted out while Morris sucked his teeth.

"Um, I don't think I see it on the menu."

"Don't stress. I got you. I'll bring a bottle of Caymus out. It's rich. You'll love it."

She believed him. She even believed he learned about Caymus from some old white man from Napa he struck up a conversation with one day.

He looked at Morris again. "A shot of Casamigos for you, my boy?"

"Damn, you know me already."

"For sure. You got a piece and an ID the bartender can hold at the bar for your tab? It's a new policy. They got the bar and kitchen operating separately right now."

Morris pat his pockets and dug out a gaudy, tattered designer wallet that had seen better days. He thumbed through a pile of cards and loose paper before he flung out a credit card and his ID and pushed it toward Anthony.

By the time she deciphered what a piece was and had fixed her mouth to ask Anthony why the restaurant and bar were operating independently in a restaurant like Vaughn's, he was already turning to leave with another sly smirk on his lips.

He passed the non-binary with the "they" pronouns on his way to the back of the restaurant. They nudged shoulders like old friends.

"I like that lil' nigga," Morris mumbled. "But that wine better be the price of that lemon drop I was gon' order for you."

She groaned out loud this time.

"What? You wanna request another waiter since you teach his snotty-nosed kid?"

"Huh? No." She shook her head, pushing back from the table. "I'm...I'm gonna go to the lady's room. I'll be back."

He eyed her stumbling out of the chair. It was the type of look the old men that hung outside of the gas station gave her. It made her want to scrape imaginary dirt off her skin.

Her toes twisted together at the front of Logan's expensive shoes, she couldn't even pronounce the name of, while she dug her cellphone out of her purse and searched for the bathroom.

"I am gonna kill her lil' ass..." she whispered, tipping past another old white couple being shown to their table. "I'm gonna yank every lash off her eyelids one by fuckin' one."

The restroom seemed light years away while she walked on the painful stilts Logan swore would make her ass look bigger.

They fucking didn't.

By the time she pushed the heavy wooden door and stumbled into the women's bathroom, she was sure there wasn't any skin left on her pinky toe.

"Answer the phone," she muttered, stabbing Logan's name and pushing into a stall. "Answer the ph—"

"I'm sorry, but the person you have tried to reach does not have a voicemail set up—"

"Oh...my...God. *'Let's manifest your perfect man, sis. Fuck Ciara's prayer, we're gonna write Venus' prayer,'*" Venus mocked, kicking the heels off and relishing in the cold floor that soothed her throbbing feet.

Her ex mother-in-law was still proving herself right: She was a mess.

"A low-down, uncouth, country ass mess, Trey," Rose used to hiss over the phone. *"All them nice gals at that school and you go and fuck a janitor's daughter who don't ever comb her hair?"*

She stared down at her chipped toenail polish while the Uber app loaded on her phone.

"Forty fuckin' dollars." She shook her head.

Forty dollars to get from midtown and back to her apartment, where Pepper waited for the recap of her disastrous date.

She collapsed on the toilet seat and curled her toes together as her phone dinged with a text.

743-22:

Your account has insufficient funds for one or more recent transactions. Charges may apply.

four

. . .

"MOM SAID she got a suit for you to wear on the big day," Mikayla muttered, poking the buttons on the point of sale machine behind the bar. "A charcoal grey one. It's a classic neutral color, and it's Tom Ford. You can never go wrong with Tom Ford."

Anthony snorted next to her while leaning against the bar. "And how much is that gon' cost me?"

"Anthony..." Her voice volleyed up and cracked.

It was the thing he hated most about fuckin' with girls like her—their vocal fry was an instant dick softener.

"What's wrong with my white button down and slacks?"

She looked at him out of the corner of her eye. "No offense, but how many court dates have you worn that same get-up to?"

He smirked, shaking his head.

He'd worn that same ole get-up DeeDee boosted out of Nordstrom years ago at least ten times, but that was something else they kept on a need to know basis. Mikayla's mama, Lynn, was the only person who *needed* to know the ins and outs of his shaky history with Atlanta's court system.

"Got that bottle of Caymus for you, nune-dawg," the sommelier, David, rasped as he came out of the wine cellar next to the bar.

He uncorked the bottle and swiped his hand across his forehead. "I just taught you cabs last week, and you already sold a bottle of Caymus? Who're you trying to finesse tonight?"

He hiked his blonde eyebrows up.

That was the thing he hated most about working with white folks.

"You in my business, D. I thought we talked about keeping it P?"

"Alright...alright." He held his hands up. "I got you. I got you. I can keep it *P*."

Anthony smirked, snatching the bottle and turning back to a red-faced Mikayla. "All you need to know is that I ain't ever pled guilty in that get-up. I know I'm Lynn's favorite client right now, but tell her I can dress myself."

Her nostrils flared like they did when they locked eyes in Josiah's suite at the Mercedes Benz Stadium earlier that year.

He had fucked her in the women's bathroom all the way through the fourth quarter and missed Josiah's game-winning touchdown. Afterward, he spent all spring sexting her over WhatsApp while she studied abroad in Spain, but then that life shit happened. Now he was walking around looking like a penguin and had her thinking their situationship was more than what it was because he had asked her for a favor he'd never be able to repay. He *hated* that shit.

"Look, she just really, really wants y'all to win this," she replied as her caramel face wrinkled with worry.

Y'all?

DeeDee had never even met Lynn in person.

He snorted. "Yeah, I bet."

Her eyes rolled down to the bottle he gripped. "Caymus? Is that for the lady with the purple twist out in your section?"

It wasn't Ms. Thibodeaux's titties spilling out of her too tight Mugler dress, the way her obviously borrowed Louboutins made her calves bulge, or the way she looked at him like she was caught red-handed on a date with somebody's lame ass unc. It was that purple twist out. The rest was just *chef's kiss*.

Tash was right. He wanted to fuck her—hard. And God knew that. Why else would she be traipsing around Vaughn's on the night he worked out of all the places in the city?

Puffy bags sat underneath her soft eyes after chasing Munch and her classmates around all day, and he liked those the most. They meant she still desperately needed good dick he couldn't deliver because she wanted to put an IEP on Munch but his dick was so flaw it still got hard for her judgmental ass.

"What you talking about?" He smirked, fingering her date's cards in his pocket and pulling them out to skim them. "What lady?"

He chuckled at Ms. Thibodeaux's date staring at him from the Georgia ID card.

LaDarius Mitchell.

He held it next to the credit card he'd thrust at him.

Danielle Jameson.

He knew that nigga was broke.

"Don't play stupid and don't fuck up your tip chasing vagina that's taken," Mikayla nagged.

"Ha!" He laughed, shoving the cards back in his apron pocket. "Ain't nobody chasing pussy... and believe me, it ain't taken."

If it was, she wouldn't have been eyeing him with an attempted escape plan written on her panicked face.

"That's Munch's teacher, anyway."

Her eyes widened. "Seriously?"

"Yeah, *seriously.*"

"She can afford that bottle on a teacher's salary?"

No, but Munch liked Ms. Thibodeaux no matter how unprofessional and broke she was, so Caymus it was.

When he fixed their Fruity Pebbles that morning, Munch had unraveled her twists in the living room while reassuring him her hair would "look just like Ms. T's" afterward. It didn't and he couldn't salvage Dre's work, so she ended up with a crooked bow around a sloppy top knot.

"Now, you *really* in my business," he said, shaking his head. "Don't do that."

Mikayla's slanted eyes softened with a follow-up question as he backed away, but she knew better. She'd only gotten as far as knowing Munch's name because Lynn had a big ass mouth and penchant for making sure that whatever he and Mikayla had wouldn't last past his "big day in court." Lynn wasn't like him. She didn't keep shit on a need to know basis unless she was in a courtroom.

The curiosity melted from Mikayla's hazel eyes the further he moved away from her.

"You're coming over later, right?" she asked, blinking hard and chewing on her glossy bottom lip. "My roommate's still in LA."

"What I need to come over for?"

Red crept up her cheeks as she crossed her arms. "Don't."

He smiled, grabbing the Casamigos shot off the bar. "Damn, 'Kayla. If you wanna fuck, then be a woman and ask for it."

She blew out a loud huff and rolled her eyes.

Shit, he had wanted to do the same after installing another battery in Dre's car before sunrise, dropping Munch off to Lola, reassuring Logan's husband Desmond he wouldn't file a complaint on Ms. Thibodeaux when he called to do Logan's dirty work, and then rushing across the city to work a shift in a stuffy ass restaurant to show Judge Montgomery he was an upstanding citizen with a regular ass penny-paying job.

He couldn't huff and pout, though.

He didn't have that privilege because he wasn't a spoiled rich girl who worked for fun money. There just wasn't enough time in the day to fuck Mikayla in her dorm—especially when she wouldn't even ask for his dick like a grown woman and make his time worthwhile.

He stalked off toward the back of the restaurant, anticipating the blood to rush back to his dick after getting another look at those puffy bags under Ms. Thibodeaux's eyes. He even skipped out on checking in on the owner, Vaughn, who only tipped him in hundred-dollar bills because he "liked the way his brain worked."

When he rounded the corner to the main dining room, that same purple twist out Mikayla mentioned poked out of the women's bathroom door.

He stopped, sitting the wine and shot onto a nearby table while watching her.

She stumbled out and leaned against the wall, trying to slip her bare foot back into her shoe.

She mumbled to herself while her titties inched to the top of that ugly ass dress he wanted to burn and it was just like the second day of school when she corrupted Munch's ears with her lame ass remix of "Wheels on the Bus."

DeeDee would've called her a "hot ass mess" while she was hunched over, twisting the too little shoe from side to side and contorting her foot in all kinds of intricate ways. Her heel wouldn't budge, though. It hung over the back of the shoe.

He shook his head while his flaw ass dick told him to make one last exception before Nuneyland closed shop for good. Meanwhile, DeeDee bitched at him in his head, reminding him to keep that shit closed—especially for police ass bitches like Ms. Thibodeaux.

"Fuck," she hissed, blowing a stray purple kinky curl out of her face. "Fuck, fuck, fuck."

He smiled and his dick might've too.

Ms. Thibodeaux cursed when people weren't around?

Yeah, his dick was *definitely* smiling.

He inched closer, but she couldn't hear him because she was too busy saying all the words he sent Munch to time out for. In fact, she and Munch were a lot alike—smart mouths, big hair, and they both had eyes in the back of their heads.

"What're you staring at?" she gritted out, looking off into the restaurant.

"You."

His response wasn't draped in want nor did it let on how much he liked to watch her. It was as messy as the predicament they were in. Of all the people in the restaurant their manager Mona could've told him to handle, God chose Ms. Thibodeaux—the judgmental teacher his dick wanted. But maybe it wasn't God after all. Lola would've said, "that shit wasn't nothing but the devil" because only the devil and Tash could justify fuckin' Munch's new teacher.

"Well, stop staring and help me get my foot back in this damn shoe," she said.

"Keep talkin' sideways to me and you'll be limping your barefoot ass back to that sweaty, peanut head ass nigga you up here grinning with."

Those words came out with all the want that was missing in the "you" he said before. It settled between his words like he had her hair between his fingers and her naked body grinding on top of his.

"Lil' boy, I will fuck—"

"Man, shut up."

It was *just* like the second day of school, except this time they were in the wild and she could fire out all the unprofessional comebacks she wanted. All that was missing was her cheap pencil skirt and brown stain over her right nipple.

"Don't tell me to shut up," she sneered, falling back into the wall.

He shook his head, smirking and grabbing one of the tiny glass bottles of olive oil they kept on the tables for the bread.

He squatted next to her and wrapped his hot hand around her slick ankle. The skin puffed up around her joints as an electric wave zapped against his palm. That was *for sure* the devil.

His mouth grew moist at the sight of her round turquoise

painted toes. They looked as good as the bags underneath her eyes.

She moaned while he pressed his fingers into her skin. "Don't do that."

"Your ankle swollen."

He turned his head, watching for Mona and then pouring a dollop of oil in his hand.

A ragged groan erupted from the back of her throat as he massaged her heel. His gaze roamed between her foot and the tension melting from her face.

"Stop looking at me like that," she said.

"Like what?"

"Like you want me to explain myself."

"If you wanna date lame ass niggas with no motion, no hoes, and fake rollies, that ain't got shit to do with me."

Her eyes blinked back open, and she frowned. "English, please. I don't speak teenager."

He chuckled, digging the tips of his fingers into her skin and sliding her foot back into the shoe with ease. "If you wanna date a broke misogynistic incel wearing a fake Rolex that only gets fucked once a year by his baby mama, then do that shit. What you do outside of school hours ain't my business."

The shame in her eyes was better than any explanation she could give him.

He slid his greasy fingers together and pointed back to her table where "LaDarius Mitchell" sat waiting for her.

"You damn right. I *can* do whatever I want. Fuck you." She huffed, tugging her tiny crossbody close and marching off in front of him with her ass teasing him in that hideous dress.

————

Misogynistic? Incel?

Kaydens knew what those words meant and how to use them in sentences?

Fuck.

Venus crossed her legs to stop the throbbing that Anthony's deep voice induced.

"I told my baby mama the phone work both ways. If my son wanna play AAU and she want *me* to pay for the shit, his lil' ass better start calling me," Morris ranted, swiping another bead of sweat from his head.

She sighed, shaking her head and taking another gulp of wine.

Those overdraft fees kept looking more and more appealing as the night wore on and she noted all the things she forgot to add to her prayer—like men that didn't wear fake Rolex watches and come with a gaggle of baby mamas he swore were the problem.

She twisted her greasy, swollen ankle around, ignoring the buzz that lingered from Anthony's fingers.

It was hard to ignore, though. *All of it* was hard—the way he kept taking care of her despite their obvious hate for each other, the expensive ass wine he kept in her glass, that "explain yourself" look he swore he wasn't giving her, and the ugly warm feeling that overtook her when that non-binary Y2K person brushed shoulders with him under the guise of "helping" even though there was nothing Anthony needed help with.

Daddy would've called him a delegator. He always said it was one of the most important traits her husband should have— the fine art of delegation while under pressure. Trey never delegated, though. He always floundered and Daddy always wondered why she'd even been attracted to him.

"It's hot," Anthony said as he walked up to their table.

He swiped a saucer of bread from in front of her and replaced it with her dinner: Parm crusted lamb with a side of couscous.

It was another dish on the menu she'd never eaten before, but it didn't matter because it rolled off Anthony's tongue. He swore it would become her favorite thing on the menu, as if she could afford to come back to Vaughn's.

Morris ranted about his third baby mama and fourth child while steam rose from the plate. The buzzing on her ankle drifted to her middle and mingled with that throb while Anthony's tongue snuck from between his lips as he switched her cutlery around. The wine had her warm, boozy, horny, *and* hungry, which was the worst combination when on a date with a man like Morris.

She reached out to adjust the plate, but Anthony slapped her fingers away in a "didn't I just tell your ass the plate was hot" kind of way.

By now the wine had her believing they were both telepathic.

She rolled her eyes at him and he smiled his best "wait until we get home" smile, as if they would end up at the same place when her hellish date ended. It wasn't nothing but that *sneaky sneaky* wine.

"How your ankle?" he asked, cutting off Morris again.

"It's fine."

He chuckled. "Hm, a'ight."

"What's wrong with your ankle?" Morris butted in.

"Oh noth—"

"She twisted it coming out of the women's bathroom. It's all good, though. I'm sure you'll take care of it when y'all get home."

"No sirrr," Morris dragged out. "I ain't a feet man. You better ice that bad boy."

Anthony shook his head with a stony expression. "You should prop it up when you get home. Those shoes ain't meant for walking."

"What the hell kind of shoe ain't meant for walking?" Morris asked.

Anthony nodded his head to her empty wine glass and his non-binary sidekick replenished it.

"Those shoes are only meant for two things, my boy—for pictures..." He smirked. "And for home."

She saw the fantasy in his head because of that weird telepathy he induced.

"Well, if that's the case, then why you wore 'em out?" Morris asked.

Anthony coughed to cover up his laughter while she sank into her seat.

How could a grown ass man be so dense?

After dropping their food off, Anthony disappeared to give them space to enjoy their meals and, unfortunately, each other's company. He didn't bother aiding in her escape plan. It was like he wanted her to suffer, to teach her a lesson in this new weird dating world she lived in.

Morris frowned and kicked around a brussels sprout with his fork. "What the hell is this?"

"A brussels sprout."

"It looks nasty."

"It's a vegetable. It's good for you."

"It looks like a lil' cabbage." He stabbed one, taking a big bite out of it and gagging. "It needs hot sauce."

She guzzled another mouthful of wine because there was no need to stay sober.

It took Morris forty-five *long* minutes to pack away every piece of meat on his plate after scraping the brussels sprouts onto a saucer. The wine had muted the flavors in her food so much so that she still had most of it left, because she couldn't taste any of it. There were no interesting conversations or debates about misogynistic incels because Morris still sounded out his words when he read—so he chewed and she drank until he stuffed the last piece of meat into his mouth.

Afterward, she smelled Anthony before she saw him because the wine had discombobulated her senses. His scent was so fervent she almost tasted him.

"You want me to take care of this for you?" he asked her, pulling her fork out of the half eaten couscous.

She shook her head, pushing it away.

"You don't look satisfied yet. What you want for dessert?"

"And how much is that gon' be?" Morris grumbled.

She caught the tiniest flash in Anthony's doe eyes, and she swore she heard him again.

Does it fuckin' matter?

"It depends on what the lady picks," he said out loud instead.

"It better be something less than—"

"You can bring the check," she cut in, dropping her napkin on the table as he took her plate.

Morris sucked his teeth and let out a deep, satisfied sigh. He sat back and pat his bulging stomach that wasn't there when their "date" first started.

She shuddered, holding onto the bile in her throat.

"Well, the lady said to bring the check, so I'm gon' bring the check." Anthony shrugged.

"Fine by me." Morris waved his hand and Anthony walked off.

It took too long for Anthony and his familiar scent to come back, but it could've been the wine playing tricks on her again. It made everything about him enticing—his mouth, his voice, his fingers, his eyes.

When he finally came back, he slid a wooden box engraved with "Vaughn's" onto their table and sat a purple macaron on top of it.

"Whenever you're ready, boss. No rush." He nodded at Morris.

She smiled at the only silver lining from the night—a macaron that matched the botched dye job she gave herself after her divorce was finalized. Purple wasn't even her favorite color. She only chose it because she knew it was a color Trey would hate.

She reached for it at the same time as Morris and their hands brushed, but nothing happened. There was no zap of electricity or snarky words—just his warm, hairy hand gliding across hers and trying to steal the only other good thing that came out of their night together.

She snatched it before his grubby hand could.

Anthony nodded to her empty wine glass. "How 'bout a glass for the road?"

"I can't just take a glass of wine out of the restaurant."

"Man, you can do whatever you want."

Their eyes locked again, and that telepathy came back. He left the rest of what he wanted to say in his head like the part about her having the ability to do whatever she wanted as long as he was around.

He snorted, shaking his head.

"Shit, for this fuckin' bill, you goddamn right you can do what you want," Morris cut through their mind-reading with a gruff. "Aye, you got to split this, neph."

Heat snuck from the roots of her hair to her swollen ankle. If she hadn't promised Michole she would stop bursting into tears at any given embarrassing moment, that nice tablecloth Anthony kept scraping the crumbs off of would've been soaked.

She dropped the macaroon on the table and swallowed while yanking her purse open with trembling hands.

"You wanna see this shit?" Morris asked, pushing the bill her way. "Most expensive meal I ever ate. Besides that one time I went to Ruth's Chris with my first baby mama."

Rubbing salt into her gaping wound wasn't even an accurate metaphor for the way Morris ranted and raved, while Anthony watched her dig her empty debit card out.

"We don't split checks," Anthony said, blinking at him.

"What you mean y'all don't split checks? Hell, even Chili's split checks."

"Right, and they charge you twenty-five dollars for two meals, too."

If she wasn't so down bad, she would've laughed at Anthony's snark. Instead, she sat there with egg on her face and her empty debit card dangling from her hand.

"Man, come on, neph. You gotta figure this shit out," Morris begged.

Anthony's eyes swept her card and then the rest of the restaurant. He tugged it from her fingers.

"A'ight. You want me to charge your half to that card you got up at the bar?" he asked.

"Yeah, yeah. Gon' head and swipe it."

"Bet that. I ain't gon' be long," he mumbled before walking away.

Five minutes.

That's how long he disappeared with her empty visa.

She craned her neck, waiting on him to breeze from the back of the restaurant with that sexy know-it-all smirk on his face and satisfaction in his voice while he announced that her card declined.

"Damn." Morris sucked his teeth. "He owe you something?"

"Huh?" She frowned, whipping her head back toward him. "Uh—no. I was just—I think I might've gave him the wrong card."

"Too late now."

Anthony swaggered back from around the corner.

Sometime between preparing to break the embarrassing news to her and splitting their check, he'd rolled up the sleeves on his black button down. Now, she was woozy as she drank in his placid expression and arms full of tattoos.

"For you, boss." He slid the receipt-wrapped cards to Morris. "And for you, Ms. Thibodeaux."

She snatched the card from his hand and shoved it deep down into her crossbody, where it needed to stay until her check hit at 2:59 a.m.

"A'ight." Morris sighed, ignoring the "tip" section and scribbling on the bottom of the receipt without glancing at it. "Let's go. Gotta make sure my car still in that parking lot around the corner. I don't think ole boy with the vest on was a real parking attendant."

"Ugh." She groaned out loud, following Anthony's fingers across the table as he picked up the last few pieces of their mess and she dug through her purse for her phone.

She tried making out the letters across his brown knuckles while Morris huffed, pushing away from the table.

"Chop. Chop." He snapped as soon as she got ahold of it.

All she needed was a forty dollar Cash App from Ginny, if she would just answer the phone or a text or a bat signal.

She swallowed as Anthony's knuckles stopped right in front of her.

Finally.

She sighed.

She saw them clearly as her eyes made themselves dizzy, bouncing between her phone and his knuckles.

THIR

He snatched his hand away.

"You good. Shawty gon' take an Uber," he bellowed, making her eyes snap up to his face.

"A *Uber*? Since when?" Morris asked.

"Since she told me." He balled her used napkin in his hand. "And that nigga with the vest ain't no parking attendant. You might wanna go handle that. Ole Joey probably down at the Citgo with the five dollars he charged you to park on private property."

For the first time that night, Morris' baldhead didn't hold all of his sweat. This time, it pooled under his armpits and drifted to the front of his shirt. His knuckles turned white as he gripped the back of his chair.

She scooted forward, hoping she could catch Anthony's words and apply them to her throbbing middle to soothe the warm sensations that kept rumbling through it.

"Who the fuck are you to tell me what my date gon' do?"

Anthony held up his hands, shrugging.

That sexy, know-it-all smirk sat on his wet lips as he and

Morris stared at each other. That smirk was dangerous and so was the "you better tell him" look he threw her way.

She took deep breaths, just like Michole taught her to do. Her stomach pushed as far as it could against Logan's tight dress.

Morris uncurled his fingers from the chair and stepped forward. "Nigga—"

"Hold on," she yelped, kicking her shoes off and pushing up from the table. "I told him I was taking an Uber."

She shook her head and scooped up Logan's shoes, remembering that she didn't have to explain herself to either of them. She didn't have to explain herself to any man anymore. She was free to do whatever the fuck she wanted in her new life.

"Actually, why am I even..." she trailed off.

Her words evaporated between them just as a boy appeared out of nowhere with a glass of wine dangling from his fingers, because Anthony really believed she could do whatever she wanted.

He held the glass out for her to take.

"Thanks," she muttered, snatching it and walking toward the door she'd been eyeing since she got there.

five

. . .

"HEY, you've reached Ginny. I can't get to the phone right now —" Venus sighed, ending another unsuccessful call to Ginny.

The grooves from the iron bench outside of Vaughn's dug into her thighs while she savored each tiny sip of wine she took.

It tasted better than all of the grocery store wines she ever chugged, and she almost felt as expensive as Rihanna except for the glaring fact that she couldn't even afford to get back home.

It was probably best Ginny didn't answer. If she did, the whole family would find out Trey won because Ginny's mouth was bigger than her brain sometimes.

The valet attendants rumbled around her, dropping off and picking up cars that belonged to people that could afford to eat there. Their voices and the pounding from Vaughn's front door blended together in a teasing way, as if they were telling her broke ass to hurry and get away from the expensive building.

"Surge pricing?"

Smoky voice. Deep Atlanta drawl. That good ass, sweet scent she'd been inhaling all night.

She looked up and found Anthony standing next to the bench.

"Yup... surge pricing." She nodded with a grimace.

He pursed his pink lips and nodded as a Kia pulled up to the curb with the Uber sign lit in its windshield. An older white couple shuffled into the backseat.

He chuckled. "C'mon, man."

"C'mon where?"

"Home. Unless you wanna sit out here until closing and beg one of my Honduran partners from the kitchen for a ride. They roll about twenty deep, though."

His black button down hung over his shoulder and his black slacks hung from his tapered waist. The plain white tee he had on under his button down was wrinkle free without a stain. If somebody would've told her that he was pronouncing obscure dishes just an hour ago, while running around a fine dining restaurant, she wouldn't have believed them.

She sighed. "That actually doesn't sound that bad."

Squeezing in the back of some Honduran's hooptie sounded a lot better than hopping on the handlebars of whatever bike Anthony had probably ridden up there. She spoke enough broken Spanish to explain to them she'd repay them as soon as she got that direct deposit notification.

He swiped a joint from behind his ear and she shook her head.

Apparently, *Vaughn's* was the type of job that let Anthony clock out with a joint behind his ear and his pants hanging off his ass.

A flash of light burst from between his fingers as he lit the joint and blew a plume of smoke out of his mouth. Afterward, he dug in his front pocket.

"I mean..." he drifted off, pulling out an ID and holding it in front of his face. "You could always call up LaDarius Mitchell and have him come back and get you."

"Who the hell is that?

Another panty-wetting smirk crawled across his top lip while he flipped the ID around, studying it. Then he dug into his pocket again and pulled out a credit card. It looked just like the one Morris had pulled out of his tattered wallet.

"You ain't take me as the type to go after bald scammin' niggas old enough to be my daddy." He cocked his head to the side, laughing.

"Once again—I don't speak teenager. What're you even talking about?" She fell to the back of the bench and guzzled the last tiny drop of wine she'd been saving to give her the courage to order that Uber with nothing in her bank account.

He thrust the cards in front of her and Morris' face stared back with a name printed next to it she didn't recognize.

She groaned, even though she was supposed to give unbothered when Anthony was around. "LaDarius Mitchell? Who is that?"

"I don't know. The nigga you came with gave it to me."

Who would've thought she'd be going tit for tat with Anthony during her first post-divorce date or she'd get catfished so badly she'd want to delete the night out of her brain? Daddy was really gonna have a field day with this one.

The iron bench rocked as he sat next to her, smothering her with weed, strawberry, and the scent of Vaughn's kitchen nestled in his clothes.

"You stole that man's shit?" She gurgled up a hiccup full of wine and dragged her crossbody to her middle.

"You got catfished in 2023?"

She yanked her purse open. "Go 'head, laugh it the fuck up."

A dopey laugh poured out of his mouth and tickled her ears. It felt as good as that warm buzzing on her ankle that wouldn't go away and she felt like shit because he looked like every bit of the Kayden he was when he wasn't scowling at her. Nothing on her body should've been warm *or* wet for his young kleptomaniac ass. But he didn't warn her that all those glasses of her new favorite wine would sneak up on her, so she couldn't even look him in his face while she covertly unbuttoned her wallet.

"What you digging through your purse for? Ain't nothing but dust on that visa you gave me, *Venus*. Be fuckin' for real."

Now she was really warm. He'd blown up her spot with her name rolling out of his bow-shaped lips. He said it like it made his dick hard that she didn't have a dollar to her name.

"You can thank LaDarius Mitchell for your dinner and the Caymus he talked shit about. He even had enough on that credit card to buy the whole kitchen rum shots."

"Are you serious?" she yelped and then groaned, dropping her wallet back to the bottom of her purse. "Why'd you do that?"

He shuffled the license and credit card back and forth between his fingers while taking another puff from his joint.

He was sly like the boys she taught her first year out of college when she swore troubled kids were her passion but the way he swiped Tori's snotty nose with his bare hand and the easy way he finessed a man twice his age told her something about him was very different from those boys.

He wet his bottom lip and studied Morris'—well—LaDarius' picture on the driver's license in a way that made her knees clamp together.

Then he shrugged. "Because what kinda man ask a woman out and talk about himself the whole goddamn time? He ain't even care to learn about what you do for a living. *Then* he had the gall to split the bill fifty-fifty. What a loser."

He blinked over at her through long lashes that curled at the tips like he'd kept a detailed log of every infraction Morris committed throughout the night. "That ain't bad business to you?"

His words felt personal and good even when they shouldn't have, just like their mutual telepathy.

He pushed his head out and raised his eyebrows, throwing out his best "answer me" expression that she couldn't fall for because he was too young and, worst of all, he was Tori's daddy.

"What'd you give him when you brought our cards back?"

Rae Lyse

He shrugged. "Nothing you need to worry about."

"So what if he calls the cops and reports his shit stolen?"

"He won't."

"And how do you know that?"

The question made a gut busting laugh roar out of him as if it were the dumbest thing somebody had asked him all day, and it made her want to laugh too.

He stuffed the cards back in his pocket while his body relaxed back into the bench with hers. "Only a dumbass would call the cops to report some shit *they* stole themselves. LaDarius Mitchell probably ain't even LaDarius Mitchell.... as if you ain't already know that."

He dropped his head back against the bench and stared up at the night sky like he was searching for the missing stars that the city drowned with its lights. He squinted and tilted his head.

Afterward, he muttered, "Munch's teacher fuckin' around with scammers on a school night. I told DeeDee they let anybody teach at that school."

She scoffed and let out her own laugh. "What are you so passionate about my fucked up night for, huh? What I do outside of school hours ain't your business, remember? Shouldn't matter if I got catfished or not or that I can't even afford my forty dollar Uber ride back to my goddamn place."

He pulled his head back as if she slapped him and then let out another one of those goofy laughs. "You done yapping about nothing? Because I'm tired and ready to go, so let's go. Cursing at me like you crazy."

He shook his head, pushing up from the bench.

———

Anthony slammed the door to an ugly, loud muscle car and rounded it with a pair of pink UGG slippers dangling from his fingers.

He thrust them toward Venus. "Here."

She frowned, eyeing the band of fur wrapped around them and then the car. "Vaughn's must pay real good, huh?"

He smirked, letting out a low laugh. It wasn't the dopey one from before that made him look his age.

"It's slow money. It pay enough for Munch to put money in her piggybank and go on Amazon hauls once a week."

He said "Munch" with the same gusto he used when he said her name. She felt the good feelings a father should have for his daughter between the letters—all the feelings Trey swore he'd have for their future daughters.

"Hm... and the slippers? I doubt your girlfriend would want some strange woman's feet in her house shoes."

It was one of those double-duty questions she used to throw out back before the dating pool had turned into a contaminated swamp full of men like LaDarius Mitchell—back before Trey. It was the type of question she should've thrown out on her date, but it had snuck its way out for somebody who wasn't even a potential for her.

"I don't date insecure bitches with low emotional intelligence —so ain't no problem on my end."

Now, she was laughing even though she wasn't supposed to, but her new favorite wine made her silly enough to think the bad words tumbling out of Anthony's mouth sounded good—all the bitches and misogyny he swore swirled within LaDarius.

"Watch your mouth." She rolled her eyes, snatching the slippers from his hands.

"A'ight, Venus." He smiled and nodded while she shoved her feet into the UGGs.

The tension in her feet melted into the wool as he walked over and opened his car's passenger door for her.

God, the bar was in hell.

The bare minimum impressed her.

His eyes grazed her legs as she pushed up from the bench and tugged her dress down.

He talked to her with his mind again, telling her he'd peel

her out of the God awful too little dress as soon as he got the chance.

He leaned against the door, waiting as she shuffled to the car and maneuvered into the passenger seat like a stuffed sausage because he had strange gentlemen-like qualities that didn't make sense in her foggy wine-filled brain.

After he closed her inside, she craned her neck for any other evidence of the emotionally intelligent girl he claimed he dated. All she found was a little pink sweater and Jodeci crooning through the speakers. Kaydens were something to behold when they shouldn't have been, and the wrongness of the entire situation didn't smack her in the face until he got inside the car.

"Where you live?" he asked, putting the car in drive and pulling out of Vaughn's parking lot.

They glided onto the dark midtown streets.

She swallowed, rattling off her address and waiting on him to put it into his GPS, but he just kept puffing on that joint he never dropped and humming along to Jodeci like he was decompressing alone after a long shift at work.

"You tryna call me old?" she rasped, smirking.

"What you mean?"

"Jodeci? Really? Were you even thought of when this came out?"

He didn't blurt out the first thing that came to mind. Instead, he waited until he stopped at a red light and then flashed a lazy, low-eyed look at her.

"How old you is, anyway?"

"Your mama never taught you to never ask a lady her age?"

"My nigga taught me that if I fucked a lady good enough, age wouldn't even be a topic of discussion."

That warm buzzing from before trickled back to her middle at the way his lips contorted to say "fuck." How could somebody she was supposed to hate look so good and say such sketchy things at the same time? It was sinful.

"Language," she gritted out, rolling her eyes and fighting a smile.

"Don't chastise me right now. I could've put you in a nice Uber Black, but I'm letting you infringe on my me-time, Ms. Thibodeaux. Let me live tonight."

"So you're saying *I* can chastise you?"

Her stomach fluttered in a way she thought it had forgotten. It'd been so long that butterflies were probably kicking up cobwebs as they fought to rise from the dead at the bottom of her loveless gut.

She remembered how to flirt?

He shrugged. "Mhmm. I'm open to constructive criticism when I need it."

The smile she fought crept along her mouth because he sounded good, even when he wasn't saying his words with gusto. She imagined he floated home from work every night in the same way—all cerebral and high behind the wheel of that stupid loud ass car.

"You'll even accept constructive criticism from judgmental bitches like me?" she fired back with the same addictively, calm tone as his.

It must've been the second-hand smoke.

"It depends."

"On?"

"What it pertains to and how you deliver it. Sometimes women think a nigga need hand holding—whole time we just be wanting guidance on how to be men without the condescending bullshit that comes with it." He shrugged. "Correct me with respect is all I'm saying."

"I don't know if I should be offended or enlightened."

"That's for you to decide. I'm just giving you food for thought, Venus."

There it was again—her name with gusto. It sounded even better when he was floating in the clouds with red hazy eyes and

Jodeci crooning because what Kayden even thought about the shit Anthony did?

She mulled over his words while the smoke kissed her face and the city's lights fluttered inside the car as they glided along quiet back streets she'd never taken.

"So... are you enlightened or offended?" he asked, rolling the window down and flicking the shriveled joint out of it.

She smiled at the way he blinked and brushed a hand across his tired eyes. It was only the second time that night he looked young and vulnerable. It disappeared as quickly as it came.

"I'm... enlightened I think."

"You think? You don't know how you feel?"

She snorted with a smirk. "It's something I'm learning again."

Trey had swiped all of that away because Rose believed good wives gave up that right. Feelings and decisions were controlled by all the good husbands who stripped their wives of their identities and gave them new ones that revolved around the institution of marriage.

Shit, what would Anthony think of such an archaic belief?

"You forgot how to feel? That ain't no good," he said.

"I guess."

"One of the best parts of a woman is how deeply she feels."

"Yeah... but sometimes life happens and we lose touch of those deep feelings. We get too busy catering to other folks and bending ourselves so much that one day we wake up and can't even remember how the fuck we like our eggs cooked because we been cooking them the same way for ten years just to satisfy another person."

They turned to each other.

It was funny how easily "LaDarius Mitchell" turned into an afterthought and the aggravation with Logan and Ginny didn't consume her anymore because she sat next to an anomaly that made her wet just from a simple conversation. After spending so long in a thought-less marriage, her brain did backflips at the mental stimulation from a man.

"So..." He smiled. "How you like your eggs cooked?"

The laugh she'd been holding shot out in a loud guffaw that made the muscles in her stomach tighten.

She wagged her finger his way. "Over easy... I like them over easy."

He nodded as if she'd given him access to her best kept secret and she didn't have time to follow up with her own questions because he'd already pulled up to the parking garage entrance of her complex.

Her stomach dropped.

She would've believed Anthony if he told her they floated all the way there with Jodeci playing in the background.

"Home sweet home," he muttered.

She fumbled with her crossbody and pulled out her key fob, opening the garage door. He pulled into the first open parking spot while she tried to ignore her flip-flopping stomach.

The universe was being as weird as Daddy always claimed it to be. It was how she ended up as a Thibodeaux and now it had her giddy in a car with Tori's daddy during the first week of school.

She reached out to pull the door handle, but paused and looked over her shoulder. "So, is this a truce?"

"A truce?"

"Yeah... an agreement to sto—"

"I know what a truce is." He snorted and brushed his knuckles against his tired eyes again.

Those letters she studied back at Vaughn's glowed underneath the parking garage's lights. Now, she could finish reading the rest of them without LaDarius' cawing to interrupt.

TY.

TH I R TY.

Thirty.

He dropped his hand back against the steering wheel. "Ain't no truce. I'm just letting you know this is neutral turf."

"Your car?"

"Nah, this space between me and you without Munch."

She glanced at the empty backseat and imagined Tori there with her eyes as wide as they were when they practiced their numbers in class. She tried to hear her voice in the space between her and Anthony, but she couldn't.

"Right..." she replied, pushing open the door until she remembered why she hated all those rowdy alternative school boys that looked at her like she shit out gold.

She turned back toward him and thrust her hand out.

"What?" he asked.

"Morri—I mean LaDarius' ID and credit card. Give them here."

"For what?"

"I know that Vaughn's doesn't pay enough for this car." She cocked her head to the side. "Just like I know that credit card fraud is a felony. If you get pulled over, ain't no cop gonna believe that stolen ID and credit card is LaDarius'—or whatever his name is—and not yours. Give them here."

"Are you discriminating against me?" He laughed. "Shit, I got co-workers that drive BMWs."

"Don't insult my intelligence, lil' boy."

He shook his head with a smile and dug the cards out of his pocket. When their hands brushed, she tried to control the shudder that coursed through her body, but it was a hard thing to do when Anthony maintained eye contact better than most men her age. Logan was right. She needed to get fucked. It was the only explanation for the embarrassing emotional roller coaster ride she let *a Kayden* take her body on.

She gripped the cards and then pushed out of the car.

"Venus?" he called out before she could slam the door.

She pulled it back open. "Yeah?"

"You gon' really walk away without explaining yourself?"

She snorted out a low laugh, glancing down at the pink UGGs she decided not to give back to whichever little undeserving girl got to sit and listen to Anthony's fascinating musings about the world.

"Explain?" She rolled her eyes up. "I divorced the last man I explained myself to."

His eyes lit and his lips grew slack. He even leaned over the middle console like he planned to drag her back inside and make her do what he asked, but both of them knew better.

This was their first and last night together. There'd be no future stolen moments between them because Paula had entered Tori's change of address into the computer for the third time and the rest of her communication with Anthony would be through Parent Connect where all of his words would be monitored for the inappropriateness he liked to weave into their conversations. There'd be no more temptation because she'd let Logan have that dreaded future meeting with him about Tori's inability to say her name.

There'd be no more mutual telepathy or silent gushing over the way his mouth moved when he cursed, pronounced fancy dishes for her, or spat insults her way. She had to be the mature one for them.

She tapped her fingers against the door and peeled her mind away from his.

"Stay out of trouble, Anthony."

six

. . .

"WHAT DO you mean she's not talking?" Lynn's eyebrows shot above her readers as she stopped typing.

"I didn't say she ain't talking. I said her new teacher said she ain't talking *in class*," Anthony gritted out. "There's a difference."

He hated he had to relay Venus' outlandish observation out loud. He had even fought with himself about it.

The door to her office creaked.

They looked up at Mikayla poking her head through the cracked french doors. She bit into her lip, staring at him because just five minutes before, he had her on her knees in the empty office Lynn's paralegals used when they weren't working from home.

Lynn cleared her throat. "Can you give us a minute, sunshine? We're talking intricate details right now."

Anthony snorted out a laugh and rolled his eyes as Mikayla backed out of the doorway. The restored hardwood floors in the bungalow creaked as she pattered away in her Golden Goose sneakers without a response.

"We're sending her to USC next semester," Lynn blurted as soon as the doors slammed shut.

"Oh, for real? From Spelman to USC. Interesting."

"They have an excellent law program. It'll do her some good to be away from me, Quentin, and ... Atlanta."

"Atlanta" didn't come out easy. She squeaked it in a high-pitched tone with a spacey look on her face, as if she wanted him to keel over and hold his shattered heart. Little did she know, Mikayla wasn't his only fling that got shipped away. He hoped Sarauniya was still thinking about him in Lagos. She swore they'd get married one day, even though he promised her he wasn't the marrying type.

"Do she know she moving?" he asked.

She dropped her pen on Munch's file and shrugged, leaning back. "Not yet. We haven't decided how we're going to tell her. She's so stuck on staying here for the rest of her life."

Her eyes bore into his face and neck. They raked across his tattoos, his jeans, his sneakers, and his mouth.

She was searching for the "whys" and "hows" of Mikayla's obsession. Parents always wondered how he did it—how he turned their preppy, worldly baby girl's brains into foreign objects that only revolved around him, but Lynn described herself as a liberal. She toted around a gaggle of women that looked like they should've been on somebody's Real House-wives cast, so she'd never ponder out loud about Mikayla's attraction to a shiesty ass nigga like him.

"This might be a wild suggestion, but maybe you should ask her how she feel about it first."

She laughed, swiping the straight bang from her pixie cut out of her face. "I'm paying for tuition, room, and board. She has no feelings in this situation. When Tori gets older, you'll under-stand. I admire your sage parental advice, though."

He wouldn't understand because he promised DeeDee they'd never control Munch's future. If she wanted to venture to New York City and try her hand at fashion design or trek overseas to explore Europe during a gap year, he'd let her do it with no fuss.

"Let her have USC. She needs it," she said.

He smirked, shrugging.

He didn't care about his and Mikayla's situationship beyond his last court date, but Lynn knew he had the last say-so in her and Quentin's audacious USC decision, despite what she said. He wasn't paying room, board, and tuition, but he *was* giving Mikayla the best dick she ever had in her young life and that trumped anything her mama and daddy said. She told him so anytime he asked.

"Now, about this problematic teacher we have on our hands," she said.

His cheek tingled at her description of Venus.

She was problematic, mouthy, sexy... and divorced, which meant she *really really* needed his dick and he *really really* wanted her to have it however she wanted it. Then, he wanted her barefoot behind a stove cooking them the over easy eggs she forgot she liked. He'd replayed her snatching LaDarius' cards out of his hand and sashaying away in Mikayla's UGGs a thousand times. It got better each time.

"What's your relationship with her like?" Lynn asked.

"Relationship?"

"Yeah. Are you in good standing with her?"

"It's only the first week of school. What kind of relationship I'm supposed to have with her?"

"Well... I'm sure you've heard the old saying—'you never get a second chance to make a first impression.' So, did you offer to buy extra supplies for the class? Offer to volunteer throughout the school year? Ask about joining the PTA? Most important, did you pretend to take her concerns seriously?"

"I ain't a brown-noser."

She laughed. "No, but you're... resourceful."

She eyed him with less vitriol, like she was reminiscing about that day in Josiah's suite at the Mercedes Benz stadium when Mikayla bounded up to her and Quentin with a dewy after-sex glow and her hands tangled around his arm. Four months later, he had Mikayla's arms hooked around his middle while they sat in Lynn's living room with her retainer fee stacked on her coffee table.

If Dre' was there, he'd correct Lynn.

Nuney? Resourceful?

Nah, in their family, he was the finesser.

"What you getting at?" he asked.

"I'm not getting at anything. As your lawyer, I'm advising you to cultivate a decent relationship with her, which includes taking her concerns seriously."

"As my lawyer, why're you advising me to waste time cultivating relationships with folks whose opinions don't matter?"

"That's where you're wrong." She held up her finger. "Custody cases are emotional and most of the time they boil down to a bunch of 'he said' 'she said' bullshit that the judge has to sift through. Montgomery doesn't want to hear from me or you how good of a parent you are. He wants factual testimonies from people who have nothing to lose, and may I remind you, there aren't many people like that in your life."

He frowned, sweeping his eyes across Lynn's desk.

Just the thought of Venus sitting up on a stand and hearing all the shit he and DeeDee kept on a need to know basis made his stomach rattle.

"Don't tell me she have to come to court?"

Her eyes grew, and she hunched her shoulders. "It's a possibility. She *is* Tori's teacher."

"Fuck no. Hell *fuckin'* no."

"Hey, we're knee deep in a war here and you're not exactly Mr. Clean. We need all the allies we can get—even allies you might hate."

And wanna fuck.

He shook the thought away.

"We're not in the business of collecting unnecessary enemies. Go offer to buy some freakin' tissue and construction paper and smile at her. How hard could it be?"

Sometimes Lynn's privilege leaked out. Offering to buy

useless shit and smiling at Venus wouldn't make her get on a stand and tell a judge how good of a man he was. Venus wasn't naïve like the neighborhood girls that worked at Munch's old daycare. She looked at him like DeeDee did sometimes and if Lynn knew anything about women who doled out those looks, she'd know that all was fair in love and war with women like them.

"All I'm saying is that you need to consider it. Calling her in as a character witness is only a possibility right now. Like you said—it's only the first week of school. She's someone new in Tori's life, but in the meantime, you need to keep her placated."

He almost groaned.

Only Munch could have him pivoting from street wars to courtroom battles and wanting to groan like a pussy in some lawyer's office.

"I'll see about it," he replied, swiping his forehead.

"Alright. Well, you better see about it quickly." She scoffed. "Is it even true?"

"Is what true?"

"Is she really not talking?"

He narrowed his eyes at her until she shrank in her seat with an eye roll.

He could've argued with her and told her just that morning he had to explain to Munch that she couldn't use the word "damn" even if DeeDee said it all the time, but he'd be wasting his breath.

"Fine." She tossed her hands up. "I told you I'm not the enemy. You have to start telling me everything. This isn't a gun charge or a probation violation and I'm not some court appointed shithead who doesn't have your best interest in mind. If Tori isn't talking anymore, I need to know because if they even get wind of something like that..."

She shook her head, looking at the floor.

As if he didn't know that.

"I told you I'd see about it," he repeated, leaning forward

and checking for Mikayla's reflection in the mirror Lynn had mounted above her desk.

She huffed. "Well, how're things at the restaurant? Or are we being mum about that, too?"

"If things were bad, Mikayla would tell you." He smiled, and she frowned.

"Would she really?"

"Of course. Ask her."

"I'd rather not. Vaughn is doing us both a favor, so keep your nose and his restaurant clean. Montgomery hates irresponsible unemployed parents—especially ones with uncooperative baby mamas that do more harm than good, and teeth that cost as much as the different cars they pull up to court in."

He laughed, and that made Lynn frown harder.

He looked between her and Mikayla in the mirror.

Mikayla sat on the sofa in the waiting area with her legs draped over the arm, scrolling on her phone while Lynn's eleven o'clock sat next to her, thumbing through a Vogue magazine. His appointment ended an hour ago and Lynn charged a grip for her time, but she'd eat the cost because that extra hour had nothing to do with his case and everything to do with Mikayla.

He stood up, pulling his keys out of his pocket, but he didn't take two steps before Lynn's frigid voice stopped him.

"Hey..."

He stared at the doorknob while the soft patter of her pen tapping against her desk filled the quiet space.

"Who's Shad?"

"Who wanna know?"

"Me—your lawyer. I wanna know," she mocked.

Her words hung between them and he let them.

"He got hemmed up in DeKalb a few weeks ago. The cops questioned him about some other petty crimes and your name came up when they asked about his hand."

He looked down at his own hand, curling his car keys into his palm.

"My contact at the county courthouse pulled up the police report from the incident. Shad told the cop in the emergency room that he never saw who walked up to his car and did it."

"I don't know what you talkin' 'bout, Lynn."

The tapping stopped.

"Right..." she uttered. "If they put charges on you, then all of this is done. You know that, right? There are only so many miracles I can make happen with this case. I got the temporary custody with no visitation, the job history to impress Montgomery, fought the motion for drug testing. I swear I've been fighting motions since you signed the retainer agreement."

He pressed his hand against the french doors.

"You should take care of that—take care of him and that teacher."

As soon as he pushed the door open, Mikayla hopped up with a relaxed grin because she was as sunny as that "sunshine" nickname Lynn gave her. She bounced over to him as Lynn's eleven o'clock glanced up from the magazine and stared at his hands grazing her ass.

"Think you can drop me off on campus?" she whispered as Lynn waved the lady off the sofa. "Daddy took my car to get new brake pads put on and I have a paper to finish."

She curled her fingers through his and pulled him outside the bungalow's front door, where she latched onto his side. The wind blew a gust of air carrying her jasmine scent and sweeping away the remnants of Shad's screams that were leftover from last summer.

He dropped her fingers.

"What's the paper about?"

"'A Raisin in the Sun.' Somebody came in clutch and posted their notes in our class' group chat."

"It's only like a hundred and fifty pages."

"How do you know that?"

"You left it in my car last week."

"And you actually read it?"

"Yeah." He shrugged.

"When did you even have the time—actually don't even bother giving me a non-answer." She laughed. "Just don't let me forget it in your car again. It's a loaner and I have to bring it back to the bookstore."

He actually didn't have the time, so he spent an hour every other Wednesday thumbing through the pages while Dre' met with his PO. He'd gifted Dre' his own car when he got out but ever since life happened Dre' insisted on encroaching on his me-time until Tash told him to stop.

They talked about a lot during those thirty-minute treks to the parole office, though—mostly about their own intricate details of Munch's case and the implications their lives would have on it. Sometimes Dre' doled out that sage parental advice Lynn mused about.

"I'mma tell you like I told JoJo—fatherhood is special. You get to have somebody that's gon' love you for the rest of your life. Don't let the world dictate your relationship with her. The only thing that matters is what you feel in your heart."

As soon as they got near his passenger side door, Mikayla pushed her small body into his and let her head fall back like they were in some corny ass rom-com.

She wanted a kiss.

He pressed his finger against her nose and smiled instead. "Don't be lame. Read the book, 'Kayla."

Thanks to Logan, Venus' classroom had turned into a battlefield.

They'd just finished inhaling their lemon pepper wings from King's Wings and recoiling at the recap of her date when Logan's office phone rang. She heard that raspy voice boom from her seat in front of Logan's and she was prepared for Anthony to spill the beans about their run-in, but he had something else on his mind that made Logan shift in her seat.

"You want to have a conference on a Friday? In the middle of the day? Have you lost your mind?" she squeaked.

Undoubtedly, he had.

Now he sat across from Venus at her class' designated Play-Doh table smelling like a pleasant medley of weed and strawberries.

Just five minutes before he breezed through her classroom's threshold, Destiny Jefferson smashed Tori's finger in the cafeteria door because she didn't hear her trailing behind her. Now, Venus and Anthony were engaged in a full-fledged war with their eyes because *Munch* wailed in the space between them. She cried so hard the veins in her neck bulged and she didn't call him "daddy" when he pressed her purple finger to his puckered lips.

"Noni!" she hollered as Logan rushed through the door with a bag of ice from the cafeteria.

"Shhhh," he whispered, bouncing her up and down. "I'm sorry that happened."

Now, Venus owed Daddy twenty dollars because Anthony had been the one to get Tori to belt out her first word of the school year.

She scooted to the edge of her seat, holding her breath for Tori to gasp out more, but she kept wailing.

"It's okay..." Logan cooed, pressing the ice pack to her finger.

There was no parent on Earth that ever made Venus squirm, but Anthony glared at her like she'd been the one that slammed Tori's tiny finger in the cafeteria door.

She twisted in her blue jeans because they didn't exist in the neutral space of his car without Tori. They were enemies again. She felt transparent—like he could see that she tossed LaDarius Mitchell's ID and Danielle Jamesons' credit card in the trash chute that morning and then fried an over easy egg in her underwear, wearing the pink UGGS that still smelled like him. Pepper even liked to rub his back against them when he thought she wasn't looking.

God, she hated his young judgmental ass again because he *was* that damn fine.

"Thanks for accommodating us, Venus. I know this whole thing was last minute, but Anthony really wanted to meet with you about your concerns." Logan looked between them while Tori croaked out a whimper.

"Sure." She shrugged, glancing at the Sesame Street clock behind her head. "No problem at all. I understand that Anth— uh... Mr..."

"Nunez," he finished for her.

"*Nunez.* I understand Mr. Nunez works so..."

That same space Anthony assured her was between them the night before, sat between her words now. She took long uncharacteristic pauses that made her cringe.

He tugged Tori closer into his chest with a smirk as if he rolled over right as the clock struck noon with the bright idea to give Logan a call and ruin their most sacred day of the work week.

It was her fuck-it Friday. She had a list of trashy reality shows queued up on her laptop for when she got off the phone with Ginny because she was sure her silly idea to date without a purpose was over.

"Right." Logan clapped, sighing. "So, Nuney, Venus shared some concerns with me abo—"

"Yeah, concerns I already addressed with her the other day. So I'm tryna understand why she felt the need to bring them to you."

She *absolutely* hated his ass again.

"I mean, her concerns are valid. She did what any of the other teachers would've done. Not to mention it's been a whole week and Tori still hasn't spoken."

"Oh, so all of y'all go around gossiping and misdiagnosing the kids here?"

Logan cocked her head back.

"Forget all this politically correct stuff, Lolo. I always

approach you with respect when it come to Shaun, so return the favor," he added.

Venus snorted out a sarcastic laugh and Logan cut her eyes at her. The tension grew between them and festered.

Logan sighed, slapping her thighs. "Okay, Nuney. What's up? My house is a mess and I need to find thirty koi fish before Desmond gets back. You trippin' on a Friday, nigga. I been mentally off the clock since ten—"

"Venus thinks something is wrong with my daughter. She think she's non-verbal," he cut into her rant. "I just wanted to give her the time and space to voice her concerns while I'm here and get your thoughts on the situation without Mo inserting himself into something that ain't his business all the way from Japan."

All the gusto was missing from "Venus," but the allure that existed in their neutral territory twinkled in his droopy, red eyes. "Fuck you" was written all along the smirk that appeared on his lips afterward because he played dirty in war. It was that telepathy again that had her reading through his expressions.

Logan's eyes got big.

"I did not say she was non-verbal," Venus gritted out. "I told him she doesn't talk in my class and, according to other staff, she doesn't talk in theirs either."

"I told you she talk at home."

"Alright," she huffed out another sarcastic laugh.

"You just heard her talk, didn't you?"

"She was in pain... and she hasn't said anything since, but whatever."

And nobody could translate what she'd even said, besides him.

Tori inhaled a deep breath and sucked up a nostril full of snot at the same time. He swiped at it with his bare hand while Venus grimaced.

"You always insinuating something's wrong with your students and making assumptions about their parents?"

"*Really?* You're going there?"

"Hey, you said it. Not me."

"Are you fuc—"

"Woah now." Logan twirled her short arms in circles. "Let's simmer down. It's getting spicy for no reason. It's Friday, y'all. *The weekend.*"

Venus rolled her eyes.

Logan was as shitty of a mediator as the one she and Trey used during their divorce, except there weren't any assets to be divided between her and Anthony. The only thing on the line was her shoddy reputation Anthony had every right to attack. She *had* accused him of being neglectful in a roundabout way, but she'd never called Tori non-verbal—at least not officially.

He shrugged. "I ain't got nothing but time."

"Well, I don't. Desmond will be home any day now looking for these fish. I'm spiral—"

"Okay, Logan." Venus sighed, grabbing her forehead. "Can you give us a minute, please?"

"Are you sure? I can jus—"

"I'm sure."

seven

. . .

ALL WAS *ALWAYS* fair in love and war with women like Venus—especially when her blue jeans cuffed the bottom of her ass as she escorted Logan out of her classroom. Her hips even swayed in a natural rhythm that made Anthony's neck hot.

As soon as she turned around from closing the door, he let out a sigh that made Munch whip her head around to stare at him between whimpers.

Venus crossed her arms, covering her hardened nipples underneath the frilly "Ms. Thibodeaux" t-shirt she probably only wore on Fridays. Today, it didn't have any mysterious stains, and he already wanted to peel her out of it.

"So, what you not gon' do is come up in here and put words in my mouth," she spat.

Next, his stomach did a cartwheel because who the fuck did she think she was talking to?

Munch rubbed her red eyes with the back of her fists and that really made Venus' feet hot. She stomped his way in a pair of Roshe Runs DeeDee would've gagged at and pulled Munch right out of his arms. Munch didn't even make a fuss about it like she normally would.

"You know good and well I did *not* call this baby non-verbal, nor did I diagnose her. That's damn near illegal." She swiped a Kleenex off her desk and dragged it across Munch's nose liked she'd wiped a thousand tiny noses throughout her teacher-life. "Shhh. It's okay. We looked at your finger. It's not bruised or broken."

She tossed the Kleenex in the trash and then pulled the bag of ice from Munch's hand, dropping it on her desk. Then she tugged at the hurt finger, wiggling it from side to side as Munch stared in bewilderment.

"Destiny told you sorry and even helped me put the bandaid on your boo-boo. Calm down so me and Daddy can understand what you're trying to tell us."

She talked to Munch like he did, but she had the feminine energy they'd been missing at home. She made him want to fly to whatever podunk town she came from and collect all the other Venuses that might've existed there with their big hair, country accents, and fat asses. If Dre' was there, they'd laugh and muse about placing Venus at the top of his 'favorite bitch list'—she'd go right under DeeDee.

Munch didn't say anything. Instead, she hugged Venus around the shoulders and her legs squeezed her wide hips. Their bodies molded together and made his mouth dry. If he could be a fly on the crooked, paint splattered curtains that covered the window in her classroom, he would. He'd watch Munch curl into her like they'd known each other their whole lives every single day, with no regrets.

They leaned against her desk and Venus' eyes brushed against his mouth. "You got fifteen minutes."

"To do what?" he choked out.

"To explain yourself before my class comes in from their impromptu recess, thanks to your lil' stunt."

He didn't even recognize his own hoarse voice, but that's what his favorite bitches did. They made him speechless with their audacity sometimes, as if he wouldn't fuck the audaciousness out of them.

He snorted out a low laugh.

"I can't correct a man with respect if he don't respect me first. Respect is mutual, and it's earned, Anthony." She frowned. "You bum-rush me on a Friday afternoon, putting words in my mouth I didn't say. Are you tryna get me fired?"

Damn.

Their conversation from the night before still danced in her head like it did his.

Venus popped her hip out. "I'm waiting."

"I hate the last bitch I explained myself to."

He didn't mean for it to come out, but the way she belted out similar words before slamming his car door made it feel okay to share something so pussy.

Hate was a strong word, but it was the only one that could encompass the hot feeling that bubbled inside him every time he saw any semblance of DeeDee on Munch's face.

Venus' eyebrows relaxed and her lip tilted up. "You're on my turf today, so watch your mouth."

She didn't ask him to explain any more, and it made his shoulders light because that explanation was something else on him and DeeDee's "need to know" list.

He swallowed at the way Munch's eyes fluttered while she snuggled against Venus' titties. He didn't blame her. He'd curl up right there too if they didn't argue so fuckin' much.

Venus didn't even need to rock her like Lola did, and Lola was an expert at soothing babies. All it had taken was the soft cadence of her voice and her deep breaths to shut Munch up and make her fall into a light sleep.

He nodded their way. "You real good at that."

"Good at what?"

"Putting her at ease."

She was almost as good as he was.

She shrugged. "It's not so hard once you get the hang of it."

"How long you been teaching?"

"Twelve years."

His mind chased after her age that she wouldn't divulge the night before until she held her hand up.

"Don't do that."

He smiled.

He missed their telepathic conversations. Even DeeDee couldn't do that shit.

"You ever had a student like Munch?" he asked.

"No..." She smiled at him and he forgot his lips were still upturned. "I never had such a perfect jitterbug who follows me around all day, helps me pass out snacks at snack time, or hums 'Wheels on the Bus' so dang good because her daddy won't teach her another song."

She didn't talk like any teacher he ever had. Her words sucked him into a frilly kindergarten world where he imagined her reading nursery rhymes in all the silly voices his elementary teachers never did. He saw the softness in her eyes when she talked about Munch and felt the longing she felt as the other kids screamed outside her classroom window.

"But I *have* had plenty of students whose voices I missed even though I never heard them."

She was trying so hard to set fire to that list he and DeeDee had created with the way she pranced around the elephant in the room much more delicately than she did the first day they met.

His eyes fluttered to the door where he knew Logan had her head smashed against it, trying her hardest to hear.

He'd known Logan since he was little, but he had learned that sometimes family ties didn't mean shit in the real world. He wasn't as enthralled with her as his little brother DeShaun was. Logan still had a job to do, a license to protect that she worked hard for, folks to report her *special* kids to, and paperwork to file that Lynn would curse at when they talked about the "intricate details" of his case. He couldn't let her in on anymore of his and DeeDee's messy ass life.

"So, how do things work on your turf?" he asked, peeling his eyes off the door. "Since you strong-arming me today."

When he looked back at her, she was looking at his balled knuckles resting on top of the table he sat at. Her eyes traced the letters Lynn made him cover with her concealer any time they went to a hearing.

No matter how much white teenagers had embraced that word because of Josiah's new NFL career, their parents still saw it for what it was. Lynn didn't dab makeup onto the "Lola" on his neck or the outline of DeeDee's puckered lips on his wrist—it was just that THIRTY that always had her so flustered but not Venus, though.

He saw the knowing in her eyes as if she was there the day Dre' told Josiah to stick him thirty times in his chest for thinking he could live with Lola on Thirtieth Avenue and not befriend them. Dre' counted each punch from his daddy's front porch and Anthony thought his heart had stopped until Dre' reassured him that if it did, his brothers were the only ones that could bring him back to life. He still believed that sometimes.

"You tell me how things work on yours first," she replied, pulling Munch closer to her chest. "Respect, remember?"

He saw what twelve years of teaching had done to her psyche. It swirled in her sable colored irises.

He glanced at the door again. "That's your friend?"

"Who? Logan?"

"Yeah."

"I mean, we just met over the summer—"

"But do you consider her a friend?"

"I—yeah. I do," she stammered out the words, wrinkling her eyebrows.

"Oh..." He nodded. "A'ight."

"Why? What's that have to do with anything?"

When he didn't respond, her face contorted into three different expressions—confusion, intrigue, and then annoyance.

"Who I consider a friend is my business, not yours," she added.

He strummed his knuckles against the table while her Sesame Street clock ticked, filling in the silence.

They stared at each other in their familiar way—trying to rifle through each other's thoughts.

"Fuck this," almost rumbled out of his mouth until Munch gasped out the deepest sigh and hooked her bandaged finger onto the collar of Venus' shirt like she hadn't slept in years. Now, instead of "fuck this," it was "fuck it" because who did she think she was, clutching Munch into her chest like that, and talking to him like he had his dick buried deep inside her the night before?

"My bitch, my business," he replied. "That's how shit work with me. Since you wanna know so bad."

She didn't gasp. Instead, her face lit with mirth. Dre' had taught him that one in a letter he'd written to him the summer he turned sixteen.

Mirth.

Dre' said his counselor's eyes "lit with mirth," when he told her how he jumped bail again because he promised Lola he'd be there for her sixtieth birthday party.

A laugh rippled through Venus' body like she heard his thoughts. It was deep and guttural, but didn't make Munch stir.

"First of all—" she choked out between laughs.

"Women ain't bitches," he finished for her with mirth on his own damn face. "I know."

"I'm glad you know. So next time you won't say that God awful word in my babies' classroom." Her laugh calmed into a chuckle. "And second of all, I'm Tori's teacher—not *your* bitch. So I'm not *your* business."

Her eyes grazed her favorite place again—his knuckles. "But I think I get it."

She did. She had the type of intelligence that transcended the pages of college textbooks and only came with life experience.

"I don't have kids but I think there's a certain type of unhealthy obsessiveness we—well, parents get when somebody else tells them that something's changed in their kid." She looked up at the ceiling. "They want to know the ins and outs and inner workings of their little brains so they can try to rewire them to go back to how they were before the change happened."

She nodded to herself and kept talking to the ceiling. "In a sense, teachers become *yours* just as much as they become your kids' because we're responsible for them seven hours a day and sometimes we become just as obsessed."

He sighed like Munch.

It was full of jealousy because his baby got to sit and listen to Venus Thibodeaux's airy voice and spacey thoughts all day. Only she could justify his irrational ass rule, that DeeDee always struggled with, and explain why he felt so compelled to make her follow it when she wasn't shit to him. She wasn't his girl, his sister, or his mama. She was just Munch's judgmental teacher whose mind he could read sometimes.

She looked away from the ceiling and back at him. "I don't gossip with Logan about everything that happens in this class-room, if that's what you're getting at. I only report things that concern me. Not that it's any of your business how I move at work, but I understand your concern as a ... *parent*."

She struggled with the word "parent" as if he wasn't quali-fied for the role, but for once, he wasn't offended by her judg-mental nature—just fascinated.

He nodded while trying to relax his stiff cheeks. His muscles fought him, though—especially since he didn't need to spell anything out for her. She lived in his head whether he liked it or not, and lame ass smiles were a requirement of her new living arrangements.

The faint sound of another teacher rounding up Munch's rambunctious class made him push up from the Play-Doh covered table. His fifteen minutes had fizzled down to one and if he could, he would've recorded this moment for Lynn just so he could say, "I told you so."

What would his favorite bitches do with construction paper and tissue? They didn't need that. They needed him to sift through their broken pieces other folks had stepped over and put them together one by one.

He strolled up to them, brushing his knuckles against Munch's brown cheek. She looked like DeeDee the most when she was deep in dreamland with her eyes pinched shut. He felt that hot bubble of hatred deep in his gut until she blew out a tiny wisp of air through her nose and reminded him she wasn't her mama.

He bent down, nuzzling his lips across hers while inhaling.

"Bye, Munchy-Munch..." he muttered, savoring the sweet scent wafting from her little mouth and its taste. "No more crying today."

He felt the heat from Venus as her chest rose and fell while he whispered to Munch, and he recognized the need in her voice when she blurted out, "I—I met him on Tinder. I wasn't looking for anything serious. I was just looking for somebody to..."

He let her unsure words hang between them before he pulled his lips from Munch's and looked up at her.

She looked at the ceiling again as if that was her safe zone. There, they couldn't hop into each other's heads and read the thoughts that drifted around in them, but little did she know he could still get in her head just from inhaling her energy.

"Pass the time?" he finished for her.

She snorted and nodded. "Ye—yeah...to pass the time. If that's how you want to put it."

The mysterious case of LaDarius Mitchell was finally solved, and it'd taken almost twenty-four hours to squeeze it out of her.

He shook his head and reached out, tugging at her t-shirt and marching his fingers along the kooky leopard printed letters that spelled her name. "Next time, don't make me bum-rush you on a Friday afternoon and put words in your mouth. You should've just explained yourself last night when I told you to—now leave my baby *and* Tinder alone."

Her mouth fell open while the tiny footsteps of her class echoed from the hallway. Logan chirped to the teacher respon-

sible for escorting them back inside while forbidden heat rumi-
nated between them.

It was something about the thrill of anybody bursting
through her classroom door to find his fingers on her and the
explanations she swore she'd never give him falling out of her
mouth. That something made their eyes heavy.

"I thought you didn't care what I do outside of school
hours?" she breathed out in a daze.

How could he not care when she made his dick stir, and
worry run rampant through his body at the power she yielded
over him just from the tiny piece of innocuous information she'd
brought up to Logan under the guise of being a good teacher?

"I lied," he muttered, giving her t-shirt one last tug and then
backing away. "You should never wanna just pass time. You
should wanna live."

The classroom door creaked as it flung open and Logan led
the way, guiding little bodies in with her hands on their shoulders. "So, should we finish this up in my office? I can get Mrs.
Maloney—"

"Nope," Venus replied, glaring at him. "Anthony was actually just leaving."

"*Oh.* Y'all worked it out?"

"Yeah…something like that." She reached out and gripped
his elbow, escorting him out just like she'd done to Logan.

Even on the walk out, with her fingers digging into his skin,
all he could mull over was the fact that some fuck nigga had the
audacity to let *her* divorce him.

———

"You met someone?" Michole looked up from her notebook.

She sat up straight and flung a braid over her shoulder.

Out of their hundreds of therapy sessions, it was one of the
few wide-eyed expressions she'd given Venus—besides that time
Venus admitted to pouring sugar in Trey's gas tank.

Venus nudged Pepper from under her computer desk, shooing him away with the soft ball of fur from the UGGS she couldn't peel her feet out of. "Huh? Oh no, I didn't meet anybod—"

"You said 'Anthony drove you home from your failed date.' Who's Anthony?"

The best thing about virtual therapy sessions was the mute button that lived right underneath Michole's chin.

Venus clicked it and released a deep groan before clicking it again.

There was a trick she'd learned with her and Trey's first therapist, Susan—if she only fed Susan the information she "needed to know," their sessions could flow a lot smoother. There was less bickering, less judgment of her awful thoughts, and less regret in her chest on their drive home.

Therapy as a single person was different. There was no one to share the spotlight. Michole reserved all of her curious energy for her, and sometimes she opened her big ass mouth and blurted things she shouldn't—things like Anthony's name that tasted as sweet as the strawberry scent that always clung to him.

"So... who's Anthony?" she repeated.

She didn't realize her mouth hung open until Michole cleared her throat.

"We don't have to talk about him—"

"He's nobody. He's one of my students' dads."

She rushed through the sentence, trying to convince herself and Michole that Anthony was another insignificant parent at Hill Elementary.

"*Oh,*" Michole replied with too much interest in her tone. "How did he end up taking you home?"

"He works at the restaurant as a waiter and felt sorry for me, so he offered to give me a ride."

"And you accepted?"

"Well.... I'm rubbing two pennies together with one income now. It was either collect more overdraft fees or get in the car with some sweaty, balding catfish named LaDarius Mitchell. So Anthony it was."

Michole winced, and Venus did too. She'd *really* wince when she realized she'd have another unpaid invoice that month.

"So, which student belongs to Anthony? The projectile vomiter, the biter, or the hummer?"

Her stomach fluttered.

"And by all means, tell me to move on from this subject if you don't want to talk about it."

"No...no. It's fine." She shook her head. "Uh, the hummer is his."

"Oh." Michole sat higher, if that was even possible.

Her neck stretched like a giraffe's and then she looked down. The faint sound of scribbling echoed through Venus' computer speakers.

"He's the parent you're having conflict with?"

"I wouldn't call it conflict."

"You said you tried to tell him that his child isn't verbal, and he shut you down. I'd call that conflict, wouldn't you?"

"Okay, sure. It's conflict." Venus hunched her shoulders and shook away the stoic look on Anthony's face from that second day of school.

It was so titillating that it made her march home after she left work, log on to her afternoon therapy session and call him every name but his God-given one while Michole scribbled in her little therapist book of bullshit. The amount of times she replayed his expression in her head that night should've been criminal. Now, her brain was stuck on another Anthony loop.

She swallowed his scent again as if he were right in front of her, scolding her for having boundaries with somebody that looked as good as him.

Michole cleared her throat again. "You know this space is yours, right? If you don't want to call it conflict, we don't have to."

"No, no. I agree. It's conflict. He continues to give me push-

back about his daughter. He even coordinated his own conference at the last minute to humiliate me in front of the counselor,
even though it's clear his child has a speech problem."

Her stomach rumbled as if she were betraying Anthony and
Tori by sharing their business with a third party.

"So what's your plan?"

"For?"

"For the rest of the school year? I mean, you're experienced.
You know that a non-verbal student is a serious concern and a
parent in denial is ..."

Michole whistled and her slender face contorted into all
kinds of satisfying "thank God, these aren't my problems"
expressions, while Venus stared at the Parent Connect portal
behind her head.

Not only did Kaydens have odd gentlemen-like qualities, but
they were also responsible in a good ass panty-wetting way that
kept her focused on them and not therapy.

Anthony Nunez ✓

There he was. Parent number two out of ten that had registered for the portal Principal Bivins swore would be the answer
to their communication problems with parents. Never mind that
half of her students still had the instructional flyer in their take-
home folders.

She brushed her fingers that had touched his elbow down the
length of her jeans. They were still hot and longing for another
taste of his skin, even though it had been hours since she nudged
him out of her classroom.

"Venus?" Michole called out, making her look away from his
name. "Is everything okay?"

"Uh... yeah. I'm good."

"I asked what your plan was for the rest of the school year. I
think I lost you."

"Plan?" she choked out, squirming.

She needed to create as much space between her and
Anthony as possible. She could request that Tori transfer to Mrs.

Maloney's class, but then she'd need a reason—a *real good* reason. The way Anthony's glowering expressions and their bickering made her want to roll her panties down to her ankles for him wasn't good enough. She could explain to Principal Bivins that she couldn't handle Tori's complex issu—

"Avoidance isn't a healthy coping mechanism. In fact, it'll only worsen the problem in the long run."

"You—you think I want to avoid him?"

"I told you this was a safe space. It's just me and you here—no Anthony."

She almost gagged at the fact Michole even knew his name. She still called Trey "the ex-husband" in their sessions. No one had the privilege of infiltrating her safe space, yet Anthony had finessed his way in just like he did with everything else.

She blew out a deep breath. "This is ridiculous. I've had worse parents than him. There's no reason for me to avoid this boy, because let's be frank—that's all he is. An immature ass lil' boy that thinks he knows better than everybody around him. He —he..."

He made her body and mind teleport back to a time before Trey—back before he tore her into tiny little pieces and blew her into an abyss where all the rest of the world's miserable wives existed.

"He... what?" Michole asked, wrinkling her eyebrows.

He made her want to do the irresponsible shit she did before Trey. Irresponsible shit...like *fuck him*.

"Nothing," she squeaked out with a swallow.

"Well..." Michole sighed. "Although confrontation is uncomfortable, it's healthy if you do it in the right way. Let's use this weekend to focus on naming our feelings, owning them, and taking the first step to *healthily* confronting Anthony about his denial and your frustrations."

"First step?"

"Yeah, the first step. As Desmond TuTu would say, 'there is only one way to eat an elephant, and that's one bite at a time.'"

Michole waved her arm before grabbing her mug of tea. "I can't tell you what the first step might be for you. Maybe it's jotting down some talking points for the next time you run into him or drafting an email outlining your concerns. You could even practice in the mirror in the comfort of your own home—noting your breathing and delivery when addressing him. I mean, the possibilities are endless, but my main concern is that you do it healthily and responsibly, Venus. You're doing the right thing by advocating for your student and you're *so* experienced—don't let anybody take that away from you. I'm so proud of how far you've come."

Her cheeks bunched up as she took a sip of her tea.

eight

· · ·

"LOOK, MUNCH. SAY 'UNCLE,'" Josiah sang, tugging Munch's thumb out of her mouth. "Come on. Why you beefing with me? Who I'm gon' watch highlights with now?"

Munch sniffled, staring at him from her cocoon on Anthony's lap. Josiah's daughter Journey leaned in with her soft eyebrows pinched together as if she'd forgotten what Munch's rasp sounded like. It'd been a while since they all heard it echoing throughout Josiah's big ass house, but then again, DeeDee had never let her stay home long enough to even get to know Journey.

She was always absent from their birthdays and welcome home parties and he was always fumbling over whatever excuses didn't sound so fucked up when they asked where she was because DeeDee didn't see her as a living baby sometimes. She saw her as a chess piece.

Dre's daughter Audriana pranced around in front of the projector in the game room.

Ever since Zeke's Aunt Toya's house got lit up last summer, Josiah's compound in Alpharetta had turned into the epicenter for their family on his off days. It was his home, but their communal space. His girlfriend Jade liked to do domestic shit there, like cook dinner and plan "baecations" that never came to fruition, so she settled on sporadic game nights that made them feel their ages sometimes.

"Say 'Dri,'" Audriana yelped, spinning in a circle with her braids flying around. "She still says my name, Uncle Nuney. She was just saying it earlier."

"Okay, but she gotta say it for us, sweetpea," Anthony mumbled, acquiescing to Audriana's tales.

Josiah tilted his head, sighing. "You tried candy?"

Twenty Tootsie Rolls, five packs of Starburst, and even banana pudding Mona shoved into his chest at the end of his last shift. She swore it would make the shyest kid talk again. Munch inhaled it and threw it all up afterward without even so much as a "thank you" and she still wouldn't talk to Josiah when they pulled up to his house after he picked her up from Lola's.

He twisted his lips at Josiah's "genius" solution and Josiah shrugged. "Message her ass back and tell her 'no.' Period."

It sounded like a simple solution, but Venus Thibodeaux wasn't simple. She was complicated, sexy, and kept him distracted every time he confronted her. She had her slender foot on his neck and refused to let up and deep down in the pit of his stomach he didn't want her to.

Her complicated ass even had Josiah flustered, and that nigga *never got* flustered. That word wasn't even in his vocabulary.

Anthony glanced at the message from the Parent Connect app that was still open on his phone.

V. Thibodeaux
Good evening Mr. Nunez,
Per our conversation from this afternoon, I wanted to
follow up and inquire about your availability next week
so we can further discuss Tori's developmental milestones
with Logan present. I look forward to hearing from you.

"Fuck," he hissed, widening his eyes at Munch afterward,

but she was so entranced by Josiah's goatee she didn't even repeat it.

She reached out and pulled at the hairs.

"Ohhh," Audriana sang, prancing by them and holding her hand out. "Gimme your twenty dollars for the swear jar."

He held in the rest of his bad words and dug a crumpled twenty from his pocket, holding it out for Audriana so she could stick it in another one of Jade's corny domestic projects: The lame ass swear jar. They'd accumulated a thousand dollars that summer because they were all home for once instead of on Rice Street, in prison, or fantasizing over the phone about how they'd finally get out of Toya's basement and up to Athens to visit Josiah in college.

Audriana snatched the money and then pulled Journey toward the doorway, leaving Munch in her new comfort zone in his lap.

"What about DeeDee?" Josiah croaked, flopping back to his side of the couch and picking up the PS5 controller he'd dropped to tend to Munch.

"What about her?"

"You take Munch to see her?"

Anthony looked back at Venus' message.

Her words jumbled together into a hodgepodge of black and white. He tried to think of anything he could do besides that. Munch's tiny finger glided across the message before she turned to him with a grin.

Today, she *really* looked like DeeDee. He had tied her favorite bow around her puff and dressed her in polka dotted overalls DeeDee liked for her to wear.

"You allowed to do that, right?" Josiah asked.

"I never asked."

"Maybe you should."

As soon as he opened his mouth to name all the reasons he shouldn't do such a stupid ass thing, his phone dinged with another Parent Connect notification.

Weekly Progress Report
Math: Exceptional
Science: Exceptional
Work Habits: Exceptional
Reading Development: Needs Improvement
Speaking Development: Needs Improvement
Notes: SPED evaluation pending upon response from
parent.

He didn't realize his heart pounded against his chest until
Munch pushed forward and turned to him with her eyebrows
furrowed, like she knew what Venus' notes said.

"You good, twin?" Josiah's voice broke through the
pounding.

He looked up.

Josiah stared at him with a worried expression because
they'd all been taught to absorb each other's problems. It was a
switch they couldn't turn off no matter how old they got.

"Yeah, I'm straight." He picked up his phone and pressed the
"reply" button.

He *had* to get Venus off that police ass app.

The cursor blinked while he mulled over all the ways he
could convince her to stop caring so much because he could fix it
—he could fix Munch without Logan, a SPED class, or Venus'
interference before their day in court.

"Why the fuck she online at eight on a Friday anyway?" he
complained. "Oh yeah, because she ain't got no goddamn life."

Josiah sputtered out a laugh while smashing buttons on the
controller. "Chill. Teachers love Fridays. Jade like to come home,
get her grading out the way, put Jour to bed, and then put me to
bed as soon as I get in…"

His voice drifted off while Anthony tried to picture Venus
going through the same boring routine. He couldn't. All he saw
was her playing on another lame dating app and getting
catfished for the second time because the world had probably

changed since she last dated. He imagined it to be a strange place for a woman just looking for somebody to "pass the time" with.

Munch pointed at the TV as Josiah stopped sifting through NFL teams and stopped on the Baltimore Ravens.

"Purple." Anthony tugged her thumb, but she wouldn't let go. "Purple like Ms. T."

He smiled, even though he didn't want to. Venus occupied the space in his brain that DeeDee and Munch didn't, because she was as complicated as they were.

"Ms. T…" Josiah muttered to himself. "Maybe her nigga will get home and fold her ass up—make snitching the least of her worries."

Anthony blew out a raspberry. "What nigga?"

"Oh… *damn*. Never mind. She gon' be lighting your ass up all night, my boy. Talk to Logan about it."

"That's her work friend. They on the same side."

Josiah grunted. "Talk to Mo about it for real this time."

Now Anthony grunted.

"Yeah, never mind." Josiah grimaced. "Don't talk to Mo about it. Ms. Dorothea gon' have the whole city in ya' business."

He bit into his lip, holding in another "fuck" while his wild eyes roamed Josiah's game room. They raked across the dolls Journey and Audriana left scattered in front of the projector, Munch's opened backpack, and their car keys on the pool table. Then, he scoured the Parent Connect app while Josiah babbled next to him about Jade and her raggedy brown Honda she wouldn't let go of for "nostalgic reasons."

"That shit really just been collecting dust in the driveway, on God. I don't get it. She got a whole Benz out there with the plastic still on the seats but want me to spend money on a new paint job for an Accord. She swear Jour gon' be driving that lemon when she turn sixteen. I ain't putting my baby in that."

His voice drifted off and blended in with Audriana and Journey's giggling as they climbed the stairs leading into the game room. He couldn't differentiate between any of the sounds because his brain was doing that "funny shit," like Zeke always said. It was connecting the dots—putting the pieces together—lining shit up just the right way to make a play.

His eyes jumped back to Munch's backpack where that ugly, bedazzled folder poked out the top of it.

"Bluey," he blurted, scooting to the edge of the couch.

"Huh?"

"The coloring sheet in Munch's backpack."

"What about it?"

He plopped Munch next to him, and then pushed up, taking long strides to her backpack. When he got to it, he pulled out the folder and thumbed through it until he found the coloring sheet he stopped Lola from tossing in the trash.

"What you doing, man?" Josiah asked distractedly.

"Shutting her ass up."

"Huh?"

"I'm gon' shut her ass up," he repeated, snatching the paper out.

"And how you gon' do that?"

He studied the paper until he found her phone number on the tiny label in size four font. "Shit, I'mma fuck her."

Josiah sputtered out a laugh. "Listen, usually I'm on your side because a lil' ratchet shit never hurt nobody every now and then. But man with everything going on, I really don't think that's a good idea."

He tuned Josiah out. Ever since he and Dre' fell in love, they thought they were the moral police. He needed Zeke. Zeke was just as loveless and ratchet as he was when Jade's annoying dick-crazy friend Kristen didn't have him locked down.

"These females got y'all soft," he muttered to himself, looking between his phone and her number.

He squinted at the tiny numbers on the label. He typed them in and then started typing the most important part: The message. It had to be inconspicuous—innocent, even.

> Hey, this is Anthony, Tori's dad. I see your messages on that app, but I can't reply. I think it's a glitch. Can we talk?

It was a silly, white lie that shouldn't have felt good to tell, but it did anyway. Little white lies always got his foot in the door —like when he told DeeDee he'd only stick the tip in, or when he reassured Mikayla he'd still wanna fuck with her, even if her mama wasn't a lawyer.

It didn't take long for those telltale dots to pop up underneath his text. He studied them, trying to follow her typing patterns through the screen.

"You know you can go cross-eyed from staring at the screen like that, right?" Josiah cracked. "But I'm tender, though? *Tuh.*"

His phone vibrated in his hand with her response.

It was a good sign for him, but bad in the grand scheme of things. She didn't take hours to think about shit she should've, and that's probably how she ended up on that Tinder date from hell.

He shook his head.

All of his assumptions had been right—*nobody* was fuckin' Venus Thibodeaux.

> 8329601846:
>
> Uh...sure? You know my phone number is only for emergencies.

Right.

He was supposed to have tossed it in the trash by accident, like the rest of the parents in the class had.

> 8329601846:
>
> But how about Monday? I can stay late after school if you have to work.

For the night

Anthony:
Nah, let's do it tomorrow. I'll buy you coffee.

8329601846:
That's inappropriate.

He smiled.
She was as easy as she was complicated.

Anthony:
A parent buying you a cup of coffee is inappropriate...even though you like coffee?

8329601846:
You don't know that.

Anthony:
I saw it on your shirt that one day after school. It was on the white button down with the gold buttons. You always be spilling stuff right there?

This time, she thought.
She typed.
Stopped.
Typed again.
She did it so much that his stomach churned.

Anthony:
We'll be on neutral turf. I can't fuck with you on neutral turf. You know that, right? We can air out our differences.

He didn't realize he'd been staring at their text thread for so long until Josiah grunted at Journey for running.

"Jour..." he warned.

"Sorry, Daddy."

The loud ping from Venus "HaHa'ing" his last message drowned them out. She snatched the reaction away before he had time to say something slick about it, like she was stopping herself before she got carried away.

> **8329601846:**
>
> Just coffee. Nothing else. I'll pick the place. Also, don't make this a habit. I value my off days.

His burning eyes darted over at Journey hanging off Josiah's neck and rambling about how she'd only been running because she wanted to get to him faster to hug him.

As soon as she blurted out her last thought, Anthony cut in. "A'ight, baby-Jade, can Uncle talk to Daddy for like two seconds?"

He held two fingers up, and Journey grinned back at him.

If they let her, she'd ramble to Josiah forever until he was the one apologizing for fussing at her.

She pressed her forehead to Josiah's and let out a light giggle.

"Twin, let me get that AMG off you," Anthony added.

Josiah yanked his head away from hers. "Nigga, what?"

"You heard me."

"I just told you I bought that for Jade."

"So? Ownership ain't never stopped no motion." He shrugged and then nodded toward the projector. "I'll even meet you where you at today. No dice."

Josiah shook his head, frowning. "Man, go 'head. You don't even fuckin' play Madden."

"I do today."

nine

. . .

ROSE HAD CONVINCED Trey there was still a sliver of Venus' brain he hadn't squeezed the immaturity out of.

I thought you talked to her," she used to hiss under her breath as if Venus wasn't a few feet away. *"She gallivanting around here in lil' bitty ass shorts, tipsy as all hell and grinning in your cousins' faces. I saw that letter from the doctor when I checked ya'lls mail. She ought to be worried about that."*

He tried to wrap his hands around that piece of her brain one last time after Rose's observation, but he wasn't successful. Now it was still there—battered and hanging on by a thread, but still craving excitement.

"I'm responsible. I'm confident. I'm mature. I can handle any obstacle that presents itself in my life."

Venus paced the perimeter of her empty living room. She wrung her wet fingers while repeating the affirmations Michole forced her to write out over the summer when she moved to Atlanta with a thousand dollars to her name.

Her heels dug into the carpet and she jumped at the clacking noise from the hallway that could've been Anthony knocking at her door.

"Fuck, I need a TV," she whispered as Pepper meowed from

her bedroom's doorframe. "Don't look at me like that. It's just talking. We're just gonna talk—that's it."

Pepper meowed back and roamed into the living room with his wispy tail sweeping back and forth. Even he knew how wrong all of it was—Anthony's messages, the fact she'd even *responded* to those messages, her outfit, and worst of all—she'd accepted his offer to pick her up.

She glanced down at the denim jumpsuit that hadn't seen the light of day since Rose convinced her that all good wives dressed modestly. It still fit all the places it wasn't supposed to—around her bust and hips, and it hugged her ass in a way Trey loved before they got married. Surprisingly, it had come back in style again, so she didn't look as dated as she felt.

"I'm taking the first step to confronting what I've been avoiding." She straightened her back like Michole. "I'm eating the elephant one chunk at a time or whatever the fuck she said. I'm —I'm meeting this dude where he's at. He's in denial. Tori still can't say more than one word. That IEP in Logan's office is still blank. I'm confronting him respectfully before Principal Bivins finds out I'm hoarding a kid who can't talk."

She looked and sounded ridiculous trying to justify the spontaneous meeting. It had been so long since sweat coated her palms because of the impending excitement of doing something just a *wee* bit irresponsible.

She grew dizzy.

Her palm didn't even get a chance to land on her kitchen countertop to quell her dizziness before the soft *tap tap* against her door made her back straighten again.

She glanced at her watch.

Of course, it said seven because Kaydens were annoyingly punctual when they wanted to be.

She clunked over to the front door and took a deep breath before twisting the locks and flinging it open with a now or never attitude.

As soon as their eyes crashed into each other's, she wished

she would've erred on the side of never, because *Anthonys* looked their best with mischievous smiles on their toasted brown faces, dressed in all the things Trey and LaDarius Mitchell wished they could pull off. He'd even gotten his hair cut down into a low taper. She wanted to reach out and touch him...to make sure he felt as good as he looked.

He wore jewelry too—inconspicuous shit only women would appreciate like tiny dainty gold huggies that dangled from his ears.

She opened her mouth, but nothing came out. It didn't matter though because Anthonys were professional Venus mind readers. He probably saw all the "shits," "fucks," and "damns" that hung out in her head while she tried to convince herself that everything that made him...*him*—was wrong—like his tattoos peeking out from his shirt's collar, his freckles the dim hallway lights caught as he dropped his head, and his stark white sneakers that would've been an abomination if they were going on a first date.

He smirked, dragging his low eyes across her face. "Hi."

"Hi."

A soft *thwack* against her leg made them peer down at Pepper staring between them.

"Go back in, Pepper," she hissed, nudging him with her heel.

She'd almost escaped the lonely cat lady label, but Pepper was just too damn nosey.

Anthony nodded at him, crouching down. "What you got goin' on, Pepper?"

Pepper purred because he liked male voices—especially deep, low timbre ones like Anthony's. Sometimes she caught him at the front door with his tiny ear at the crack, listening for any men that might pass by. The cat rescue she adopted him from told her his old owners were a gay couple named Ronnie and Ray, as if that explained why he craved men more than she did sometimes.

"What's that your mama was saying before I pulled up,

Pepper?" Anthony leaned in, being careful not to intrude on his personal space. "Oh, for real? *Swear to God?*"

"What are you, the cat whisperer or something?" She chuckled, nudging Pepper again.

"For sure. The black Jackson Galaxy at your service." He looked up at her and saluted. "Shit, I can do more than whisper to it if you let me sho—"

"Don't start." She frowned, waving Pepper back in. "Why the fuck do you know who Jackson Galaxy is, anyway? You're such a strange lil' boy."

His goofy laugh made Pepper stick his pink nose through the crack for one last peek before she pulled the door shut.

And just like that, Anthony broke the ice between them because that immature part of her brain was addicted to the dead butterflies he figured out how to resurrect with silly double entendres and stupid shit he only thought about like Jackson Galaxy.

He wasn't high and cerebral this time—just sober and flirty with the afternoon's possibility in his eyes. The funniest part of it all was that she'd take either version of him because they were both enticing enough to make her crave him when he wasn't around. She couldn't even remember the last time she craved a man.

He let her lead the way out of the building as if he hadn't found his way to her apartment on his own. Despite being out of practice with men, she knew his eyes brushed her ass the entire walk. Trey used to tell her it was impossible for men not to watch when she walked because she swung her hips in an infuriatingly sexy way he hated, so he convinced her to forget how to do it.

But a month after her divorce, Michole made her learn how to walk all over again. One foot always went in front of the other —heel down first, toes down second. They agreed it was the perfect way to walk away from the things and people that didn't suit her anymore. The quiet chuckle Anthony uttered confirmed her practice had been worth it. She still walked in that infuriat-ingly sexy way—she still had it—maybe.

When they approached the busy side street next to her build-ing, she strained her neck searching for that ugly loud car she'd gotten into two nights ago, but it wasn't there.

She turned at the sound of Anthony digging a pair of keys from his pocket. These keys weren't personal to him. They had a key fob and dealer tag hanging from a Mercedes Benz keychain.

He pressed the fob twice and another expensive car he shouldn't have been able to afford chirped. It was all black with modest tint and nothing that screamed, "illegal!" It looked like something she used to dream of driving back when Trey would feed her all of the promises a man who reeked of potential would—all of the, "you'll be driving that once I get this job" potential.

"Anthony..." she gritted out. "Don't have me in no shit."

She didn't even realize she'd been wagging her finger at him until he gripped it and tugged at it.

It was the second time their skin touched in two days. She shouldn't have been counting, but Logan theorized that being dick-less did strange things to a woman's brain.

"And I'm telling you not to be wagging your finger in my goddamn face unless you want me to bite that motherfucka." He smiled, brushing his eyes against her décolletage just like he had at the restaurant while he massaged her hot finger. "You not correcting me with respect right now, Ms. Thibodeaux, and I don't like it."

His voice didn't even match the words he spat out. He talked in the same tone he used the night he brought her home, but this time there was a brusqueness in it that told her she'd met the yin to her irresponsible yang that Rose hated. They were too close and too hot for one afternoon that was supposed to exist as a neutral space for them to air out their grievances.

"Is this your car too?" she asked.

He nodded with a smile as sweet as Tori's.

"Are you telling the truth?"

"The paperwork is in the glovebox."

"Yeah right. I'm not riding in that."

"Why you ain't text me and tell me what you wanted to ride in, then?"

A light breeze tickled her face as a group of girls came out of an apartment and passed by them. They giggled and eyed him as if he were theirs because, in a sense, he was. He was their age, their speed, and the girls he should've been entertaining.

"Because I don't sit around texting all damn day like a teenager," she spat back, fighting that annoying smile he always conjured up while avoiding the girls' gazes on their close bodies.

"Oh, so you like to sit on the phone then? Why you ain't tell me that? I would've called."

"Because I think you're confusing this with something that it's not." She pulled her wet finger from his grip.

He stepped back, furrowing his bushy eyebrows and swiping his tongue across his bottom lip. "So you mean to tell me you just be getting dressed up for any ole dude and I'm not as special as I thought? Damn, Pepper lied to a nigga's face."

He talked as if he were delivering a soul-stirring monologue to an enthralled audience, but his performance was just for her as they stood underneath the hazy mid-afternoon sun. His emotionally intelligent little girlfriend must've been entertained often because Anthonys were lit with a certain humor that only existed in people that "lived" like he'd mused about.

"He most definitely lied." She smirked, shrugging as if it hadn't taken her an hour to work up the nerve to pull the jump-suit up her thighs. "And I'm *most definitely* not riding in that car."

His lips drew down, and he nodded to himself. "Fine. Go back upstairs then."

Her face fell because it hadn't caught up with the responsible part of her brain yet. She was supposed to feign indifference and march back upstairs just the way she had marched down—one foot right in front of the other because they shouldn't have agreed to do something so damn silly, anyway.

Cars honked in the distance and zipped past them as they frowned at each other.

She almost heard her own heavy breaths until his lush lips crawled up into an annoying smirk. "I'm just fuckin' with you."

"You said you wouldn't do that."

He cocked his head back, beckoning her closer. "You right. C'mon with yo' federal ass."

"I don't even know what that means."

"Good. You don't need to know," he murmured, yanking the passenger door open.

He stooped down and flung the glove compartment open while she shuffled back and forth on the sidewalk, preparing to turn back at any semblance of bullshit—for real this time.

"Here." He turned around, nudging a piece of paper toward her.

When she didn't take it, he tugged at the same finger she wagged in his face. "My lil' brother borrowed my other car for the day."

She hiked her eyebrow up. "He can drive that car?"

"He'll drive a goddamn tractor as long as it get him to see his lil' girlfriend. I probably ain't gon' see it 'til tomorrow night."

"What if he gets pulled over?"

He shrugged, smirking. "Chill. If you don't put it out in the universe, it won't happen."

He whistled, tugging her by the finger with the paper hanging at his side. "Now, what else you wanna know, Officer Thibodeaux?"

She smiled against her will—a breezy one that made his eyes low. "So who's watching Tori? She with her mama?"

"Wrong turf."

"Fine." She rolled her eyes up. "What's that paper?"

"The title."

He unfolded it and her eyes raked over a name that didn't belong to him.

Josiah Joseph.

She frowned and yelped. "You stole a football player's car?"

"Stole? Man, you trippin'." He howled, deciding one finger wasn't enough to convince her to get in the car, so he grabbed another. "JoJo is my brother. I just ain't got the title changed."

She raked her eyes over his face, searching for the "gotcha!" but it never came.

The Josiah Joseph *she* knew was plastered on the cover of that month's *Essence* magazine with poreless brown skin and cherry kissed lips. She breezed past it in Publix after work the night before on a wine run. He was young—*too* young, but it didn't stop grown women from swooning over his accent and the way he loved on a girl that looked nothing like the chicks his peers obsessed over. The possibility of him leading the Falcons to the Super Bowl and his declaration to *Essence* that he would never "leave his family" was the icing on top because everybody knew he wasn't pandering—he was just being him.

She searched Anthony's face for the life they'd lived together that had bound them together as "brothers." She stopped as soon as he reached up and brushed his knuckles against his eyes.

See, Josiah was shirtless in that *Essence* spread she'd thumbed through in the checkout line. The number thirty stretched so far across his chest that she'd cocked her head to the side, studying the way the ink dipped between his abs and wondering why his agent hadn't made him cover it yet.

"So you borrowed your brother's car, who just so happens to be the quarterback for the Falcons while your *other* brother has your car?" she asked. "Interesting."

"First of all, I ain't never borrowed nothing in my adult life. I won it. Ironically, that nigga is ass in Madden, but he plays in the NFL. That shit should be illegal because how the fuck you lose a whole car?" He tsk'd to himself. "Good thing I have a meeting with a teacher who always wanted to drive a Benz, though—an AMG, to be specific."

He muttered the last part.

"Ho—how do you know that?" she stuttered, trying to wrap her brain around the fact she kept flirting with a guy who still played video games.

He snorted. "Come on. Don't act like you don't be in my head too."

"So you hustled your brother?"

"I don't hustle people."

"So, what do you call what you did?"

"My lawyer would've said I was being resourceful."

Lawyer?

She shook her head, looking down.

Now, she was flirting with a guy who had a lawyer for reasons unknown.

God, the bar was in hell.

"Come test drive it."

He pulled away and walked to the driver's side door, yanking it open.

She didn't begrudgingly get in this car. Instead, she floated right past him and eased behind the steering wheel. When he shut her inside and swaggered around the car, she counted out her deep breaths like Michole would've suggested. In *onetwothree*. Out *onetwothree*.

He snatched open the passenger door and fell inside next to her.

The car smelled like new leather and him. It was impersonal, with twenty miles on the odometer. Tori's belongings still weren't in the backseat and there was no Jodeci crooning this time. It was quiet and waiting for her to bring it to life.

She pulled the seatbelt over her chest while he watched her.

"Don't be staring at me the whole time I'm driving either," she complained, gripping the steering wheel hard. "I will park this bitch and go back up to my apartment."

He laughed in the goofy way she was getting used to because he didn't take offense to anything she said unless it involved Tori.

"If you knew what I wanted to do every time you cursed at me, I bet you wouldn't do that shit no more."

"Behave..."

"You first."

"*Anthony.*"

He snickered, reaching on the floor in front of the passenger seat and pulling a strawberry kiwi Snapple from a plastic bag while leaning the seat back.

"I was thinking we could just go to a coffee shop nearby. One just opened around the corner. I pass it every morning on the way to school. It looks quaint... and neutral."

And far enough away from Hill elementary, so they had no chance of running into a nosey staff member.

He slurped out of the Snapple bottle and stared through the window while she pulled onto the street. "Quaint?"

"You got something against quaint places?"

"Only when controlling kindergarten teachers can't just be soft. Why you be so hard all the time?"

"Pardon me?"

"You really think I would invite you out and have *you* make plans for us? How presumptuous of you, shawty."

Presumptuous?

She smiled to herself, staring at the road.

When he talked like that with his accent dipping in and out of each syllable of whatever enticing word he used, she got warm in places she shouldn't have and didn't give a fuck if he hustled his so-called friends to impress her.

"If I wanted us to go to a quaint coffee shop, I would've planned for that, but I'm reasonable, so we can go after dinner if you still want coffee."

She choked on a wild bead of spit. "Dinner?"

"That's what I said. I can't talk on an empty stomach. What, now you gon' tell me you fasting or some shit like that?"

She laughed, and it made him whip his head toward her with the Snapple to his lips.

The sun cast a bright glow on his face. She couldn't believe they'd found themselves in the same space outside of Hill elementary again.

"Make a left up here and get on the e-way," he muttered after a swallow.

And she did, reveling in the smooth way the car glided across every pothole and dip in the street. It felt nothing like her Honda and it was laughable the emotionally intelligent little girl she was always wondering about got to enjoy Anthony's unpredictability and all the nice toys he was always driving around.

"Your girlfriend know you taking Tori's teacher to dinner?" she blurted, trying to pry into that part of his life just one more time.

She wanted to know *too* much about the girl who had Tori's eyes and got the cerebral parts of him more than she did.

"If my ole lady wanna know where I'm at, she gon' know where I'm at. I ain't answering no more questions from you, Officer. You don't hear me asking you about the nigga that let you divorce him."

He smiled and reached out, turning on the radio while she swallowed his words.

Let?

ten

. . .

"SHE GAVE ME A C. Can you believe that?" a soft voice murmured.

"Yeah. You ain't follow the rubric in the syllabus," Anthony replied. "It was under the assignment prompt in big, bold ass letters. You know bold usually means important, right, girl?"

She huffed out a giggle.

Venus eyed him out of her peripheral. He had stretched out in the passenger seat with his arm tossed behind his head, staring out of the window.

He looked his age again with sleep laden eyes. Every now and then, he'd swipe his hand across his head and stare wistfully at a random maple tree.

"I asked you to proof it. Why didn't you point out that I missed half of the rubric requirements?"

"Be specific next time. You said to proof it—not confirm that you followed the instructions. How you gon' get in law school if you don't even read the whole syllabus? The professor could write *anything* in there and you wouldn't know no better."

She giggled again. "Leave me alone. Nobody sits there and reads every syllabus they get, baby."

Venus' stomach flipped as if the girl had called her such a soft nickname. She hummed it out like they were in bed together.

"I would if I was in college."

"Then come to college," the girl replied.

"No."

He said the word with finality and Venus tried her hardest to picture him on her own college campus with the Texas heat baking his skin to a nice reddish brown and the possibility of him pledging some fraternity he'd blend seamlessly with. They'd sit next to each other in biology and he wouldn't waste half the semester staring at her before asking for her number—he'd just do it on the first day of class. She understood the wistfulness in the girl's voice, even if she didn't want to.

When he synced his phone to the Bluetooth connection in the car, she expected to be ambushed by more R&B or a bunch of aggressive mumble rap, but she got something worse: Mikayla J.

The emotionally intelligent UGG owner that made her blood pressure hike wasn't intelligent at all—emotionally or in a traditional sense. She was just a spoiled girl that hung on to every word Anthony dangled her way, and there was no way she was Tori's mama.

Mikayla sighed so deep it filled the car. "Where are you, anyway?"

"Out."

"Where?"

"Didn't you tell me to mind my business when I asked where you was at last weekend when you wasn't answering my texts?"

"I was matching your energy." She huffed, and he laughed.

"Can't do that if you in your feelings, 'Kayla."

"Yeah, whatever."

She felt Mikayla's bashfulness through the phone as he little girled her.

"Don't get into anything or Mom will have a fit," she added. "Call me when you're done with whatever you're doing."

The call ended with no promises from him.

All the sour laughter Venus had been holding in came out as she drove down a winding street in Druid Hills.

Who would've thought Anthony Nunez had a thing for spoiled college girls that still cared about what their mama's thought?

"Thought if your ole lady wanted to know where you were at, she'd know?" she blurted between chuckles.

"A teacher who can't read between the lines. Interesting..."

"Are you shading me?" she yelped, smiling too big.

"Nah. I'm telling you that you too grown to not know when I'm talking to my woman and when I'm choppin' it up with a vibe." He thumped her thigh.

"So, that's not Tori's mama?"

"So, you really served your ex-husband with divorce papers?"

She sputtered out another sarcastic laugh. "Funny."

She tapped her fingers against the steering wheel while her mind ventured to the forbidden places it kept wandering to ever since he came into her classroom raising hell. In those places, she imagined him in uncharacteristic scenarios where he fucked preppy college girls who felt comfortable enough to introduce him to their parents.

"Turn on this street up here," he said.

She turned down a picturesque street without signaling and cringed. Her eyes darted to the rearview mirror, even though he assured her the car was legal.

"It's the house at the end of the cul-de-sac," he added.

She wasn't an expert at Atlanta no matter how many summers she'd spent with Ginny, but she knew there was no restaurant nestled on the street he mentioned—only citizen-led neighborhood patrols. There were only two houses—the one he directed her to and another off to the right that looked dwarfish in comparison to the brick one she drove toward.

Its rainbow-shaped driveway looked like it should've been staffed with a valet and a doorman, but it was empty. There weren't any cars or people awaiting their arrival. She expected a lone bunch of tumbleweed to blow past the car when she pulled into the driveway.

"Where should I park?" she asked, swallowing her other questions.

"Right here is good."

She pressed the car's brakes and put it into park when they stopped in front of the massive front door.

Nobody burst out of the house with excitement to accuse them of trespassing. Nothing happened except the sprinklers sputtering on to coat the lush grass.

She pulled the visor down to make sure she hadn't licked all the gloss off her lips as they drove.

Anthony stretched his arms up and cracked his knuckles while she gave herself another once-over Trey was usually in charge of. He'd complain about her unnecessary cleavage, the heels that made her two inches taller than him, and her hair. He liked it slicked back into a bun the best. It was nondescript, librarian-like, and made her blend in. Today, it was wild, purple and free.

"You look sexy as hell," Anthony grunted out lazily while smacking his lips.

Just like that, he extinguished all the critiques that had spread like a wildfire in her head, even though Michole taught her to stop seeking validation from men. There were no Anthony clauses in her lessons, though. Validation sounded *so* good wrapped in his smoky voice that she wanted him to give her more because the weird thing about it was the way she automatically agreed with his opinion. Her wild hair, ample cleavage, and heels *were* sexy, and they *were* just for him like he'd mused about, but she'd never tell him.

"C'mon before this nigga change his mind." He pressed the push to start button and the car's humming engine stopped.

In the short time it took him to get out, round the car and

open her door, she counted out five deep breaths while trying to forget what "sexy" sounded like coming out of his mouth.

She couldn't.

It was still lingering in her head, wrapped in his accent and deep timbre.

When she climbed out of the driver's seat, he eyed her up and down completely this time, as if his compliment was his warning that he'd admire her in the open for the rest of the evening, so she'd better get used to it. Afterward, he smirked and held his arm out like a chauffeur.

They glided to the front door with her marching in front of him again. She clenched her calves and glutes so he could admire the ways a divorce had restructured her body. Stress eating had given her an ass Ginny admired any chance she got, and living on the fourth floor had replenished the little muscle she lost after college.

He chuckled to himself as she climbed the steps to the porch. When they made it to the front door, he hooked his hand around her waist and leaned over her to pound on it. She took the time to inhale him until somebody flung the door open.

"You allergic to being on time?"

The "nigga" Anthony had mused about was a handsome bald man who looked like the Morris she'd been longing for at Vaughn's.

He grinned at her in his slacks and white shirt. She looked up at Anthony, who smiled at him.

"That's how you greet your best employee?" he asked the man.

"Best employee?" she hissed at him. "This your boss?"

The man stepped back, inviting them inside with a nod of his head.

Anthony tapped her at the center of her ass, and her stomach jumped. It happened so fast she couldn't even decide how she felt about it. She stepped forward, and he nudged her into the massive house that felt lush inside, with its gaudy chandeliers and hardwood floors.

The man ignored Anthony's quip and her question and zeroed in on her cleavage that Anthony assured her was sexy just minutes before. It didn't feel that way standing in front of a man that was his boss, though.

"I'm Vaughn." He grinned and scooped her hand from her side.

Oh no.

She *really* shouldn't have been there.

His thumb stroked the backside of her hand while he stared through her. "You're beautiful."

The old her would've melted at the way "beautiful" rolled off of his tongue, but she heard the sleaziness in it. He probably used that same compliment on every moderately attractive woman he came across, and she saw the void look in his dark eyes.

"Nice to meet you." She smiled a crooked grin, backing into Anthony's middle. "I'm Ve—"

"Now why the fuck would a beautiful lady like you agree to dinner with this asshole?"

She widened her eyes until Anthony snorted out a low laugh and pressed the small of her back.

Her shoulders dropped. "I didn't, yet here I am."

Vaughn stepped back and waved them further inside. As soon as Anthony closed the front door behind them, he squatted next to her.

She tried not to grow dizzy from his hands that had somehow traveled from her ass to her ankles in just five short minutes. They still hadn't slowed down long enough for her to process how she felt about *any* of it.

"Every week, I beg this dude to have dinner with me—to pull up on me—to come kick it. Every. Single. Month. And it takes a female to get him here—no offense, beautiful."

"None taken... I think."

"Good. Sometimes I speak before I think."

"Right," she replied breathlessly.

Vaughn swiped her hand again, pressing his puckered lips to it while Anthony slipped her heels off and she shrank to her normal height.

He lined them up beside the front door but kept his sneakers on, and then Vaughn dragged her deeper into his massive house by the same hand he kissed. He squeezed it as they passed a kitchen with a full staff and a puff of onion and garlic billowing out of it.

"This dude is something else ya' know?" he asked.

Boy, did she.

She glanced over her shoulder to make sure Anthony was still there. He was—with his eyes back on her ass as he trailed behind them.

They locked eyes just as Vaughn tugged her into his dining room and she caught the lust in them.

The inside of the massive dining room looked like a florist had thrown up all over it. Any in season flower she could think of sat bunched on the twelve foot wooden dining table that was set for three with charger plates and expensive cutlery. It smelled like springtime and made her feel for whoever the lucky lady was he was trying to impress with such an extravagant display.

"This dude never answers my phone calls, but he expects me to answer his. He called me up at the last minute last night, telling about some female who came to my restaurant and had a fucked up time there with a lame she met online. So I ask him, 'what the fuck it had to do with him?' You know what this nigga told me..."

"Venus," she filled in the blank for him so she wouldn't be reduced to "some female" again.

"Venus! I like that." He snapped his fingers, yanking out a chair at the table and then nudging her in it. "You know what he tells me, Venus?"

She shook her head with a bated breath.

"He tells me, 'well, OG.' That's what he calls me—'OG.'"
Vaughn smiled proudly. "'I ain't never been on a date with a
woman as fly as her and I think that's what she really likes—
dates.'"

She turned around to search for Anthony's eyes again, but he
was too occupied with the Newton's Cradle on the console table
next to the dining room's entryway. He pulled at a ball as if
Vaughn hadn't just proclaimed something so embarrassing out
loud, but somehow, after knowing him for only a few days, she
knew he wouldn't be embarrassed at all.

Vaughn laughed, tapping his knuckles on the table. "Then he
tells me, 'I wanna take her on a proper date to make up for that
lame ass nigga. You think you can make that happen for me,
OG?' As if I ain't have a flight to catch to New York tonight for
my friend's soft opening in Brooklyn. So here we are... a special
dinner for Venus."

The words sounded more romantic and less abrasive coming
from Vaughn and she doubted Anthony said something so g-
rated, but all she wanted to know was, "why?"

Why did it matter to Anthony that she liked to go on dates—
cheap ones, expensive ones, or apologetic ones when Trey
fucked up? Or why Vaughn would cancel such an important
flight to meet the demand of a lowly waiter from his restaurant?

———

It was only the first week of school and somehow Venus had
ended up on a date with Anthony Nunez at a restauranteur's
house. Once again, the universe was being as weird as Daddy
always said it was.

Vaughn sat across from her and Anthony while his staff
served a full course meal that wasn't available on his restaurant's menu. It was a meal that would only come out of his
kitchen and, according to him, nobody else in Atlanta could
replicate it.

"These are my grandma Adele's recipes," Vaughn said, reaching over and sitting a beautiful bowl of shrimp and grits in front of her. "They've been passed down for generations. They're completely different from what's being served at Vaughn's. I'm thinking of going in a more home style, family oriented direction for the Sandy Springs concept."

He talked so fast she kept wanting to ask him to repeat himself, but she was too stuck on the fact she *actually* let Anthony label their meeting a date and she was *actually* in Vaughn's dining room.

She glanced at Anthony out of the corner of her eye because glances were the only thing she could muster. She wouldn't survive if she looked him in his face, so she settled for fleeting glimpses. His arm draped across the back of her chair and every now and then, his fingers scraped at the little hairs on his chin.

"What you think about this?" Vaughn asked, looking up at Anthony.

This was her go-ahead—the one moment where she could study Anthony while he studied her food.

He blinked at it while the blasé fog lifted from his limbs and he leaned forward. "You missing something."

Afterward, he cocked his head to the side and for only the second time since she'd met him, he sort of looked like Tori.

"Something like..." Vaughn trailed off.

"Something green—like scallions."

"Scallions?"

"Yeah... and it's too flat. The chef say you supposed to add height to the plate. You probably should rethink the plating."

Vaughn shook his finger at him with a grunt that doubled as a deep laugh. "Been hanging out in the kitchen again?"

Anthony snorted, easing back into his chair as if he didn't want to get caught in such a compromising position again. Like how dare she witness him talk about plating cuisine in such a delicious way?

He shrugged. "I pass through when I take my smoke break sometimes."

"Yeah, whatever, nigga." Vaughn twisted his solid body and gripped a staff member's shoulder, pulling her in close.

She was an older black woman dressed as casually as the rest of his staff in jeans and a t-shirt with her hair slicked back into a ponytail.

"Grab some scallions for me, Sheryl. My boy says we need color…and height, apparently."

Sheryl smiled, nodding at Anthony. "How you want them, baby? Chopped?"

"Yeah—chopped." He nodded back while Venus held in a scoff at another woman calling him that soft nickname he always defied.

"Scallions it is. Be back."

Two minutes later, she was back with a little silver bowl of scallions that Vaughn sprinkled over her shrimp and grits.

"There we go," he muttered, tilting his head again as if he were studying a work of art.

She paid Anthony another glance to see if he was as enthralled as Vaughn.

He was.

But not with the food.

Instead, he stared at her, stroking his chin again. "What you think?"

"It…it looks…" She hurried to look at the concoction he and Vaughn created with her dinner. "It looks great."

"I'm not talking about that. I'm talking about his idea for the restaurant in general."

Oh. That concept he kept rambling about like he was pitching a business plan to Anthony?

"I think it's a great idea."

Anthony smirked, flinging his tongue against his bottom lip and holding a finger up. "You boring my date, man."

Vaughn held up his hands, dragging his eyes against her chest. "My apologies, Venus."

"No need to apologize. I get it. It sounds like you work real close with your staff and you value their opinions."

"I don't," he replied pleasantly.

She flung her head over at him while Anthony crunched on his salad between them. "I ain't never had dinner at any of my boss's houses."

"Well, Anthony's a special case."

"Oh yeah? How?" She stuck her fork in the shrimp and grits, inhaling the tangy scent. "I wanna hear all about Anthony Nunez being a special case."

Anthony chuckled next to her.

"Before I tell you, tell me, what's your ideal role at your current job?" Vaughn asked.

It was an odd question to ask a stranger, but after doing a stint at a private school for a short year, she'd learned that wealthy people were weird like that. There was always a lesson woven within their cryptic statements and questions.

She tilted her head, ignoring the tension that crept up her shoulders from his question while picturing the little brown faces that greeted her every day in the hallways at school.

The smirk Anthony gave her out of the corner of her eye made her drop her fork. "Would you judge me if I told you I didn't have one?"

"Maybe." He laughed. "I don't know what it is you do, but you don't aspire for more in your career?"

"Nah…"

"Never?"

"Nope."

Their eyes bore into her face. Those words were never something she would've said out loud to anybody before her divorce, but now they flowed out as freely as they drifted around in her brain. She didn't even smile to ease Vaughn's uncomfortableness. Michole would've been proud of her.

"My daddy built us a chicken coop when I was little. It was a big one. I liked to help him clean it and feed the chickens, but when it was time to sell the eggs or slaughter one, I'd holler like hell."

Anthony laughed first, and then Vaughn followed. Their chuckles made her chuckle.

"One day he got so frustrated when I wouldn't let him butcher one. He told me 'you care too much. People like you can't ever be a politician or...or a lawyer because you wouldn't be able to stomach the wrong you gotta do to survive in those positions and ain't nothing wrong with that. You just care too damn much.'" She shrugged. "So, here I am, big and grown, still caring too much and not aspiring for much else but to be a good kindergarten teacher."

A syrupy smirk coated Vaughn's face. He almost didn't look sleezy anymore.

"Venus—the girl who cared too damn much." He hummed.

"The *woman*," she corrected him.

She wanted to blurt that getting Tori the help she needed would feel as good, if not better, as somebody offering her Principal Bivins' position, but she remembered what happened the last time she blurted something about Tori she shouldn't have. So, she gave Anthony her own little smirk and picked her fork back up to take a bite of the grits.

She chewed, savoring the flavors and the fact that Anthony's brain was colorful enough to find food plating interesting.

"Well, you just blew my goddamn speech out the water with that one!" Vaughn exclaimed.

"I didn't mean to, but I also didn't wanna lie. Being a teacher was enough for my mama, so it's enough for me. Not everybody is constantly aspiring for the next big thing in life."

"Is that what you think too, Anthony? Is that why you won't accept my offer?" Vaughn asked.

She didn't savor the grits for long before she swung her head to look back at Anthony.

She'd be dizzy by the time they left.

Anthony didn't rush to finish chewing to stammer over an answer. He kept chewing and stared at the obscure painting hanging on the wall in front of the dining room table. His eyebrows dipped into a thoughtful expression until he swallowed and wiped his mouth with the cloth napkin, she didn't even realize he had draped over his thigh.

"I appreciate the offer, but now's not a good time for me to take on such a big responsibility."

Well thought out. Respectful. Succinct.

His response was way better than the "I can't" she would've blabbered out at his age and *that* made her body hum. He was a chameleon.

"What's the position?" she asked.

Vaughn smiled like a proud daddy. "I offered him a general manager position for my new concept as soon as we broke ground, but I guess he has the same ideologies as you. You must be rubbing off on him."

Anthony shrugged, tossing his arm back behind her chair. "It ain't even like that."

Vaughn's smile got bigger as he swiped his glass of bourbon off the table. "You see?"

He tilted the glass at her. "He won't tell you he can run a restaurant with his eyes closed, but I know he can—everybody up there knows. I guess that's one joy of black boyhood. We all got that irrational fear of being seen doing all the shit the world says a black man shouldn't do. The lucky ones blossom out of it."

He let his heavy statement linger before he took the last sip of his bourbon to the head.

She believed him.

She heard the way the names of luxurious dishes rolled off Anthony's tongue, noticed the easy way he read the situation with her and Morris, and somehow in a restaurant full of people, he made her feel as if she was just his to dote on.

"General manager?" She whistled. "That's a high-level position."

"Well, he's a high-level thinker," Vaughn replied. "You know, when my friend called me asking for a favor, I just knew she'd got involved in some bullshit when she popped up with him at her side."

"Your friend?" she asked.

"Yeah, Lynn Jarrett. A menace or an angel, depending on where and how you cross paths with her. She's a beast in the courtroom. We go wayyy back. I knew her husband Quentin first." He twirled his empty glass around. "She likes to test my generosity sometimes by sending me on side missions like teaching her daughter the value of a dollar or giving this stubborn knuckle-headed nigga a server's position that he wouldn't just take. He wanted to interview for it with no fuckin' fine dining experience."

She raised her eyebrows. "Interviewed?"

"Oh yeah." Vaughn chuckled. *"Interviewed."*

She looked at Anthony again and tried to imagine him in a job interview with a hotshot like Vaughn. He was still relaxed and handsome.

"What'd you ask him?" she asked.

Her question made Vaughn laugh harder. "You don't ask a nigga like this if he knows the difference between a salad and dinner fork, but we talked—found out we knew some of the same folks, and found out he dabbled in some of the same shit I used to, back when I was young and lost. We're the same type of man, you know?"

He sat his glass down.

Anthony's blasé demeanor faded for the first time that night. He sat stock straight, swiping the back of his neck. It was fleeting and something the old her would've never noticed because he went right back to being relaxed.

Her brows wrinkled as she mulled over the details of his

secretive life that Vaughn yapped about as Sheryl breezed back into the dining room.

"Second course should be out in a second," she drawled, replacing Venus' drink with another and then nodding toward Anthony. "You ain't drinkin' nothin', baby?"

"No ma'am. Water is good for me."

"Alright then. Holler if you change your mind. I'd like to think you old enough to drink."

Venus held in her laugh.

It would've been criminal for him to be that fine and plot against her if he couldn't even drink.

eleven

. . .

HE COULDN'T FUCK VENUS.

She cared too much—about chickens, eggs, Munch, and about shit most folks didn't give a damn about...just like her daddy said.

She tossed her head back, laughing at another story Vaughn told about his old club promotion days. The light from the dainty chandelier hanging above the table illuminated her slender neck Anthony decided he wanted to kiss.

"Anybody ever told you your laugh is contagious?" Vaughn asked, smirking and pushing back from the table.

Vaughn liked her. He liked her hair, the twang in her voice, and the way her titties sat up in the jumpsuit she wore with the crease from her cleavage teasing him. His eyes brushed her chest for the third time that night.

"Just my daddy, but he don't count. He's supposed to make me feel special." She chuckled.

"I wanna hear more about him after I check on this dessert."

He breezed out of the dining room and down the hallway that led to his kitchen, leaving them alone.

"Shit, this is a nice ass house," she hissed, leaning forward to squint at the Kehinde Wiley piece on the wall.

She'd gotten so comfortable that she sat with her leg shoved under her ass while she sipped on her third espresso martini. She never even had one before that night.

"Can you imagine living in a house like this?"

He stretched his neck, looking around the gaudy dining room, searching for all the wonder she fawned over—plush curtains that cost more than his rent, original hardwood floors Vaughn probably used as a talking piece when other rich folks visited, and a china cabinet that screamed, "wanna be old money."

He shrugged. "It's cool."

When he looked back at her, she was staring at him with a close-lipped, tipsy smile that made his dick twitch. She studied the arm he had draped across the back of her chair and the gap between his spread legs.

"Are you hard to impress, Anthony Nunez?"

"Absolutely."

She sputtered out a laugh and fell forward. "I don't know why I expected anything else to come out of your mouth."

"I ain't never impressed by what somebody got because I never know what they did to get it."

"Wise words." She snorted. "Your nigga told you that one, too?"

"Nah, my granny did."

"What kinda trouble you in that got you waiting tables for this rich ass mysterious man, anyway?"

He snorted this time, tilting his head to the side to stare at her mouth. He wanted to remind her of how sexy she was again, but he kept it to himself this time.

"The kind that can make you indebted to folks if you not careful."

"Do you even like waiting tables?"

"I like anything that make me see the world different, Venus Thibodeaux."

She squinted her eyes at him and tilted her head sexily, mirroring him. "That sounds too good and too rehearsed."

He laughed harder while she kept squinting at him.

"So, are you indebted to your lawyer, Lynn Jarrett? Is that why she got you giving these rehearsed answers and waiting tables for Vaughn?"

He rolled his eyes, smiling.

Vaughn had a big mouth, but Anthony got it. At his age, most shit didn't matter anymore except his businesses, the money in his pocket, and the harem of women he fucked. Vaughn wasn't bound by that list he and DeeDee were. He could talk about the favor he'd done for Lynn to make himself look appealing to Venus.

She took another sip of her drink. "So, who'd you meet first? Her or Mikayla? It's gotta be Mikayla, right?"

"What you talkin' about?"

"That's how you scored this once in a lifetime gig. You're fuckin' Lynn's daughter—Mikayla J—the lil' girl that got you proofreading her papers even though she says she wants to go to law school like her mama did."

She was so player with it, he didn't even catch what she said until the silence settled between them and he replayed her words back in his head.

It had only taken her three espresso martinis and one drawn out conversation with Vaughn to connect some of the dots in the trifling saga he couldn't escape. She wasn't good at modern dating, but damn, she might've been a pro at reading niggas.

"I'm on to you..." she uttered, pursing her lips and staring at him with a tiny smile that didn't reach her eyes.

He could've played dumb. He could've feigned innocence. He could've even pretended like she had it all wrong. Instead, he reached over and gripped her thick thigh, tugging it until she let him pull her leg from underneath her ass.

He lifted it and sat it across his lap, staring at her freshly painted toes.

Rae Lyse

Tiny dots of turquoise peppered the cuticle of her pinky toe. This time, he could savor her foot. He didn't have to relinquish it to some random Tinder nigga, hoping he'd take care of it. He could do it himself.

He rolled her ankle between his fingers while she studied him and he replayed what she'd said in his head again.

She didn't go home and mull over their night together and then get all passive aggressive. She said that shit right to his face as soon as she realized what was going on.

Damn.

"You tryna fuck me too, huh?" she spat. "You never planned to talk to me about Tori today. It was always about fuckin' me to get in my head to distract me from the issue. You don't actually like me. You just like what me and my pussy can do for you."

She said it all without emotion. There was no finger pointing and yelling and he *really* couldn't fuck her now.

He picked up her other leg and laid it across his lap before going for that ankle. Then he made his way to her slender toes. He kneaded them in tiny circles while sweat formed on the palm of his hands. He'd never sweat there before—not even while gripping his car's steering wheel when twelve trailed him, but somehow Venus conjured it up.

"You gon' say something?" she drawled.

That country twang made his heart stutter in the same weird way his stomach did when they crossed paths.

"Yeah, you right," he finally replied.

"About all of it?"

"Nah, just some of it." He reached over and tugged up the zipper on her jumpsuit.

It had eased down throughout the night as she talked, laughed, drank, and ate. His eyes had been competing with Vaughn's to get a closer look at her titties all throughout dinner.

She glanced at his fingers as they pulled it up. Her mouth twitched like she wanted to say something, but Vaughn breezed back in before either of them could say anything else.

"Wardrobe malfunction?" he asked, laying a decorative towel down and sitting a skillet of bananas foster in the center of the table.

They hastily looked at Vaughn and then back at his hand on her zipper.

Anthony smirked, dropping his hand. "Nah—just a lil' lover's spat."

"Maybe I can help," Vaughn replied, dusting his hands together.

"I think you can."

"Oh, no. It's not even like tha—" Venus started, pulling her legs away from him.

Anthony gripped them until she stopped moving. "He said he could help. Let the man help."

"Okay, I'm all ears. Tell me what the problem is." Vaughn's face lit and he hooked his hands on the back of the chair next to him.

Anthony smiled. "She think I'm scared to get fired from your restaurant."

Vaughn leaned forward against the table, crinkling his eyebrows. "Okay, I'm not following the problem here."

"She thinks..." Anthony pointed at Venus and then at him, wagging his finger between them. "That I won't air you and yo' beautiful ass house out if you don't keep your goddamn eyes to yourself, OG."

Venus sputtered out a shocked laugh until she realized he and Vaughn weren't laughing with her. They eyeballed each other instead and her laugh sputtered into a hiccup.

The hardness in Vaughn's eyes that made Anthony call him "OG" the first day they met in his office reappeared. He was real good at hiding it, but Dre' always said "a dog gon' recognize a dog"—especially in the wild and especially when a woman was involved.

Vaughn's fingernails raked against the wood and he folded his bottom lip under his front teeth. "I ain't know it was like that, neph."

Venus squirmed out of the corner of his eye, rubbing the back of her neck and looking between them.

"I thought it was just…you know," Vaughn finished, glancing at her.

"Well, now you know it's like that." He nodded toward the forgotten bananas foster, pulling her legs closer into his stomach. "What kinda rum your granny put in there?"

———

Existing on neutral turf was freeing.

It's where Venus switched in front of Anthony and then giggled nervously when he swatted Vaughn's hand away from her shoes as they neared his front door.

"You sure you don't want the flowers?" Vaughn asked her. "They're for you."

"Oh…nah. Tell Ms. Sheryl to take 'em. I don't have a green thumb to save my life."

She scraped her fingers across Anthony's head as soon as he squatted to strap her heels back on her feet. Her nails grazed his scalp while he tried to keep his dick in check. Tipsy and soft, she placed her weight on him as if she were testing him out to see if he was strong enough to hold her up.

"You'll be back, right?" Vaughn asked.

"Uh, I don't know." She sang, marching her fingers across his head. "I gotta ask Anthony."

"Don't tell me you're an 'ask permission' type of gal."

"I'm a 'keep the peace' type of gal."

Or maybe they weren't existing on neutral turf. Maybe they were finally existing on *their* turf where she accepted Vaughn's carefully worded apology, left her legs in Anthony's lap while she ate her dessert, and understood that he liked her more than he was supposed to even when he was trying to manipulate her.

Anthony buckled the clasps on her heels and rose from the

floor. Vaughn smiled, giving them a once over like he hadn't been trying to steal Venus the whole night.

Afterward, he reached up and gripped Anthony's shoulder. "Think long and hard about that offer. As long as you're still here, it'll always be on the table."

Anthony nodded, doing his best not to internalize the longing in his voice. There'd been other men in his life like Vaughn—probation officers, COs, and men Lola dated that saw the potential in him that Carlotta didn't.

"Don't give Lynn too much hell. She'll get you out of whatever this mess is you're in," Vaughn added, letting go.

Anthony nodded again. "I hear you."

Venus waited patiently, looking between them with tense shoulders.

Before Anthony could pull the front door open, Vaughn's voice was already piercing his eardrums with that melancholy longing he was always running from at the restaurant.

"Pull up anytime you need something, neph. You know I'm good for it. Oh, and send D and Clo' my love."

"I got you."

When they stepped outside, Venus sucked in a deep breath and exhaled as if she'd been holding it in throughout dinner. She kept a foot of space between them until they got to the car and he opened the passenger door for her.

She moved to get in and he brushed his fingertips against her ass one more time in case she came to her senses and made sure it was the last time he'd do it.

As soon as he rounded the car and climbed behind the steering wheel, she blurted, "why won't you take Vaughn's offer?"

That was it. That was the question she'd been holding in with tense shoulders. Out of all the revelations and stupid declarations that came out during dinner, that's what she wanted to know.

"Because slaving eighty hours a week collecting slow money

from some ex-drug dealer turned CEO ain't my focus right now."

"Oh." She nodded, biting into her lip. "And being *resourceful* is? I don't see the sustainability in being resourceful for the rest of your life. Most of the resourceful men I know are—"

"Dead or in jail."

She folded her lips under her teeth like she was thankful the words came out of his mouth instead of hers. Finally, she let go and her lips popped from underneath her teeth, begging him to taste them, but she had other plans.

"What's wrong with collecting a steady, predictable paycheck and going home to Tori every night? Us grown folk do it every day. It's life, baby boy."

He cut his eyes at her. "Since you know so much about life, you should know I can't come up with Lynn Jarrett's retainer on a waiter's salary or even a restaurant manager's, no matter how nice the place is."

"Oh, you don't get pro bono services for dicking down her daughter?"

He doubled over in laughter, even though there wasn't a hint of humor in her voice. She sounded like a scorned wife for the second time that night and in some odd way, he wished she was his scorned wife to argue with.

"Fuckin' her only got my foot in the door."

"Ouch. I would've thought lil' Mikayla had more pull than that."

He hunched his shoulders up, snickering at the shade she threw. It was the first time he could laugh about the fact that Lynn Jarrett's services were its own damn bill in his household. Her retainer agreement was in the same drawer as the light bill, cellphone, and rent.

"Why don't you just ask Josiah for the money?" she asked.

"That's my brother. He not an ATM just because he got an NFL contract now. He helped me enough over the years. You ask all of your rich friends for money every time you get in a bind?"

"I don't have any rich friends."

"Well, I wanna chop it up with you when you get 'em. I wanna absorb all this audacity you got." He chuckled, shaking his head. "Fastest way a nigga go broke is by carrying every one of his brother's burdens."

"Does Josiah think that?"

Nope.

Josiah carried the world on his shoulders and he'd be damned if he added his problems to the load.

"It's not about what he think. It's about what *I* think and *I* think I can take care of myself. I don't borrow large sums of money from friends—especially rich ones. It's too many emotions involved."

"So you're prideful?"

"Ain't every man?"

She tsk'd and looked away. "Yeah, until God humbles 'em."

Venturing out of neutral territory and into this space was sobering. He smelled the coffee and vodka on her breath and saw the curiosity on her face. She probably squeezed every thought out of her ex-husband's head with the expressions she wore.

"You on the wrong turf anyway," he muttered, starting the car. "Mind your business."

"Well, you did just threaten to shoot your boss and his house up for staring at my titties. I think we graduated from that 'mind your business' shit."

He shook his head, partly at himself and partly at her.

Yeah, he'd really done that crash-dummy shit.

"And *actually*, I'm doing what we initially agreed to do, which was to talk about Tori. If we talk about Tori, then we gotta talk about you first." She flung her head back against the head-rest, sighing and closing her eyes. "You wined, dined and mind fucked me enough tonight. I drove a Benz, ate at Vaughn's massive ass house, let you touch my ass since you can't stop staring at it, *and* somewhere along the way I think you confessed you liked me. I behaved. Now the least you can do is hold up your end of the original deal."

She opened her eyes and turned toward him. "What do I gotta do to get that? You want me to explain myself to you again?"

"Go 'head." He shrugged. "Do what you want."

He smiled, replaying the way her confession toppled out of her mouth in her classroom's doorway.

"I guess you want me to tell you that sometimes I do irresponsible stupid shit that gets me in trouble too...like go on dates with my student's daddy or fight my ex-husband's girlfriend."

His eyes widened.

This explanation was better than the LaDarius Mitchell one. This one explained so much, yet not enough.

"Your turn."

Instead of following her lead, he picked up the lone manicured finger she'd been wagging in his face earlier that day and tugged at it.

"Ms. Thibodeaux curses outside of school hours *and* fights?" He tsk'd to himself. "And you really thought I ain't like you?"

"Let's be clear, the old me fought."

"Oh, you a changed woman now?"

"I'm a work in progress." She rolled her eyes, smirking.

He *had* to move her up on his favorite bitch list. Dre' would tell him that because of this new revelation, she and DeeDee were neck and neck.

"You know it's unfair when you do this shit, right? You can't bum-rush me at my job, trick me into going on a date with you and then not give me what I asked for in return. I just wanna talk about Tori."

She was right. It *was* unfair—even if his head kept telling him to ignore his emotions and his dick because they would have him down as bad as Josiah and Dre' but there was no time for him to give in before his phone rang through the car's speakers.

She looked at the car's screen, reading the caller ID with a confused smile. "Fulton County Jail?"

"Don't tell me you have a jail girlfriend, too." She belted out an uneasy laugh. "How do you even keep up with all of their problems? What's next? You gon' bail this one out after you fill out Mikayla's law school application?"

She murmured the last few words while taking it upon herself to reach for the screen like she was that scorned wife he'd been craving. He tried to grab her hand, but she pressed her finger against it before he could stop her. Their hands fell against the gearshift.

Static rattled through the phone until the call connected.

"Hello, this is a pre-paid collect call from... *Deeanna...*"

His stomach fumbled in the most grueling way as he glanced at Venus. A frown spread across her face in a slow crawl.

"An inmate at the Fulton County detention facility. This call is subject to recording and monitoring. To accept this call, press one—"

No!

Too bad automated systems couldn't read human brains, or that Venus didn't understand there was a reason DeeDee existed at the very top.

She pulled her hand from underneath his and reached for the screen again. He tried to stop her lone shaky finger, but it pressed the "one" before he could.

The call connected.

DeeDee's deep breaths rattled through the speaker. "So just fuck me, huh? Carlotta said you would put up my bail today."

He kept his eyes on the Benz's flat screen, inhaling Venus' scent he'd swallowed all night. If he could disappear into that leather seat, he would, but Deeanna didn't believe in letting him do anything alone. She'd be right there trying to disappear with him.

He should've hung up, but blind loyalty came with all of his favorite bitches. It was the reason he was their favorite, too.

"I never said that," he replied.

"*What?* I sat up here waiting around for you looking like a goddamn fool!"

"What else was you supposed to do? Go take a stroll around the block?"

"Don't—don't fix your fuckin' mouth to say no shit like that."

"Don't fix yours to assume some secondhand information is true."

"Nuney...I swear to God—"

"You swear to God, what?"

She growled out a frustrated moan that turned into a high-pitched whine that sounded too much like Munch's.

"You ain't even talk to me about it. You talked to her," he added. "I put money on your books. Your own mama and brother ain't even do that. I did more than what I should've done and you trippin'?"

"You know what, you right. *Fuck you!* Where's my baby?"

"Safe."

"Anthony... where is Toriana?"

"With Tash and Dre'."

"I told you to stop letting that bitch and your friends babysit. You couldn't call Keem, huh? Or... or my mama?"

"Your *mama*? You must think I'm stupid, and Keem don't even got her own kids half the time. What makes you think she'll drop what she doing to watch yours?"

"Mine? Oh, that's how we talking now? What, you got a new girl? I ain't been gone but a couple months and you already letting hoes get in your head? Who is it, huh?"

"The only hoe I let in my head snaked me. Keep on and you'll be in there until both of them court dates hit."

"Oh really?"

"Yeah, *really*."

"You a bitch, Anthony!"

He scoffed.

It took one to know one.

"I hate you!" she yelled.

"Good."

The funny thing about the top of his list was how much hate equated to love there. The two were intertwined and he and DeeDee played tug of war with each emotion. Hate...love...that shit was all the same at the top.

"What else do you fuckin' want from me?" she screamed. "I got on my knees and begged your ass for forgiveness! I do everything you tell me to! I'm sitting up here like a fuckin' fool while you take your time getting me out! I—I told him to stop all of this! I don't even love him! I love you! I'll fuckin' die for you, Anth—"

twelve

· · ·

VENUS FELT the buildup of thousands of other angry phone calls in the slap Anthony gave the Benz's screen.

The loud thwack made her body jolt.

This was it. This was *her*—the emotionally intelligent girl that didn't mind if Anthony called her a bitch. She was the girl that had Tori's eyes, and maybe she had her sweet demeanor at one point. She was the last woman Anthony explained himself to— the one he hated.

She had an angelic voice. It was soft and poised, even when she screamed out for Anthony. The desperation in it made goose-bumps prickle Venus' arms.

Her teeth ached as she unclenched them and glanced over at him.

He sucked in hard breaths, like he had just finished running a marathon. They were the breaths she'd gasp out after arguing with Trey. They'd be full of the rebuttals he refused to hear, and she probably sounded like Deeanna back when she'd let Trey lead her into dark pits and make her wallow in her anger inside of them.

"I'm sorry," she blurted.

Sorry for getting comfortable enough in his space to answer

his phone, sorry Deeanna was in jail, sorry they were okay with disrespecting each other, sorry that Tori still wouldn't talk.

"Man, fuck her!" He whipped his head toward her and she wished he wouldn't have because she wanted to touch him—to wrap her hand around his face and tell him Michole said the best way to move forward was to soothe himself until he calmed down.

"I hate her ass."

He looked more youthful under the glowing moonlight. He looked every bit like the "baby boy" she'd let slip out earlier—red faced and mad at the world as he slammed his head against the headrest and closed his eyes.

His loud, ragged breaths overtook the silence until Deeanna decided she wanted more from him and had the audacity to call back. They let his phone ring, and then let it ring again when she called for a third time.

Venus gulped.

Fuck that sliver of immaturity in her brain she just couldn't outgrow. Now she was stuck mulling over Deeanna's angsty confessions and the way Anthony made her feel. If only she could rewind time—not to five minutes ago—but back to the second day of school. She would've held in her observation of Tori and only told Logan, but now she was caught up with Anthony...and he liked her.

"Anthony?"

His eyes fluttered beneath their lids. He clenched and unclenched his hand.

She held her breath for him to lash out at her and make her pay for whatever Deeanna had done because Kaydens were a lot like her kindergartners—they didn't know how to process emotions that were bigger than them.

He kept his eyes closed and frowned harder, as if he were hiding. She didn't blame him. She'd hide too if he ever heard the nasty shouting matches she and Trey had.

Rae Lyse

Instead of yelling, he murmured, "I thought I was baby boy?" in a husky voice with his words running together.

It wasn't the tongue lashing she expected, and warmth spread between her legs when it shouldn't have.

"Hmph." She smirked, looking down at the hand he'd been brushing across her ass and feet all night, and replaying the way he held onto her legs after reminding Vaughn she wasn't his to gawk at.

He didn't move like a baby boy at all.

"Why you hate Tori's mama so much? What she do to you?" she asked.

"You interrogating me again, Officer Thibodeaux?"

"Nope, just wondering what kind of magic you got that got girls getting on their knees for you and begging for your forgiveness, even though you hate them."

He laughed, pinching his eyes tighter, and her shoulders lightened.

She had decided she probably wouldn't get her conversation about Tori. Deeanna had shut it down with one phone call, and Vaughn had unearthed a heap of feelings between them that had them distracted.

He peeled his eyes apart and rolled his head over to stare at her. "You first. What kinda magic you got that made you serve ole boy his walking papers? I bet he ain't wanna sign 'em."

"Aht... aht. I already went first."

"Oh yeah." He laughed. "I forgot. You be going Mike Tyson on hoes."

"*Boy*." Her wagging finger came back and snuck into his relaxed face.

When it got too close to his lips, his low eyes got even heavier.

"I think you want me to bite it." He snickered.

"I want you to answer my question."

And bite it.

She folded her finger back into her palm and waited.

142

She felt stagnant like Deeanna did in that jail because Anthony had a strange superpower that kept them obedient and hanging onto his every word, even when they shouldn't have.

He pulled his bottom lip under his shiny teeth. "You ever been with somebody that looked at you like you was the second coming of Jesus?"

She shook her head and whispered "no."

He balled up his face. "Once again, what kind of fuck nigga did you marry?"

Laughter shot out of her. "Now, you the one that needs to mind your business."

"We past that, remember?"

"Fine. I married a man I thought would take care of me."

"And..."

"He wanted me to look at him like he was the second coming of Jesus."

"But..."

"I couldn't because he couldn't protect me, respect me, and he didn't know how to be the man I needed."

"That's a vague answer, but I'm gon' let you live." He smirked. "So why'd you say 'yes' when he proposed, then? He changed after y'all got married or something?"

"You wouldn't understand. You're too young."

"I bet I would."

She believed him. It's why they couldn't climb their way out of each other's brains, no matter how much they tried.

She sighed, glancing back at Vaughn's quiet house. "Because I didn't believe I deserved more."

"Expound..."

"*Expound?*" She snickered. "Go back to speaking teenager, please."

"Explain yourself."

"Ugh." She groaned, cursing Michole and all the introspection she'd pulled out of her. "For a long time, I had settled with the idea that it was him. That he was the problem. But I was to blame, too, because I didn't believe I deserved more than him. So I settled—tried therapy, tried to make things work, but they didn't."

She narrowed her eyes at Vaughn's lush grass until another gruff of words came out of Anthony.

"Sound like he still wreaking havoc up there."

She tore her eyes from the tall blades of grass and looked back at him. "Up where?"

"Up in your head."

"Maybe..." She shrugged, ignoring the 'yes' she wanted to scream out.

Getting over her marriage shouldn't have felt like she was recovering from war, but alas, she still suffered from PTSD, and Trey wouldn't let go, no matter how far she ran.

"Now, it's your turn. No more running from my questions," she added.

He turned his head away and closed his eyes again, and she let him.

"Tell me about the lil' girl that looks at you like you walk on water. I can't be the only one in this parent-teacher relationship telling my business."

When he gulped, she swore she tasted the breath he swallowed.

"And tell me in english, please. No teenager talk."

She rolled her eyes, but deep down her pussy longed for all the weird lingo that came out of his mouth without effort.

He smirked but still didn't answer, so she helped him along like he'd done to her.

"So... she worshiped you?"

"Yeah. I was the nigga that could walk on water with an ankle monitor on, turn our empty pantry into a Publix all the way from Rice Street, cure her self-consciousness with new titties and teeth, love her ass even when I shouldn't have."

"And now?"

He peeled his eyes apart and looked back at her with his eyebrows raised. "You heard her, didn't you?"

He didn't have to repeat Deeanna's desperate words. They were still ricocheting off the soft sides of her brain so she accidentally blurted, "how does somebody even get to that point? To —to wanna *kill* for another human being and admit that shit on a recorded line?"

She had her fair share of puppy love, good dick, and even an entire marriage, but Daddy would kill her if she was ever so down bad over another person.

"Hm." He snorted. "*Again,* what kinda fuck nigga did you marry?"

"Apparently just a mere mortal and not black Jesus." They laughed together until she caught her breath with the one question she'd been dying to ask on her lips. "Are you and her still..."

Were there any words to even describe such an intense love affair? Deeanna was the mother of his child, for God's sake. She still harassed him from jail and shouted her love for him from deep within her gut.

"They say Judas betrayed Jesus, right?" His eyes raked over her lips.

"So I'll take that as a 'no'? She must be Judas in this blasphemous metaphor."

He laughed, thrusting his head back. "Betrayal always feel good in the moment until you wake up from your rampage and see all the damage you caused. Then that shit don't feel as good because now you gotta deal with the fallout and that fallout is a motherfucka."

She gulped, like she'd done whatever Deeanna had.

"Is that lawyer you have for her?" she muttered.

"Nope."

"So, it's for you then?"

"Sneaking your toe on the wrong turf again I see." He snorted. "It's getting late..."

"But—but we didn't even talk about Tori."

"We can talk about her another time. Let me get from in front of ole boy's house before he try to drag you back in."

Her stomach dropped from its safe cocoon to her knees even though he promised her there'd be more times between them, but she knew better. This had to be it. She *really* had to be the mature one for both of them this time.

He laughed. "Don't give me that look. I hate that look."

"What look?"

"You know what look I'm talking about."

Had they known each other long enough for her to have looks he hated?

She glanced at her reflection in the moonlit window and caught the desperate dip in her eyebrows. She was proving Rose and Trey right. That immature part of her brain needed to be dealt with, even if Anthony didn't agree.

When she looked back at him, he had a complacent smile resting on his lips.

"Tighten up," he muttered. "That look gon' get me in trouble."

Tighten up?

How could she when he had her so loose and curious?

"You still didn't tell me what look you're talking about."

"I'm talking about that, 'Daddy, don't leave me' look." He tsk'd shaking his head.

Warmth spread from her limbs and settled between her legs again. It was an innocent statement, but the vibrato in his voice made it taste raunchier as it sat at the seam of her lips, waiting for her to repeat it and analyze it.

"It take a Happy Meal and a hundred kisses to get that look off Munch's face. Now, how I'm supposed to get it off yours?"

He could promise her he'd stop playing so many games that tempted her, fucked with her head, and put her job in jeopardy...that's how. But that was the mature part of her brain talking.

"Tell me where you going," she murmured as desperately and as needy as Deeanna.

Shit, she had to keep her body from leaning over the middle console. It was the only way she could stop herself from touching him. He was making the irresponsible part of her brain do cartwheels and back handsprings after treating their "date" so delicately, even though she wasn't delicate at all, according to Trey.

"I'm going to work."

"Work?" She glanced at the clock on the car's dashboard. "Vaughn's is closed."

He laughed, shaking his head. "Nah. Not my play work. My work *work*."

"'Play work?'" she mouthed to herself until the lightbulb went off in her head. "You talking about the *work* that got you that ugly, loud car?"

"Why you always thinking the worst of me?"

She balled her lips to the side and crossed her arms.

"Shit, it's the *work* that paid for your date tonight, too. If you must know."

"You paid Vaughn for this?"

He smiled another soft smile. "Of course I did. Ain't no such thing as a free lunch. Didn't you learn that in economics, teacher bae? If I would've let him put on this theatrical ass dinner for free, he'd think I owed him. I don't collect debts from folks."

She smiled against her will. "Is that why you interviewed for your position?

He nodded.

"Why'd you bring me here, anyway? We could've had dinner anywhere and I would've been okay with it."

"Because when all your homegirls yap about 'Vaughn's this' and 'Vaughn's that,' you can tell them you ate at Vaughn's dining room table, drank out of his expensive ass martini glasses, and got eye-fucked by the man himself until your date had to check his ass."

She inhaled, trying to breathe his scent from his place behind the wheel. She *almost* had it. There was his saccharine strawberry scent. God, he probably tasted as good as he smelled.

"So, how I get that look off you?" he asked, swiping his tongue across his lips. "I know you don't fuck with Happy Meals and you'd kill me if I kissed you, so now what? I got something I need to take care of."

In some sick way, she got it—the longing in Vaughn's eyes when he waved them off into the night and the curling of her insides when Anthony talked about "work" wasn't for nothing.

"Take me with you," she said.

He let out a gruff laugh, waving his hand and then reaching into his pocket. "Hell nah. Here...go for a nightcap at that coffee shop on me—"

"No."

The word still didn't feel as empowering as Michole claimed it should, but the way Anthony's eyebrows bunched together made her body tilt forward like it'd been wanting.

"What you mean 'no?'"

What she meant was that she wasn't Deeanna, Mikayla, or even Tori. She had a voice in their weird parent-teacher relation-ship despite all the times Trey told her it held no weight in their house.

She thrust her hand under her chin and stared at the tiny smatter of freckles that teased her from his cheeks. "You wanted to know how to get the look off my face and I'm telling you how. You can't leave if I'm not okay with it, either. That's not how it works with us."

For a minute she understood Deeanna—not the Deeanna that betrayed him, but the Deeanna that couldn't let go. How could she? He made them both want to hang onto the hem of his t-shirt and beg to go wherever he went.

A goofy smile spread across his face and made his eyes light up in an 'aha' type of way until they remembered they could admire her in the open now, so they skirted to her breasts and lingered there.

"You bad business, Ms. Thibodeaux. You know that, right?" He wagged his finger like her and shook his head. "Sit back and put your seatbelt on."

———

"What's this place?" Venus asked, looking out of the car's passenger window.

"The best place to take nosey ass kindergarten teachers— neutral turf."

"In an empty warehouse?"

It didn't take a Happy Meal or a hundred Eskimo kisses to get Venus out of her head. Anthony didn't know what had got her out of it. He was *so* sure he had fumbled her after DeeDee called, screaming about numbers four, five and six on their list until those words rolled from between her pouty lips.

"Take me with you."

Didn't she know he'd take her ass to Venus *for real* and make love to her there?

Out of all his favorite bitches, he'd never had a teacher. Venus Thibodeaux was the first, and she came with all the qualities he imagined a teacher would.

She turned to him with her pert nose crinkled. "Do I need to hide my purse?"

She was judgmental.

"Who you here to meet?"

She was nosey.

"There's not even a sign outside the building. How you know you in the right place?"

She was perceptive.

"You sell drugs, Anthony? If I get into any shit with you, I swear to God…"

She was cute.

"You know, Munch don't be giving me all this lip when I let her ride with me to run errands," he replied, turning the car off.

She rolled her eyes over to him with a curious expression that made him want to give her anything she asked for—even intel about his little munchkin who woke up one day and forgot how much everybody loved her voice.

"She's five. Of course she don't. All she knows is she's with her daddy."

"Then fall in line. How you let a five-year-old outdo you?"

He chuckled, pulling her purse from the floor and grasping the handle to the glove compartment. He pulled it open and rifled past the title he'd stuck back in there until he touched the cold metal he'd been searching for.

When he pulled the pistol out, she hissed, "Anthony."

He looked over his shoulder. "What?"

"Hell no." She shook her head with her lips poked out. "Put that shit back. Are you crazy?"

It was a serious moment, but his mouth wouldn't cooperate. A permanent smile had settled on his lips.

"Didn't you say this place was neutral? What you need a gun for?" she added.

"What you think I need one for?"

"I *think* you better use them Thirty branded knuckles you always flashing around if some shit goes down."

He belted out another loud laugh, pushing the pistol back into its place and closing the glove compartment. "You don't get tired of being the feds?"

"Don't start with me—"

He pushed out of the car mid-sentence and closed the door with her purse dangling from his hand. Her lips moved in frustration behind the dark tint while he laughed harder until she couldn't help but laugh too.

When he opened the passenger door, she stared up at him with the same glint in her eyes that showed up when he admitted how sexy she looked out loud. It was never supposed to come out, but he couldn't help it—especially not after watching her walk in heels. There was a worldliness in her walk that wasn't in DeeDee's or Mikayla's and it made him blunter than normal.

"Where the hell you have me at?" she muttered, pushing out of the car and pulling her purse strap from his hand.

He ignored her and nudged her in front of him while locking the car. They trekked to the building's front door in silence because he wouldn't entertain her questions. They were the left-over scraps from her marriage—intrusive thoughts she was used to belting out at her ex-husband while anticipating his answers. She didn't know how to just live like he'd mused because she was too used to existing. She was a lot like Lola after her divorce —scathed and insecure.

When they approached the door, she eyed the words pressed into it. "A recording studio?"

"Mhmm." He pulled his phone out and glanced at the text from Zeke.

He punched the four-digit code from the text into the keypad next to the door and when it turned green, she pulled the door open for them.

The frigid air tickled his skin and made her cross her arms across her chest. Her wild curls brushed her shoulders as she looked around the deserted lobby.

"You been here before?" she asked, wrinkling her eyebrows at the pictures of artists that lined the lobby's walls.

"Yeah, a couple times."

It'd been more than a couple, but he only remembered his sober visits. The other times were blurry in his memory. Josiah's cousin Dominic let them camp out for days while he recorded nonstop, because sometimes he couldn't get the inspiration he needed in his studio at home. Anthony liked to joke he'd be on Drake status before they knew it. He'd be so rich that niggas couldn't relate to half the shit he rapped about.

The loud, musky smell from the studio session lingered in the air.

"C'mon," he muttered, cocking his head toward the short hallway.

He led the way, and she followed. Her heels click-clacked against the hardwood floors while he fought his brain and tried not to conflate it with his emotions like Dre' always advised. He was breaking the most important rule in their family, after all.

"Outside folks don't have no place in our business," Dre' would say.

He glanced over his shoulder at Venus and her wandering eyes. She studied the plaques on the wall and suddenly she wasn't full of questions anymore.

When they reached the last door at the end of the hallway, his hand lingered on the doorknob while he tried to decide if he should tell it—not all of it—but at least enough for her to understand why he couldn't accept Vaughn's offer, but Dre's nagging voice wouldn't let up.

He pushed the door open, letting the pounding bass and cloud of smoke trickle into the hallway.

They ambled into the studio where Meezy and his homeboys laid around. When Anthony turned to look for Venus, he found her with her arms folded across her chest. Instead of focusing on what he was there for, he went back to calculating her age, even though she told him not to do that. It was hard, though, because he didn't see her as anything less than twenty-five.

Meezy repeated the bars he'd just laid on a track and paced in the center of the studio while his stringy haired engineer pressed the keys on a computer. When he looked up, he nodded at Anthony but smirked at Venus.

"What you doing here?" he yelled over the bass, raking his eyes over Venus' wide hips.

"Zeke told me you said to pull up whenever," Anthony replied. "So that's what I did."

Venus didn't budge and her eyes didn't light up in recognition. She stared at Meezy with the same unimpressed expression she probably gave any other young dude she came across. He imagined they all looked the same in her eyes.

"You still got time to chop it up, right?" Anthony asked.

Meezy nodded, darting his eyes between them and then around the hazy studio.

It was a rare night where the girls that hung around him and his newfound fame were scarce, so Venus was the only female in the space. Anthony nudged her at the center of her ass like he'd done at Vaughn's.

Meezy smiled at her this time—big and bold, like they were out and about and he needed to get her attention before she ran off, never to be seen again.

"What, your ole lady don't listen to rap?" Meezy teased, studying the way his hand wouldn't leave her ass.

"Not this kind," she replied, rolling her eyes.

"*This kind?*"

"Yeah...you know, the kind that sounds like everything else that's out."

That bold statement made all the slumped bodies in the studio sit up.

Maybe he should've explained *some* of it to her—like how blatant disrespect was the quickest way to dissolve neutral turf.

He tapped her on her ass—once in the center—and then three times on the side with his other hand. In his and DeeDee's world, those taps meant to 'shut the fuck up,' but Venus didn't speak their sordid language.

"You got you a big mouth bitch, huh?" Meezy asked.

"Nigg—" Anthony started.

"'A big mouthed bitch?' Really? That's all you could come up with?" Venus tilted her head. "*Yawn.* My kindergarten students have better insults. I would've been more impressed if you called me a poopy headed do-do bird."

Anthony really shouldn't have, but he chuckled.

Venus didn't give a shit about rapper's egos and she had no

clue that her big mouth would get him in trouble. It didn't even matter if he couldn't calculate her age. The bottom line was that *she* was grown and none of that shit mattered to her because she looked at all young dudes the same, just like he figured.

Meezy narrowed his eyes at her and the engineer cut the music. The haze of smoke floated between them. It was so quiet he heard the squeaking from the leather loveseat as his homeboy sat up further to stare at them.

A quiet studio was a weird place, but what was even more weird was the tender look on Meezy's face.

He let out a deep laugh, pointing at Venus. "Yo ass 'bout as goofy as hell."

The rest of the room lightened.

thirteen

. . .

BAREFOOT.

Anthony decided he liked Venus the best that way. Barefoot and goofy as hell with that twang in her voice.

He sank back into the leather couch, focusing on her ass as she leaned over Dan, the engineer's shoulder.

Nobody cared to figure out his name until she thrust her hand out toward him and asked.

"I'm Venus," she'd said, shaking his hand like she was meeting the president. *"Venus Thibodeaux. What's your name?"*

Dan's face had turned strawberry red, because somehow Venus made all men feel special even when they weren't. It was like a feminine superpower she harnessed. After he introduced himself, she kicked her heels off, talking about how bad her feet hurt while eyeing the studio equipment like Munch eyed the drinks at the Sugar Factory.

"So, she like white boys?" Meezy asked from beside him, looking away from Venus' ass.

"What you mean?"

"I mean...do she *like* white boys?"

In their world, "like" was never used in a literal sense. It was

always bad business anytime DeeDee liked somebody—
even him.

"She a teacher," Anthony replied. "Her brain don't even
work like that."

Meezy laughed, nudging him in the side. "A teacher?"

"Didn't you hear her when we came in?"

"Man, you know how females lie."

"About being teachers, nigga?"

"I'm just saying." He shrugged. "A teacher? With ass like
that?"

"I ain't know ass size correlated to somebody's occupation."

"Correlated? Occupation?" Meezy guffawed. "Who the fuck
you is? Obama?"

Anthony rolled his eyes while fighting the urge to swipe his
moist hands down the length of his jeans as both of them looked
back at Venus' ass. There it was again—that sneaky sweat she
conjured up.

"Man, I came here to talk about that thing you asked Zeke
about—not about who I came with."

"A'ight... a'ight... a'ight. Damn. I was just wondering." He
eyed Anthony's hands.

Anthony swiped them down his jeans anyway while Venus
belted out a loud cackle, swatting Dan's arm.

Now angst gripped his chest and squeezed it, wringing out
all the leftover distress DeeDee left there because he didn't
know what to do with that feminine superpower Venus
carried.

The first time he learned what angst meant was after Munch
was born.

"That girl got you all angsty," Lola said, shaking her head at
the way he obsessed over every move DeeDee made. *"It ain't
good for you."*

And it still wasn't.

"Listen Anthony," Venus called out, pulling her arm off Dan's
shoulder. "This is a drum."

She glanced over her shoulder and smiled while Dan looked at her like she put on that jumpsuit for his white ass.

"Anthony?" Meezy snickered beside him. "You practically delivered her to me, then turn around and say I can't have her when she dangling all that ass in my face. Now she calling you by yo' government name? You sure that ain't yo' bitch?"

She was climbing there and if she called out his name like that again, he'd nudge her ass past DeeDee.

"Show me that other thing again, Dan. I wanna show Anthony that, too." She bit down on her pointer finger—the one he'd been gripping—the one that kept him in line like she wanted. "Make it sultry. He likes slow jams."

The biting, the way her ass had spread as she leaned over Dan, and how every eye in the studio kept zeroing in on her, *really* made him understand what Lola meant when she said angst wasn't good for him.

"Yeahhh, like that." She smiled as if she didn't feel their low eyes stroking her body. "Bet Lil' Try Hard over there can't rap over nothing like this."

"Goofy ass." Meezy chuckled and flicked a lighter, holding the flame to the end of a blunt. "I ain't never fucked on a female that pretended to be a teacher. On God, that shit kinda sexy."

He laughed harder, taking a deep toke from the blunt while Venus' ass seemed to get wider because angst fucked with Anthony's eyes something serious.

Anthony huffed, frowning. "You wanna talk or not?"

They were getting further and further away from the topic and venturing to spaces where Meezy thought Venus was free to roam. It was just like being at Vaughn's again, and now he was really convinced there was no way her ex-husband let her go without a fight.

Meezy's mouth grew slack as he slid further down the couch. "What you got?"

Not as much as he had before.

There was that Hellcat DeShaun was driving around town.

He was holding it for a girl he'd met at a takeover until she got her next paycheck. Then there was Jade's AMG that would be easy money that night.

"What you want?" he asked.

"I don't know. Something sexy." He tilted his head to the side because Venus shifted her weight to her right hip. "I heard you Mr. Make it Happen."

"Anybody ever tell you how much you favor Justin Bieber?" Venus cooed over Dan, cutting into their conversation.

Dan's face turned an even brighter shade of red and he smiled so big Anthony felt a tingling in his knuckles.

"Wait...no...no." She snapped. "You favor a young Brad Pitt. You even old enough to know who Brad Pitt is?"

Meezy snickered. "Maybe I'll take whatever Venus like. That's a sexy ass name—*Venus*."

Anthony shook his head.

Lola was right. Angst was fuckin' terrible.

He scooted to the edge of the couch where Venus' round ass swayed three feet away. It almost had him under the same spell as Meezy until he remembered he didn't have to talk for her to hear what he was saying.

He reached out the three feet and dropped his hand on her ass in a solid *smack*. The force made her flesh ripple underneath the denim and his dick twitch.

She flung her head around with feral eyes until they locked with his. Her top lip curled like she wanted to say something. If she was a keep the peace type of gal like she told Vaughn, she'd read his mind loud and clear.

He narrowed his eyes at her.

Tighten the fuck up.

Because niggas were testing him again and now, they were questioning her because they didn't have the same couth Vaughn had.

"C'mere." He blinked, chewing on his bottom lip. "This stupid nigga think you need him to buy you a car."

Her feral eyes widened until they settled on the tiny space between him and the arm of the couch. He saw all the panicky thoughts running through her mind as if he'd play wingman and deliver her to some lame ass rapper that couldn't even walk into a dealership and buy a car outright.

She smiled an apologetic smile at Dan, stepped over her shoes, and squeezed between Anthony and the couch's armrest. They sat back together, and she sank into his side as if they always sat that way with his arm around her neck and her head against his chest.

Meezy leaned forward, grinning. "Did I get you in trouble, baby?"

She crossed her legs with a disgusted frown. "Don't call me that."

Meezy held his hands up with the blunt dangling from it. "My fault."

"So, like I was saying... what you want?" Anthony asked. "I got an AMG sitting outside, if that's what you on. It ain't modified, but it's clean and brand-new."

Meezy curled his lips under his teeth and whistled. "And how much that's going for?"

"It depends."

"On?"

"If you help me out."

Meezy screwed his face up. "Help you out? I ain't no do-boy."

"Did I say you was?" Anthony shrugged. "I can always take my business somewhere else. I mean, Zeke said you was solid."

"Yeah, solid with my bread. I ain't tryna get involved in none of the shit y'all be on. I just got signed."

Anthony looked from him to his homeboys still lying around. None of them were folks that hung around him when he was just snotty-nosed Malcolm.

"I heard. Zeke say he be with y'all—going to your shows. Especially when y'all be hitting them cities outside Georgia."

"He do."

"Yeah, I guess he ain't explain that's not a free service."

"The fuck you mean? A service? Me and Zeke been cool for a minute."

"Right... *y'all* cool, but me, you, Dre' and JoJo ain't. I guess he ain't explain that. So, you saying I should talk to him about how he markets our services?"

Meezy blew out a breath, rolling his eyes. "Man, come on. I'm not getting in the middle of this shit with y'all and them."

Y'all and *them*? At this point, *they* were just another tiny piece of the trifling saga at hand. They were a part of those loose ends Lynn said he needed to tie up.

"You know I don't get involved in neighborhood beef."

The more Meezy's tone hiked, the more tense Venus grew beside him. He just needed her to hold whatever thought she had for five more minutes, but that was a lot to ask a woman who wrangled five-year-olds all day.

"So, it's like this—tell me what you want, I guarantee the delivery, and then I tell you what I want. After that, we do good business, and you keep Zeke and this lil' image you tryna portray and everybody ends up happy."

Meezy blubbered out a groan while shaking his head and looking around the studio at his friends. They were as clueless as he was because they were used to obnoxious physical threats.

"Goddamn it, Zeke," Meezy muttered to himself.

It was shiesty, but all was fair in the streets, just like in Venus' classroom.

"What you want?" He sighed. "The label ain't even gave me all my advance yet so I don't even got it like that, bro—"

"I want you to call Shad."

"I'm telling you, I don't keep up with them dudes."

"But that's your cousin. You was just keeping up with him the other night from what I saw on IG."

"Man, come on..."

Anthony shrugged. "I'm trying to, but you ain't working

with me. I heard you got a show down in Houston next month. It'd be real fucked up if you had to go deal with them niggas down there without Zeke. You check in with them and all of a sudden they got you by the balls, gon' have you repping they shit and involved in they beef. At least with us you know what it is."

He reached for his pocket. "As a matter of fact, let me call Zeke and tell him you good on hi—"

"A'ight, a'ight, a'ight—damn. Fuck!"

The last few curses he hurled out made Dan glance over his shoulder. He didn't look at them for long before he turned back to the computer to mind his engineer business.

Anthony nodded before turning to Venus. She sat with her back straight, arms crossed and mouth in a moue. He concentrated on that moue, drinking in the slick smoothness of her bottom lip while they argued back and forth in their heads about all the distasteful shit they'd done throughout the night.

Damn, he couldn't fuck her... *or could he?*

Maybe she was as fluid as DeeDee. Maybe she could blend into any space and do whatever he wanted without having to ask out loud.

He pulled her into him. "Earlier when Meezy thought he could afford you, he wanted to know what kind of car you liked. Help him out. He ain't got the best taste."

She frowned while he mentally begged her to keep it together and play along. There were two cars and only one made sense in this situation—just one.

"That loud one I'm always talking about," she muttered. "That's what I like."

Fuck.

She for sure wasn't DeeDee.

She cared too goddamn much.

———

Suddenly, Venus' pussy had a heartbeat, and silly things made her new heartbeat hammer against the crotch of her jumpsuit—like the way Anthony's palm ricocheted off her ass and the clever ways he reminded other men they'd never have a chance with her no matter how successful or audacious they were. They were silly, silly immature things that Rose would scoff at.

Anthony locked her head in a vise grip in the crook of his arm while he swiped through the pictures on his phone of that ugly, loud car she wanted him to get rid of, even though she wasn't supposed to care that much. She actually wasn't supposed to care at all, but he made her care in some weird way she couldn't explain. It was probably just another silly thing.

"It's clean, right?" Meezy asked, wrinkling his eyebrows. "With a new title and a VIN?"

The smugness had melted off of his chubby face after Anthony laid out the terms and conditions of doing business with him because Anthony was a no-nonsense "businessman" with an intricate operation that made the swag in Meezy's voice disappear.

"Shad still on his way, right?" Anthony asked.

Meezy nodded.

"It ain't no paper title. I already took care of the VIN and plates, though. That's all you need and you'll never get pulled over—trust me. I can't be careless."

Shad—whoever he was—had been on his way the whole time, but businessmen like Anthony needed their suspicions confirmed, so he made Meezy call him.

"Didn't I tell you I was gon' pull up when we talked earlier?" Shad asked breezily. *"I'm dropping Sicily off at work first. Then I'm coming. I got the King's—lemon pepper wet, all flats."*

If Daddy was there, he'd laugh and tell her how Meezy and his friends wouldn't bust a grape in a fruit fight because they were the real baby boys.

"Twenty twenty-three redeye wide body. I wrapped the car and swapped the VINS myself, so I ain't bullshitting you,"

Anthony said. "It ain't nothing but a thousand miles on it. It don't even have a GPS. I just drive it to my gig and to run errands for my baby girl."

He was talking about Tori, but Meezy's eyes fluttered toward her. She shuffled closer to Anthony, relishing in the soft way he talked about Tori like she owned him.

"It's clean, but I'll get it detailed before I drop it off to you. I don't usually do that, but you cool so…"

Meezy didn't even want the car anymore, but it didn't matter because now he was wrapped up in a business deal he couldn't afford and she'd seen her first real life extortion. It wasn't as volatile as the crime shows on Netflix made them seem. Everything with Anthony was subtle—even the way he coerced folks. It was in the way he maintained eye contact with Meezy, the careful way he thought before he spoke, and the inflection in his voice that warned Meezy he better not do anything stupid.

Dan paused the beat he had been playing on a loop and pushed away from the computer, but before he could stand up, the studio door clicked and they all looked toward it.

"Why it's so quiet in here? I thought you said you was record—"

Shad had a marred hand with a nasty scar that zig-zagged across it. It didn't spread all the way when he pushed the studio door behind him. It stuck up unnaturally. She wouldn't have even noticed it if it weren't for the plastic bag full of styrofoam to-go boxes dangling from it.

His brown eyes turned ice cold when they landed on Anthony and then jumped to Meezy.

"You hit your head or something?" he asked him.

There was no "hey, cousin!" like she greeted Ginny.

Meezy shook his head. "Nah."

"So what the fuck is this, then?" Shad gestured between Anthony and him.

"He just popped up on some fan type shit. For real."

"Fan?" Anthony pulled his arm from around her neck and sat forward, staring Meezy down.

Goosebumps prickled her arms.

"Nigga, don't insult me like that. You got one song that my five-year-old know from TikTok. Be fuckin' for real if you gon' cap. Tell your cousin what you told Zeke."

Dan's shoulders hunched up to his ears while she covered her mouth. He didn't even spin around in his chair. He looked straight ahead at the paused beat on the computer screen.

"You told him to pull up?" Shad asked, stepping forward and dropping the bag on the table.

"Just to talk about cars. That's it. I didn't think he would actually come."

His voice was different again—more suburban and even less abrasive.

Shad's eyebrows wrinkled, and he pointed at him with his good hand. "If you tell a nigga like him to pull up, what the fuck you think he gon' do? Think about that shit, Malcolm."

Meezy tossed his hands up.

Her and Anthony's heads swung back and forth between them.

Their family was imploding, and she didn't even have a bag of popcorn to enjoy the chaos Anthony caused.

"This ain't them private school niggas you roll with," Shad added.

Private school?

Damn. Now she needed a drink to go along with her imaginary popcorn.

"Take them niggas and go get me a Sprite from the store."

Meezy pushed up from the couch without hesitation and the rest of the baby boys followed with big eyes. They marched past her with frowns. Once the door clicked behind them, Shad looked at her and the hand she had unconsciously laid against Anthony's back.

She should've taken her ass with them.

He took a step forward and swiped a black gun out the front of his jeans, clunking it on the table next to the wings.

She didn't realize she'd gone stiff until Anthony snuck his hand around her thigh, kneading it and using their weird mutual telepathy to tell her not to worry because they were on neutral turf. It was its own place, with its own unwritten rules where regular folks like her and Dan could exist without harm.

He gave her leg one last squeeze of reassurance.

"I thought you was a waitress now?" Shad snorted. "I knew niggas was lying."

"How your hand holding up?" Anthony replied.

"Fuck you."

"I just gave your lil' cousin the best deal of his life." He laughed. "But it's 'fuck me?'"

"Yeah, fuck you and Dre'. Both y'all some lame ass niggas… and that lil' dyke, too."

"Hold up, not too much on my lil' sis. I know you wanna keep that other hand."

There it was again—that eye contact and thoughtfulness and inflection—all the silly little things Rose's son couldn't do.

She didn't even know who Shad or Dre' was or what had happened to Shad's hand—all she knew was somewhere along the way she had decided she didn't just want to fuck Anthony. She wanted to keep him and his hardness, too.

Shad's nostrils flared. "C'mon bruh, what you want?"

"I want you to keep your mouth shut. I heard it's been looser than normal these days."

"I don't know what you talking about."

"You got hemmed up in DeKalb and somehow my name came out your big ass mouth for no reason."

"Who told you that?"

Anthony tsk'd. "Now you know better than that. I look like you?"

Nope.

He looked like a grown ass man sitting next to her with his

hand on her thigh, nothing to protect them but his fists, and belting out a mouthful of shit she didn't know nothing about.

Shad chuckled, swiping his nose and looking away. "They asked me a question, and I answered it. I can't control what they do with my answer."

"Man, come on." Anthony laughed, shifting forward and waving his hand. "I thought we was better than this? I mean, I am the one that saved your other hand. That should count for something, right?"

"You a sick motherfucka."

Anthony laughed even harder.

He laughed so hard that he squeezed her thigh to calm himself. "All I'm saying is my nigga is real serious about that lil' dyke you still in your feelings about. If it was up to him, you'd be handless. Gimme some credit."

"You ain't do that shit for me. You did it for yourself. Everybody know how you and DeeDee move."

Trying to follow their conversation was like watching a tennis match. They fired out responses so fast she struggled to keep up until he said Deeanna's name and the little game they played stopped.

She waited for Anthony to fly off the handle, but he stared at Shad instead.

"Niggas been talking about y'all..." Shad smirked. "Is it true?"

Now she was the one going stiff and leaning forward into Anthony's back. She pushed her chin against his shoulder and she didn't even know why. It all came to her like second-nature.

She didn't know enough about him and Shad's history to interject, but she knew that taunting tone Shad questioned him in. Rose had asked her the same question, in the same way, when she heard she'd finally moved out of her and Trey's house and back in with Daddy. That tone was universal.

She raked her fingers across Anthony's hot back while his jaw clenched.

He reached out and flicked Shad's gun.

"You know, me and Dre' debate a lot—about how irrational I can be and how hotheaded I get when I'm tested." He shook his head. "I don't give a fuck 'bout your hands or your cousin that you promised to keep an eye on. You keep playing with my name and Ms. Ann gon' be on Fox 5 crying about how good of a boy you was, because it's one thing in life I don't take lightly and right now you dancing *real* close to it…."

She gulped for Shad as chills coursed through her limbs. She felt the tension hovering between their bodies and saw the fear in Shad's eyes.

Shad shook his head. "Fuck you, *Nuney*."

fourteen

· · ·

VENUS HAD BEEN MISTAKEN.

There was one Kayden-like quality that existed in Anthony.

His hot stare penetrated her back as she pushed out of Meezy's studio session. It singed the spot where Dan had pressed his hand and then grazed her ass where Meezy couldn't stop staring.

She peeked above his head at the security camera mounted on the ceiling while holding in her questions about Shad and his hand. Afterward, she took off down the hallway that somehow seemed longer. She stopped when she didn't feel Anthony's warmth at her side.

She turned around and regretted it because Kaydens weren't supposed to look like *that*, and she wasn't supposed to want them after learning about the dangerous shit they were capable of.

Kaydens weren't supposed to lean against walls with their heads cocked to the side, studying her in the ways grown men didn't. They weren't supposed to make threats so easily or smile at her after everything she saw behind those studio doors and worst of all...they didn't understand how complicated women's brains were.

"Where you going?" he asked in a huff, pinching his eyes together.

"To the car."

"No." He shook his head, laughing. "No ma'am. *Hell nah.*"

He pointed down at the open space in front of his sneakers before he could get the rest of his words out, but when the words came—they *came.*

"You got ten seconds to explain yourself right goddamn now and on God, I don't wanna hear that 'you first' bullshit."

She gulped as her new heartbeat bopped.

"Ten... nine... eight..." he counted.

Her feet moved along to the not-so menacing countdown he belted out while the beat Dan let her tinker with started playing again. She marched along to the sound of it and Anthony's voice until she ended up right where his finger had pointed.

He had a glower in his eyes, as if he were twice his actual age and they both had some explaining to do.

Thanks to Meezy, he had a contact high, and he looked even better with sullen heavy eyes and curled lashes she could count all day.

"I... I," she stuttered over the words she didn't have while he kept smiling.

His lips even moved along with hers and she wanted him to touch her *so* badly she kept imagining he already had. She felt his fingers pressing into her neck, his hand coaxing her new heartbeat to a calm rhythm and his mouth on hers.

"A'ight, let me help you out," he muttered, leaning down next to her ear. "Tell me his name."

"Trey," she blurted.

The earth didn't feel as if it stopped spinning. Time didn't come to a halt, and her stomach didn't turn for the first time.

He nodded, biting his lip. "Hmph."

"Hmph? What's that supposed to mean?"

"Nothing. I just figured a nigga that caused so much havoc would have a more opulent name."

She laughed.

Trey *was* a basic name. There was a time it used to make butterflies flutter in her belly and her pupils dilate when Daddy would bring it up in disdain. Now it meant nothing to her—not even when she stared at it on the screenshots Ginny sent her of his new life from Facebook.

Anthony waved his arm out. "Continue..."

"Don't start that again."

"Well, stop running from the explanation."

"Oh, like you running from our conversation about Tori? Like you about to run from our conversation about whoever the hell that was in there and what type of shit you be in?" She tossed her thumb back at the studio door.

He raised his bushy eyebrows, and she felt him again because her body inched forward without her even realizing it. Her fingers even found their way onto his eyebrow. They twirled between the hairs and journeyed down its tail. The heat from his body she had missed engulfed her, and she didn't mind drowning in it this time.

"I couldn't even smile at a man without him accusing me of flirting and starting a fight afterwards," she blurted out, explaining herself anyway.

"So that was your way of testing me out in there after what I said to Vaughn? What, you was tryna see how I'd react to you flirting this time? You wanted to see if I'm as immature as you always thinking?"

She pinched her eyes shut, shaking her head. "I—no, and even if I was, it wouldn't matter."

"Why not?"

"You know why."

It was all so stupid. None of it would matter because he wasn't courting her. She needed to stop wasting her double-duty questions and childish tests.

He smirked, laughing to himself. "If it's just us for the night, then let it be that. I ain't telling nobody we went on a date if you not."

Whatever night they were having was just that—*a night*. They were done after this. Then again, she said that the last time they ended up in the same space. At some point, she had to be the mature one.

His head fell against the wall and her fingers went with it because even the innocuous parts of him felt good. The soft strands of his eyebrow glided against her fingers as his tongue darted out to wet his bottom lip.

He pulled her hand away from his face and nudged it back to her side.

"Were you jealous with Deeanna?" she asked.

"Nah. I didn't need to be. She made me feel something else."

"Well excuse me, Mr. Mature."

He shook his head. "It wasn't even like that."

"What you mean 'it wasn't like that?'"

"You wouldn't understand."

"*Expound.*"

He frowned, looking down at the polished hardwood. "Nah...you too judgy for me to be doing all that."

She grunted out a laugh that made him laugh.

"For the hundredth time. I am not judgmental...damn."

Her last few words came out in a whisper and their laughs simmered into slight chuckles until he wet his bottom lip again.

"If you my woman, then that's just what it is. It don't matter how many men you flirt with behind my back or in front of me. I always exist at the top."

She smirked. "Oh yeah? How do you stay at the top, then?"

"Flirting is about curiosity. It's about the possibility this new man might satisfy something inside of you I can't. Maybe you think this random dude you met is a bigger catch, or maybe you just flirting to learn something about yourself or your man—like if he'll start realizing you can't control another man's eyes... or how sexy you are." His cheek lifted as if he could see all the screaming matches and pointed fingers between her and Trey. "It doesn't matter the reason, though. It all gets handled the same way."

Her breath had grown shallow with each word he spoke. "And how do you do that?"

He shrugged. "I just fuck the curiosity out of her when we get home."

Another "how" got caught in her throat. She knew better than to let it come out and give him the chance to *expound* again. He said "just," like fucking the curiosity out of somebody was easy—like he did it every time Deeanna decided there might be somebody better out there for her.

"Maybe Trey ain't know that one of the worst feelings in the world is walking into a room and knowing that all the other men in there can't keep their eyes off you, but the best feeling is knowing that it won't matter because you're his. It's a mental thing."

At some point between his words, she pressed her body against his because he kept her in a perpetual state of neediness without even trying hard. They were pelvis to pelvis with their eyes locked, and he still hadn't even touched her.

She heard Logan yapping in her head, reminding her that going so long without dick was blasphemous, but she didn't understand how unholy it was to not have Anthony's dick.

He dropped his head, peering at her middle pressed against his.

Then he tsk'd and wagged his finger at her. "I told you I was the cat whisperer. Now I gotta housebreak her, too. Bet Trey ain't never even did that shit."

Her head fell back as she grunted out a deep laugh. "I told you not to have me in no shit."

"*Me?* You got me in all kind of shit. Up in there, bent over, running your mouth about stuff you don't know nothing about. That was some reckless shit you was doing in there."

"You know what I was trying to do."

"Yeah, I caught your game," he said, sliding his hands along the widest part of her hips and making her exhale at their heaviness. "That car you gave up in there wasn't meant to be given up. You was supposed to give up that AMG I'm letting you joyride so I can get you another one, and another one, and another one..."

His voice trailed off into a low murmur. He felt good and looked even better, pleading his case and tugging her body closer to his. When his warm hands slid to her ass, her pussy's new wild heartbeat bopped in a slow, hard rhythm.

"You better not get me another anything unless you pay for it." She shook her head. "I'm sorry I don't know the ins and outs of all your illegal proclivities."

He laughed and squeezed two handfuls of her ass.

Her stomach jumped. "So now what?"

"Now I gotta get another car 'cause you wanna play Mrs. Nunez."

Mrs. Nunez.

Damn. Now, she was the jealous one—jealous of the fact that some girl would get the chance to get called that if he stopped being resourceful long enough to do something crazy like get married.

"*Anthony...*"

They should've been shouting at each other, but instead they stood face to face with smiles on their faces that were as dopey as his laugh.

Nothing was funny about the predicament they were in or the things he'd promised to do to Shad, but he thought it was *hilarious*. It was another Kayden-like thing she overlooked. Anthony didn't take life as seriously as Trey had taught her to— he just lived like he told her she should've been doing.

"I'm only an hour into work and you fuckin' up all my motion. The *hell* is you doing, Ms. Thibodeaux?" he muttered between laughs while pawing her ass in a rough way she didn't even know she liked. "No more take Munch's teacher to work days."

———

Anthony felt different from any other man Venus had ever experienced.

He felt *good*—kind of like a nice ass tropical vacation she didn't want to end. He made her feel soft and feminine, like God intended. He reminded her of how good a man's hand felt between her legs—not in a sexual way, but a comfortable one because they were comfortable now — *too comfortable*.

"I gotta make another pit stop," he mumbled, chewing the end of a straw he got from their first pit stop at a random McDonald's.

While there, he ordered them iced teas so they could wash down the want they'd been choking on.

She glanced from the intimidating condo building to his hand cupping her in the center of her legs.

It lived there even though they hadn't kissed, exchanged loving pet names, or fucked. It went along with all the cat double entendres he liked to joke about. It shouldn't have been there, but she'd been the one to let him touch her first, so he was just following her lead after all.

"You have to go in that building?" she asked.

"Mhmm." He hummed, pulling the straw out of his mouth and sitting it on the empty console under the radio.

She held in her questions, reveling in the building's luxury while Total crooned through the car's speakers.

He drove toward the building, and then down a winding driveway that led to an underground parking garage. He stopped at a keypad, letting go of her long enough to type in a code while her body hummed for his hand to come back.

Going so long without sex made the desperation ooze out of her. She swore it was even in her breath when she exhaled.

The keypad *dinged* and the gate's arm lifted, granting them access. They drove through the maze of a parking garage while she tried to hold in her desperate breath.

"You good over there?" he asked, pulling into an empty parking spot and pushing the car into park.

She nodded stiffly. "Yeah."

"Then let's go."

He pulled the key fob from between their drinks in the cup holder and got out.

They'd only been together for a night, but that's all it'd taken for her to learn the way he'd move as somebody's husband. He opened doors. Closed them. Took her shoes off. Put them back on. Paid for things no matter how small they were. Sang R&B songs she forgot existed, and he obsessed over the weirdest parts of her, like her feet.

He pulled the passenger door open.

This time, before she stepped out, she didn't have to count out any deep breaths because she wasn't hard anymore. He'd taken his time and melted her down to a mound of lusty putty.

He leaned against the car door, smirking, and holding his hand out for hers. "No questions this time?"

She sat her hand in his warm one. "Nope."

"We'll see how long that last." He snickered, pulling her up and out of the car.

He closed the door behind her and then picked her hand back up after hitting the lock on the fob. His hardness she'd been relishing and fighting all night engulfed her.

Holding hands?

What was wrong with her? People in relationships held hands.

She glanced at his calloused fingers tangled between hers.

He tugged her his way until she was between him and the cars parked along the wall. They walked until they came upon an elevator. As soon as they stepped inside, she tugged her hand out of his.

"Where you tryna go?" he asked, pressing the button for the lobby.

"Nowhere."

"A'ight." He snickered. "What Trey gotta say now? He don't let you hold your date's hands?"

She didn't realize she had a breezy smile plastered on her face until she caught her reflection in the elevator doors. "*I* ain't held a man's hand in a long ass time—let alone a date's."

"Oh, I'm a man now?"

His smug smile reflected in the elevator doors next to hers and she rolled her eyes.

"'Preciate it, by the way," he added.

"'Preciate what?"

"You letting me pop your hand holding cherry for the second time. They say the second time around is the most fun."

He smiled placidly as the elevator doors opened like he knew that out of all the hands she'd ever held, his were the most enticing.

She shook her head.

What the hell did she get herself into?

As soon as they stepped into the bright lobby, a peppy brunette pulled her face from between the pages of a Colleen Hoover novel and squinted until they got close enough to the marble desk she sat behind.

Anthony smacked it.

Her squint turned into a wide-eyed stare and then she smiled so big that all thirty-two of her white teeth almost showed. "Well hello, handsome."

It was his second pet name of the night—*handsome*. It made her stomach turn just as much as Mikayla's "baby" did.

The girl dropped the book next to her pink tumbler decorated with Tri-Delt stickers. "Long time no see."

"For real, it's been a minute."

"Been busy?" She eyed Venus out of her peripheral.

He smirked in response.

"Right." She giggled. "Busy being good or bad?"

"Always good."

"Tuh. If that were the case, I wouldn't like you so much."

She didn't even sugarcoat the shit. She just came right out with it.

Anthony held his finger to his lips. "Shh. You tryna scare my date away?"

"Date?" Her arched eyebrows shot up, and she looked over at Venus directly this time, frowning. "I guess there won't be any emergency concierge calls to 3520 tonight."

They'd fucked.

Based on the way the girl tilted her head, they'd fucked several times while Anthony did whatever he did in unit 3520.

Venus crossed her arms. "Don't worry, you can have hi—"

"Unless..." The girl cut her off, smirking at her cleavage that had found its way to the top of her jumpsuit again.

She studied her chest in a way that made the hairs on Venus' arms stand. Venus sucked in a gasp and clumsily reached for the zipper, but Anthony beat her to it.

"Aht, Aht," he hissed, tugging it harder than he did at Vaughn's.

The girl rolled her eyes and puckered her pouty, glossed lips. "Fine. You never let me have any fun."

"Nah. You be having *too* much fun."

He wasn't having a "lover's spat" with this girl. This was something else. It had the same vapid energy as his conversation with Mikayla did. It was filled with nothing but vague words and the lust of past encounters.

"I'm always on my best behavior with you, you know that."

He laughed, gripping the back of Venus' neck and tugging her to him. "Sometimes."

She rested her chin in her palm and they stared at each other, with Venus standing between them. She eyed Anthony with an expression that Venus couldn't read.

"What's on your mind, Priya?" he asked, tightening his fingers around Venus' neck as she relaxed against the desk.

"You know, Mr. and Mrs. Dennison from 3260?"

He nodded in her peripheral.

"They left for Italy today." She smiled and picked up her book again, skimming the page she was on. "They'll be there all month."

Anthony whistled, pulling her body into his. "The Amalfi Coast?"

"Probably. If my husband had enough coin to take me to the Amalfi Coast, I'd be the happiest girl alive. Mrs. Dennison is always such a bitch."

Venus choked on a snicker that made Priya look up from the book with a mischievous smile and then go back to reading.

"Still? What you do to her, Priya?"

"I can't help it that her husband wants to fuck me." She smirked. "She yelled at me because FedEx lost her Saks package the day before their flight left."

Her green eyes scoured the page and her voice got featherlight. "I heard she has the nicest collection of Birkins, though. Such a shame an evil wench like her gets to carry so many bad ass bags. Their housekeeper, Olga, says she doesn't even lock them up when they go on vacation. She has them propped up like little thirty thousand dollar trinkets and makes Olga dust the hardware every day."

Her words would've sounded noncommittal to anybody passing by—like she was shooting the shit about the building's most annoying couple. Venus imagined the Dennisons breezing through the mid-century modern lobby draped in ornate furs and snapping their fingers at Priya and the rest of the staff.

Priya giggled at something she read and then looked up at them, biting into her bottom lip. "Mr. Dennison gave me a key last month for *emergencies*. Just tell me when and they're all yours, Papa. It'll solve that little problem you told me you had."

Venus swallowed a lump in her throat at the abrupt change in her tone.

No wonder Deeanna was going manic in jail. He had a whole roster of little girls that felt just like she did.

He laughed off Priya's bold offer and pulled Venus by the neck. "You crazy, Pri."

"Thank you." She batted her lashes and then winked toward Venus. "Enjoy the rest of your night with your date, Mr. Nunez."

He tugged Venus away from the desk.

She swung her head from Priya to him as they stumbled toward another elevator. Their hands intertwined as he pulled her inside.

She tsk'd and shook her head as soon as the doors closed. "A crazy thieving Tri-Delt? Really? How many lives do you live?"

She was undoubtedly in the *Twilight Zone*.

He laughed, tossing his head back and squeezing her hand.

She accepted his non-answer this time. The less she knew about him and Priya, the better.

When they passed the thirty-second floor, one of those questions she'd been holding in came bubbling up. "So, what's this place?"

"The best place to lay your head between plays."

"You're talking teenager aga—"

The elevator chirped out a shrill ding, and the doors opened to a private hallway with one black door at the end.

He pulled her out while she studied the crown molding and muted grey accents along the walls. When they made it to the door, he pecked another keypad and entered a code he didn't even bother hiding from her.

The door swung open and unit 3520 smelled like peonies and looked like a Pottery Barn ad with its comforting neutrals, wooden console tables, and lush throw blankets. It was so spotless she didn't want to move past the entryway.

"You want a glass of wine?" he asked.

Her body jerked, and he laughed.

"Whose place is this, Anthony?" she hissed.

"My big brother's."

"There's another one? What the hell does this one do? Play basketball?"

He spurted out that goofy laugh she liked and squatted down next to her. "That nigga wish he could shoot a ball."

He pulled her shoes off and tossed them on a shoe rack she hadn't even noticed. It held other shoes—Jordans, heels, and little pink girly sneakers. If she didn't know any better, she'd think the whole family was home.

He walked further into the condo, leaving her barefoot and confused.

She ambled behind him through the entryway, glancing at the family pictures and plaques on the wall while he flicked up some of the light switches, illuminating the open floor plan.

"I'm not much of a rap person, but I recognize this guy." She sat her hands on her hips, tilting her head at the framed *Billboard* magazine cover where he'd buried his caramel face behind his tattooed hands.

"Oh yeah? So you recognize D, but you ain't recognize Lil' Try Hard?"

"Lil' Try Hard ain't win a Grammy. This guy did, though." She pointed up to the portrait of Dough. "I saw his speech."

She didn't know much about him—only what she saw when scrolling on social media and his songs she heard on the radio. There were times she thought he was cute. Other than that, she didn't think much of him or the people around him.

"You know a lot of famous people," she added.

"Nah... a lot of famous people know me," he replied, slamming a cabinet shut.

"Smart-ass lil' boy." She huffed under her breath, snorting. "So, what, he just pays you to house sit?"

"No. The family is busy nowadays, so we all just pop in when we can. It used to be JoJo's mama's place, but she decided she wanted to move out to Dunwoody. D's girl say a condo ain't the best place to raise kids and she'd rather keep her house in Sandy Springs. So we stuck with it until D decide what he wanna do."

"Hmm... you talk about it like you put money into it."

"I put my time into it and my time is just as valuable as my money."

She smirked. "Oh really? Who told you that one?"

"Myself."

She studied another picture of Dough cradling his girlfriend, their newborn, and their pre-schooler. The pictures were intimate, and the world had probably never seen them. They made her want to guzzle that wine Anthony hunted for when she should've been cooing over how beautiful their family was.

"No wine." He slammed another cabinet shut. "You drink clear or brown?"

"Clear."

"Patrón... Casamigos... Don Julio."

She turned around and found him pulling his jeans up at the waist. It was another silly thing that turned her on. He stared at a bottle of Patrón, turning it over in his hands.

She bit into her lip as his brows furrowed. "You know you never answered Ms. Sheryl back at Vaughn's."

"Answered Ms. Sheryl about what?"

"About you being old enough to drink..."

He looked up at her. "I'm old enough for you if that's what you tryna ask."

She couldn't remember the last vacation she went on, but she knew it wasn't like this one. This one made her want to do every forbidden thing she was supposed to do in paradise—like all the shit Anthony wouldn't let her leave without doing.

She ignored her heavy tongue and his piercing stare and stepped further into the living room. Her bare feet sank into the rug and the spotless beige furniture beckoned her to it.

She ran her fingers across the soft suede until she noticed the city sparkling outside the balcony doors. She walked toward them.

The building's lights reflected off the blue water from the pool nestled on the condo's balcony. All of it went along with the allure of the pretend tropical vacation she was on.

She pressed her fingers against the glass, squinting at the city and the pool. "Jesus..."

"You should get in."

She turned around at the sound of his voice. "Hell no."

He stood in front of her with a handful of stuff he'd dug out of the kitchen—a lighter, the Patrón bottle, and a Ziploc bag full of weed.

"Damn. There Trey go again—ruining all the fun. I coulda swore you said you was gon' let it be us for the night." He shrugged, nudging her to the side, twisting the lock on the balcony door and pushing it open.

"I didn't say that. You did," she talked to the back of his baby blue shirt as he strolled to a chaise and collapsed in it, dropping everything he held.

"Maybe. I be getting our thoughts confused sometimes." He kicked his feet up, laid back, and pulled his phone out.

She sighed to herself at the purring noise the waterfall made at the end of the pool.

"Get in," he repeated. "I'll wash your bra and panties when you done swimming."

"You do laundry?"

He smirked. "For *sure*. I specialize in intimates."

"Don't be talking fresh—"

His phone rang, and she hoped he didn't hear that tiny voice in her head she kept trying to hide from him. It taunted her and beckoned her toward the pool while he answered.

"What's the word, twin?" he drawled.

"Oh yeah? Let me talk to Munch."

Her breath hitched in her throat at the immediate smile that spread across his face while he babbled on the phone about nothing.

She wanted to tell him to put the call on speakerphone. She needed to hear that Tori could tell him how she felt about being without him for the night or hear what "daddy" sounded like coming out of her little mouth but Anthony was like all the other delusional parents she'd came across while teaching—haughty and abrasive when it came to his kid.

"I talked to Mama, and she said that if you got your thumb out your mouth, Daddy could buy you that puppy you keep asking for." He paused, letting the phone fall into the crook of his neck. "Gimme a kiss."

She shuffled from inside the condo and pulled the balcony doors closed behind her because Anthony was demanding kisses. Now, she was the delusional one.

"*Muah*," he belted into the phone with puckered lips.

He met Tori where she was at. He talked to her like the five-year-old she was, in a soft cadence whether she talked back or not. He didn't blabber about Deeanna's distressed jail call. They talked like all was well in their little world while her hand snuck its way to the zipper dangling from her jumpsuit.

She didn't think while she glided toward him because he told her he was old enough for her.

He could make the purring between her legs stop. He could make her tighten up when they were around other men, he could make her shoulders light, he could make her stop asking so many questions, he could make her stop drafting those emails to Principal—

Her shin knocked against the chaise as she stood at the edge with her hand hanging onto the zipper.

fifteen

. . .

"LET ME DO IT," Anthony mumbled, moving his phone to the opposite side of his neck. "You gon' hurt yourself tryna get to me."

Venus' body heated with hot, embarrassing desperation.

He knew all about it and had been knowing about it, since they sat in Vaughn's driveway, but he made it seem like a good thing—like it was good for her to fall in line with Mikayla, Deeanna and even Priya even though she was too old to do something so stupid. Those girls were young, and she'd been there and done that. She'd begged for love when she shouldn't have, chased men who didn't pay her any mind after they fucked, and did stupid things under the guise of being in love.

"Come right here," he murmured this time, patting the space between his spread legs.

She rounded the chaise and tried to think before she did anything stupid, but he hooked his arm around her thigh and pulled her down before she had the chance to.

She sat on her knees in front of him while he divided his attention between her and the phone. His hand moved little by little until it reached her zipper and pulled it.

Its purr rose above the sound of the waterfall in the pool. She swore she was the only one that heard it because he was still lost in his phone. Tori had run off after he begged her to go to bed, leaving him to talk his night over with his friend.

"I lost the cat," he said, eyeing her breasts that spilled out and kissed the night air.

His friend belted out a loud, "how the fuck you do that?"

Her body tensed as she waited for him to explain what happened and then for him to realize she'd really been the one to fuck things up for him.

Sometimes it took Trey's anger an hour or so to build up. He'd go on about his day until it registered in his brain she'd done something stupid he needed to correct. She'd run off to Daddy's or sneak a cigarette while she waited for the explosion, but this time she had no choice but to wait right in front of Anthony.

He smiled at the black lacy bra she threw on at the last minute. His eyes stroked her chest so hard her nipples puckered behind the cups.

"Don't even worry about it, twin," he blurted, laughing. "Shit happens."

His friend's voice volleyed up and down in a deep, melodic cadence. She couldn't make out any more of his words and she didn't know if it was because Anthony's hand had crept under her bra's wire or if he had turned the phone's volume down when she wasn't paying attention.

"What you mean what I'm gon' do? I'm gon' go out and get another one." He laughed again. "*Or* I could just not give him the shit. I already got what I wanted. That nigga soft as hell, Dre'."

So this was the infamous Dre' that Shad thought was a bitch even though he had deep talks with Anthony and babysat his child while he ran around the city? They'd made him sound almost mythical back at the studio.

Anthony smacked his lips and "mhmm'd" while Dre' probably talked about that shit Anthony said they always debated about.

The stress from his problem lived in his hands. They glided to places they weren't supposed to while he listened to Dre' and she let them.

"It'll be my last one for the summer. For real. I can't risk it no more."

His stressed hand found one of her hidden nipples. He brushed his thumb across the lacy cup before yanking the rest of the zipper.

The jumpsuit's straps fell down her shoulders and he leaned back to watch her peel the rest of the fabric down her midsection, but apparently he knew she wouldn't do it right.

"Watch out." He nudged her fingers away.

His responses to Dre' went from complete sentences, to errant words, and then to hums because he'd ran into a problem. The jumpsuit stopped at her hips and he couldn't divide his attention between her and Dre' anymore. It was too much stress for his already stressed hands.

"Go get in," he muttered to her. "I ain't gon' be much longer."

She got up and yanked down the rest of the fabric with trembling hands before trekking to the pool with hard nipples and wet panties.

She stuck her toe in the tepid water and ear hustled as he fired off short, rapid responses to Dre' that would've sounded like nothing to anybody who hadn't been around boys like Anthony, but she'd spent a whole summer with them once. Stupid fuck ups had to be reported to somebody, future reckless plans needed approval beforehand, and nothing was ever spelled out just in case square ass people like her were around to hear.

She laughed to herself and eased into the water.

As soon as she turned around to dangle off the pool's edge, he hung up and yanked his shirt over his head in one motion.

She almost choked on the air at the sight of his solid chest. It looked better than she'd been imagining.

He rifled through the stuff he had laying on the chaise, picking up a pack of rolling papers and pulling one out while she tried to quell her watering mouth.

She cleared her throat, holding onto the edge of the pool and kicking her feet out.

"This other job you got is pretty boring, huh? Hustling perpetrating rappers, threatening their scary cousins, house sitting, fuckin' the building's concierge, getting high..."

His tongue stopped against the rolling paper and he looked at her. "Every night can't be a movie. Slow motion always better than no motion."

"You talk in punchlines. Maybe you should ghostwrite for Lil' Try Hard."

He snickered, licking the paper again, dropping a clump of weed in it and then rolling it between his fingers. "I ain't crazy enough to be a rapper. That's a hard job—especially when you gotta cosplay a lifestyle."

She laughed to herself, thinking about the sudden change in Meezy back at the studio. She'd have to tell Ginny about it one day.

She tilted her head at the way he concentrated on the joint he rolled.

A mist of sweat covered his taut stomach from the humid night air. She followed the dips in it and tried to remind herself that just one minute ago he was on the phone with Tori—the same Tori that sat in her classroom five days a week. That thought didn't help because she'd gotten distracted by how much age changed men's bodies. Stress and life had turned Trey's flat stomach into a round pudge she thought she liked until she saw Anthony shirtless.

He looked like he should've been hanging in an exhibit in the MoMA that depicted the physique of the perfect black man. He had washboard abs covered with hoards of stupid tattoos, but he probably didn't even go to the gym, and there was a jagged scar that peeked from under his armpit. He made her want to ask him stupid shit, like if he ever wanted to visit a place like the MoMA. He'd say 'yes' because his brain was always in places she never expected it to be.

"What happened to your arm?" she asked, fighting the urge to ask if she could taste the skin there.

"Broke it fighting JoJo when I was little."

"The football player is a fighter?"

"Yeah... that ugly ass nigga always tryna fight somebody."

"What'd you do to piss him off?"

"You know, if we gon' be in this whole parent-teacher relationship, you gotta have more faith in me. I don't do nothing to provoke people." He looked up, smiling. "You always thinking the worst of me."

She pursed her lips until they burst into laughter. After not laughing with a man for so long, she was getting used to the feeling again with Anthony. They were always laughing about one thing or another.

It wasn't until he lit the joint and laid back against the chaise that he confessed, "I stole his bike... *allegedly*. I look like a thief to you?"

"You really want me to answer that?"

He huffed out a loud laugh while blowing out a plume of smoke. "Fuck what you talking 'bout. Munch say I'm the 'bestest daddy in the world.'"

She expected heart emojis to pop out of his eye sockets just from the mere mention of Tori, and it made her new heartbeat bop at a mile a minute. It was a juxtaposition compared to the terror in Deeanna's voice when she screeched through the phone, wondering where "her baby was." Now she had even more questions than she did on the first day of school when she asked Tori her name and Tori looked up at her like nobody had ever asked her that before.

"Where you get that nickname from, anyway? *Munch...*"

"I don't know. It popped in my head the first night she came home from the hospital. We sat outside looking at the sky for hours that night. It was the only way she'd go to sleep. I used to tell her I'd steal the moon for her and I still would. That's just my lil' munchkin, my sidekick, my right hand, no matter what tricks her mama try to pull, you know?"

"Tricks?"

Another cloud of smoke escaped from his nose while he stared up at the moon like he was plotting on how to wrangle it from its place in the sky just for Tori.

She didn't hold her breath for him to explain, so she tried to fill in the blanks between him, Deeanna, and Tori on her own.

Maybe it was as simple as Deeanna being a bitter baby mama or him being a bitter baby daddy?

She shrugged, sighing to herself, and mentally adding 'absolutely no baby mamas' to that sad prayer Logan forced her to scrawl out on construction paper.

The water from the pool purred while she undressed him with her eyes, yanking his jeans to his ankles and then rolling his briefs down. As soon as she tried to paint a picture of what his dick might look like, he dropped the shriveled joint on the end table next to the chaise and popped up with all the energy of a guy who swore he was old enough for her.

"It's enough room in there for me?"

She stretched an arm out in the massive, empty pool. "The world is yours, baby boy."

"Yeah, sometimes I be forgetting that. 'Preciate the reminder." The moon hit his shiny teeth as he opened his mouth to smile.

They gleamed while he stood up, unbuttoned his jeans, and kicked them off with his sneakers.

He didn't give her enough time to study the bulge in his black briefs before he took off in a sprint and canonballed his way into the pool beside her. Water splashed onto her head and her perfect twist out dissolved into coily ringlets that flopped in her eyes.

She pushed them up. "Anthony!"

He glided underneath the water like a tattooed fish, making her twirl around in circles until she got dizzy and tired of their bodies not touching.

Parlaying around with Anthony was frustrating. He evoked an itch deep inside of her she needed to scratch, but nothing good would come of it if she did.

She kicked her legs out, brushing them against his body and reveling in that hardness she missed.

He pushed back to the surface, gasping for air with his eyes pinched together. "C'mon. Come swim."

"Hell no. I ain't swam since I was in college at some off campus pool party." She giggled.

Her.

She was giggling.

The last time she probably giggled was the last time she swam.

"Good," he replied.

"How is that good? I sound old."

"Nah, you sound sexy and nostalgic as fuck. I hope Trey insecure ass wasn't there."

She laughed harder. "He wasn't. We were broken up that weekend. My cousin Ginny caught him coming out of her dorm earlier that week. It was an all girls dorm. He said he was there working on a group project...at midnight."

She could laugh about it now, but back then her fragile, naïve heart shattered when Ginny showed her the damning pictures of him pushing out the side entrance of her dorm. It was their first breakup of at least a hundred and the first time he twisted her thoughts so she could blame herself for his indiscretions.

"You got your lick back at the party, though, right?" he asked.

They floated with their faces inches apart while she shrugged. "Maybe."

"*Maybe?* Oh, you fucked somebody there?"

She giggled again, splashing a handful of water at him. "Shut up. I don't kiss and tell."

"Not even to me? Come on...it's me."

"*And?* Who you supposed to be?"

He blinked away the water she splashed in his face with a mischievous smile before nodding his head at her. "I'm your date for the night."

"You're actually Mikayla's date. I'm just borrowing you tonight."

He balled his face up and floated closer to her. "Hell nah."

"What's so bad about that? She sounds like a sweet girl with her head on straight. Shit, she's in college and she wants to be a lawyer."

And she wasn't sitting in jail or offering to steal some rich lady's Birkins for him.

Somehow, she knew what Mikayla looked like without even seeing her in the flesh. She had perfectly coiffed hair she kept in a silk press and a lithe body she curled around him while she purred out "baby." She probably spent her time trying to rescue him. She'd gone to college with plenty of Mikaylas.

"Mikayla wants a husband and I ain't that."

"Then what are you?"

He smirked. "I'm married to the game."

"You're speaking teenager again."

"Fuck love. Is that clear enough for you?"

"You're too young to be philophobic."

He smiled bigger at that word coming out of her mouth. "And you too young to be scared of falling in love again."

How'd he even know what that meant?

The only reason she knew what it meant was because of Michole. It was a constant topic in her weekly therapy sessions. No one warned her about the day she'd wake up with a sinking feeling in her stomach at the thought of falling in love again just to fall out of it.

He swam to the edge of the pool, where he left the unopened bottle of Patrón.

He picked it up. "C'mere."

How could she not when he looked so damn good?

She floated through the water toward him while she eyed the bottle in his hands.

He broke the seal with his teeth and she tried to breathe, but each breath kept getting caught in the back of her throat. As soon as he yanked the cork out, his lips covered the bottle's rim, and he took a swig.

"The objective is for you to stay sober enough to drive me home, Mr. Nunez," she murmured, studying the way he sucked his bottom lip after he swallowed.

"Open your mouth so I won't be so tempted then."

Rose was right. That sliver of immaturity in her brain would never leave. It was like a leech she couldn't peel off, so she opened her mouth, just like he suggested.

The bitter liquor trickled down her throat while his other hand held her in place around her neck. The Patrón burned because she hadn't tasted its tart flavor since her last hoorah, right before she told Trey she didn't wanna try anymore.

When Anthony decided she finally had enough, he yanked the bottle away and stared as she swallowed the last few drops. They were too close again, and she needed her brain to understand that if she kissed him, fucked up things would follow.

"How you do that?" he asked, taking another swig.

"Do what?"

He twirled the bottle in front of her, swallowing. "How you marry somebody that ain't appreciate all this?"

After drinking boxed wine for so many months, the hard liquor smashed into her brain like a sledgehammer. It paralyzed her tongue and made her crave his lips even more.

She blinked and looked down at the "all this" he was refer-ring to—a soft body that had changed right along with Trey's over the years. Now Anthony could see all the rest of the ways divorce had changed her body.

"I don't know," she muttered lamely with a frown.

"That's bad business. This ain't like that egg metaphor you gave me in the car the other night, is it?"

She smiled. "Why do you even remember that?"

"I remember everything."

"That's impossible."

He shook his head and then took another swig of liquor. "I thought you knew that *anything* is possible when I'm on the job."

This giggle shook her chest so hard that it grew sore. "That sounds like some ghetto ass plumber's jingle."

She forgot Patrón made her handsy and loose, so she toppled forward into his chest.

He didn't move away. He let her rake her fingers down his skin while she reveled in the way it reddened under her nails.

"What job are you even talking about? You're getting further and further away from the objective, Mr. Nunez..."

And when did her voice change into a throaty whisper?

"I'm talking about the job you told me about," he replied, staring at her fingers while sitting the bottle back on the edge of the pool.

"I told you about a job? When?"

"On the second day of school."

She frowned, sifting through her second day of school memories.

Over the days, they became muddled, blending in with the first, third, and fourth days, yet somehow her memories of Anthony always survived. She'd even mastered the art of pulling his smell to the forefront of her mind so she could experience it over and over again while laying on her couch at night. She even remembered the way he balanced Tori on his hip in the front office while he scrawled on the transportation form with his left hand.

Jesus, since when did being a lefty turn her on?

"But we never talked about a job that day." She cocked her head to the side, frowning. "Are you trying to extort me like you did with Lil' Try Hard?"

He laughed so hard that his abs pushed against her stomach and made her thrust her arms around his neck to steady herself.

"I don't extort women. That's lame."

They were getting further and further away from the topic at hand, and she kept getting closer and closer to him. Finally, he had enough of her and her dick hungry ways and picked her up. Her legs rushed to curl around his waist and her body melted into his because she finally wasn't dreaming about it in her empty apartment. It was there—hard, agile, and reassuring her she wasn't being stupid.

"On the second day of school, you said you needed somebody to remind you how to live," he muttered. "So I accepted the job."

He twirled their bodies around in the water and she sighed. "And how do you expect to do that in one night?"

"Truth or Dare?"

"What? Hell no, I'm not playing Truth or Dare with you." She giggled again. "Nope. I am too old for that shit."

"Here you go again."

"I'm not expecting the worst out of you. I promise."

"Then tighten up." He smiled. "Truth or dare."

Her stomach jumped.

No man had ever told her to do that, but when it came out of Anthony's mouth, there was no room for negotiation—only enough space for her to do what he said.

"Fine... okay...okay...dar—"

He pulled their bodies underwater without warning and she almost gasped until he pressed her lips together with his fingers.

Somebody once told her falling in love was a lot like swimming. She couldn't remember if it was Ginny or Daddy. All she remembered was how flippant they'd been when they told her it was impossible for her to forget how to do either—even if she was philophobic. She didn't know why the thought crossed her mind as they disappeared underwater, but it came like a fleeting little leaf that blew off in the wind.

His nails dug into her ass as the water gushed into her ears and the pressure made her clamor to get closer to him, even though she couldn't possibly get any closer. Their heartbeats were one.

When her eyes popped open, he was there, eyes wide open, clearer than the clearest picture she'd ever seen with his baby face that wasn't really babyish. It was just so fuckin' beautiful.

He let her go.

What was the dare again?

Was it to swim? To hold her breath for as long as she could while not losing herself in his eyes? Or was it to stay sane while he rolled his boxer briefs down his legs with a smile?

Her eyes sagged as they followed his movements. The fabric slipped from his fingers and her eyes zeroed in on the one part of him she hadn't been able to picture in her head…his dick.

It floated with the rest of his limbs while she fought the urge to grab it, study it, and figure out if it tasted as good as it looked.

He didn't give her time to fantasize about it before he reached out and tugged at the sides of her panties that dug into her skin.

Now it was her turn.

What were the rules again?

The last time she played, she didn't remember being light-headed, confused, or horny. And they were supposed to take turns, right? She was supposed to choose her own destiny and then he would choose his. That was the whole point of Truth or Dare. They weren't even playing it right.

She curled her fingers under the sides of her panties and rolled them down as bubbles fluttered around them from the breaths they blew out.

The fabric tangled around her ankles until she kicked them away and shuddered at the water flowing in places she was supposed to keep covered. Next was her bra. She reached behind her back and unclasped it, one hook at a time.

As soon as her breasts escaped, she expected him to reach out and touch them. Instead, he smiled with his eyes pinched shut, as if she'd blessed him with the perfect gift. Then he grabbed her fingers and tangled his through hers, pulling her back to his body until they were skin to skin. She melted into him like he was the first man she'd ever touched.

She wanted to ask Michole if every divorced woman turned manic after being in a drought for so long and was she supposed to wanna fuck Anthony every time he breathed her way? Also, was it normal to read his thoughts without him having to teach her?

But if she admitted any of that to Michole, then she'd have to admit all the bad things she'd done to get to that point—all the games, the flirting, and the rule breaking.

His dick bobbed between her legs, sliding against her slick folds. Every time she curled her body into his to chase it, he dug his fingers into her ass to remind her she'd better not. He even fought against the pressure of the water and smacked her right cheek until he decided they'd held their breaths long enough and pushed them up.

They gasped together as they bobbed to the surface. He reached out and swiped his hand across her eyes, wiping the burning water out of their corners and pushing her curls back.

"Truth or dare," she blurted while panting.

He smirked, carrying her back to the edge of the pool. "Truth..."

She studied his face, knowing his truth had conditions because every other part of him did. She couldn't jump right into the juicy stuff. He was the type that made her tread lightly and trudge through the gunk he kept around his heart to protect it from strangers. He was guarded like Daddy.

"What really happened to your arm?" she whispered, eyeing the jagged scar that looked better up close. "I know Josiah didn't break it."

"My daddy broke it when I was fourteen because I did something he ain't like."

"Like?"

"I took something I wasn't supposed to take."

"What'd you take?"

"Nuh uh. No more." He nudged the Patrón bottle toward her. "Take a shot."

She picked it up without fighting and took a gulp.

It burned even worse than the first time while she tortured herself over the things he could follow her nosey questions with if she picked truth or the suggestive shit they could do if she decided on a dare. There was the scar from the summer she fell on the gravel outside her house after brunch, or the invisible scars leftover from the times she tried to make Trey happy but her body wouldn't cooperate.

He snatched the bottle away from her lips. "Truth or dare?"

She grimaced, pinching her eyes shut, fighting the burn in her chest. "Da—no. Truth."

"So, how'd Trey like his eggs cooked?"

"Ugh. Scrambled with cheese."

"Go figure." He snorted. "The nigga is insecure, and he eats cheese. On God, you got terrible ass taste in men."

Her eyes popped open. "At least he ain't in jail."

His face fell, and she pulled her lips into her mouth to stop any other low blows she'd have to take back. "I'm so—"

He pounced on her and she swore she swallowed his strawberry taste as he picked her up and shook her like a rag doll, with that goofy laugh echoing through the night.

"You taking another shot just for that!"

"Anthony!"

She screamed so loud she knew the neighbors would

complain, but it wouldn't matter because Anthony had Priya curled around his finger, just like every other girl in his life.

He was an anomaly—an eccentric deep thinking anomaly that made her regret her Kayden hating ways.

sixteen

. . .

FOUR TRUTHS, three dares, and five shots later, Venus had learned Logan's theory about men who liked the Braves wasn't true because Anthony liked the Astros.

He'd never even been to Houston *or* Texas, though. According to him, he was "always on papers" when Josiah played there, which meant he couldn't leave the state—not even to see his best friend play football.

"I'll bring you one day," she hiccuped, squeezing his cheeks between her hands. "You can talk cars with my daddy. He's a car guy too."

Somehow she'd ended up on the ledge of the pool with him between her legs while she kept ignoring all the reasons she needed to get her ass up and get out of there. She forgot how much tequila coddled that immature part of her brain, though.

"What's his favorite kind?" he asked.

"Maseratis—some shit that me, you, or him can't even afford."

He shrugged. "That don't mean I never drove one before, though."

She tightened her hold around his cheeks, tilting his head toward her. "What's with the cars?"

"What you mean?"

"You know exactly what I mean. Ain't no cameras or cops around this pool. Tell me why you like taking cars so much. That's why your daddy broke your arm, huh? That was the thing you took."

She eyed the scar, trying her best to keep her tongue in her mouth.

She'd been around him for so long she'd gotten used to talking in punchlines, riddles, and half-statements. Nothing that came out of his mouth was ever straightforward, but the Patrón had her determined to get it all out of him for this one night.

"They easy licks." He swiped his tongue out and smirked like he had her exactly where he wanted her.

"Stealing a whole car is easy? I'm clearly in the wrong fuckin' profession."

He laughed, yanking his face from her hands. "I better not ever catch you trying to steal no car."

"You never know, maybe I'll be as good at it as you." She shrugged, looking up at the sky like he had.

Tori's moon hung above the pool while her mind wandered to Anthony and his sticky fingers. It made her smile, even though it shouldn't have.

"They wasn't always easy, and I didn't always steal cars."

"So you're a kleptomaniac?" She giggled, thinking of Logan's description of a six-year-old *Nuney*.

He grunted out a loud chuckle. "Fuck no."

"Then why you like stealing so much?"

She looked back at him, easing her face closer to his and cocking her head from side to side in a teasing way. He almost let her push her nose against his, but when they were an inch apart, he pulled away.

"My mama worked at Publix all my life," he muttered. "She ain't the most ambitious person... or the brightest and ain't nothing wrong with that, but it seemed like we always needed more than what a minimum wage check could pay for—sometimes it was either rent or electricity, clothes for me or clothes for my brother Shaun, sneakers so I can stop sharing with my niggas or groceries, a suit for Shaun's prom or the car note. It was never both. Neither of the men that gave her babies is worth shit. One of 'em got a wife and kids back in Mexico and the other one..."

He shrugged. "Somebody got to go out and get it. So, I was the man of the house until she kicked me out. Then she had Shaun thinking he needed to be the man of the house until Desmond got ahold of him the last time I went to jail. Them generational curses be real."

Now, she really wanted to smash her nose against his, but she nodded instead.

"I get it," she whispered. "My mama died while giving birth to me, so it was always just me and my daddy. He's been a janitor all my life—we never had a lot. We always had just enough. My ex mother-in-law threw a fit when I told her he couldn't afford to pay for an entire wedding on a janitor's salary."

"She sounds..."

She held her breath as she waited for whatever word his mind would conjure up to describe Rose.

"Exhausting," he finished.

She exhaled and her shoulders drooped because she still carried parts of Rose with her like she did Trey.

"If only you knew," she sang, smiling. "So why you stealing 'em now if you got a job at Vaughn's?"

He chewed his bottom lip and stared at her so intently that it made her shift against the warm concrete.

"Wrong turf?" she muttered.

He nodded with that perfect little smirk she swore she'd became obsessed with.

"At least tell me how you do it," she whispered. "I won't tell."

"Tell you how I do what?"

"Steal them—the cars."

Instead of answering, he rested his face on his hand. She wanted it in her middle—right along the apex of her thighs. Her body was warm, wet, and it hummed every time his callused fingers touched her, even though he was being modest with his touches.

She reached for the bottle again, waiting for him to explain himself, but he nudged it away before she could take another swig.

"Tell me..." she sang. "Tell me how you do it."

"No."

He said it in the same brusque tone as he did when Mikayla asked him about college. The fog from the liquor lifted just enough for her to see the twinkle in his eyes.

"Why not? I told you I won't tell."

"How I know that?"

She thrust her arms up. "Look at me. I ain't in the position to judge nobody right now. I'm butt ass naked in front of my student's daddy. You can go off and snitch on me for all I know. Neither one of us are saints."

He looked off, shrugging. "It ain't like how you see it in the movies."

"Well duh. I mean, what do you do? Prowl parking lots and bust the person's window? Or—or are you one of those lil' boys that learned how to hot wire cars from TikTok?" She chuckled. "Or do you—"

"I just take 'em."

She rolled her eyes. "I *know* that, but ho—"

"I take them, Venus."

It wasn't until his fingernails dug into her thighs that she stopped and looked back at his stoic face. His tongue snuck out again and his chest pumped in and out in a calm rhythm while his words echoed in her head—"*I. Take. Them.*"

The weird part about their mutual telepathy was how sometimes there were no words playing in his head—just pictures. She gulped in his smell and the night air like she was the last person he'd taken from with a cold barrel to her forehead.

"You always take them?" She breathed out.

"I don't always have to do something if I got somebody that would do anything for me."

"You talking about De—deeanna?"

She didn't know why it came out in a stutter, because she'd heard similar things come out of other stupid men's mouths—but those men weren't Anthony. They didn't look like him, talk like him, or even breathe the way he did—calm and labored while he stroked her thighs like he was trying to reassure her he wasn't always so damn reckless.

"Yeah..." he replied in a breathy voice. "Why risk it all every night if I can get my bitch to walk in a dealership and get whatever I want? A pretty girl with a brilliant mind is a lot more dangerous than me, you know that, right?"

She almost choked on her tongue.

"Happy?" He murmured from between her legs, nudging them open and staring at all the places she kept trying to hide.

She shook her head, studying him because there were still parts of him she wanted to unearth.

"What you want out of life, Anthony?"

He pulled his eyes from her middle and looked up at her, smiling and shrugging with that baby face that only appeared sometimes. "To be happy for the short time I'm here. Now, it's your turn. Truth or dare?"

———

He'd failed the objective for the night.

They were drunk—loud, sloppy ass drunk. The type of drunk that made for a good "you remember that one time" story. If they were meant to last past the night, Anthony imagined Venus would giggle with Munch one day, telling her about the night she got drunk and fell for her crazy ass daddy even after he told her some shit he shouldn't have.

"Can you stop studying my vagina while I'm truth or daring?" She giggled, nudging his head away.

"Why? It's pretty."

All of her was beautiful, but he stuck with pretty because she was the type of woman that ran from the B word. Men like Trey had soured it for her and stripped her down so much so that she learned to settle for inferior ass compliments like "pretty."

She had dimples in both ass cheeks and cellulite that had settled around the widest parts of her ass. He even got cross-eyed when he tried to follow the trails of her stretch marks.

"First of all, I ain't had a wax in God knows when. Ain't nothing pretty about the situation I got going on down there."

The "situation" wasn't shit but a few coarse curls that waved at him from between her legs and made him want her even more.

The last legs he had his face between were DeeDee's. There were some days he lived there—especially when she was pregnant with Munch. She'd beg him to fuck her or to let her suck his dick, but he couldn't. It was a weird, sneaking urge that made him want to drown in her taste and walk around with her smell attached to him. Lola said it was fixation. He was *fixated* on DeeDee.

"Fuck a wax." He rested his chin on the pool's edge, studying the curly hairs and tiny scars from the waxing and shaving she did over the years to make it look pretty enough. "Who said you needed a wax?"

"*I* did."

He smacked his lips. "That's the problem. You think you know everything. Are all teachers know-it-alls?"

She giggled again. "I'm older. I'll always know more than you."

"Nah, that's just a false belief society wants you to conform to."

She mouthed the words he said with a small smile and then reached out to scrape her fingers through his hair. "Who even thinks of shit like that?"

"Me."

"You're such a strange ass thieving lil' bo—"

His mouth covered her pussy without warning. He swallowed her stupid ass theories about him being too young, too strange, and too close to her job for him to taste her.

She gasped so loud that she choked.

His tongue darted out, and he tasted her unique flavor. It was a musky sweetness that made him sigh. He was tired of holding out and pretending to be the gentleman he'd never been. He was exactly what Tash said he was—a menace.

"Anth!" she shrieked, choking on the rest of his name and falling back on her elbows. "You—you—can't..."

He could.

He could kiss her pussy before he kissed the lips on her face. He could lap up every trace of wetness that had been sitting there all night while she danced around her attraction to him. He could trace his tongue between her folds and french kiss her there until she tried to scream his name again.

He pulled away, hovering over her slick mound. "Shit, I can do whatever I want. The world is mine, remember? *You* said that."

He kneaded her thighs while she gasped like she'd came, but he knew she hadn't. It was just the shock of it all—the way he had her naked and stretched underneath the moon with her legs spread open while she panted. And the way he kissed her somewhere he shouldn't have without warning her.

She reached for his head again, but he nudged her hand away while blowing a puff of air on the spot he'd made out with. "The game ain't over yet. Truth or dare?"

Her breasts swayed back and forth as she shook her body instead of her head.

"Why not?" he asked, pressing his lips against her thigh.

"Because it's gonna get us in trouble."

"So? I ain't scared."

"Anthony…"

This time, she shook her head. He recognized that shake and euphoric look on her face. It'd been a minute since a man ate her pussy and meant it.

He suckled on her thigh, talking around her flesh. "You knew I was trouble when you replied to my text, Ms. Thibodeaux. Don't play stupid. Truth or dare?"

"Tr—truth…truth," she gasped out, arching her back off the warm cement even though he hadn't even dove back in.

"Truth? You sure about that?"

"Yes!"

"A'ight then… truth." He smirked. "You a runner?"

"What're you talking about?"

"When you cum, do you run from it?"

"I… I don't even know what you mean."

"Damn." He shook his head, falling back between her legs and covering her with his mouth.

Now, she tasted like the ripe tangerines he picked off the tree in Lola's backyard the first spring after Carlotta kicked him out. DeeDee never even tasted that sweet. There was a tartness underneath Venus' sweet taste that kept him wanting more.

She panted and writhed underneath him, thrusting her hips against his mouth and she talked. She talked through high-pitched moans while he tried to find her weak spots.

"Ant… we're not supposed to—to…"

"Not supposed to what?" he murmured against her, pushing her legs wider. "How you thought the game was supposed to end?"

"I don't know." She sighed, arching her back toward the moon. "I don't know. I don't know."

She chanted because he'd found her weak spot—her clit. He obsessed over it like he obsessed over her—swiping his tongue against it, covering it with his mouth, sucking it until her fingers fell from his head and landed between her legs. They slid against his tongue and clumsily stumbled around. He let them, while she cried out in tiny gasps until he slurped them into his mouth for being in his way.

She was out of practice, just like he figured. He tasted it and smelled it, but that was the fun part because she wouldn't forget him when she finally got that "man" she'd been chasing. He was the one that had ended her drought and made her squeal noises she hadn't in so long. Shit, he'd be the one she thought about when that "man" crawled between her legs to do all the boring shit Trey did.

She snatched her fingers from his mouth and smacked them against his face before shoving them back between her legs.

"Why're you—" she hiccuped, fumbling over her words.

He pulled his lips from her and slapped her fingers away. "Why what?"

"Why'd you do that?" She whined, sighing. "Why...you can't just..."

"Why, why, why." He laughed. "Why you taste so good? Why you always talking so much shit to me? Why you thought it'd be us for the night and I wouldn't taste you? Why you asking so many goddamn questions instead of enjoying this?"

He shook his head and stopped torturing himself with her problems because that's what they were...hers.

He raked his fingers down the length of her body while studying her tilted mouth and wide eyes. She stared at him like she couldn't believe he had her spread open.

Finally, she smiled, thrusting her head back and staring up at the moon with a tipsy smile. "I *told* you not to have me in no shit. I told you."

That shit broke him.

It made him pick her foot up and study her toes until he felt cross-eyed and had no choice but to kiss them until she squirmed. It was the other part of his fixation. He wanted to taste the parts of her that scared other men. He wasn't like LaDarius Mitchell. He was a foot man, an ass man, a leg man, a throat man, a hand man. He was committed to tasting every part of Venus Thibodeaux.

He started with the smallest toe, covering it with his lips while his other hand made up for his mouth's absence and stroked her between her legs. Next, his mouth grazed her other toes—the ring one, the middle one, the long one.

"Ant..." she garbled out.

"Ant?" he asked around her toe. "Who that?"

"You...you-uh."

"What you calling me that for?"

"'Cause I—I can't finish." She sighed in exasperation when his tongue skirted between two toes. "I can't say—oh!"

"*Oh.*" He smiled as one of his fingers slipped and fell inside of her—at least that's what she'd probably tell herself when she woke up the next day so he figured he'd better savor her in that moment and the way she screamed out, "Ant!"

Nobody ever called him Ant. It sounded square, but he wanted to kiss her for thinking he was worthy enough to be called such a lame nickname that didn't sound so lame when she moaned it. It'd sound even better if she choked on it, but that was another problem for a day that wouldn't come.

He dropped her foot and dipped down to taste her again because he wasn't satisfied. That's how his fixation with DeeDee started. He stayed between her legs that first time for so long, chasing the satisfaction of fulfillment, he got dizzy. It was the good dizzy that threw off his equilibrium and made his head spin, though.

His tongue rammed inside of her.

"Ant!" she screamed, squeezing her legs around his head. "Ant! No...no...no...no...no..."

She sounded as possessed as a woman who couldn't remember the last time somebody made her cum.

Her body shook as the shockwaves from her orgasm rolled through her. She panted and writhed again and ran from his tongue because she was a runner and she didn't even know that shit before she met him.

"Stop! Stop! I—I..."

He pinned her down at the waist and talked against her weak spot. "Stop running from it."

She dragged her body against the cement as if it would make him let go, but it pissed him off instead. How could she sacrifice her soft skin because she was scared of all the fun shit he could make her body do?

Her legs squeezed around his head so tight he thought it would pop from the pressure. He smiled as she thrust her hips against his face and tried to scoot away from him at the same time.

"Stop," he gritted out. "Be still."

"I can't... oh my... Ant!"

And she likened him to God when all of her pent up frustration squirted out of her and landed in its rightful place.

He swallowed her taste while wishing she wasn't such a "by the book" type of woman, so he could drown in her and grow dizzy every day while searching for that fulfillment.

Her legs shook.

They vibrated back and forth against his arms while he stared in awe because it'd been a while since he'd been inspired enough to do something so audacious. DeeDee always swore it was a power move. It was his favorite way to fuck her head up right after she fucked his up.

"Ride it out..." he muttered as she tried to fight against it.

"Why?" she groaned. "Why?"

"Because if you don't, you'll kill the high—"

"Why'd you do that?" she asked in agony, kicking her leg against his chest. "Why the fuck would you do that?"

Her words didn't match the euphoric slack jawed expression on her face and it made him smile.

"Because the real objective for the night is for you to cum over and over again, Ms. Thibodeaux. That's why."

"That's impossible."

"Damn, you forgot my ghetto plumber's jingle already?"

She laughed in a huff that sounded painful and tried to curl into a ball, but he pulled her legs and nudged them back open.

seventeen

· · ·

ANTHONY BELIEVED orgasms had the power to cancel hangovers.

"It's the endorphins, the oxytocin, and the serotonin. But they have to be mind numbing intense nuts—not that frilly shit you might get from your fingers." He raked his fingers against Venus' scalp while they laid on a chaise beside the pool.

A mild breeze tickled her bare breasts.

"How do you even know this?"

"I used to fuck a girl who wanted to be a sex therapist. She was majoring in psychology. Sometimes she left her shit in my car," he replied huskily, staring up at the yellowing sky.

"Was this before or after Deeanna?"

"I don't know. Somewhere in between."

His tone was vague, but she felt it wasn't on purpose. He and Deeanna's relationship sounded like any other one that had gone on well past its expiration date, yet they kept trying to resurrect it, hoping it'd turn new again. It sounded familiar.

"What else you learn?"

"That sex is mental more than physical."

"Oh yeah? Is this like your curiosity metaphor you told me about back at the studio?"

"Nah..." He chuckled, thrusting his head back more and pulling her closer to him. "Women have a more emotional connection to sex than men. A woman's mental state can control her sex drive and most of y'all don't even realize it. It's wild."

She pinched her eyes shut and savored the vibrations coming from his chest.

"Stress, anxiety, the reversal of roles in the household, money problems..." he droned. "I'd be stupid to think my woman would wanna come home and fuck me if she stressed out and always doing my job."

She didn't know if he knew it, but he was a *blerd*—a sexy, tattooed manic one that could steal the moon from the sky. She couldn't believe it took her five days to realize it.

She gasped, shooting up from his chest and gurgling up a burp of Patrón.

"You keep popping up like that and you gon' make yourself dizzy."

"I'm already dizzy." She groaned, rubbing her sticky legs together. "What time is it?"

"I don't know. Seven maybe? You asked me the last time you came."

Another groan fell out while she tried to understand why everything that came out of his mouth sounded perfect—even irresponsible unsureness.

"I did?"

"Mhmm." He stretched his arms up and her eyes grazed his body under the hazy daylight.

It was still hard and beautiful. There wasn't any part of him that was soft. She counted each pack on his abdomen while he rubbed his red eyes.

"You said, 'Ant, what time does the moon stop showing up in the sky?' Shit, I guess that's the same as asking for the time."

She clicked her heavy tongue against the roof of her mouth, searching for his taste, but there wasn't any straw-berry or weed, just bad drunken shameful breath. Fuck, he didn't even kiss her. Shit, he didn't even fuck her. He had the self-restraint of Jesus and it made her brain foggier because he didn't even ask her for it like most other men would have.

"You always so poetic when you riding nigga's faces?" he asked. "Or you just that way for me?"

Just for him, obviously.

She couldn't even remember talking when she and Trey fucked. He didn't evoke leg spasms, sexy nicknames from her, or worship the mundane parts of her body.

She wiggled her sticky toes.

Sometimes he couldn't even make her cum because their bedroom was no longer sacred. Maybe Anthony was right. Maybe sex really was mental.

She sighed.

Close your eyes, Venus.

They wouldn't listen because Anthony's morning wood shot toward the sky. It looked better in the soft morning daylight. Now she could get a better look at it—it's girth, it's tawny color, and that infamous curve. She didn't even get to taste it. Damn, Logan would be so disappointed in her.

"Oh God..." She whined as her heart drummed against her chest.

Logan.

School.

Tori.

Principal Bivins.

"Why you calling for God like that? You see this sunrise?" He yawned, gripping her love handles and pulling her back onto his chest as if her world wasn't on fire and her job wasn't at risk. "You ever stop to be grateful for the sun?"

She shook her head.

She never had time, no matter how much Michole tried to shove mindfulness down her throat.

"We weren't supposed to do this. We were supposed to talk

about Tori," she babbled. "We were supposed to talk about... about..."

She couldn't even get the words out like she had the first day they met. That day felt so long ago.

The annoying thing about that sliver of immaturity still attached to her brain was the "oh shit" part that came after all the good feelings wore off. This was her first "oh shit" moment as a divorcee and she was sure it wasn't supposed to feel so good.

"She likes you," he blurted, picking up a stray curl that had flopped into her eye and tucking it behind her ear.

"Huh?"

"Munch likes you."

"She does? I mean... I figured she liked everybody. She's always smiling at us."

They'd only been in school for a week, but she smiled at the janitor, the lunch ladies, at Paula, and Logan. She smiled so much Principal Bivins had already nicknamed her "Smiley."

"There's that lil' smiley face." He'd grin when he poked his head into her classroom.

He never stayed long enough to notice that she didn't chirp out a "hey Mr. Bivins" like the rest of the kids, though.

She looked up and found Anthony staring at the sunrise he kept bragging about. He looked at it like he wanted to steal it for Tori too, while he rubbed the back of her neck.

"She always been that way. My granny says she's just a happy baby, that's all. She says it's a blessing. Munch is happy, even when it's nothing to be happy about."

"Like her mama being away?"

He shrugged.

"Or does she think she's on a really long vacation?"

"She knows that DeeDee in jail and she knows to call you 'Ms. T' because we saw it in your Welcome Letter. We practiced in the spring after me and DeeDee registered her for big girl school so she wouldn't forget. She still can't say Thibodeaux, though. My granny say it's too big of a name for her."

Big girl school.

Her ovaries jumped.

"Is Anthony too big of a name for her too? That's why she calls you 'Noni'?"

"Nuney was. She was always tryna say it when she first started talking and that's what would come out. Now it's just one of those nicknames she won't let go."

"Did she tell you she liked me being her big girl teacher? Is that how you know she likes me?"

"She colors all the shit at the crib purple." He lifted that same purple lock he'd tucked behind her ear. "My J's, the walls, the fuckin' baseboards—"

"Puss in Boots?"

"Yeah. Munch ain't one for vocalizing every soft ass thing she feel. She'll show you, though."

"Like father, like daughter, huh?"

He lifted his head, looking down at her with his eyebrows raised and a tiny smirk. "You throwing shade at me now?"

"Maybe."

"Don't get back on my bad side." He squeezed her neck and pulled her up by it.

Her body knew what that notion meant before her brain did. That's how quickly he'd trained her.

"Believe me. I do *not* want to be there." She scoffed, shuffling up his long body in a drunken crawl. "I see how that is."

"What's that supposed to mean?"

"Why won't you just go bail the girl out?" She sighed, tossing her legs over his face.

"Why you care so much about another woman when you with me?"

"Little girls need their mamas. Tori needs her."

She was drunk, desperate, *and* horny now. It was all in her words. She was dumping her own shit into his situation when she should've been savoring their last moments together.

"I'm tryna make you cum one last time and you worried about DeeDee? Lying, trifling ass DeeDee? Still being Officer Thibodeaux, huh?" he murmured, digging his nails into her ass.

She'd have permanent scars there, and she didn't mind it. They were probably red, angry scratches that stretched across each cheek. It would be her reminder of their stupid one night rendezvous he tricked her into.

He smacked both cheeks.

It was a smack as angry as the one he'd given the screen inside the car. Tremors rippled through her body and sent her surging forward over his face.

She gripped the chaise's head with a sloppy, "oomph."

"Fuck Deeanna," he gritted out, biting her inner thigh. "She knew what would happen when she had the cops call me to pick up our kid while she sat in handcuffs at Phipps for swiping other people's cards. I done did some shit, but I ain't never did anything when my baby was with me."

God, it was even messier than she expected.

"And you think I shouldn't make her sit down for trauma-tizing my child? You don't think she got a mama, brother, and a nigga to put up the money for her? You see how y'all women try to fuck my head up? She gon' sit there as long as I tell her to."

She was sure she was one of those women he ranted about because she was dickmatized and bickering with him over his baby mama and she hadn't even had his dick. She was a silly delusional ass woman who was hoarse from moaning so much in one night and wet at the possibility of him wielding as much power over her as he did Deeanna.

"Ant—uh," she rasped out as soon as he pulled her slick mound over his mouth. "You being hypocritical. You...you can't drive your baby around in a stolen car and get mad at her fo—"

"Mind your business."

She let out a sharp hiss. "No. We graduated from that,

remember? You said cor.. correct you with respect, so I am. It's called accountability."

"You want me to go bail her out to satisfy you, since you know everything then? You want me to forgive her for fuckin' me over?" he murmured between french kisses and sloppy slaps. "Tell me to and I'll go be a simp and do it. Then you can put up with her."

"I don't know every fuckin' thing. Fuck!" she yelped out in a hoarse rasp while her legs shook.

It didn't even take an orgasm to make them shake. It came as soon as he started his shit. It was good shit, though. The type of shit Trey shied away from and the shit only Anthony could get away with.

"The world ain't Ms. Thibodeaux's classroom. It's mine."

She felt the onslaught of pressure building in her abdomen and pushed up, even though she knew better. She was already running from it and it hadn't even hit yet.

"Where you going?" he asked against her clit. "I thought we agreed you wouldn't run from it no more?"

Four hard smacks pounded against her ass. They landed against the scratches he'd scraped on her skin. He delivered them without mercy because she couldn't follow simple ass instructions like, "keep your legs open" and "hurry up and cum for me so we can go."

That last one was the one that did it. He said it so casually, like he doled out orgasms to her all the time.

"Ahhh..." She thrust her head back, trying her damndest to prolong it before she succumbed to all the endorphins, oxytocin, and serotonin he swore was in an orgasm, but the world had other plans.

His phone vibrated against the chaise.

"*Fuck,*" he gritted out. "Hold on."

She didn't have a choice.

Her vibrating legs gyrated over his face while he grabbed the phone off the end table.

If he were hers, she would've pried it out of his hand and begged him to start over because they didn't get to relish in her orgasm like he'd taught her. They couldn't sit in it and bask in the way her arousal poured out of her. She didn't get a chance to watch him drink it or listen to him brag about how good she tasted because of his stupid phone.

"Yeah?" he spoke into it, pulling her down onto his chest.

"Bro..." a girl rasped, yawning. "Where you at?"

Her body tensed.

Another one?

She was too drunk to survive *another* girl.

"I work a real job now. My flight leaves in three hours and Dre' already left to head to the shop for his eight o'clock."

"I'm coming."

He smiled, running his hand across her ass and kneading it while she stared up at the tiny brown hairs that sprouted from his chin.

"Yeah, whatever. This ain't no twenty-four-hour daycare, nigga."

"Aye... fuck you."

"I love you too, funny man."

His smile settled into a content smirk, like she said those words to him often and didn't care if he said them back.

"Oh! I think you'll be happy to hear there weren't any accidents. Dri's mattress is still icy white," she added.

Tori was a bed wetter?

"Oh yeah? How you did that?"

"Called my daddy. He said no juice before bed."

"I already do that," he grunted back. "Thought you'd have more insightful advice."

"Fine...maybe it was luck. She still beefing with everybody, though."

Beefing?

"She'll come around," he muttered.

The fog from her almost-orgasm wore off while she tried to

read their moods, understand their lingo, and fight the guilt that crept up her chest from laying with him.

"Anyway you can bring us some chicken minis for the win! Don't forget the honey."

"A'ight." He groaned, hanging up and sitting up on his elbows.

He looked off from the sunrise he had bragged about and then down at her. The glimmer that had been in his eyes since he picked her up dimmed.

He gathered her hair with his free hand and traced her lips with his eyes. She followed every blink and dip.

Kiss me.

The thought sat on her tongue. She'd never wanted to taste somebody so bad. Her scent seeped from his pores and she wanted it to stay that way for Mikayla and any other little girls to smell when they draped their bodies over him.

"You satisfied now?" he asked.

"Satisfied about what?"

"Now you know *too* much about me and Munch."

———

What was the word for that feeling between guilt and shame? Was there even a word to describe something so torturous?

Venus squirmed against her chair while staring at the wall across from her desk in her classroom. On a typical week, it was a plain, white cinder block wall that needed repainting, but this week it was like a movie screen that replayed every dirty little deed she and Anthony had done over the weekend.

Every time she blinked, she saw his freckled face disappearing behind her, in front of her and on the side of her on that cinder block wall. Sometimes she heard him humming in her ear when there were lulls in the day.

"Can I make you cum, Venus?"

Yes!

The answer was always a resounding yes, even with the school's employee handbook splayed across her desk.

Conflict of Interest.

There it was in big bold letters.

She couldn't fuck Anthony no matter how good he sounded, how sexy he looked, or how much money he spent on her in one night.

She'd found the handbook sitting under Pepper's crate in the corner of her bed-less bedroom next to a box of Trey's t-shirts she meant to burn. If it had been any other school year, that handbook would've already been in the trash, but the universe was being weird again. Now it was stuck in her desk drawer on top of that week's lunch menu. She pulled it out anytime she needed to remind herself of how wrong Anthony was for her.

Her heart drummed against her chest while she tried to come up with all the ways she'd try not to awkwardly greet Anthony at the next school event he might come to. And there were a lot of them—meet the teacher night, family fun night, lunch with dad, and that evaluation meeting about Tori they still hadn't accomplished because she'd gone and fucked him instead of doing her job.

Well, she didn't *exactly* fuck him.

Did head count as sex? Did he know if anybody found out what they did that she'd potentially lose her job? Hell, did he even care she was rambling in her head? Of course he didn't because he didn't even kiss her—not even after buying her breakfast and coffee and walking her back to her apartment door that Sunday.

"Take care of yourself, Venus," he'd muttered, gripping her ass one last time. *"No more dating apps or secret meetings with Logan to talk about my baby—for real this time."*

She'd even been trifling enough to wear that denim jumpsuit and fantasize about his hand on her ass throughout her entire special standing Sunday appointment with Michole that she begged Michole to accommodate when she thought she was dying from heartbreak.

"Ms. T?" Treshawn squeaked from his small group. "Tori peed. I told her to tell me when she had to go and I'd...I'd tell you, but she ain't do that."

Venus cleared her throat and tried to shoo her inappropriate thoughts away. "Okay, Tre. Keep practicing your letters. I'll come get her."

She rolled away from her desk as Tori stared at her from beside him with her thumb stuck in her mouth. It was the first time they'd caught eyes all week because Venus couldn't look her in the eye without those conflicting feelings rolling through her.

Now she wanted to know even more about Anthony and Tori —like if it had been him that picked out her leggings and rainbow dress and which girl that played on his phone had taken the time to comb her hair for school that day. Had he kissed Tori goodbye that morning? Did he even make it back home that Sunday?

She grabbed the Clorox wipes from her desk and then maneuvered through the other kids until she got to Tori.

"Bug..." She crouched down, pulling her out of her seat. "Why didn't you tell me you had to go to the bathroom?"

She shrugged, glancing down at the wet circle in the crotch of her leggings.

Venus sighed and swiped the wipe across the chair.

At least she answered this time.

"Let's go get your change of clothes."

Tori pushed out her hand and Venus took it, throwing the wipe into the trashcan along the way. They walked to her designated cubby, where her extra clothes sat folded in a Walmart bag in the storage nook beneath the cubby.

As soon as Venus tugged the knot loose, Anthony's smell floated out of the bag. She felt just like he had described her that

Saturday night—nostalgic and sexy in her faded slacks with a marker stain across her chest.

She tried to focus on the task at hand, but he'd made that impossible all week. She forgot her lunch on the counter at home on Monday, sent Ciara to the SPED teacher at the wrong time on Wednesday, and now she was nostalgically running her fingers across Tori's denim dress because she wanted Anthony again.

Tori pulled the dress from her fingers without spitting out her thumb.

"Go 'head," Venus whispered.

Soft knocks made her tug Tori by the shoulder before she walked off.

Paula cracked the door and peeked inside. Her eyes swept all the kids until she found Venus. She cocked her head back, beckoning Venus to the door.

"Go into our bathroom and change your clothes. Then we gotta call daddy, okay?" Venus said.

That stupid, immature part of her brain didn't think she'd have to face Anthony so soon. Now she had to call him and tell him about Tori's unfortunate accident while pretending like nothing had happened between them.

She sighed to herself as Tori walked toward their classroom's bathroom and she met Paula in the doorway.

"What's going on?" she asked.

"It's a lady in the front office. She say she got a delivery for you, but she can't leave it with us."

"Are you sure it's for me?"

Paula eyed her up and down, smirking. "Uh...ain't no other Venus Thibodeauxs that work here."

Her face grew warm, like Paula could tell that the same Anthony she'd ogled in the front office had his hands on her all weekend.

"She look like a process server. They the only ones that come up here tryna deliver stuff directly to folks. You ain't getting served, are you?"

"Why would you think that?"

"I'm just asking. I know you and your husband separated and all. You know how niggas are. They just take and take until they can't no more," Paula whispered, thrusting her hands against her pudgy sides.

"Huh? Who told you that?"

"Oh, girl." She waved her hand. "You know how folks around here talk. Anyway, I tried to call your desk, but the line kept giving me a busy signal."

Venus squinted her eyes at her. "That phone hasn't worked since I got here. Sit with my class while I go see what's going on. I have to make a phone call, anyway."

"Mhmm...alright, my lunch starts in five minutes, though."

"Yeah. I doubt you'll keel over from starvation." She took off without bothering to acknowledge Paula's loud lip smack.

"Tori's in the bathroom changing her clothes. She knows to go back to her group when she's done," she called over her shoulder, relishing in the sterile hallway air.

She needed the reprieve even if she was walking into some unknown process serving situation. The whole debacle reeked of Trey, just like Paula hinted at, but there was nothing left of their dissolved marriage for him to serve her over. He took the house, the Tahoe, and even gave her Maltipoo to his fuckin' mistress.

Principal Bivins marched up the hallway toward her in his drab brown suit with a coffee mug, despite the day being halfway over.

"Paula came and got you?" he chirped.

"Yes sir. I'm headed that way now."

"Good deal. Let's have a chat after you grab your package. We can have Paula take her lunch in your classroom."

"Uh...sure, we can do that." Her neck heated as she passed him and pushed inside the front office, looking for the mysterious delivery person.

It was quiet inside.

Principal Bivins' assistant, Tamika, pecked away at her

computer and Jillian, the school clerk, hovered at the front desk, staring at the nameless blonde courier that sat waiting for her.

Jillian pat the desk and pointed at her. "Right here, Ms. Thibodeaux."

"Yup, I see her," Venus replied in a sing-song voice.

Jillian crossed her arms and leaned into the desk as if she didn't have a paper to file or a phone to answer.

"Jillian." Tamika tugged her glasses down her nose and looked up. "Go on and take them to Principal Bivins' office so they can have some privacy. Principal Bivins says he's gotta have a chat with Ms. Thibodeaux, anyway."

"Oh, there's no need to tie her up." Venus smiled while Jillian rolled her eyes. "It's a package. I'm sure it'll be quick."

She turned toward the poor nameless girl that had to deal with the unorganized mess that was Hill elementary and gave her an apologetic smile. "I'm Venus Thibodeaux. Somebody told me you had a package for me."

"Ms. Thibodeaux, I'm a process server with Thomason Legal Services, and I have some documents to hand over to you." She pushed a manila folder her way, but Venus didn't touch it.

She stared at it as if it were a pile of crap stuffed into a folder and frowned.

Tamika stopped tapping her computer keys and Jillian hummed out a "mmm," because Paula's nosey ass was right.

"May I ask what this is regarding?" Venus asked.

"Sorry, ma'am. They just hire me to deliver the paperwork."

"Of course they do," she gritted out, snatching the folder from the girl's hand.

As soon as Venus took her eyes off the folder, she caught the back of her blonde waves sweeping down her back while she left out of the office to go serve more poor unsuspecting souls around the city.

Principal Bivins nodded her way as he came inside, catching the door to the office before it shut.

"No flowers?" he asked Venus, smiling.

"Nope," Venus replied, tugging at the metal clasps on the folder and pulling the papers up to glance at them.

She kept a neutral expression while Tamika and Jillian burned holes into the side of her face.

"You tell that boyfriend of yours he's got to do better now," Principal Bivins rambled as she followed behind him into his office and eyed the top of the paper.

"Witness..." she muttered to herself, reading. "Witness to what?"

"What was that, Ms. Thibodeaux?"

"Oh... nothing. Just talking out loud to myself."

"Everything okay?" He shuffled behind his desk and she kicked the door closed with her foot while trying to make sense of all the legal jargon in front of her.

"Yep. All good on my end."

"Just making sure. Your face is saying one thing, but you're telling me another."

It was just like the lead up to her divorce all over again— fancy lawyer talk, a nauseous stomach, and a court date.

She clicked her tongue against the roof of her dry mouth and sank into one of the leather chairs in front of Principal Bivins' desk.

She skimmed and skimmed until she got to the only familiar name on the document.

Nunez.

"Nunez vs. Torres," she mouthed to herself.

"I wanted to get your thoughts on Toriana Nunez," Principal Bivins interrupted.

The folder crumpled under her sweaty fingers.

"Douglas said she's not talking during PE. I looked at her file and I didn't see an IEP or a request for an eval. I guess the IEP went down with all the other docs in the great basement flood. Any insight on the situation? Does she talk in your class? Anybody else said anything to you about it?"

His questions came barreling out like missiles while she folded the subpoena in her hand.

"Have we talked to mom and dad?" He stopped to scratch his salt and pepper beard, looking off behind her.

"I—" she started.

"Listen, between me and you, we don't have the capacity to take on another SPED student. We're stretched thin. Can you do some one on one work with her or...or send her some take home lessons? I just don't see us being able to swing *another* kid."

Venus cleared her throat and slid the envelope onto his desk. "There's something else going on at home with Tori. I think you ought to read this."

eighteen

. . .

"YOU WANNA DO THIS SHIT—*FOR* real?" Zeke frowned, staring at the three white girls standing in front of his car.

The red-headed one had smiled Anthony's way as soon as she climbed from their backseat. They'd parked their spotless blue car beside them with its engine humming. It looked like the car Venus had dropped in Meezy's lap—the one he'd delivered to him the day before in a Zaxby's parking lot. He didn't wanna give up the keys, but Dre' always said to be a man of his word when doing business—even when he did shiesty business.

"Just go change the title and sell the AMG," Zeke said.

"That ain't gon' fix my problems …" Anthony mumbled from the passenger seat, shrugging.

"Don't play like you can't go get another whip if you sell it."

"Yeah, and you know how long that shit'll take while I wait and stack paychecks from that job? I told you I gotta lay down after this last one, but I need some contingency money—*like now*."

"Contingency money? What the fuck is that?" Zeke groaned. "I told Kris I was coolin' tonight."

"Fuck Kristen. It's easy money. She'll understand."

Shit, "take me" might as well have been written on the car's windshield.

"Don't be a crash dummy, bro," Zeke replied.

"Crash dummy? Why I can't be a daredevil like Evel Knievel?" Anthony replied, licking his lips and searching for Venus' taste even though it was her fault he was there.

He'd licked them so much the bottom one had a red streak across the middle that worried Munch.

"I don't even know who the fuck a Evel Knievel is, twin."

"That nigga jumped over fourteen greyhound buses." Anthony whistled, twirling his lanky finger. "And you mean to tell me you don't know who he is?"

A hazy cloud covered the interior of the car. It was so thick he lost Zeke's dark face until he bobbed forward, fanning the smoke from the joint they shared and widening his droopy eyes in disbelief.

Anthony laughed at his expression and turned toward the crowd. It swayed along with the Mustang spinning in the middle of it. He caught bits and pieces of the smoke the car left as it burned circles into the pavement. It went round and round and made him dizzy until he blinked.

Dominic's voice blared through its speakers, overpowering the voices from the crowd. The song was one of Anthony's favorites—2:30. It was an old cut where Dominic rapped about how much money he could make in two minutes and thirty seconds.

"Hm…" Zeke hummed. "You really believe that man jumped over fourteen buses?"

"It's in history books, dumbass. They don't wanna talk about slavery, but got a whole chapter on a fuckin' white daredevil."

"You would know. You was the only nigga in Mr. Peterson's class that read the book."

Anthony rolled his eyes and stared up at the car's roof.

If Venus was there, she'd call him a "strange lil' boy" with a silly Cheshire grin and ask him some lame ass teacher question.

He needed to stop thinking about her because their night was over, but he underestimated how addicting she'd be and how angsty she'd make him. She'd even reiterated their *thing* was over in an uptight call from one of the school's phones while he worked his shift at Vaughn's the morning before. The call had rolled to voicemail and he let the recording play twice on his smoke break.

"Tori had a potty accident today during small groups. Can you send an extra change of clothes with her on Monday? And I... uh... I also talked with Principal Bivins about what you and I've been discussing. He...he says he doesn't recommend an evaluation for Tori and he'd like for me to send extra work home. He thinks Tori might just need some extra nudging to come out of her shell. I'm sure you'll be happy to hear that. You can email me or contact me through Parent Connect if you have any questions I can address."

She sounded serious and sexy while she talked in her professional voice. The puff of smoke Zeke exhaled looked like the tips of her curls without the purple coloring, and then he saw her face in it. She went on about Munch with her eyebrows wrinkled, telling him in so many words she was done playing with him and he needed to convince himself to be done with her, too.

"Aye..." Zeke snapped his fingers in front of his face. "You can't be zoning out on me like that."

He blinked and Venus disappeared.

He really needed to stop smoking. Before he left Munch with Lola, he'd promised her he wouldn't smoke because she hated the way the smell clung to him. She said it made him smell like a "skunk."

"My fault," he croaked out, dusting a smatter of ashes off his pants just as the redhead eased against the car's hood.

She flung her hair over her shoulder and blinked at him through the windshield with a smirk.

"You ever fucked a red head?" Zeke laughed.

"Not a natural one."

"I guess it's a first time for everything."

"Maybe…"

His phone vibrated.

He pat his pockets, holding his breath for Venus' number to show up on the screen. He pulled it out and turned it over in his hands.

Wishful thinking.

"Mikayla…" Zeke snickered from beside him, looking over at the phone. "You never told me what that's like."

Anthony ignored the call and pushed the phone back into his pocket. "College pussy—I'm her first stupid nigga so she think she in love. She don't even know what love is."

Zeke doubled over in laughter.

It'd been her third call since they parked. At work, she'd sidled up next to him and tried to pull his mind away from Venus, but Venus was impossible to forget. Her taste was one of those once in a lifetime ones he'd never get over. Mikayla would understand when she was older and found a man who made her believe the same thing.

"So what you think?" Zeke flung his finger up at the girls sitting on his car. "You tryna go snowboarding tonight or what? I'm tired of playing eye footsies with these bitches."

Anthony cocked his head to the side at the sliver of shoulder the red head had exposed. It didn't tempt him like her friend's car or Venus' purple hair. It was just a pale ass shoulder she kept trying to thrust his way and make him catch.

He touched the door handle as he looked from her shoulder to the humming car they'd gotten out of.

"I *think* you should put your shit in reverse when I get in their car and meet me at White Boy's. It's already late, and I gotta go pick up Munch."

Zeke gripped the steering wheel. "Mannn… them white girls gon' call the cops on your black ass as soon as you touch that door handle."

"Good." He shrugged. "Put your hand on the gearshift."

Zeke's Adam's apple jumped as he gulped.

Lola told Anthony Zeke's mama was just giving her testimony about him last Sunday in church and thanking God he was off papers... *again.*

Zeke shook his head and looked down. "How much contingency money you looking for?"

"I already paid a twenty-thousand dollar retainer—you do the math."

His eyes bulged. "Man, are you *for sure for sure* about this shit with DeeDee?"

Zeke asked him that same question at least once a week because he wasn't as soft as Josiah or as understanding as Dre'. He'd always seen DeeDee for what she was.

"That girl got your mind going in a million different ways," Zeke would say, shaking his head. *"Have you really thought about this shit?"*

Every time Munch cursed, sucked her thumb, or cried for him, he thought about it. Zeke didn't get it, and Josiah told him most folks never would.

"I need to go pick up my baby," Anthony rasped. "Put your hand on the gearshift, ZeZe."

Zeke shook his head and plopped his hand on it.

The other two white girls scooted closer to their red-headed friend and took their phones out. They lifted them in the air, recording the crowd as Anthony pushed open the passenger door.

The screeching from the tires and loud music spilled into Zeke's car. It drowned out any unsure thoughts that tried to squeeze their way into Anthony's head and slow him down. He'd seen too many folks get fucked over by unsure thoughts.

He crouched down and waddled to the girl's car, leaving a crack in his door for Zeke to deal with.

There wasn't any time to look back at Zeke and reassure him they were good. That was some shit they'd have to work out on their own. They'd probably used up all their luck and prayers to

God. Lola said God was sick of their black asses and the stunts they pulled, anyway.

When he touched the blue handle, he heard Venus and her haughty, judgmental voice, but she wasn't asking about the car or his plans for it.

"You sure you gon' make it home?"

That's all she wanted to know.

He yanked the car door open and climbed inside.

His body moved faster than his brain as he looked around at all the people in a trance outside. As soon as his foot slammed on the gas and the engine revved, the redhead whipped her head around in a slow, dramatic turn he couldn't process because he'd already pushed his foot on the brake and pushed their car into reverse. The tires dragged against the parking lot as he tried to ram a hole in the car's floor.

He breathed hard, inhaling the girly scent stuck in the car's interior. It was another thing he couldn't process because the smell would be gone before the next day and the key fob would be in Matthew's hand.

He didn't check for Zeke in his rearview mirror, but he heard the sirens in the distance. He was sure Zeke would make it, but even if he didn't, Zeke wouldn't trip about it. It was that whole brotherhood thing they'd drilled into each other's heads.

"My brother is right, even when he's wrong."

It went along with that whole Thirty omertà shit.

He looked in the rearview mirror as he coasted through back-streets in a trance. Beads of sweat trickled down his back and leaked through his shirt while he dashed between cars.

Nobody ever talked about how adrenaline made time creep to a halt. It made the ten-minute drive to the shop feel like ten hours. Streets that were only a mile long seemed endless, and every flashing light made him press the gas harder. He and Zeke used to joke that it was just God trying to make them rethink their stupid ass decisions.

He turned the steering wheel with two hands, swerving down another long road with too many cars.

"Shit," he hissed as a rickety Corolla drifted into his lane.

He didn't bother laying on the horn. Instead, he whipped from behind it, passing it up and veering back into the lane. He did the same thing four more times to four other cars until the fifth one slammed on its brakes.

"Oh shi—" He whipped the steering wheel so hard the car jerked into the passing lane.

The blinding lights from oncoming traffic came straight toward him.

His eyes widened, and he gasped, tugging at the steering wheel.

He couldn't make out the cars that came his way—only the colors—blue, silver, brown, and finally red.

Tires screeched until metal crunched against metal and somehow he became suspended in the air. He thought he'd closed his eyes, but he saw the world Venus told him was his. It floated beneath him while he flew through the air.

He tried to count the seconds, but that part of his brain stopped. He couldn't conceptualize numbers or time—only memories—like the kiss Munch had given him before he left, the sunshine cascading over Venus' brown body…and her voice.

"What you want out of life, Anthony?"

Before he could tell her, he fell back to Earth and landed with a loud *smack*.

His body thrashed around the car—up and down while the crunching and shattering burst through his ears and made them ring. His head swirled in an endless loop until it couldn't anymore, and the world got so quiet he started searching for that light they talked about in church sometimes.

"Call 911!" somebody yelled in the distance.

"No." He groaned, but it wasn't loud enough because they kept yelling it.

"Are they still in there?" they asked.

"Jeez...he had to have been going about a hundred. I tried to miss 'em, but it was too late." Another muffled voice snuck through the wreckage.

"Hello! Are you okay?"

A sliver of orange light peeked through the car's busted windshield and landed on his face. A white lady stared at him with glossy eyes.

"He's alive! I see him blinking. Sweetheart, we're gonna get you out of there. Just hang on, okay? Keep breathing."

"Fuck..." he croaked, searching for the door handle in the clump of metal.

He found it next to his foot, dangling from the door.

He gasped, sucking in the bit of fresh air that drifted through the hole in the windshield. He wiggled his toes, then his fingers, and looked around at the crumpled metal that was once some girl's dream car. The furry dice she had hung from the rearview mirror laid on the floor next to his head.

Heat bubbled up his arm as he reached toward the hole in the windshield. Glass scraped against his skin, but he didn't feel the punctures.

"Hold on! We almost got you!"

A pale hand grabbed his wrist, yanking his limp body through the hole and pulling him from the wreckage. The round, balding man fell back as Anthony fell forward on top of him.

Anthony rolled off of him and crawled toward the night air, breathing in through his nose and out through his mouth just like Dre' had taught him the first time they'd done something stupid.

"Are you okay?" the man asked. "The ambulance is on their—"

He pushed off the ground and took off.

His feet pounded the pavement. People shouted in the distance. Smoke rose from the wreckage. The tart smell from the airbags' gas got caught in his throat.

More sirens wailed.

"Fuck, fuck, fuck."

He ran faster and rounded an empty warehouse as the sirens got closer.

He slapped his pockets for his phone and keys and then took off in a full sprint toward the metal fence behind the warehouse.

He jumped.

His fingers curled through the fence's holes and he crawled as fast as his brain would let his body. It was still muddled from smoking, so all he felt was warmth and wetness on his arm.

Once he was on the other side, he let go and landed on the concrete. His ankles tingled from the drop and his body folded into itself until he caught his breath and rolled over to stare at Munch's moon.

nineteen

. . .

"SO... WHAT DO YOU THINK, COUSIN?" Ginny whispered, elbowing Venus in her side while flinging her auburn locs over her shoulder. "He's cute, right?"

He was a snooze—a muscle headed corny snooze ... and possibly a hobosexual based on the vague answer he'd given Venus about his living arrangements and how quickly he'd invited himself to her place.

"Oh, he's great." Venus shrugged with a tight-lipped smile and turning stomach.

He didn't look like he could give her back-to-back leg shaking orgasms, and he was probably one of those incels Anthony talked about.

Ugh.

Why was she still thinking about Anthony?

It had been a week since their "date." There were a million reasons she needed to stop thinking about him and the most glaring reason wasn't even the fact he was embroiled in a custody case with his baby mama, who was in jail—there were more.

Victor glanced at her from the crowded bar as Ginny's

husband Chris tugged him into one of those cheesy "bro" hugs. They were probably having a similar conversation while they waited for the bartender to fix their drinks.

The dive bar wasn't Vaughn's expansive dining room and Victor didn't know the owner of the place. It was just a basic ass first date—or like Ginny called it, an introduction.

Ginny snickered. "You think he's lame."

"He's a cool dude. Really."

"What's wrong with him? He's one of Chris' best looking friends. I mean, looks wise, he's the complete opposite of Trey. I thought that's what you wanted." Ginny blinked at her.

"Who said I wanted the complete opposite of Trey?"

"Uh... that divorce on file with the Harris County Clerk's office. Isn't it in our nature to stray from what's familiar after being hurt by it?"

"Don't get philosophical on me."

"I'm just saying..." She shrugged, wrinkling her nose. "You have to at least get your feet wet. Dating ain't what it used to be. We're not exactly sexy coeds anymore."

As if Venus hadn't cried about that very notion to Michole. She was starting from scratch while her peers were having oodles of fat-cheeked babies, taking endless family vacations to the Caribbean with their other married friends and posting the pictures on Instagram to torture her.

She glanced down at her basic black romper and T.J. Maxx sandals. "Yeah, I know."

It wasn't her hip hugging denim jumpsuit that made Anthony's dick hard, and Victor hadn't even told her she looked good in it. He'd complimented Chris' sneakers more than he complimented her and he'd committed one of Anthony's first date infractions by not appreciating her sexy post-divorce body as soon as he laid eyes on it. He was so corny.

"See, that's why you need to get out there. You're still young. You still have time to get married aga—"

"Hold up. Slow down."

"Look, you'll never know what you want in another husband unless you date again."

Venus held her hand up. "Who says I haven't been dating?"

She regretted the words as soon as they came out because she'd finally left Morris and their embarrassing date in the past. Now Ginny was going to make her relive it.

"Oh," Ginny chirped. "Well, what's tea? You should've been told me to shut up. Who you been dating?"

Venus looked around the crowded bar. "I've... I've been on a couple dates here and there. You know."

"No, I don't know. Hurry up before they come back."

The longer she took to stammer out an answer, the more Ginny's soft face wrinkled into a frown.

"I'm picking up some energy and it ain't good. What's wrong with the dude?"

Everything!

Because Anthony was right. She had terrible taste in men and she needed to shut up.

Ginny reached out and gave her shoulder a squeeze. "Damn, girl. Is it that bad?"

"It depends on how you look at it."

"Uh..." Ginny cocked her head to the side. "Is...is he *ugly*?"

"What? No!"

"Well, Jesus, girl. What is it?"

"He's... he's young," she muttered without thinking.

It was another thing she regretted because her one night with Anthony didn't count in her quest to "get her feet wet." He was a vacation from everybody's stupid expectations of her new dating life.

"Okay, how young?"

Venus' eyes rolled to the ceiling. "You're about to judge me to hell."

"I won't. Now, the rest of the family might if they find out, but not me, cousin."

Venus knew better than to say it out loud, but she needed to hear how ridiculous it was for her to want Anthony. She couldn't tell it to anybody else—especially not Logan.

At the end of her meeting with Principal Bivins, he'd given her one piece of advice: Keep her conversations with Anthony and about him to a minimum until he talked to their district lawyer and that was *if* their district even had one. Ginny wasn't just anybody, though. She was her loud-mouthed cousin who didn't need to know the complete story with Anthony—just half of it.

Venus swiped her hot neck and glanced at Victor again, hoping his brown skin and bulky forearms would make her feel like Anthony's body did.

She shuffled against the stool, trying to nudge some sense into her pussy, but it was a mental thing, like Anthony said. According to his philosophy, curiosity made her agree to this stupid introduction.

"I don't know how old he is. I just know he's young... maybe a lot younger than me."

"You didn't ask him?"

Venus bucked her eyes out. "Sort of."

"And?"

"He said he was old enough... for me."

Ginny let out an obnoxious purr and bat her lashes. "And then you fucked him, right?"

"Ginny... *please*. He... he ain't the most suitable dude."

"Girl, at our ages, how many men are? I mean, look at Chris."

They looked over at him, taking their drinks from the bartender. His dimple sank into his cheek as he grinned at the girl. Not in a suggestive way—just a friendly "I'm taken" one. His wedding band gleamed under the dim lighting in the bar.

"It took us some time to get there, but with my molding, he's now Mr. Right. He's safe and at our age, that's what we need—safe."

She heard the years of complacency in Ginny's tone. Chris

was what Trey had convinced their friends and family of being. Daddy always said he was like a wolf in sheep's clothing.

"He has a job, right?" she asked.

Venus swallowed and nodded.

"No kids?"

She hesitated, but then shook her head because the conversation needed to end.

"Well, shit." Ginny waved her hand. "Sounds like he's doing better than eighty percent of the male pop—"

"It doesn't matter. We hung out, it was cool, and now we both moved on."

And Anthony wasn't safe. He was just trouble—sexy, dangerous trouble with a kid that she taught.

"Perfect. So you're free to date Victor?"

"I didn't say that."

As soon as Ginny opened her mouth to argue more, Victor and Chris emerged from the throngs of people crowding their table.

"One lemon drop for you," Victor sang, sitting the drink in front of her and sliding back onto the empty bar stool next to her. "We weren't gone too long, were we?"

"Nope!" Ginny chirped. "You guys came back just in time. We were talking about double dating next weekend. Y'all down?"

Venus kicked her bony shin under the table. Ginny cringed, mouthing "safe."

"I'm down." Victor grinned. "Where we going?"

"I keep seeing this restaurant on my feed every time I open Instagram." Ginny stuffed her hand into her purse. "Vinny's... Vino's..."

"Vaughn's?" Venus uttered, shuffling against her stool again.

"That's it! It's right up my alley—sexy tapas, gorgeous drinks, rave reviews from all my favorite food bloggers, a reason to buy a new outfit—"

"And expensive, right?" Chris butted in, flinging his arm around her as she pulled her phone out.

Victor swiped the back of his neck. "How expensive we talking? I mean, I'm cool with a nice little steakhouse, but spending my car note on one dinner sounds wasteful. I bet we could have a better time at Venus' place."

Ginny raised her eyebrows this time while Venus took a sip of her lemon drop and looked away.

"Aw... come on, man." Chris whined. "Let's treat the ladies so they can do their lil' Insta flexing and brag about how their men took them to the hottest spot in town."

Their men?

Venus choked on the tart drink.

"You good?" Ginny asked.

"Yeah, yeah. It went down the wrong way."

"Better watch how you're handling that drink." Victor winked, sliding a napkin her way. "I don't wanna have to drive you home."

"Oh, you won't. I am a-okay."

And not desperate enough to have him do anything that would give him the opportunity to ask to sleep on her couch.

Chris chuckled. "You sure you're not tipsy? I know how you and Gin can get."

"Uh..." Ginny cleared her throat. "Let's do a rain check."

Venus' apprehension must've been on her face and Victor's brokeness must've been on his. Everybody realized except Chris because airheadedness was one of his safe traits Ginny tolerated.

Venus pulled her purse from around the back of the barstool. "Yeah, let's do a rain check. I'm gonna head out. I have an appointment in the morning."

Getting up on time for her special standing appointment with Michole sounded much more exciting than spending the night running away from Victor.

"Fine." Chris groaned while Victor smiled a little too big.

"I'll walk you to your car," he chirped.

She forced a smile onto her face.

———

As soon as Venus slammed herself inside her Honda, she let out the ragged gasp she'd been holding the entire walk through the parking lot with Victor.

This couldn't have been the curiosity Anthony talked about. She didn't wanna flirt with Victor or even tap her lips against his. She wanted to run far away from him and all the other safe men pretending to be good.

She squeezed the steering wheel and then shook it. "Fuck love and fuck finding it. I'm not too young to be philophobic, Anthony."

She thrust her head against the headrest and smiled because back-to-back orgasms made her talk to his ghost.

Maybe she should've said more that Sunday when he dropped her off. She should've made the first move and tasted him to get him out of her system for good. His lips probably weren't as soft as they looked anyway—he was a smoker.

She balled up her face.

He probably tasted like all the shit she'd outgrown.

Her tongue darted out, and she squirmed like she'd done on that barstool, but now she wasn't squirming to make her pussy cooperate. She was squirming for Anthony and his oddball ways.

Her phone dinged and her body jerked forward.

"Tighten up, Venus Thibodeaux," she mumbled. "You acting like Mrs. Nunez right now and you are *not* that girl."

She dug her phone out of her purse, squinting at the bright screen.

Ginny

Lmk when you make it home. Per Chris, Victor thinks you're "cute." Childish, I know! But give him a chance. I mean, at least he's kid-less since you're going the whole child-free bachelor route.

"Cute?" She rolled her eyes, swiping the notification off her screen and groaning.

Meanwhile, her non-cooperative pussy hated her for trying to force it to be curious about another man. It was overdue for attention and here she was, tearing it away from the one man it *ached* for. Dramatic, but true. If she hadn't sworn to herself she'd stay away from Anthony, she decided she would have to beg for him, just like Deeanna. She would have to get on her knees at her big age and beg for his dick. That was it. That was the one thing she had in common with Deeanna, Mikayla, and Priya. He made them all fuckin' crazy.

Sometimes she still felt remnants of his lips on the intimate parts of her body he explored—like her toes.

She wiggled them in her sandals, smiling to herself while turning her phone over in her hand until she stopped.

She looked back at it, swiping out of her and Ginny's text thread and scrolling through useless messages about Pepper's pending catnip delivery and Daddy's prescription refills until she got to the one place she didn't need to be.

Her finger lingered over her and Anthony's text thread she'd been meaning to delete. The last text was her sharing her address with him like the irresponsible wench Rose said she was. The thread felt unusually quiet compared to all the talking and confessing they'd done in their one night together.

She sighed. "What the fuck, Anthony?"

He didn't even have anything snarky to say about the spicy voicemail she left him from Principal Bivins' office. Hell, he could've at least warned her of the subpoena coming her way, but then again, he was just a parent and she was just his kid's teacher. They didn't owe each other anything.

She pressed his name, staring at his texts as if they'd help her read between the complicated lines in his life. Her finger hovered over the empty message box. She swallowed and pressed it, typing and then erasing different variations of the same question until she remembered who she was fuckin' with.

> Truth?

Her body started all the weird things it did when she was being immature—sweating and aching in odd places but she needed to know what was going on and she needed to hear it from him.

Finally, she held her breath and pressed the blue arrow, sending the message out into the abyss of Daddy's universe.

She didn't sit there and wait on his reply like some needy lame chick. Instead, she tossed her phone into the passenger seat, cranked up her car, and drove out of the parking lot. Two blocks away from the dive bar, she started talking to herself again.

"You're pining, Venus," she muttered, turning down a dark street. "He's out doing whatever it is dudes his age do—hanging out, fuckin' Mikayla, waiting tables, hustling rappers—"

Ding.

Her foot jerked, and she pulled into a Publix parking lot.

There was nothing so profound he could text that she needed to read at that moment, but he had her brain convinced that he always needed her undivided attention.

She double parked and snatched the phone from the passenger seat even though it could've been Ginny again. In fact, there was a tiny part of her brain that needed it to be Ginny so she could rant and rave to herself about Anthony Nunez being a ghoster.

She turned the phone over.

> Tori's dad:

Truth

Of course, he wasn't a ghoster. Any man who made out with her pinky toe wouldn't dare be a ghoster.

Venus:

Did you make it home to Tori tonight?

It was a safe question. They always started with the safe ones —even when she wanted to ask dangerous ones like why he was trying to take Tori from Deeanna.

Her eyes burned from how wide they got as that torturous little bubble popped up while he typed.

Tori's dad:

Not yet.

His reply wasn't clever, groundbreaking or mysterious. There wasn't any flirtatious banter. It was as flat as it should've been because they had nothing left after their one night together. It was obvious he was reminding her of the terms she'd set.

"See...you were trippin' for nothing," she murmured. "Now you gotta go back, lick your wounds, and go on that second date with Vi—"

Her phone vibrated in her hands and "Tori's dad" covered the screen.

She held it like a newborn baby and stared at it while tossing all the "what-ifs" back and forth in her head. It stopped ringing and dinged with another message.

Tori's dad:

Answer the phone.

There still wasn't any flirtatious banter, but he called *again*. Now all the "what-ifs" she'd been tossing back and forth turned into "maybe I shouldn't haves." This time, she hesitated, but swiped to answer the call.

When she put the phone to her ear, he didn't let her get a word out before he huffed into it. "You good?"

He talked between deep breaths.

"Um, are *you* good?" she shot back.

"Yeah... yeah. I'm good."

"You don't sound good. You sound out of breath. Do you wanna call me back?"

"Nah, you texted me, so I thought something was wrong. You not a texter, remember?"

She thrust her head against the headrest and smiled until he coughed out a quiet, "shit."

"Are you working or something?"

"Nah," he replied distractedly. "Where you at?"

She frowned and looked around the empty parking lot. "At Publix."

"Publix is closed. Where you at for real? It's late, Venus."

She felt the anxiety in his voice.

"Okay, so I'm not just hanging outside a closed grocery store like a bum. I'm in my car... and I'm grown."

The jingling of loose gravel crackled throughout the line while she tried not to get lusty and distracted by him because something was wrong.

"Anthony..." she called out, pushing the car back into drive. "Are you... are you working *working*?"

She sighed and drummed her fingers against the steering wheel while staring at the dark Publix.

"Yeah, but I fucked something up. Stay on the phone with me while you head home."

"Are you sure?"

"Where you coming from?"

"I... I went on a double date at some di—wait a minute. Did you get the voicemail I left you?"

A door slammed on his end of the phone and he coughed

between loud breaths. The noises made her wipe her hands down her romper and look around like he was headed her way.

"Yeah, I got it."

"And?"

"And what? *You* broke up with me, Ms. Thibodeaux, yet you still on my phone telling me to share my opinion with you about something that's over with. Didn't you call me from the school phone like you ain't have my phone number? What you want me to say?" he murmured huskily.

She smiled. "Listen, lil' boy, we'd have to be in a relationship for a breakup to occur."

"Occur? Look at you using your teacher voice. Did it ever occur to you I don't put my mouth on every pussy I come across?"

"Stop changing the subject. I... we should really talk about that conversation I had with Principal Bivins... and I need to talk to you about something else."

A car's engine hummed and a nasally suburban voice shrilled in the background.

"What the fuck, bro? You're fucked *up*. That was you speeding off on that girl's Insta story? That shit was crazy! You parked it in the cut off Shaker, right?"

"Nah, man. You don't hear all them sirens?" Anthony replied while she held her breath and pushed her ear closer to the phone. "It's gone."

"Fuck!"

"Yeah, fuck is right."

Their voices quieted until the nasally one perked back up.

"You need a ride?"

"Nah."

"Anthony?" she whispered, interrupting their back and forth.

"I'm here, Venus."

Even with her blood boiling from the weird predicament he was in, she felt that "I'm here" in all those forbidden places on her body he claimed as his.

"I'mma send you my location. Come get me and we'll talk about whatever you wanna talk about," he muttered, hanging up.

Her phone vibrated with the message he promised. She stared at the blue dot on the map and sighed to herself.

———

Twenty minutes later, she spotted him from the road. He stood in front of a nondescript warehouse with one dull flickering light outside it. The voice she heard in the background of his call wasn't there—nobody was.

Her tense shoulders hunched up to her ears and Logan wasn't there to convince her to relax them, so they were stuck.

As soon as he noticed her car, he power walked toward it, looking behind himself after every step until he yanked the passenger door open.

She frowned as he hawked up a glob of spit before he pushed his long leg inside. A fresh outside scent clung to his clothes and filled her car when he closed the door.

The full moon cast just enough light inside for her to rake her eyes across the gash on his arm and the grass stuck in his hair. She tried to piece together his night without getting caught up in his eyes, but he made it hard because he stared at her so intently it made her uneasy. The uneasiness left her with a rawness that made her heart bang against her chest.

"Look at you..." he said, smiling with swollen lips and bloody, sparkling teeth. "You got your romper on and shit. Why you always look so...*sexy*? I don't remember saying you could go on a date."

The more she watched each word come out of his mouth, the more that rawness crept up her throat and her mouth watered for him. She never had so many conflicting feelings at once for Trey.

"You wore your hair up," he muttered, eyeing it from

different angles and then reaching out to tug the top of her romper. "Why you do that?"

Specks of red wept from the raw skin on his pink knuckles. Fresh blood trickled over old dried blood and his tattered shirt dangled down his arm, exposing his scar.

"What the fuck, Anthony?" she choked out. "Do you think you fuckin' invincible or something?"

twenty

. . .

WHEN VENUS THIBODEAUX WAS ANGRY, heat seeped out of her pores and radiated off her body. It was so intense that when Anthony inhaled, he swallowed it.

She stared at his busted lip like he'd fucked around and betrayed her, and she wanted to know if he thought he was invincible.

"Sometimes," he croaked out, staring at her under the moonlight and then swiping mascara from underneath her eye.

"Well, you're not!" She held her finger up like she wanted to ram it into his forehead.

It hung in the air while her face scrunched behind it in agony.

"What you all upset for? We can talk about the voicemail—"

"I don't know what the fuck you been in, but whatever it is could've killed you! Does that ever occur to you when you doing fucked up stupid shit?"

Nope. It never did.

Lola used to tell Carlotta it was a shame he wasn't afraid to die. It was the only worthwhile thing Miguel taught him before he was deported. He always said he didn't need to fear life or death because he was *infinito*.

"What the fuck is wrong with you? Look at your face and... and your arm!"

She didn't even fight like Deeanna. Deeanna tried to gut him with her hands more than her words, and she held his love for Munch over his head. She dangled it there, taking Munch away from him when she felt like it and bringing her back when they couldn't handle the world without him. She didn't care about none of the lame shit Venus cared about because Venus moved off of emotion. There weren't any ulterior motives behind anything she said. It was in her eyes.

He picked his arm up, twisting it around and marveling at the redness spreading from his elbow. A dull pain throbbed under the skin. He wanted to tell her at least it wasn't broken, but that'd make it worse.

She shook her head, looking down. "Where I need to bring you? It's late and I need to go home."

He pointed toward the road next to the warehouse. "Go up there and make a left."

She drove off and gripped the steering wheel so tight her fingertips turned white.

He leaned against the passenger door, staring out of the window and holding in everything he wanted to say because being in a confined space with a woman and her heightened emotions was delicate.

They drove for two blocks before she huffed and slammed her foot on the brakes at a red light. "I'm so stupid."

She talked to herself when she was angry, too.

"This is why I need to be dealing with a grown ass boring man with no baggage, no crazy baby mamas or pending court dates."

"What you talking about?"

"Nothing you need to worry about. Where do I go from here?"

"That's a figurative question or a literal one?"

She slapped the steering wheel. "A literal one! Where the fuck am I driving to?"

Trey was so bitchmade he must've given Venus plenty of reasons to disrespect him when they fought.

She breathed hard, staring ahead at the road while she waited for him to answer. The loud silence in the car made his ears ring while the light flickered and turned yellow.

She whipped her head toward him. "Hello! I asked you a question."

He shook his head and leaned back into the passenger seat, letting the light roll to red. "I don't know what type of date you been on that got you thinkin' you can disrespect me, but don't do that."

That finger he thought he loved came back. It shook as she poked it over at him.

"I'm not a child."

He chuckled. "But you throwin' a tantrum about somethin' that don't have nothin' to do with you. Respect me."

A dark car whizzed past them and laid on the horn. She jumped with wide eyes, hesitating to lean closer into him.

All of it made him shake his head.

They weren't supposed to be there. He promised himself he'd never go *there* with another woman after DeeDee, but then again, he never expected to find another woman that made him as angsty as she did—especially not a woman who cared about so much trivial shit.

"Keep straight until you get to thirtieth," he said.

She slammed her foot on the gas and the car jerked forward.

"I'm letting a lil' boy that won't even kiss me because he's too afraid of real intimacy get under my skin and call me childish? What the fuck is wrong with me?" she whispered to herself.

He sat forward. "What did you just say?"

"You heard what I said. You sitting right next to me."

"Yeah, but I want you to repeat it and stand on it."

"Oh, please. Go somewhere with tha—"

"I ain't going nowhere. Be a grown woman and stand on whatever you got to say, Venus."

She jerked the steering wheel and turned down twenty-ninth street instead of thirtieth. "Don't talk to me like that."

"Like what? Like a reasonable motherfuckin' person? You think you the only one that get to correct? Nah..." He shook his head, laughing. "You should watch what you say. You don't even know what you talking about."

"That's the problem! You won't *let* me know and then you *let* me get blindsided! I gotta beg to know shit and sometimes I even wonder why I care so much!"

Sometimes he did too.

She wasn't really his. She was free to move around, to find a "grown man" that would take care of her, to breathe without his burdens wearing her down, but there was always that little thread that kept them strung together and pulling at it to get each other's attention.

"They subpoenaed me to be a witness in whatever bullshit you and Deeanna got going on," she rasped. "What the fuck I'm supposed to get up on the stand and say when they ask me about your parenting, huh? What the fuck am I supposed to say?"

Emotions were wild. They were never black or white. Sometimes they were purple like the ringlets that sprouted from Venus' head and other times they were a ghastly ashen brown like her face when she finally pushed him far enough.

"Say I'm a good parent!"

Emotions were reckless, too. They made things that were supposed to stay in come out—like that little thing that was at the very top of him and DeeDee's list.

"Tell 'em that's my goddamn daughter no matter what anybody say! Tell 'em that I try and I won't stop trying just because her sperm donor wanna take her away from me! I signed her birth certificate, Venus! I always been there! *Always*! I'm the only daddy she know."

253

Emotions made his deep voice climb to an unnatural shrill.

"Even when DeeDee take my baby and tell me I can't see her for months at a time to punish me, I'm still there—calling, begging, pulling up to her mama's house! That's what the fuck you supposed to say! But you don't ever go up for me!"

He leaned over the middle console, pointing like she always did. Her eyes widened at his finger nearing her face and for the second time in his life, he didn't know what to do with all that angst Lola had snickered about.

"But you wanted me to go bail her out, right? You wanted me to dig in my pockets and bail her out of her bullshit like always? Even when she fuckin' some other man, but calling me because I'm the only one who don't hold her fuckin' feet to the fire and make her grow up! He was supposed to leave his wife for her and Tori, you know that, right? That's what he told her the last time she hopped off my dick and climbed on his!"

He laughed hard, like that day he came home to an empty apartment. She'd even taken the curtains off the walls and Munch's pink butterflies off of her bedroom door. It took him weeks to get the strength to get another place.

"Now she fucked up and I'm bailing her out again. I picked our baby up so they wouldn't take her. I found the lawyer. I threatened to kill a nigga over my baby right in front of your face! I'm fightin' so we can keep *our* baby that he tryna take and blend with his family that he never planned to leave. He never leaving his wife, Venus. *Never*. A mistress and an outside baby don't fit into his image as a family man and doctor."

The car glided down twenty-ninth even though she steered it. She was just paralyzed from him, from DeeDee, and from Trey still in her head, making her believe he was some lil' boy who'd run from intimacy with her.

He shook his head. "Oh... and did I mention he was a grown man just like you want—a lying, cheating, grown ass man with a private practice and all the money to take my world away? He even sped up the fuckin' custody trial with his money, Venus. That's why I'm still doing the shit I do!"

"Ant..." she muttered, shaking her head.

"Don't! Don't call me that shit!"

"But, I'm sorry. I didn't know."

"Yeah, I ain't know I was supposed to go around shouting from the rooftops that my daughter really ain't my fuckin' daughter."

"I'm *so* sorry."

It was the first time anybody ever apologized for the way DeeDee had set his world on fire. *She* wouldn't even do it. There were no "sorrys" or "my bads" or remorse in her eyes for holding onto a bomb of a secret for ten long months. She never even flinched when Lola asked why Munch didn't have his freckles or when Josiah kept asking if his niece would ever start to look like her daddy. It'd been so long that he'd given up on ever hearing that word from her or from God for ever dropping her into his life and fuckin' it up.

His hand trembled and fell onto Venus' warm leg. He scraped his bloody fingers across her soft skin.

"You tell Trey that I can't kiss you," he murmured. "Because I know he still up in your head just like DeeDee be in mine. You tell him that if I kiss you, I won't be able to stop ... and if I keep kissing you, then I'm gonna wanna make love to you... and I won't be able to stop that either. And then you know what?"

"What?" she asked, hanging on to his every word.

"Then I'm gon' wanna put a baby in you and Lord knows we don't need that."

A hot tear rolled down his cheek. Over the years, they'd gone from blinding, gushing tears that made his head hurt to solitary ones that rolled out every blue moon when he thought about how much damage DeeDee had done to him.

Venus dropped her hand on his, but he nudged it away and cupped her middle. Her pussy was so warm he was sure it would singe his hand and if it did, he wouldn't give a fuck. At least it'd be another thing that bound them together.

"Now go 'head," he mumbled, stone-faced and needy. "Correct me."

She shook her head and looked down at his hand cupping her center. "Ant..."

"What?"

"I...how...how long?"

"How long what?"

"How long you been knowing she's not yours?"

"Long enough to contemplate so many scenarios in my head that all lead to the same ending. Long enough to get used to the strange looks my niggas give me every time they realize I don't wanna give her up. Long enough to realize what I don't want in a woman—now correct me like I said."

She jerked the steering wheel and pulled over onto the shoulder while cars zipped past them.

He had a love-hate relationship with angst because all of his favorite bitches made it feel so good that he lost himself inside them while running from it.

She pressed the brakes.

He pushed the gearshift.

She tore her seatbelt off.

He yanked her romper down.

Her breasts spilled out, and she gasped.

They were so in sync he couldn't differentiate her thoughts from the words that came out of her mouth.

"I'm supposed to stay away from you," she breathed out, crawling into his lap. "Fuck. I need to stay away from you."

"Who said that?"

"My common sense, my boss, my head."

"You tell them how good I make you feel, though?" He reached out and yanked her bun, rolling the hair tie down her strands.

Her poof of hair exploded as she shook her head. "No."

"That's bad business."

"No, *you're* bad business."

"How you gon' correct me if you always thinking the worst of me?"

"I don't always think the worst of you," she gritted out.

It was too late for her rebuttal because he'd already started leaning forward. He pushed his face between her breasts and inhaled. She smelled like everything he needed in the week they were apart.

"Yeah, you do," he muttered into her skin. "But it's cool."

He hadn't even done anything, and she was already scraping her fingers through his hair and murmuring out that nickname she'd given him.

"I don't, Ant..." she whispered. "I promise I don't."

He closed his eyes and tried to push his head so far into her she wouldn't be able to go anywhere else without him. It didn't work, though. It just made him look desperate.

She massaged his hot cheek. "Let me see your mouth, baby."

Her "baby" didn't sound like Mikayla's. Hers had that obsessiveness underneath it that DeeDee's did. It was the kind that made him give them everything he had, even when he had nothing left to give. Lola always said it was dangerous.

He pulled away and looked at Venus.

She reached out with her eyebrows knitted together and pulled down his bottom lip, grimacing at the gash he'd been soothing with his tongue while they fought.

"What would Tori do without you and a mama that's in jail?" she asked, studying the torn skin. "What's she gonna do if you don't come home one night? Huh? Then who's gonna fight for her, Anthony?"

She didn't say anything he didn't already know, but that wasn't the point. The words were wrapped in her feminine voice and they came from *her*—her mind, her heart, and her soul.

She raked her fingers through her hair with wild wide eyes. "Don't you understand how fuckin' beautiful your brain is? You got a damn millionaire enamored with it—enamored with *you*. Use that shit! Be fuckin' resourceful in places that matter!"

Beautiful brain?

Now, that shit was new. Nobody had ever told him that one.

"Come here," he muttered around her fingers. "Gimme your tongue."

She stooped down and pressed her lips against his, plunging her tongue into his mouth and grinding against his dick.

He didn't realize how long he'd been craving her taste until the days, hours, minutes and seconds danced behind his eyelids. He breathed in all the time she'd spent not knowing of his existence. Her apology was intertwined between the tiny moans she emitted and the sucks she gave his tongue, but in their short time apart, he'd forgotten how emotive she was when he made her feel good.

"I'm sorry," she uttered, pulling his bottom lip into her mouth and soothing the gash.

Her hand wandered down his neck and onto his stomach, where she ran her fingers across it. "I'm sorry, Ant."

When she grabbed the button on his jeans, he figured she wasn't even apologizing for DeeDee anymore.

"Nuh uh," he hissed, squeezing her fingers. "No."

"Why not?"

"It ain't enough room in here."

She twisted her neck around her car, surveying the space until she stopped on the backseat. She grabbed hold of the driver's side headrest and lifted her leg to climb over him.

"Where you going?" he asked, yanking the hem of her romper. "I told you it's not enough room for us."

"I don't think you remember what the objective is, Mr. Nunez," she grunted in that teasing voice he missed.

He let go of her hem long enough to slap her ass and drag her back onto him. "And I don't think I remember telling you that you could go on a date. Come explain yourself because I ain't Trey. I'll die before I sign some motherfuckin' divorce papers."

"I thought you were married to the game?"

"Nah, not on our turf."

She laughed, and it felt good—*she* felt good with her body draped over his. He'd learned to savor times like this where he caught glimpses of the Venus she was before Trey—with her wild hair and warm voice begging to be fucked on the side of the road after fighting about the shit in their lives that frustrated them.

A truck zoomed past, shaking the car.

He smacked her ass again because of the predicament they were in. She flinched as his finger inched past her hem and pushed inside of her. She was still tight and wet for him even after he confessed the thing that haunted him the most.

"Babyyy..." she groaned in frustration.

He'd never get used to her calling him that. It was sacred, just like "Ant" was.

His dick stabbed the inside of his jeans because it was as frustrated as she was.

She didn't understand that the way he made love was too robust for the backseat of a Honda Civic with factory tint. He wanted to yank her out of that romper, plunge inside of her and never come up for air, but he settled on adding another one of his throbbing fingers instead.

"You satisfied?" he hummed, pumping his fingers inside of her in a slow in and out motion that made her slack jawed.

"What you talking about?"

"You satisfied you went on a date with a *grown man*?"

A car's headlights flickered inside as it passed them. It cast just enough light for him to see his blood coating her plump lips.

She bit into her bottom lip and sucked it like she was happy she'd finally gotten part of his DNA. "You satisfied you still making my job difficult?"

"What's his name?" He pushed harder inside her, taking her

chin into his mouth while she squealed and squirmed, running away from his fingers.

"What time you go to work on Monday? I need you to come in and tell Principal Bivins that you want an eval for Tori. He's neglecting your baby because of campus politics."

There she went again—caring too damn much.

He smiled against her chin and let go. "This how it is when you play Mrs. Nunez? You gon' tell 'what's his name' how you come home, put the pussy on me, and make me do shit I don't wanna do?"

She couldn't answer because sometime between his words he squeezed a third finger inside of her that made her gasp. Wetness seeped down his fingers while she clamored against him and fell into his neck.

"No, but I'll make sure I do that when we go on our next date," she uttered against his skin, thrusting her hips. "I'll tell him how Mr. Nunez is a pretend daredevil. He's brave enough to do the craziest shit to save his world, but too scared to fuck the curiosity out of me in my backseat."

He laughed and cupped the back of her neck.

As many women as he'd fucked and almost fucked, he'd never had a full-blown conversation while knuckle deep inside any of them. Maybe that's what real married couples did when they made love? Maybe they laughed, bickered, bargained, and eventually acquiesced.

"I go to work at ten," he whispered, pressing his lips against her hot forehead. "And I ain't doing shit at that school unless you there—no Logan."

She gurgled out a ragged moan as he found her hotspot and massaged it. "Baby—ugh. Behave."

"No, now hurry up and cum so I can get you off the side of the road."

twenty-one

. . .

VENUS NEVER HAD an orgasm that made her sing so loud her vocal cords tingled from overexertion, but then Anthony came along being all passionate, carefree, and so selfless that she was dizzy and maybe even a little ditzy for him.

"That's my granny's house right there." He lifted his hand from between her leg and pointed. "Pull in the driveway next to the AMG."

Darkness coated the outside of the house besides one naked lightbulb dangling from a wire sticking out of the house's siding.

A plump brown-skinned woman sat on the porch smoking a cigarette under the flickering yellow light. She swatted at a bug while yelling out something to a lanky boy dribbling a basketball in the driveway.

He looked up at her car rolling to a stop and started trekking their way with a scowl until Anthony rolled the window down, exposing his face.

"Damn. What happened?" The boy whistled, shaking his head. "JoJo been on your head again? Duck and weave next time, stupid. Ya' mouth 'bout as bloody as hell."

"Shut up. Who in the house?"

"Granny and Munch."

Anthony nodded his head as the boy shoved the basketball under his arm and stooped down to look inside her car. His locs flopped over his eyes, but she saw the resemblance between him and Anthony—toasty brown skin and symmetrical features she couldn't help but stare at. All he was missing was a smatter of freckles.

She swiped at her mouth to wipe Anthony's sticky blood from her lip.

"Who that?" the boy asked, nodding at her and then glancing at Anthony's hand sliding back between her legs. "She look familiar."

Anthony glanced over his shoulder at her while she shifted under their gazes. "That's Venus."

"Like the planet?"

"Yeah, like the second one from the sun, dumbass." He reached out and nudged the boy's head. "What mama over there running her mouth about?"

The boy rolled his eyes and shoved the ball against the driveway.

"I hear you," Anthony replied, even though the boy hadn't said anything at all.

He just ambled off.

"I can stay in the car," she muttered.

She'd already gone too far and the spot between her legs where his hand had been made her want to go further. She wanted to do all of those things he admitted to in the car because he needed it after what he'd screamed at her—they both did.

He glanced down at the gash on his arm and then out toward the dark street. "Nah, come in the house with me."

"No. I... I can sta—"

"Munch ain't gon' wake up and catch you." He smirked, reading her mind. "She a heavy sleeper... and if she do..."

He shrugged. "She's five. Tell her she dreaming."

"That's deceptive."

He chuckled. "It's parenting."

He pushed out of the car and she followed, pushing out too. She trailed him until he stopped on the porch in front of his mama and snatched the pack of cigarettes off the crate she'd been using as an end table. He stole one and tossed the box back where it was. A man prattled on the other end of her phone, talking in Spanish to somebody in the background.

She blew out a plume of smoke and got up. "Miguel, your son just pulled up. Let me call you back."

She didn't give Miguel a chance to ask about Anthony before she hung up.

"That lawyer lady been calling the house phone for you all day." She frowned, squinting at Anthony's face.

Next, she looked at Venus.

Her eyes glided over her body and face in an icy trail like Rose's used to. "And DeeDee called too."

Anthony stuck the cigarette behind his ear and reached back for her, squeezing her hand. She didn't realize how much she missed their mutual telepathy until their fingers locked together in a lazy loop. Her small ones melted into his and he tugged her into his hot back while reassuring her she'd survive this.

His mama side-eyed their conjoined hands. "I know your phone ain't broke 'cause DeeDee ain't out to break it. Why you been ignoring everybody calls?"

"I been busy all day."

"Right, I see it on your face. The laws ain't gon' be coming around here, is they?"

"Not unless they coming for you."

She swatted his shoulder. "You ain't funny."

Venus took advantage of the lull in their conversation to thrust out a shaky hand. "I'm Venus."

Cigarette smoke suffocated her while his mama stared at her outstretched hand like it was nothing.

Anthony watched them until his mama took another long drag from her cigarette and then pushed her hand into Venus'. She snatched it away before their hands could even embrace.

"Carlotta," she uttered, reaching up to rake one of her kinky curls back into her ponytail.

"Nice to meet you."

"Mhmm...you too."

Satisfied with their lackluster introduction, Anthony looked over his shoulder.

"Come in the house, Shaun!" he yelled, pushing the front door until the hinges creaked and it swung open.

Shaun stopped bouncing the basketball, and they all ambled into the house behind Anthony like they'd been waiting for him to show up so they could go in.

It was hot inside, but she could've been imagining it because she was on his and Tori's turf for real now. Tori laid sprawled on the couch in the living room with a box fan blowing on her exposed back while a Barbie commercial played on the TV.

Anthony pulled her hand, and they walked over to Tori.

That weird pang came back to her middle as she peeked at his tortured face when he grabbed Tori's backpack from the floor and leaned over her.

Tori wasn't his, and it felt wrong to even think those words. She didn't have deep brown eyes with curly lashes like him. Her mouth didn't curve in a perfect bow and her skin wasn't the color of Daddy's banana bread. She didn't have smatters of freckles. She didn't look anything like Anthony. It hurt in a belly aching way that made her nauseous and want to give him that baby he talked about back in the car, no matter how ridiculous it sounded.

He picked Tori up from the couch and slung her over his shoulder without letting Venus' hand go. She held her breath, hoping and praying Tori wouldn't crack her eyes open to see her.

Carlotta trailed them from the living room to the cramped kitchen that was even hotter. Anthony flicked on the lights just as a roach scurried under the refrigerator. Venus' eyes darted from the roach to her smiling face on the welcome letter the school had mailed to her students over the summer. Somebody had tacked it onto the fridge next to a calendar.

She gulped.

"You gon' go pick up DeeDee tomorrow?" Carlotta asked from behind them.

She was like a gnat he kept trying to swat away, but she wouldn't leave.

A line of blood trickled down Anthony's arm while he balanced Tori on one hip, hoisted her backpack over his empty shoulder, and held Venus' fingers. Venus wanted to wipe the blood and pull Tori's backpack off his shoulder so he could yank his jeans up and get himself together, but she thought better of it.

"I'm not talking about this with you right now—" he started, letting go of her hand.

"But I told her you was gon' take care of it. It ain't right to have her sitting down there."

"Why you making plans with my money?"

"I'm not!"

"Mama..."

"I just don't think it's right."

Tori's limp body dangled in his arms while he swiped the cigarette from behind his ear and grabbed a lighter from the kitchen counter. "I don't remember asking what you thought about it."

Venus wanted to shake him by the shoulders and tell him to tell *Carlotta* to bail Deeanna out, but that's how she and Rose's beef started. Rose said she was always overstepping her boundaries.

Warmth buzzed off Anthony's body, and he breathed hard as he struggled to light the cigarette.

"Next week, my check is supposed to be decent. I can help you pay half—"

"Pay me the half and then what? Then who gon' pay your bills?"

"Don't talk like that in front of folks." She eyed Venus.

"What you talking in code for? She know who DeeDee is and where she at and she know Brian can bail his own baby mama out."

So that was his name.

It didn't sound opulent to her, just like Trey's didn't to Anthony.

"Call him up and tell him to go get her and then you can put your money toward my lawyer's retainer since you wanna help so goddamn bad."

His deep voice got louder and Tori shuffled closer into his neck like she knew whose arms she was in. She moved just enough to give him space to light the cigarette, but Venus couldn't take it anymore.

She tugged Tori's little body until Tori uncurled her fingers from his tattered shirt and sank into her chest because she was a professional overstepper. She couldn't help it when Rose stuck her nose too far into Trey's business and now she had another crazy mama with the same twinkle in her eyes.

"She made a mistake," Carlotta said. "When you gon' move on?"

"*A mistake?*" He huffed. "I don't think you understand what the definition of a mistake is."

"Don't talk to me like I'm stupid."

He blew out a cloud of smoke, shaking his head. "A mistake is something done in error... a misstep... a blunder. A *mistake* is unintentional."

They were veering into an uncomfortable territory that made sweat pool at the small of Venus' back. She wanted them to talk in code again because the more she found out about Deeanna, the more she judged her.

He pointed at Carlotta with the cigarette dangling between his fingers. "You done sat on the phone all month and trauma bonded with that bitch because she stuck in jail and now she convinced you that cheating on me, having a baby with another man, and convincing me it was mine her whole pregnancy was a mistake. Me and you must got different definitions of the word 'mistake.'"

He belted out a sardonic laugh that made the hairs on Venus' arms stand.

"We all make mistakes. How long you gon' hold this over her head?" Carlotta asked.

"When you gon' learn her? Huh? You hated her when you thought CPS was gon' take your grandbaby, but now y'all back cool, because she call you every day and pretend to be interested in what you got to say." He nodded. "And now I should forgive her? Bet."

Carlotta had struck a nerve in him but he was still the Anthony she'd grown to know—cool, calm, level-headed and running mental laps around his mama despite being so young. That beautiful mind was at work, even when he was angry and tortured.

Tori shuffled in her arms and let out a tiny whimper that made Anthony beckon them to him with a lazy wave. They shuffled toward him while Carlotta threw icy daggers their way. It almost seemed like Deeanna was there—giggling at all the trouble she'd caused from jail.

She'd never known a girl who could warp folk's minds without being in their presence and wreak so much havoc on a man that he'd turned into some sort of philophobe himself.

He took a lazy drag from the cigarette and pushed her curls out of her eyes until a door creaked from somewhere in the house. His hand dropped to her neck, and he pulled them into his chest like he was protecting them from a brewing storm.

The storm in question rounded the entryway of the kitchen and shuffled inside—silver haired, brown-skinned and freckle faced like her grandson.

"I don't remember my kitchen being a communal space for you all to meet, bicker, and air out your dirty laundry in," she said.

Her voice was like a splash of cool water on Venus' hot body.

She'd forgotten all about Anthony's granny because Carlotta and Anthony's saga had her distracted.

His granny dragged her house shoes across the tiled floor and stopped at the refrigerator, flinging it open as if they weren't there. She pulled out a bottle of cranberry juice and popped its seal. After taking a swig, she turned on her heels and eyed them all like they were children. When her eyes swept across Venus, they stopped on her hair and she squinted.

"You always so involved in your student's family drama?"

Venus' eyes got big, and she choked on her tongue. "No...I..."

She raised her eyebrows and took another sip of juice. "You what?"

"No... I'm not."

In her twelve years of teaching she'd came across kids her heart beat differently for and fine daddies that made her question her loyalty to Trey, but she'd never had an Anthony. He made her feel foolish for ever thinking she'd forget how to swim.

His granny drew her lips down and nodded. "Good."

Next, her eyes shot to Anthony's bloody face. "I'm not asking and I for damn sure don't want you telling me. One of these days you gon' end up dead."

He leaned back against the kitchen counter and they sparred with their eyes until he backed down and ashed his cigarette in an ashtray next to the sink.

"Take your baby and her nice teacher home and have her get you together, Nuney," she said, pulling her robe taut. "I'll explain to Carlotta why it'd behoove her to stay out of you and Deeanna's drama."

———

Rain pelted Venus' windshield as she trailed the Benz she drove the weekend before.

Just fifteen minutes before, they'd walked out of Anthony's

granny's kitchen with Carlotta's eyes searing into them. His granny's voice had floated out the door with them.

"Let him figure this shit out with Deeanna on his own, Carlotta. He was violated — not you."

Her words sobered Venus even if she wasn't talking to her. It was the first time she'd ever thought of what Deeanna did as a violation, but the more she mulled over the strain in his voice when he confessed, the more she saw it for what it was.

Her eyes crossed from the heavy raindrops and his brake lights as she drove into the entrance of an apartment complex and pulled into a parking spot two spaces away from where he parked. She shook her head to clear her vision and reconcile with the fact she was actually going to his place.

She was being stupid again. He made her that way, though. It was easy for him.

"Come home and talk to me," he'd said after strapping Tori in her car seat and turning to her.

"I don't think that's a good idea."

"Come on...you can't let it be us for another night?"

She could.

She was grown, and he was too, and her new heartbeat told her it was best she let him quell its erratic beating because she saw the fire in his eyes.

Instead of letting her make up an excuse, he curled his arms around her waist and then palmed her ass in that boorish way she'd grown to love. He dropped his face into her neck, swiping his lips against her skin.

"Let me have you for one more night."

When he said it that way, she couldn't say no. He had damn near begged and she knew that Anthony Nunez wasn't a beggar, just like he wasn't a ghoster.

He lived in a quiet complex about a mile from his granny's. It was midsize, and he felt comfortable enough to leave her, Tori, and his running car downstairs while he ran up to his apartment. He came back with an umbrella over his head.

When he saw her reaching for her door handle, he shook his head and waved his hand for her to sit back. He balanced the umbrella and unloaded Tori and her things before trekking to her car with Tori clinging to his chest as the rain fell around them.

As soon as he got to her car, he stooped down and pulled her door open, but she couldn't move to turn the engine off. She was stuck because she was stupid enough to have missed him...even her body did.

He frowned and cocked his head back while staring at her through a pair of glasses he'd thrown on when he went inside to grab the umbrella. They solidified his *blerdiness* and were another thing she was happy to learn about him—he wore glasses—sexy black frames that made her kill the ignition.

He didn't give her a chance to step out before he tugged her arm. She stumbled outside and into the other side of his chest. The wind picked up as they moved together, stomping up the stairs and spilling into his apartment.

The first thing she noticed was the smell. It smelled sweet inside, just like them.

She took a deep inhale, swallowing the strawberry scent, and then cautiously peeled her wet sandals off her feet.

She looked around.

So *this* was their turf—a cozy two bedroom with a sectional and the absence of a woman's touch. Deeanna's shoes weren't sitting by the door, and there weren't any decorative vases or flowers to brighten up the neutral decor. It was just him, Tori, and the culmination of all their stuff from their busy week lying around. They even had more furniture than her.

"Let me go put her down," he rumbled from beside her, kicking his muddy sneakers off and dropping Tori's backpack on the floor. "Go in my bathroom. I'll be in there in a minute."

He resurrected those struggling butterflies in her stomach again as he walked off to a door with a fuzzy T hanging off the doorknob. Tori dangled from his arms in a daze. She opened her eyes long enough to give Venus a confused blink and gurgle out a whimper that made Anthony "shush" her and cradle her head.

Venus dropped her purse beside her sandals. She shuffled into the living room and picked up a plush giraffe while Anthony's deep murmur floated from Tori's room. She imagined he was telling her frilly little lies to coax her back to sleep.

An empty, pink plastic bin sat in front of the patio door, so she tossed Tori's odds and ends inside. Afterward, she lined his sneakers next to the front door and straightened the pillows back against the couch. She'd almost made it to the kitchen until Anthony pushed out of Tori's bedroom, shaking his head.

"You must want me to keep you for more than a night," he garbled out, closing the door.

She paused, with his hoodie dangling from her hand, and looked back at him. His eyes swept the living room rug that was hidden underneath their clutter before she got there. When Daddy said marriage had done a number on her, he should've told her about all the things she'd never unlearn, no matter how hard she tried.

"Did she see me?" she asked, wringing the fabric between her fingers.

"She won't remember it."

"We shouldn't sneak around in her space. It's not right."

"Ain't nobody sneaking around but you." He walked up to her and tugged the hoodie out of her fingers.

She studied his battered face again, pulling her bottom lip into her mouth to taste him. "I guess tonight wasn't one of those slow nights, huh?"

He nodded. "I told you to go in my bathroom. I'll be in there."

"It must be gold in there. We can talk in here. You know that, right?"

He laughed at her foolishness.

Talk?

She actually thought she could avoid the inevitable.

He grabbed her face, studying it and clicking his tongue. "Who got you curious enough to go on a date?"

She'd forgotten all about Victor and that dive bar, but Anthony hadn't. He'd probably been thinking about them ever since she blurted that she'd gone out. It must've been hanging out in the back of his head between his confession, the drive home, and the walk upstairs. She'd actually gone on another date in Atlanta... and it wasn't with him.

Her mouth grew dry at the thought of him fucking the curiosity out of her like he said he used to do to Deeanna. She tried to swallow, but he controlled that too.

"Go 'head," he muttered, nudging her face to the side. "Put your stuff in my room."

She even liked that. Trey never did shit like that.

This time she listened and grabbed her purse and shoes from beside the front door before trekking toward the bedroom opposite Tori's.

She nudged the door, and it creaked. After learning Anthony, she didn't know what to expect behind the darkness because he was so different from any man she'd ever known intimately. He was much more than Logan's "eccentric" label.

When she flicked on the light and saw his made up bed and Tori's purple portraits lining the bottom of the wall above the baseboards, she smiled.

"That girl..." she muttered, knowing Anthony hadn't made a fuss about it.

According to his philosophy, life was too short to worry about silly things like baseboards.

She eyed the only other furniture in the room—a floor-length mirror and a tufted chair that seemed out of place. There were no video games or things from other women lying around. It was all him.

She sat her purse and shoes in a small nook beside the bedroom door and walked inside the bathroom, looking around.

There wasn't toothpaste slathered inside the sink or gunk

splattered on the mirror. Daddy would've said he was a good dude. He thought all good dudes were neat freaks like him.

She gripped the edge of the sink, studying herself in the mirror—her wild hair, bruised lips, and wrinkled romper.

"No more after tonight, Venus." She shook her head. "No more."

A quiet tap on the door made her jump.

He didn't give her a chance to pull herself together before he pushed inside shirtless and holding a frilly bath bomb.

She grinned wryly. "A purple cupcake? Who's that for?"

"You. It's lavender. If you ever dye your hair back black, I don't know what Munch gon' do with all this purple shit."

He pushed her at the waist and closed the door behind him.

"Is that from one of her infamous Amazon hauls?"

"Yeah." He glanced at it, turning it between his fingers. "It turns the water purple."

Her middle turned in that painstaking way again at the thought of some other man whisking Tori away.

"Does...does Brian know she likes purple?"

He thrusted his head up with his lips twisted. "You ever talked to Brian Torres? He ever called you up to request a meeting so he can know who's teaching his baby five days out the week? Is he fighting you and Logan about goddamn SPED evaluations? Did he pick my baby up when you kept her off the bus?"

She gulped and looked down as her breath grew shallow. "How'd you even find out?"

"In a fight after asking her why the fuck 'Midtown Family Health Center' kept blowing her up after business hours when that wasn't even the clinic her OBGYN worked out of." He chuckled, avoiding her gaze. "It wasn't no dramatic type shit, but I guess your girl yelling, 'that's why she ain't your baby anyways, nigga' would cripple any man in a fight. I damn near dropped to my knees."

She reached out, running her hands across another smatter of blood on his face. "Oh, Ant..."

"She told me she was done with me over the summer for real this time because she was tired of all the back and forth, the fighting, the making up and breaking up. She told me the Rolex she'd been wearing was a gift from him and that he was gon' leave his wife for her. The next day, I came home to an empty apartment. A month later, the cops come calling me talking about they at Phipps and they taking my girlfriend to jail and if I don't pick up our daughter, DFCS was gon' take her. So I went and picked her up. Then the next week, a sheriff at my granny's door with papers saying Brian wants full custody of my daughter."

She had *so* many questions. There were so many blanks she wanted to fill in but couldn't because only he and Deeanna could. All she could do was accept the tiny bits of their history he gave her.

He left her at the sink to turn on the bathtub's faucet and toss the bath bomb inside. The water turned a deep purple that fascinated the little Venus that still lived inside her and quelled some of the aching she felt for Anthony. She'd have to buy Tori another one.

"C'mere," he muttered.

She shuffled toward him and then let him roll her romper down the length of her body.

It wasn't like that first night they spent together, where hesitation laced her every move. This time she moved fluidly against him, propping her hand on his shoulder and leaning in so close she wanted to taste him again.

Afterward, he helped her into the warm water and nudged her back. She sank down, trying to remember if there was ever a time she wanted to be in a space meant for relaxation with Trey.

There wasn't.

Her eyes sank and her shoulders sagged until she saw darkness.

A hard thud from a cabinet slamming made her eyes jolt open.

"What's his name?" Anthony asked.

"Who?"

"Your date."

His fingers weren't inside of her, so there was more bass in his question this time.

"Victor."

"Hmm... Victor." He chuckled, sitting on top of the toilet.

"Is that opulent enough for you?"

"Is it for you? You the one that's gon' have to live with it."

"Who says I have to live with Victor?"

"So you saying I have to live through more of these first dates with these so-called grown men that got you texting me as soon as they over?"

He talked like their fling would last forever, but it was just the playful flirting she'd gotten used to. They weren't meant to last.

She watched him through heavy lids as he leaned over the sink and poured a stream of alcohol over his knuckles. He winced, and she did, too.

He glanced up while sitting the alcohol down. "What, you can't hear or something? I asked you a question."

The question felt as good as that nudge he gave her face in the living room.

"Yes, I can hear, Ant." She smiled. "I'm not allowed to go on dates?"

He shrugged. "I ain't say that."

"It's allll in your tone. You're being unreasonable."

"Baby" lingered at the seam of her lips, but she didn't let it slip out this time.

"*You're* being unreasonable."

"How?"

"I ain't the one looking for somebody to pass the time with."

He turned on the sink's faucet and shoved his fingers underneath.

"You don't get it."

"Then make me get it. I don't wanna do shit else tonight but get it."

She wiggled her toes underneath the purple water and smiled.

His bickering even felt different.

He turned back to her, shaking the water off his red fingers and then dipping them into her purple water.

She sighed. "I woke up one day at thirty-five and realized the life I had wasn't mine anymore. It was gone—*poof*—just like that. Imagine starting over at thirty-five—no house, no kids, nothing to show for all the years I invested in a marriage. I ain't exactly a sexy coed anymore. Maybe...maybe I need to date with a purpose and Victor was a start."

She scoffed as her voice cracked and stared at the bubbles in the water, waiting on him to say something.

He snorted, dragging his fingers through the water.

"What's so funny?"

"You internalize too much of other people's fucked up opinions and expectations." He flicked the water at her and then grabbed a loofah that hung from a hook he had tacked to the shower's wall.

She smiled, flicking the water back at him. "*Expound*, Mr. Smarty-pants."

"Imagine starting over at thirty-five without being attached to some insecure, cheating ass man who was incapable of taking care of you," he mumbled, dragging the loofah against her legs.

He studied them so hard the new heartbeat she'd grown to love pitter-pattered from between her legs.

He picked up the loofah and squeezed it over her breasts that bobbed above the water. "Imagine waking up with the world in your hands and some stupid ass young nigga in your phone who don't want nothing from you but to bathe you, make love to you, and remind you it's okay to live. Can you *imagine* that shit, Venus Thibodeaux?"

twenty-two

. . .

ANTHONY WASN'T PERFECT.

Daddy said perfect men didn't exist. They were all flawed and some of them were broken, but that didn't mean they couldn't love. Venus didn't know why the thought came, but it did, like a fluttering leaf caught in the wind just like the night they stared at each other underwater.

"How long it's been?" Anthony murmured, tugging his towel off of her body while they stood in the middle of his bedroom.

Their brains had synced together so beautifully that she already knew what he was referring to.

"A while," she replied.

He wiped the water off her back instead of responding to her embarrassing answer. Next, he swiped the towel down her legs, massaging them as he wiped.

"Ain't nothing wrong with that," he finally muttered.

He wasn't God or some all knowing entity, but she believed him. It was okay that she couldn't remember the exact amount of days or months since the last time she had sex. It was okay, just like starting over at thirty-five was okay.

When he finished drying her off, he studied her body while

she studied his red eye. The bedroom light shined against her skin and she opened her mouth to rally against it, but he shushed her with that bass in his voice that she loved to hate sometimes.

"How the fuck I'm supposed to see you when you doing all that?"

"All...all what?"

"All that insecure shit you did with Trey." He snorted, wagging his finger at her. "That ain't part of the objective tonight."

He took a step forward, and she took one back, bumping into that random tufted chair. He grabbed her hand and then reached around her, gripping the chair at the top.

"C'mon," he muttered, pulling her from in front of it.

Her breath grew shallow, and her legs shook as she turned around and walked. He trailed behind her with the chair.

"Right here," he said, making her stop in front of the floor-length mirror that rested against the wall.

He turned the chair around so the back faced the mirror.

Finally, she got it.

Those three random pieces of furniture weren't random at all. They all had jobs. The tufted chair belonged in front of the mirror and the bed was where he tossed her towel, his jeans, his glasses, and then his boxer briefs.

He didn't even give her a chance to study his dick again. All she wanted was to make sure it was still pretty and curved like the last time she saw it.

"Truth?" he asked, gripping her wet curls in a tight hold and nuzzling her neck.

He walked them in front of the chair as she stuttered out, "yeah...tr... truth."

"You gonna be quiet enough, or am I gon' have to make you be quiet?"

Goosebumps swathed her arms as he swatted the back of her leg. She lifted it into the chair and let him push her over the back of it. Now she couldn't escape their reality because it stared at her in the mirror as he stood behind her.

They looked like they'd made love thousands of times in a past life—like he'd given her the babies she deserved—like he'd came home after work and told her to go to their room so he could relieve the stress that had built up throughout the day while she took care of home. They looked like perfection.

Her eyes sank as he pushed his lips against her neck and twisted her hair. "Answer me."

"You gotta make me be quiet," she muttered, quivering underneath him.

"I can do that." He yanked her hair tighter, and she felt his bulbous head sliding against her slick folds.

His first stroke took the wind out of her and it wasn't even a stroke. All he'd done was slide his dick inside of her and make her feel complete. It throbbed against her walls and she exhaled a ragged breath at the way they fit together.

"You feel perfect," he whispered, meeting her eyes in the mirror and tugging her hair.

It was such a simple statement, yet no other man she had sex with had ever said it.

"You feel *so* perfect," he double downed. "And you look so fuckin' good. This what you been wanting?"

Yes!

And it felt exactly how she imagined it would. It filled her to the brim.

And that curve she'd fallen in love with?

It hit every wall Trey neglected throughout their marriage.

"Answer me." He pulled out and rubbed against her, teasing her so much she squealed.

"Nuh uh." He smiled, shaking his head and pulling out. "Fuck. Don't move."

She couldn't help but smile back when he stumbled from behind her and picked up the remote from underneath a stray pillow on his bed. When the TV came on, it was already on a random channel playing the type of music he liked.

It had been so long since she made love that she felt her heart beat in her throat while some R&B song she hadn't heard since junior high played. She closed her eyes until he got back to her.

He gripped her sides, positioning her at the perfect angle. She gasped when he plunged back inside of her, but Jaheim's crooning overpowered it. Her heart fluttered in wild spasms while she fought against the lethargy his dick caused. Its flutters were in sync with her new heartbeat and she closed her eyes to bask in them being together.

He hooked his hand around her throat. "Open your eyes and look at us."

Her fingers dug into the chair's soft fabric while she pried one eye open and then the other.

"You see how it's supposed to be?" he asked, pushing in and out slowly.

An ugly mewl fell out of her mouth.

"It's only supposed to be me inside you like this—nobody else, Venus. Fuck Victor. He ain't me."

"I...I know," she huffed out.

Her body folded into itself because it'd been so long since a man made her feel anything while making love.

Fuck. There it was again.

Love.

It floated around and went in and out of her head in the same rhythm as his strokes, and she couldn't jokingly refer to him as a boy anymore because boys didn't talk like him. They didn't make her clamor to get away because she couldn't take so much pleasure at once, either. It was too much.

"Don't run from me. You not a runner no more. Remember?" he grunted, digging his fingernails into her skin and hoisting her back up. "Show me how good you can take my dick. I'll be patient while you get it together. I promise."

A moan as ugly as that mewl she let out came barreling up her throat, but he caught it with his mouth.

His tongue stabbed against hers and he swallowed it with a laugh while smacking the back of her leg. "Shhhh."

She couldn't. Not when he kept slow stroking her into oblivion and talking to her in a way she never knew she needed because the men in her past didn't understand mental foreplay. None of them could talk a lake into her panties like Anthony did.

"Come on... arch your back."

He pressed the small of her back until it contorted into the perfect curve he approved. She pinched her eyes closed and waited for the inevitable, but nothing came except for a hot, stinging slap on her ass that made her yelp.

"Look at me."

She pried her eyes back open, and they crashed into his.

"Ant..." she whimpered.

"Did he touch you?"

She shuddered at the thought of Victor's hands on her body. She hadn't even wanted their arms to brush as if Anthony was in that dive bar watching and waiting for her to do something as crazy as that.

"No, baby." She shook her head with too much enthusiasm. "I didn't...I wouldn't. I swear."

She wouldn't?

Her words sounded foreign, and her body looked different. Who was this person staring back at her all disheveled, drunk off a man... and *sexy*? There was a time she couldn't look at herself in the mirror when she made love and now she hated she couldn't keep her eyes open to stare at this new woman Anthony created.

Her eyes sank again.

"Look me in my eyes and tell me." He pulled her back by the neck so he could torture her with their perfect reflections while he ground into her like he was making love.

Her mind wandered to all kinds of strange and beautiful places where she agonized over crazy shit like the fact other women had gotten the chance to make love to him in the past.

They looked into each other's eyes and she saw a softness in his. It made that fleeting thought she kept trying to get rid of come drifting back.

"I...I didn't let him touch me."

"Why'd you do that? Huh? Why you go out with him?"

"I...I told you why..." She gasped again. "I thought it was the right thing to do."

He scoffed. "The right thing? D'you forget you was my business?"

"No...no."

She could never forget that hard and fast rule he spat in her classroom.

It should've been embarrassing that something like that would ever turn her on, but on Anthony's turf it was okay to like it, to like him, to like the way his thumb fell between her glutes and dipped inside of a place no other man's thumb had been. Everything bad was okay.

She felt a fullness that made her back dip lower.

"Pretty ass arch..." he murmured, letting her wet hair go and planting a hand in the middle of the dip in her back. "Look at how beautiful you look when I'm inside you."

She'd never made love to a man that paid so much attention to the innocuous details of her body and talked about them like he did.

She watched his reflection while he studied the parts of her she hated, like the dimples in her ass. He massaged them and the rest of the shit she agonized over when she got dressed some-times—her cellulite, her stretch marks, and the extra weight that came with age.

"You was really tryna leave me over some subpoena, huh? Over a court date?" he asked. "That's why you agreed to go out with him? You was trying to forget about me…about my baby… about us."

"No, I wasn't."

"Don't get on your fuckin' knees and lie to me, Venus."

When he said her full name with his dick and thumb nestled deep down inside of her, her stomach turned like she'd been called to the principal's office.

"That's the worst place you can lie to me. You know that?"

"Yea—uh…"

Deeanna's voice reverberated through her head.

"I got on my knees and begged your ass for forgiveness!"

She fell forward until he gripped her hair back into his free hand and yanked her up for thinking about Deeanna while they made love. She was so used to their mutual telepathy that hearing the shit he wasn't saying out loud felt like second nature.

"You'd leave me over something silly like that? Don't tell me you a fickle wife."

He leaned over her and covered her mouth with his. Their tongues intertwined, and he controlled the rhythm of the kiss while pushing himself so deep inside of her, she choked.

"Ant…" she garbled into his mouth.

He swallowed his name and the rest of the jumbled words she wouldn't remember when she woke up.

"Don't call me that if you not gon' stand on it." He ground deeper inside of her and hit a wall she didn't even know existed. "Now, explain yourself. You really thought you could leave me?"

"I…I was scared…about my job. My boss told me to…to… stay away from you. I can get fired if he finds out about us."

"You don't trust me to take care of you if something happened? Huh? You think I'd let you stress about money?"

"No! *Fuck.* You don't understand!"

He let go of her hair and delivered a smack that knocked the wind out of her. "Then make me understand."

She whimpered out a pathetic "baby" without all the bass attached to it.

"I wasn't gonna leave you. I swear."

This wasn't the playful banter from inside her car. This was the side of Anthony she didn't know. *This* was where all his insecurities came out—all his Kayden-like tendencies he kept under wraps until he got pushed too far.

"You lying to me, huh? She do me the same way...always running off trying to find somebody better... always disappearing when I need her. Always *fuckin'* lying."

"No, Ant. I...I...I'm not her. I promise, baby. I'm not."

"Then fix us." He yanked his thumb and dick out of her right as an orgasm teased her. "Show me how you gon' make us right again after all this stupid shit about court and...and some ugly ass nigga named Victor. Show me why you the only wife I'd ever accept."

————

Venus was perfect.

Lola always said women like her existed—gentle women who wouldn't stomp on his manhood and make him rethink life, women that cared if he made it home and didn't shame him for obsessing over another nigga's seed. Anthony swore they were unicorns until Venus came bursting into his life with purple hair and a stained white button down.

She crawled out of his chair with raw knees and circled him so fast he didn't have time to bask in the way her naked hips swayed or appreciate the gentle nudge she gave his chest.

He fell back into the chair, swallowing her scent as she climbed onto him. He tasted all the innocuous parts of her— the notes that made her the woman she was—like her divorce, the disappointing men that kept finding their way into her orbit, and the secrets she kept from him about her life with Trey.

"Shhh…" she moaned, throwing her legs over his and squatting onto his dick. "I'd never lie to you."

Her promises felt too good, like DeeDee's used to when they made love.

She gripped his face between her hands and pecked his lips. "Why you talking like that, huh? You want me to talk it out with you first? I promise I'll ask how you feel about it next time, okay?"

Her promises were too perfect—as if she'd actually ask for his permission to date other people when *they* weren't even dating. He didn't know what they were doing, but he knew it felt right.

Her promises made his heart beat in loud *kabooms* that vibrated up to his head and made him dizzy. They reminded him he wasn't supposed to fuck her. He was never supposed to fuck her because he was supposed to make love to her just like this, in all the positions that made her feel him deep in her chest.

She hooked her arms around his neck and shuddered as his dick disappeared inside of her. "You talking crazy, ba…baby."

When she called him that, it felt like somebody had wrapped a warm blanket over his body and swaddled him in it. There were other women who called him "baby," but theirs didn't sound like Venus'. Hers were draped with that worldliness that came with being a woman who had been with stupid ass men before him. Those men got to see her at her most vulnerable—before she knew how to kiss, how to fuck, or how to love.

He closed his eyes as she nuzzled his neck, bouncing up and down. "You always come first. That's the objective tonight, right, baby? To show me how stupid I was to think I could ever put another man before you. I can't do that, Ant."

She rode dick like she danced for a living and spat sweet nothings better than he did when she realized how far gone his mind was. He could've died right there with her on top of him and he wouldn't have given a fuck how compromising it looked when the coroner came.

"*Fuck*," he grunted, letting his head roll back while she rocked back and forth against him.

She raked her fingers through his hair, still grinding to the imaginary rhythm that only existed in their heads. "You really think I'm a fickle wife? If I was a fickle wife, I wouldn't have picked you up, got judged by your damn family, held you accountable for the stupid shit you do, or...or... cared so much about your baby. I'm a 'till death do us part' type of wife and I think deep down you know that."

God, he did.

He wanted them to exist in another universe where he was the man she told that to, at the altar, because that's how making love warped his brain.

Her nails scraped against his scalp and his nails scraped her ass while he tried to fight through the spell she cast on him.

Her softness was the perfect juxtaposition to his hardness, and they were doing the same shit they'd done in her car, but this time she stole his voice so he couldn't fight back. All the crazy things he wanted to say got crossed up on their way from his brain to his voice box while she planted little wet kisses on his neck with a soft hum.

"What're we doing? Huh, baby?"

He opened his mouth to remind her they were making love like they were supposed to, but a deep guttural moan came out instead.

He didn't even recognize the sound coming out of his own mouth because he'd *never* moaned while making love—not even the night he swore he got DeeDee pregnant with Munch.

The moan made Venus rock her hips back and forth in another one of those moves he'd been side eyeing until he remembered she had lived more life than he had. She'd perfected the art of riding and pillow-talking to those other men he hated. It was an irrational hate that made him clamp his nails deeper into her ass and meet her next grind with a deep stroke.

Their skin slapped together in an intoxicating clap that made his dick harder. She swiped her tongue against his neck and pulled the skin into her mouth, sucking on it until he trembled.

Damn.

Did he even know what making love was before he met her?

"I've never lied to you—*ever*. I'm too fuckin' grown to do that shit, Ant."

He thought he'd been making love to DeeDee, but he hadn't. Venus was teaching him—slowly and passionately, like she did with everything else in her life she loved.

Love?

He grunted, shaking his head as she rolled against him.

That word just wouldn't go away when she was around.

"I never felt like this before…"

Her words trailed off and his chest pumped out. Out of all the men she'd been with, he'd been the one to fill her and stretch her out so much her eyes rolled to the back of her head.

He shot up from the chair with her dangling from his waist and stumbled toward the bed.

"Wait…wait…" she yelped, trying to clamor up his chest.

He needed his voice back.

He needed to tell her she was the sexiest woman he'd ever had the privilege of burying his dick inside. He wanted to tell her he didn't know what to do because she was miles ahead of DeeDee on that list she'd probably scoff at. She'd crept forward and solidified her spot long before he even realized it. She'd set up shop there with his heart in her hand. He needed her to understand he didn't have it all figured out, but he'd try for her even when her promises sounded too good to be true.

Tiny gasps of air flew from the back of her throat while he bounced her up and down…and up and down. His name got sandwiched between them while she thrust her head back and begged for him, even though she already had him.

"Baby…please…I—don't let go of me."

They fell back onto his bed, where he landed on top of her

and pushed her legs open. She writhed around with her eyes closed and her fingers against her nipples—twisting and pulling.

He stood between her legs with his throbbing dick inside her —watching her get off like she was still alone in the world—like she didn't belong to him. He took note of the tiny nuances that came with making love to Venus Thibodeaux. Her crinkled pert nose, wild hair, and most importantly, the way she could feel again.

"You feel so good…" she whispered to herself, grinding against him. "Stay right there."

He'd live right there if he could.

"See how I listened to you and I'm fixing us? You should want a wife that'll always be willing to work things out with you."

She talked like he'd go out and search for an actual wife when she'd already ruined that idea for him. It would be impossible to find another Venus.

By the time he found his voice, he didn't even recognize it. It was warped and tired from fighting to come out while she taught him how to make love.

"Look at me, Venus," he croaked out. "Look at me…"

She didn't make him beg for long. Her eyes popped open, and she reached for his face, scraping her nails down his cheeks.

"You not fuckin' leaving me tonight," he whispered.

Or ever.

twenty-three

· · ·

DADDY'S IDEOLOGY about flawed men always hung in Venus' head when she'd convince herself to stay with Trey.

"I'll never get a perfect man," she'd tell Ginny. *"If I go out searching for a perfect man, I'll drive myself crazy. I...I wanna try and make it work. We're gonna go to counseling."*

Daddy never prepared her for a flawed, broken man that felt perfect even when he wasn't, though.

A loud, blood curling childish scream sliced through her dreams about flawed perfection and made goose pimples bubble up her arms.

"Baby—Ant." She gasped, shooting up with her body tangled in his sheets that smelled like him.

"Ahhhhhhhh!"

There was that scream again.

She pushed her dry curls out of her face and looked for him, but all that was left was the aftermath of their second night together.

His jeans dangled from the bed and her towel hung off the back of that chair she'd never forget.

The bright morning sun trickled inside through his blinds

and cast a glow on the TV. A pitter patter of little feet pounded across the floor and then the humming came.

The wheels on the bus go 'round and 'round, 'round and 'round.

"Munch, baby, I thought we was playing the quiet game," Anthony's voice boomed from the living room and her body vibrated in response.

She peeled her sticky legs apart, ignoring Rose and her finger pointing at that immature part of her brain.

Yeah, she'd let Anthony dive into her raw—over...and... over again. She didn't need Rose to remind her of how stupid she was to let it happen because it was bound to happen. Anthony told her it was every time he woke her up for more.

"Why'd it take my dumbass so long to make love to you?" he groaned out, planting kisses along her neck. *"Let me feel you again. You make me feel so full."*

That was the perfect description of their lovemaking— fullness.

Her body jerked from that stupid fleeting word again. It shouldn't have been there, but it wouldn't go away. It kept fluttering around them, no matter how many times she swatted it away.

She slid out of the bed, pulling the sheet taut around her breasts.

"My keys..." she whispered to herself, limping around his bedroom. "My phone...my purse."

She picked up his jeans, shaking her head at the splatters of blood on them and then folding them in a neat square out of habit. Next was his briefs. She raked her fingers against them and tried to ignore the warm vibration in her middle from breathing him in the next morning.

"You're getting distracted," she muttered, folding them up too. "Stop getting distracted, Venus. Your purse..."

She remembered seeing it resting against the wall in that little nook between his bathroom and closet.

She looked at it, but it was empty.

"Where's my shit, Ant?" She limped toward the space. "I can't stay—"

The door burst open, and she held in her gasp, staring at the floor. She tightened the sheet around her breasts.

"What you looking for?" Anthony drawled.

He sounded curious in a domesticated way, like she was rummaging around their house for something mundane, like her house shoes.

"My purse. I thought I dropped it here last night."

"What you need it for?"

"Ant..."

She couldn't turn around. She didn't want to. If she did, he'd win whatever game he was playing with her. She couldn't look at him.

"Did you take my purse?"

"What I need to take your purse for?"

"I didn't say you needed to. I know I sat it right here—"

"What you need your purse for? Where you going?"

Home.

The word got stuck in her throat as she turned around. Right as her hair brushed her eyelids, Tori came crashing into the back of his legs.

She needed to go *home*, but she wanted him again. He was battered, bruised and shirtless in daddy-mode, and for some odd reason, she felt like she was already home.

Tori smiled at her like she did in the mornings when she marched inside her classroom.

The air grew still between them and sometimes Venus wished everybody else's brains were like her kindergartner's. They didn't know anything about compromising situations and they weren't as jaded about the world as she was.

"I asked where you was going, Venus."

He and Tori stared her down with invigorated expressions as if she wasn't naked underneath his bedsheet. She gulped, but "home" was still stuck in her throat like a glob of dry sludge that wouldn't go down.

Tori's soft humming started back as she curled her arms around his legs and waited for the grown-ups in her life to do grown-up things.

"Anthony..." she breathed out, shaking her head.

And Bug.

She couldn't leave Tori out, but if she put them together, she'd sober up.

"I...I have an appointment with my therapist I gotta get—"

"Reschedule it," he said, laying his bruised cheek against the doorframe. "I wasn't pillow-talking last night. Go take a shower and put on some clothes. We been waiting for you to wake up."

———

Sundays weren't supposed to be like this. The possibility of them *ever* being like this vanished, just like Trey did as soon as he fell in love with somebody else.

As a newly single philophobe, Venus had decided she'd live the rest of her Sundays waking up to Pepper pawing at her feet, watching Keion Henderson sermons on her laptop, and cooking an over easy egg to go with her morning coffee.

She pulled open Anthony's refrigerator, and it felt just like his living room did when they came in the night before—absent of a woman's touch.

She shook her head at the lonely carton of eggs, pack of bacon, and gallon of milk. There were other odds and ends like maybe he'd try to cook a meal once, but never twice, and they had Fruity Pebbles—three whole boxes.

Tori hummed again and the soft scratching from her coloring the pages in her coloring book made Venus nostalgic for a time that never was.

Tori's antsiness had radiated off of her when Venus opened Anthony's bedroom door after showering and texting Michole, a pathetic "family emergency" excuse. She sat criss-cross apple sauce outside the door with that same beaming smile she wore at school until Anthony called for her to help him make up her bed.

He didn't keep an iPad shoved in her face to keep her out of his way and she didn't own a cellphone like most of the kids in her class. Instead, she helped him with all the things her tiny hands could handle, and that made Venus smile. Daddy would've said he was an old school parent—*kinda*.

She glanced at them at the dining room table as she pulled the eggs and bacon out of the refrigerator. "Please don't tell me y'all eat McDonald's every night."

He frowned, picking at the rubber bands that kept Tori's twists together. "Nah, we eat it every other night, smart-ass."

Tori balled her lips and looked up at him with bulging eyes. They mean-mugged each other until he stuck his tongue out at her and she giggled.

"I can say that word. Not you," he muttered, rolling the rubber band off of her hair.

After spending the morning with them, she understood why Anthony believed Tori talked at home. Her quiet personality was so big that it was easy to read her thoughts on her face, but she still hadn't said a word.

"You can go to the store if you want," he added.

"You took my purse."

"You still won't tell me what you need a purse for."

"There's this little thing called money." She shook her head. "I need it to buy those groceries that are MIA in your refrigerator."

He chuckled, raking his fingers through Tori's hair. "Oh, I see."

"What're you talking about?" she asked, sitting the carton of eggs and the bacon on the counter.

"Tell Trey I pay the cost to be the boss around here. We don't do that fifty-fifty shit." He smacked his lips. "Why none of your *grown men* ever act like grown men?"

A high-pitched giggle shot out of her and she felt that good feeling again—like she was on vacation. A wave of tropical air blew against her face as she walked to the stove. It tasted like him.

"You got two options. You can go to Walmart, get whatever you need, and make us late...or you can use what's in there and we can get out of here on time. Neither of 'em will bother me none. It'll bother JoJo's girl, though. She real, real punctual." He snorted.

She leaned against the edge of the stove and studied him as he studied Tori's hair behind his glasses. His tattooed biceps flexed while he moved in a relaxed way, like the good future husband he was.

Sundays *weren't* supposed to be like this.

She wasn't supposed to want to snuggle with Tori and then put her down for a nap so she and Anthony could sneak away to make love. She wasn't supposed to force herself to ask questions like, "what're we gonna be late for?"

"It's Sunday, and it's pre-season. The Falcons play the Lions. We supposed to meet up with everybody at eleven."

She turned to the cold burner in front of her. "We are?"

"Mhmm. Ain't you from Texas? Don't you know Sundays are for family, football, and Jesus?"

She gulped a mouthful of strawberry air while a bunch of excuses flew around in her head.

He hadn't told her he loved her nor had he asked to date her, but she was doing shit for him she promised herself she'd never do for another man... and she was supposed to meet his family today. Not the folks she'd already met, but the ones she saw every time her eyes brushed his knuckles.

"Now what's wrong?" he murmured in another one of those lazy domesticated slurs. "You want another option?"

Her heart sped up, and she stared at the cold burner on his stove until her vision grew blurry.

"Ms. T thinks something's wrong with our stove, Noni."

Her heart stopped.

Tori's little voice was light.

She'd whispered the words as if it was just her and Anthony there gawking at Venus fumbling around.

Tori talked?

Venus' shoulders drooped, and she whipped her head toward them, but Tori had already gone back to concentrating on the purple dog she'd been coloring as if she said nothing at all.

"Is that true?" he asked Tori, tossing a rubber band on the table and then gliding toward Venus.

Venus shuddered when his body heat cloaked her. His clean, soapy scent made her want to sink into him and her hard nipples pressed against his t-shirt she wore. They begged for his mouth.

He brushed her hair to the side and leaned over her to turn on the burner. "What's wrong with the stove?"

The burner lit up with a bright red ring around its edges. She shook her head because she didn't trust herself to not say another domesticated thing to him.

"Hmmm, so it ain't the stove then. It's you." He reached over her again, picking up a clean frying pan that'd been on the counter, and sitting it on the burner. "It's that egg metaphor again, ain't it?"

It was that egg metaphor and so much more. There was no way he could understand how terrifying swimming was after so long.

"You like your eggs over easy," he huffed out, running his hand across her stomach and massaging it. "You like to call me 'Ant' when I make you feel good and you call Tori 'Bug' sometimes, but you ain't told me why. Earlier, after you took a shower, you said 'baby, are y'all hungry?'"

Oh yeah.

She did say that after walking into Tori's bedroom and finding Tori nuzzling her little nose in his neck like she couldn't believe he'd made her sleep alone.

He leaned in closer to her ear. "And then I said, 'yeah, you gon' cook us breakfast?'"

She tried to turn her head to make sure Tori didn't see them so close, but he wouldn't let her. He kept his hand on her waist.

"You remember that?"

She nodded.

"We can't sit around while you mull over whether we're right or wrong about this shit. I only got you for the day, so let me have you."

The tense muscles in her shoulders relaxed in a way that couldn't have been good because Anthony did bad shit to her. He made love to her in a way that made her stupid. His fingers touched places they were never supposed to. His mouth said things she should've hated...and he gave her options—endless ones that made her understand what he meant the morning they woke up with the sunrise on their skin. How could she not want to do domesticated shit when he took care of all the everyday things that consumed her brain as Trey's wife? Now she had time to contemplate silly things—like the morality of their situation.

"Come on. You cookin' or you want me to buy somethin'?" He squeezed her stomach. "Decide before I do it for you. I'm hungry. I ain't ate since yesterday morning."

Her new heartbeat throbbed angrily as he breezed back toward the table and pulled at another one of Tori's twists.

"Bug," she choked out, glancing up to meet Tori's placid eyes. "You ever had Fruity Pebble French toast?"

twenty-four

. . .

JOSIAH WANTED TO MARRY JADE.

"I wanna watch her push her left hand in front of some thirsty nigga's face and blind his ass with the rock I put on her finger. Then I wanna watch her scribble 'Jade Joseph' on something stupid like a permission slip from Journey's school … and I wanna watch her do the shit over and over again for the rest of my life."

He was high when he blurted that ridiculous shit out. In fact, they were both high, sitting in his backyard, watching Jade and Journey walk around the pool.

Anthony had told him it was a dumb ass thing to say. There was *nothing* he wanted to watch the same woman do for the rest of his life. At least he didn't think there was until he met Venus.

She did all the boring wife and motherly shit DeeDee talked about, but was always too distracted to do. DeeDee didn't cook, clean, or read Munch bedtime stories. Shit, some days she didn't even get out the bed.

"Okay, this is Daddy's plate," Venus uttered, helping Munch divvy up the bacon she had fried.

He needed to ask Josiah if Jade made breakfast spreads out of nothing like Venus did? Did she fill their house with so much light that it felt dim when she wasn't home? And why did everything feel so much better when Venus did it? The sheets looked tighter when she made the bed, the living room somehow looked neater when she cleaned it, and the kitchen smelled like heaven because she had cooked. It was the simple things.

"This is your plate, Bug. We gotta make happy plates this morning, remember?"

And was it normal to wanna hold her so much she would have to peel herself off of him every day?

He swiped his wet hands down the length of his fleece shorts as she strode toward him with Munch in tow and their plates in her hand.

She sat his in front of him while he shifted in his seat to keep his dick from popping up. If he ever got the chance to run into Trey, he'd hem him up until he got the answers he wanted.

How the fuck could he have ever divorced Venus Thibodeaux?

Munch climbed in the chair to the right of him with her eyes set on the Fruity Pebble french toast Venus helped her cut into tiny squares. She'd held her hand over Munch's little one and guided the butter knife through the bread while his stomach twisted in knots.

"What're you waiting for?" Venus asked him, swiping a dollop of syrup from Munch's plate and licking it off her finger as she waltzed back into the kitchen.

"You."

She smiled around her finger and chuckled. "You said you hadn't ate since yesterday morning, so eat...boss."

He shook his head, smirking.

He wanted her *bad*, and he wanted her in that nauseating dumbass way Josiah talked about. He wanted Venus to talk shit while whipping up his breakfast every Sunday morning. He wanted her to play Patty Cake with Munch while they waited on the bacon to finish frying and for her to call him "Ant" every time he watched her too hard.

"I can't make magic with you staring at me, Ant," she'd complained from behind the stove. *"Ain't that right, Bug?"*

Munch nudged his leg under the table and raised her bushy eyebrows at him.

He was embarrassing her in front of her favorite human on a Sunday by being so thirsty he couldn't even think straight.

Sundays were usually spent preparing for Mondays where Munch got to float into school to see Venus, but now she'd gotten her a day earlier in a way her classmates never would and that privilege didn't go over her little head. He needed to tighten up or he wouldn't hear the end of how "annoying" he'd been because Munch was in her angsty kindergarten phase. Anything she didn't deem normal was "annoying."

Venus sashayed back to the table with a meager two slices of bacon, a piece of french toast and scrambled eggs.

He swallowed the ball in his throat.

"What am I supposed to wear for this football thing today? I don't have anything here." She sighed, sitting in the chair to his left. "And I need coffee."

"Whose fault is that? If you would've came home after the first night, you'd have clothes and a coffeepot here."

"Behave." She wagged her finger at him until he grabbed it and squeezed it and she smiled.

Munch giggled.

"Daddy's on a fast track to timeout. You know I make troublemakers like him sit out at recess."

She yanked her finger out of his grip and bowed her head over her plate while he and Munch stared at her like the heathens they were. Silent words fell out of her mouth until she felt their stares and one of her eyes popped open.

Her mouth curved into a gentle smile as her other eye popped open. "Do you know how to bless your food, Bug?"

Munch blinked back at her.

"It's easy. I'll teach you like my daddy taught me, but we have to close our eyes."

They looked at him and he didn't argue about it. How could anybody argue when Venus talked in her sexy teacher's voice?

He looked over at Munch's serious expression and then closed his eyes. Venus grabbed his hand, and he grabbed Munch's.

"You can repeat after me...or you can say it in your head. Whatever makes you happy," she muttered the last part and for the first time since Munch came back home, he hoped she would talk to somebody other than him because Venus deserved it.

She deserved to experience all of Munch.

"God is great. God is good."

She paused to give him room to breathe and to give Munch the space to decide if she wanted to chime in. She didn't.

"Let us thank him for our food."

Venus paused again.

He squeezed Munch's hand, but she wouldn't budge even though she could talk to Venus because Venus was like him. Shit, after the night they had, she *was* him. He couldn't breathe without tasting her.

"By his hands, we are all fed."

He shouldn't have been thinking like he was while she talked to God, but he couldn't help it.

"Give us, Lord, our daily bread."

How could they go back to normal after Venus left?

"Amen."

She squeezed his hand, making him pry his eyes open. He blinked in a disoriented way and found her rolling her eyes at him.

"I'll teach you the grown-up version later. With the type of work you do, you ought to be praying to somebody," she mumbled.

God wouldn't like that his dick woke up at those words.

"You got a washer and dryer?" she added, biting into a piece of bacon.

"Why?"

"So I can wash my clothes...or do I have options for that too?"

"You always got options when you with me."

Her eyes lit up like no man had ever given her that luxury and, deep in his gut, he knew they hadn't.

———

Damn, they even had an orderly coat sized laundry room that sat in the very back of their kitchen. Venus was still schlepping her shit to the laundromat every Saturday.

She leaned against the washing machine, rolling her eyes up. She was alone, so she could mull over all the shit Anthony didn't want her to.

His voice trickled underneath the door while he left her to deal with her clothing dilemma. Thirty minutes before, he doled out more options to her after Tori had gone to her room to play while they sorted out their grown-up problems.

"Hm... the mall opens up at twelve and we supposed to meet at eleven. Take Munch with you. She likes the mall." He'd grunted, thrusting a wad of money at her while they stood in front of his bed. *"I think you want us to be late."*

She'd shaken her head and pushed the money away until he grabbed her at the waist and pulled her into his middle while they debated.

"You want me to wash your clothes, then?"

No man had ever offered to wash anything that belonged to her except Daddy. The old Venus still harbored the archaic beliefs that Rose had beat into her head, so of course she couldn't let Anthony touch her clothes or the pile of laundry he'd left above his washing machine. Rose didn't believe in a good man doing "woman's work."

She fingered Tori's tiny pink leggings that were strewn across his black button down with "Vaughn's" stitched across the breast.

She smiled.

Sundays weren't just for football, family or compromising

situations—they were also the start of the work week for Anthony.

He pushed into the laundry room right as she dumped his and Tori's clothes on top of hers and closed the washer's lid. His phone dangled from the crook of his neck while a voice she recognized prattled on the other end.

"Mhmm." He hummed, swiping his tongue out to wet his bottom lip. "All I asked was if you could cover the first hour of my shift, not interrogate me."

His hand glided across her ass while he stooped in front of the laundry basket she'd emptied and sat on the floor. "You was the one that told me we don't have to tell each other where we been or where we going—so I don't. I don't understand why we have this same conversation every other week."

"Because I changed my mind," Mikayla huffed back.

And caught feelings.

Venus snickered.

He frowned at the empty basket and looked up at her, pulling the phone away from his mouth. "You seen a black button down in here?"

She wanted to kiss him.

She'd *never* wanted to kiss a man questioning her about his laundry while another woman bickered for his attention.

"Can I ask you something?" Mikayla chirped while he stared at her with his eyebrow raised.

"Baby…" she whined from the phone. "You're not listening to me."

Baby?

All the negative self-talk Michole used to scold her about came into her head while she leaned against the washing machine, staring at some other woman's future.

"What's wrong?" he replied to Mikayla. "I'm listening to you."

And that was a problem—a huge one.

Now she wasn't mulling over whether they were right or

wrong, whether she'd scarred Tori, or what their lives would look like after she left. Now she was mulling over all those feelings she supposedly left behind after she signed her divorce papers.

"Mom sent me some news article…about…about a stolen car at a takeover last night. The person who took it crashed."

"I don't know what you even talking about right now, 'Kayla." He stepped forward and gripped Venus at the waist. "My shirt…where is it?"

Mikayla smacked her lips.

That hot turning in Venus' stomach made her shove her arm out and brace herself against his taut abdomen. His muscles contracted against her hand and he frowned harder because he didn't understand how that sliver of immaturity in her brain worked.

She scraped her nails across another stupid tattoo that sat above his bellybutton.

"Who has your shirt?" Mikayla asked. "I can bring you your other one you left here. I had Mom drop it off at the dry cleaners with my stuff last weekend."

He must've seen the fire in her eyes, because he shook his head like Mikayla could see him. "Nah, I just need you to cover that hour, not bring me my shirt. Can you do that for me?"

"And what will I get if I do it?"

"What you want?"

"You."

A jagged red trail prickled across his stomach while Venus dug her nails into his skin harder than she should have. They dropped further and further until they got to the exact place she wanted them. When she gripped his hard dick, she remembered why she was in the predicament she was in.

"Anthony?" Mikayla chirped.

Venus squeezed it until his teeth sank into his bottom lip. He was already rock hard and waiting for her to figure her shit out.

All those soft, feminine feelings came surging through her at once and settled between her legs where they pooled into the crotch of his shorts she wore.

"Yeah, what's up?" he answered Mikayla gruffly while blinking at her.

"I *want* you and I'm communicating that to you because you're always bitching about me not saying what I want. I miss you. You haven't been over here in two weeks."

Their mutual telepathy was back, but she didn't think it had actually gone anywhere. She'd just gotten used to it and she knew what those blinks meant.

Correct him.

Because Mikayla was getting beside herself and he was letting her. The girl didn't even know how to do his damn laundry. She probably didn't know how to cook or clean or how to make him belt out unrealistic shit when they fucked. Mikayla wasn't the wife she had hoped God would send him when everything between them was all said and done.

She squeezed him again and he let her explore him with no interference. There was even a proud little smirk on his face, like he was happy she'd gotten so revved up from a stupid phone call.

She yanked his shorts and briefs down in one swift motion and eased onto the cold floor. Being on her knees had never felt so satisfying and she'd been on them plenty of times before to please Trey and other unworthy men.

There weren't any mundane breakfast or clothing dilemmas for her to ruminate over. Tori had hummed herself into a nap while playing and the next day's problems didn't exist yet, so Anthony was all she had to focus on. Maybe she was finally practicing that mindfulness Michole always talked about.

"Let me hit you back," he muttered into the phone.

"Why? What's wrong? You sound upset."

"I'm...I'm not."

"Are you mad at me? Talk to me."

The bulbous head of his dick sat right in front of her lips

while Mikayla pleaded for him to do something he'd *never* do. She leaned forward with wide eyes and ran her lips across its smooth surface.

It was still beautiful.

She'd never get used to its beauty.

He cupped her chin and tugged her face up. That same little smirk danced across his lips as he shook his head.

"Hang up," she said, pressing her hands on her thighs. "Now."

Once again, she didn't recognize the woman who said those words.

Who was this chick?

He laughed, and she would have too if she were him. He had one on the phone begging for him and another one on her knees, and he didn't even bother to keep them separate. It was the beautiful privilege of being a man. She didn't hate it for him because he was much more deserving of that privilege than most other men she knew.

"Hold up, who you talking to like that?"

His words felt like that nudge he'd given her cheek the night before.

She smiled, leaning into his hand. "You."

"Anthony, who the fuck is that?" Mikayla squawked.

"Why you talking to me like that?" he asked, looking down at Venus.

"'Cause you not minding your business right now."

He laughed harder this time before murmuring, "I'm trying to get my shit ready for work so I won't have to do it later and you ain't playing fair."

"I'm talking to you, Anthony!"

She rolled her eyes and pulled her face out of his grasp. She'd be damned if she listened to another Mikayla conversation with one of her favorite parts of him resting in front of her face.

She grabbed his dick and he let her squeeze it while he stumbled over some stupid response to Mikayla, all because he wanted to spend an extra hour fuckin' around watching football with his friends.

"Look...let me call you ba—"

He sucked in a deep inhale as soon as she swallowed him.

His phone toppled to the floor in a dramatic fall. It crashed against the laundry detergent next to his feet and slid across the floor with Mikayla still seething on the other end.

He throbbed in her mouth and she savored it.

There was something about making love to him that made time standstill. As long as she was with him, she'd be thirty-five forever. He tasted like life, and she didn't want to inhale any other man.

He fell forward, gripping the edge of the washer. It vibrated against her back as their laundry spun out.

"Fuck," he hissed, digging his nails into the back of her hair and pushing her head down until she choked.

She'd never sucked dick with so much conviction nor was she ever interested in learning how Trey liked for her to suck his, but that wouldn't fly with Anthony. She wanted to learn it all for him, no matter how crazy it sounded.

"Why you not playing fair?" he breathed out, pulling himself out of her mouth and smearing her spit along the seam of her lips with the tip of his dick. "Now she over there trippin'. I ain't gon' hear the end of this shit tonight."

He didn't let her answer, but she didn't think he ever planned to.

He bent down and smashed his mouth against hers like it was the last time he'd be able to. His tongue tangled with hers in a sensual dance that made her belt out a moan.

As soon as he gave her the space, she swallowed his dick again and reveled in the way she almost brought him to his knees.

"And you expected me to let you leave?" he gasped out, laughing. "Fuck no. You ain't ever leaving me."

twenty-five

. . .

THE DRIVE to PDK was a grueling thirty minutes, but getting out of Anthony's apartment felt even longer. It had taken too long to pull his dick out of Venus' mouth and too much self-restraint not to bend her over his washing machine like she deserved.

He shuddered behind his steering wheel at the thought of some stupid ass lucky nigga getting head from her for the rest of his life.

"Did I..." Venus muttered to herself, looking at Munch in the backseat while gripping her lip gloss. "Okay, I thought I had put a bow on your head."

How the fuck did it all ooze out of her—motherhood, wifely duties, sexiness, magic?

He raked his fingers across his head as he drove along Peachtree.

"Oh, I hung your shirt up in the laundry room above those shoes Tori colored," she talked around swipes of lip gloss. "I pre-treated the shoes, just put them in a white pillowcase and throw 'em in the washer when you get a chance tonight."

So she wouldn't be there to do it for him while he stared at her?

"I own pre-treatment?"

"Ain't you the laundry expert?" She laughed, holding the lip gloss wand above her lip. "I'll explain how I did it later."

"I'm a *thong and bra* laundry expert. I don't know shit about washing no shoes."

She fell into the middle console, laughing and digging through her purse he'd finally let Munch take out of her closet and give back to her.

He swallowed again while Munch kicked the back of his seat and hummed.

Venus twisted her neck, turning to her in the backseat. "Bug?"

She stopped humming.

He wanted to turn and see Munch's big starry eyed look too. That shit never got old.

"I loved the beautiful purple artwork you created back at home, but we don't draw on our mommy's and daddy's things. In fact, we don't draw on anything but paper unless they buy you something special to draw on. Remember the no-no list in our classroom? Drawing on other people's belongings is on that list."

This time he couldn't help himself, so he took his eyes off the road for two seconds to catch the tail end of Munch's happy nod.

He wasn't supposed to feel warm or picture himself and Venus when she said "mommy" and "daddy," but it came as naturally as making love to her did. He needed Lola there to swat some act right into him because that angst was back. It's the only way he could explain the weird thoughts he kept having about parenthood and marriage when he should've been thinking about the fact he had a final custody hearing in four weeks.

"Why don't you hum Daddy the 'Quiet Song' we learned on Friday? I think he'll like it, 'cause Ms. T has had enough of 'Wheels on The Bus,'" she mumbled the last part, but he heard it and laughed.

Munch eased into the "Quiet Song" without arguing. He

didn't know the song, but it sounded like another silly nursery rhyme he wanted to hear Venus sing with her.

"Let me find out you taught them the 'Quiet Song' just for that reason." He smirked, pulling into the airport's entrance.

"Listen…when you're responsible for eighteen little people, you have to find creative ways to stay sane. I'm sure you do it in your own way at home."

"Maybe. Sometimes I like that insane feeling, though. Life is too quiet when she not around."

She smiled and raised her hand like she wanted to touch him, but put it down like she thought better of it.

Afterward, she looked away, frowning at the building. "Peachtree-Dekalb Airport?"

"Mhmm." He hummed, taking the short route to the terminal that he knew by heart.

Ever since Josiah had gotten drafted, PDK had become like a second home during football season. Shorter trips were easier to keep away from Dre's nosey ass PO, and Josiah liked to see Jade and Journey after away games. It made him less homesick.

"I thought we were going to watch football?" she asked.

"We are."

"Like, watch it at your people's house."

"Nah…" He shook his head, pulling into a parking spot next to Jade's Range Rover at the terminal. "We watching it at Ford Field. You ain't scared of flying, are you?"

Her throat jumped as she swallowed and sat forward. "Ford Field as in Detroit's Ford Field?"

"I don't know no other one."

Munch giggled at the way she grasped the dashboard and twisted her neck around.

Afterward, she glanced down at herself.

"Now what's wrong?" he asked.

She shook her head and then turned to look at the jet they'd be traveling on—a Gulfstream G700 that one of Dominic's NBA player friends gifted him.

"Nothing, nothing's wrong."

"We ain't separated yet, you know that, right? You can tell me."

"Separated? That's what we're gonna call it when I leave—a separation?" She snorted. "No more Avant for you."

"Mhmm. Whatever. Go 'head and explain yourself."

"Anthony…"

"Don't call me that."

"Don't be difficult."

"You the one being difficult."

He stared and waited until she poked her lips out and glanced down. "I'm wearing last night's clothes."

"I told you that you ain't have to wear last night's clothes."

She rolled her eyes. "And now I'm about to go on this nice ass plane to meet your people and I…I…"

It came out sloppy, but a burst of pride exploded inside his chest because they'd surpassed the point where Trey controlled that part of her brain. Explanations came easily now.

"You what?

"I…I'm a lot older than them."

He cocked his eyebrow up. "You are?"

"I'm being serious right now, Ant."

"And I ain't?"

She thrust her head back against the headrest, smiling at the roof of his car.

He studied her, waiting on the problem that she stuttered out to become a problem in his head. He searched hard for it, combing across her smooth brown complexion, moist curls, full lips, and her eyes. No matter how hard he tried, he couldn't see what she did. In his mind, time wasn't linear, and they existed in the same space where there was no such thing as age.

He looked in the rearview mirror. "Munch?"

She quieted and smiled back at him.

"Cover your ears, baby."

As soon as she slapped her little hands over her ears, he turned to Venus.

"I probably need to cover mine, too." She groaned.

He folded his fingers into the palm of his hand because he wanted to march them across her legs while they convened over the boring shit pretend married couples bickered about.

"Why you so concerned about trivial shit? Your age… your clothes… who gives a fuck?"

Her head lolled to the side and her cheeks perked up. "Damn, you're such a romantic, baby."

They laughed together.

He let her chuckle until her shoulders fell and her mind only buzzed with thoughts of him.

Finally, he smirked. "Truth?"

"Ugh, don't start that here. Especially not while I'm having a moment that should be reserved for my therapist."

He blinked, raising both of his eyebrows at her.

They were already running late. There was no time for her to have a quarter life crisis while everybody waited on the jet.

"*You* don't start. It's Sunday, and I only got you for…" He glanced at the time on the dashboard. "A few more hours. Tighten the fuck up."

She thrust her head back. "Fine… truth. My heart can't survive a dare from you right now, anyway."

He glanced at Munch again, but she was too busy staring at a ladybug that had fluttered onto the backseat window. She pressed her nose against the glass with her palms planted against her ears.

He took the reprieve they had to lean closer to Venus and stare at the delicate skin on her chest that glistened with Munch's baby lotion.

Don't touch her.

Give yourself a minute to come down.

He cheated and stroked his finger across her soft skin. "How you feel when I make love to you?"

"Like the sexiest woman in the world," she exclaimed without hesitation while tilting her head. "Like I don't even recognize myself."

He believed her.

His dick got hard anytime those sneaky flashbacks pounded through his head from the night before. They came back in spurts where he saw her wide-eyed and gaping at her naked self in the mirror.

"So why you don't feel that way now?"

"Because we're not making love, Ant. We're...we're doing domesticated shit." She huffed and fluffed her hair. "And I still can't figure out if I feel sexy because of you or because of me."

"Wait a minute...wait a minute. You can't feel sexy, doing domesticated shit? And what's wrong with me making you feel sexy?"

"Listen, I've spent a significant amount of time unlearning a lot of shit, and not basing my worth or sexiness on the opinion and actions of a man is one of them."

She skipped his first question so smoothly he didn't catch it until he leaned in closer to her while she mulled. It seemed like she was always pondering about shit he never thought about.

He stroked her powdery scented chest again, letting the weight of her statement sit between them. Nobody had ever prepared him for life with a woman that was broken and trying to put herself back together. It was beautiful but high-key terrifying sometimes because she made him think about shit DeeDee hadn't lived long enough to experience.

Her eyes followed his wild finger as it drew imaginary circles along her slick skin. "Well...are you gonna say something?"

He stopped stroking her and let his head fall to the side. "It sound like you already got your mind made up about how you feel. Why would anything I have to say matter?"

She folded her lips under her teeth and glanced at the jet again.

Despite what he thought, Trey was still up there with her

brain in a vise grip. He was a sneaky motherfucka. Every time Anthony thought Trey had left, he popped back up under the guise of some silly insecurity she thought she buried. This time he made her believe age was more than just a number and that it was wrong for her to revel in the way he admired her.

She sighed, rolling her eyes around the car in a flurry.

Munch let out her own restless sigh. If it were just the two of them, Munch would tell him she was tired of him keeping grown-up secrets from her, but she had to impress Venus, so she kept quiet.

He shook his head at them.

His pretend wife needed correction and his munchkin needed to touch that ladybug's wings.

He reached out, tucking an errant purple curl behind her ear. "If a nigga don't wake up and obsess over the little breaths you take when you sleeping after he makes love to you or fawn over the way you toss your hand on your hip when you cooking him breakfast, then that's a fuckin' problem. Nobody on that jet knows how old you are or what you wore last night, but what they do know, is that I stepped on there with the sexiest woman they ever seen. You a fly ass bitch when I'm making love to you, when you cooking my breakfast, when you doing my baby's hair, and when you wearing yesterday's clothes, Venus. Own that and forget all that feminist therapy shit for a minute. Ain't nothing wrong with a man making you feel sexy in and outside the bedroom. It's what I'm supposed to do. I'm supposed to make you feel untouchable."

She squinted at him and leaned in so close her minty breath kissed his nose.

He leaned in closer to her lips, but she pulled back with a teasing smile. "Why you always got me in some shit, huh?"

What she really meant was why did he always make her feel so fuckin' good, but he needed to get out of her head for a minute. It was dangerous there.

Venus' fear of judgment was irrational—stupid even. Michole said it was the aftermath of choosing to stay in such an unhealthy relationship for so long. Trey had chipped away at her self-esteem so slyly she hadn't even noticed until one day she woke up and couldn't fathom the thought of somebody liking her for being herself.

Tori grasped her hand and bounced against the hot concrete as they stood on the tarmac.

They laced their fingers together while she stared at Anthony, locking the car up.

She drank him in and replayed those perfectly imperfect words he spat in the car for the millionth time. He looked mannish today. He looked like *her* man, dressed in an all black short set and sneakers as if he wasn't about to get on a private jet.

She swallowed, still tasting the tart sweetness of his essence on her tongue. She swore his cum even tasted like strawberries.

While his back was turned, she glanced at her basic outfit again because self-esteem didn't magically replenish itself because of a pep-talk.

"You look at that outfit again and I'm gon' make you sit with me the whole flight," he said.

She gasped and smiled to herself. "Is that supposed to be a threat?"

"I wouldn't know. I ain't no threatenin' type of nigga."

She snorted, rolling her eyes. "Right. Just like you never stole JoJo's bike?"

He turned around, wagging his finger at her. "Hold up. Don't speak our business, Venus. I'd hate to do you like I did Lil' Try Hard and his cousin."

She missed him saying her name with so much gusto and she still got silly butterflies when she thought about the night she met Lil' Try Hard.

He smiled at her while his eyes stroked her basic outfit one last time.

He shook his head, keeping his thoughts to himself, but it didn't matter. They'd been sharing brains for two weeks.

"Daddy *really* wants to go to timeout, Bug," she muttered in a sing-song voice as she tugged Tori and walked off.

Their walk to the jet was too short. Her palms grew moist and suddenly, she was Daddy's jitterbug again. She wanted to fidget to quell the wild feelings that coursed through her body.

She and Tori swung their hands in the air while Anthony trailed behind them.

As soon as they neared the airstairs, a flight attendant came down and met them at the bottom. She was peachy and blonde like Venus imagined a flight attendant for a private jet would be.

Her glassy blue eyes found Tori first, and she painted on a breezy smile. "Well, aren't you the cutest in your glitter bow and fun tights?"

Tori replied with a close-lipped smile and popped her thumb into her mouth.

"Why don't you and Mom step on up? Everybody's waiting on you guys."

Venus gave her a lop-sided grin. "Oh, I'm not he—"

Anthony's hand pushed into the small of her back and she shut up. Not that he was signaling her to, it was just that her brain had blurred the lines between parent and teacher.

He exchanged pleasantries with the flight attendant while tapping her on the ass to make her heavy feet move. She lifted Tori with one hand and they moved, trekking up the steps. His hand stayed glued to her ass the entire walk into the interior of the jet.

It was rowdy inside and much more spacious than she expected because she'd only ever flew budget airlines and went through TSA like the other regular folks she knew. Just the thought of taking a day trip three states over in the tiny plane made her dizzy.

A melee of voices blended together until a curly headed blonde girl noticed them shuffling inside. She shot from the back of the plane in a getup that *really* made Venus feel decrepit— casual sneakers outfitted in Falcons' colors, sweats and a crop top.

Venus forced her lips into an awkward smile when she walked up to them.

She threw her arm around Anthony and tugged Tori's puff.

She had porcelain skin with the type of features she didn't have to make up. She could roll out of bed just like she was and people would still do a double take when they saw her.

"You and Kris are neck and neck in the 'who can piss Jade off more' race," she muttered, leaning into Anthony. "I just got off a flight and made it here before y'all did."

"I had to wash clothes."

"Yeah, okay, and I heard what happened with the Benz, too. You play too damn much." She snorted, glancing over at Venus.

She eyed the way her and Tori's hands were intertwined. Her eyes trailed over Venus' body and then stopped at her hair. Venus' fingers itched to reach up and make sure one of her curls hadn't found itself in an awkward position.

Finally, she grinned. "Hi, teacher bae."

"'*Teacher bae?*'" Venus' awkward smile melted.

"Mhmm. Nuney did a terrible job of describing how fine you are."

Her neck grew hot and Tori probably felt the sweat on her palms, but she ignored it.

Anthony hooked his arm around the girl's neck and raked his fingers through her curls, shaking them around until she let out a raspy giggle.

"I'm Tash, the best babysitter and sister in the whole world," she gasped out, leaning into him again.

Now, Venus could finally put faces to names, descriptions and voices. Tash was the "lil' dyke" Shad hated and Dre' was her man.

Venus thrust her hand out like she always did. Tash looked at it and then laughed before pouncing over Tori and pulling her in a too tight hug that eased the bubbling in her stomach.

All the rest of her introductions were uneventful. Nobody cared about her trivial insecurities like Anthony said. Jade only cared about making it to Detroit on time, and the rest of them had their own concerns that Venus caught through bits and pieces of conversations like a shifty parole officer and a messy breakup.

"Hm." Anthony grunted, tapping a leather chair in the middle of the plane. "Sit here."

She didn't actually want to.

She wanted to be up under him while she experienced the second most luxurious experience in her life, but they were with mixed company, so she had to share him while also being social.

Tori was still attached to her legs, so she couldn't even sit down.

He smiled at Tori, tickling the underside of her chin. "Go sit up in the front with Jour. She missed you."

Staying true to her velcro ways, Tori shook her head and clamored closer to Venus' legs.

"I got her," she said. "She can sit next to me."

twenty-six

. . .

THE INSIDE of the jet felt like a cozy living room.

Venus tried to control her gawking, but it was impossible, so she settled on staring around in a wide-eyed trance. She wanted to memorize every morsel of the plane so she could savor the memories once she went back to her regular life of monotony and basic airplane rides.

As soon as the jet reached cruising altitude, the flight attendant unbuckled Tori from her seat and let her sit on Venus' lap. Venus inhaled the fresh scent from the leather furniture and reveled in the way she and Tori melted into her seat.

Jade and her best friend Kristen sat across from her, Tori, and Tash. That nostalgia Anthony talked about came back the more they talked about their budding careers and all the shit that came with being a black girl in emerging adulthood.

Their friend group was a weird mismatched bunch that seemed to have started with Jade and Josiah falling for each other. The girls felt like Venus' college friend group who were all still trying to find their way in the world and it was obvious they came from different backgrounds than the boys.

They were all attractive, though. Dre' had green eyes that pierced her soul when he looked her way and Jade had reddish brown skin that glowed from the happiness that came with having a doting NFL player boyfriend. Zeke had the type of face that made her do a double-take because she didn't appreciate its rare beauty the first time around with his deep skin and full lips. He had the unique features of a high-end model—but even still, none of them looked as good as Anthony.

She stroked Tori's hair as Tori leaned against her chest and stared off into the clouds outside the plane's window. The stomach-dropping turbulence didn't faze her and that obsessiveness Venus told Anthony about hovered between them.

How many flights had Tori been on with him?

Tori pressed her nose to the window like she'd done in the car, staring at a puffy cloud that floated by. She rode Venus' lap like an expert until she fell back into her chest and drifted into a light sleep.

The flight attendant breezed by and sat a wineglass on the mahogany table that separated their seat from Jade's and Kristen's.

She didn't remember ordering a drink, but then again, she'd been plagued by a strange brain fog ever since she woke up in Anthony's bed because everything that ever seemed out of reach in her life was suddenly attainable.

She glanced over at him.

He had his legs splayed open while he and Dre' had a spirited back and forth on the couch. Dre' grabbed the back of his head to get a closer look at the ugly bruise on his face.

He didn't wince while he twisted Anthony's face back and forth, examining it from every angle. "It's ugly. It'll still be there. Tell your ole lady to cover it up for you. Judge gon' be looking at you sideways if you pull up to court like this."

He could've been talking about Mikayla, but her whirling stomach told her she was being stupid again. He was talking about her.

She shifted in her seat at his words and tried to tune back in to whatever Jade and Kristen had been squawking about since the plane took off.

"All I'm saying is that I'm in my wife era," Kristen said, taking a shot of clear liquor to the head. "I will not be somebody's eternal girlfriend. They not gon' be 'special friending' me in my man's obituary."

There were two separate vibes on the flight. If it weren't for Anthony, she would've snuck to the front of the plane to sit with Jade's baby Journey and her nanny. They had snacks, a cozy blanket, and a movie playing on Journey's iPad. It would've been better than listening to some twenty-something's first world problems, no matter how nostalgic it made her feel.

Jade grimaced. "I think you're being dramatic."

"Doubt it. Statistically speaking, my chances of getting married dwindle each year. He was wasting my time."

"Y'all were only dating for a year, Pooh. You sound unhinged," Tash rasped, hopping from her seat, crossing over Jade's outstretched legs and making a bee-line toward the boys. "You need longer than a year to know if you're going to marry somebody. Let's be real and get off of those soft life socials where the girlies are bragging about covert narcissists proposing after love bombing them."

The baggy sweats she wore swallowed her frame and made Venus smile.

"I don't even know what that means," Kristen replied.

Venus snickered and took a sip of her wine while the girls dissected Kristen's love life because she was clearly the needy friend—the pretty, desperate, *needy* one. Every friend group had one. Kristen had a face that belonged in one of those old Macy's catalogues. It was angular, blemish-free, and the perfect shape for the long braids she wore. She'd eyed Venus up and down when Anthony introduced them.

Venus pulled Tori in closer to her middle and smiled as the dry wine calmed her frazzled nerves. They were the only two things keeping her above the brain fog.

Tash had flopped between Anthony and Dre' and leaned over Anthony's shoulder.

"What you bring me and Munch back from LA?" he asked, looking over at her.

Tash's answer got lost between Kristen's loud declaration that she needed another shot of whatever the boys were drinking —except "the boys" weren't drinking. Only Anthony was. Zeke had thrust the bottle of tequila into his chest as soon as they flopped onto the couch.

"*For your arm,*" he'd said, eyeing the leftover scrapes and cuts from the night before, and then looking over at her.

Kristen repeated herself and looked over at the couch the boys were smooshed on, but Tash grinned in Anthony's face, taking all of his attention.

Venus sat her wine down, nudging it away to give her brain time to process everything she saw and heard.

It was easy to let alcohol and good sex cloud her judgment, but there was *something* there she couldn't put her finger on. Or it could've just been Trey and Rose reminding her that her insecurities had always been ingrained in her identity.

They'd only been on the plane for thirty minutes but now and then she would catch Kristen's eyes trailing Anthony while laughing a little too hard at one of his jokes, because on his turf he was "Nuney" and Venus didn't know Nuney. She knew Ant.

"I heard what happened to my new truck, Nuney!" Jade exclaimed, interrupting him and Tash.

He looked up and flashed a shiny, placid smile at her. "What you heard, sis?"

"Didn't we all agree to stop gambling with my household items—cars included?"

"JoJo a snitch, bro." Anthony smacked his lips. "Just tell him to worry about this game. I got a stack on the parlay and he better not fuck up."

"Really?" Jade frowned. "The game hasn't even started yet."

"And Tash already ain't fuckin' with y'all," he replied.

"Keep her," Kristen chimed in, waving her hand at him. "She ain't for me, anyway. She wants me to be an eternal girlfriend. I guess she doesn't think I'm good enough to be a wife."

"Say man, get off my partna' head before we knuckle up. We ain't on no battle of the sexes type shit right now. Save that for after the game."

They belted out laughs at him because he was the light in their friend-group. It illuminated from within him and made her miss him when he was only ten feet away.

He hooked his arm around Tash, talking in her ear. They were always talking, but Tash never looked at him like Kristen, Priya, or how Mikayla probably did. She gave him googly-eyed sister stares like she was supposed to.

She grinned until Dre' pulled her away and made her slide into his lap like he was separating his two most problematic kids. Lucky Tash could sit in Dre's lap without worry because they weren't just fuck buddies for a night.

Her stomach grew woozy again.

Zeke kicked his foot up on an ottoman resting in front of their sofa, rolling his eyes. "That's her problem. She always projecting and blaming other folks for her shortcomings. She can't ever take responsibility for the shit she do, but she worried about being somebody's wife."

He mumbled the words, but Kristen lurched forward in her seat and squealed, "Are you talking about me?"

He shrugged.

"What's that supposed to mean?"

"It mean exactly what it mean."

"Let's not rehash old shit, Zeke."

"Nah...*let's.*"

"Let's?" She laughed, slapping her knee. "Okay, fine. We would've had to have been dating for me to do anything to you. I was free to date Tony. You need to let that go."

There it was.

Kristen didn't even bother doling out their tea little by little.

She dumped it right out with no qualms and justified Venus' insecure thoughts about being on the wrong side of the plane.

"If I pay any of yo' bills, then you mine. Period."

"I don't ask—you offer. And I only date with the intention of marrying these days. All you wanna do is fuck and hang out. You haven't made any indication that you wanna—"

"On God, y'all gotta wrap this unrequited love shit up before we get to the game," Anthony interrupted. "I ain't goin' for it."

"Shut up, Nuney. Nobody asked for your input," Kristen yelped.

"You needed my input when you ain't know what a narcissist was. Grow up, bruh."

"Ugh, Jade. Shut him up." She huffed, turning to Jade, whose head was buried in her phone. "He has the smartest mouth. I swear he always has something to say."

There wasn't actually any malice in her voice, because she was curious about Anthony. It was in the relaxed look she flashed his way.

"Shut me up?" he repeated, pushing his lips out with a thoughtful expression. "You must think I'm that architect nigga you been begging for a ring."

Kristen pushed up from her seat and sashayed over to them like he'd beckoned her with those menacing words, but Zeke was the only one captivated by her. He stared at her slack-jawed and in love, even though she kept flirting with somebody else.

Damn, that sexy nostalgia wore off quick.

She was right back in college, wading through messy friend groups muddled with frenemies, fuck buddies, and layers of drama that had accumulated in the time they'd gotten to know each other.

She held in her scoff and took another sip of her wine, even though she told herself she needed to stay sober to deal with their *Young and the Restless* drama.

She'd have to add Kristen to the list of little girls that hung on to Anthony's every word—even his insulting ones.

Kristen snatched the tequila bottle that sat on the floor between his legs. "Don't get beside yourself just because you brought company."

It was a slight dig that made Venus chuckle and Jade look up from her phone. Jade smiled at her apologetically. It was *exactly* why Venus needed to be at the front of the plane.

Anthony waved his hand in a shooing motion. "Ain't no company on here. Go'on with that."

Kristen huffed and took a swig of the liquor. She placed her lips right on the rim where Anthony's had been and even closed her eyes for good measure.

Warmth crept up Venus' neck.

Anthony blinked up at her with a bored expression. "You can have it, shawty."

"Since when are you so giving?"

"Since you started with this weirdo shit." He turned to Zeke, giving him the "get your chick" look that most men had ingrained in them, but Venus forgot she was immersed in *Nuney's* world where silly ass disrespectful shit came out of his mouth on a whim.

"Oh, that lil' pussy got you tender as hell, huh?" Anthony turned to Zeke, shaking his head. "Stick your chest out, nigga. She not even being covert with the disrespect no more."

Tash sputtered out a sloppy laugh until Dre' gripped the back of her neck, making it simmer into a snicker.

"Aye..." Dre' snorted. "Y'all chill out."

She didn't know what the worst part was—the fact Zeke couldn't defend himself or the fact the whole side of their plane knew Kristen wanted to fuck Anthony because of some silly little game she and Zeke played. She was like a middle school girl trapped in a grown woman's body, and she wanted to encroach on her territory just to make Zeke jealous.

Her territory?

Venus shook her head.

She sounded like that strange woman she didn't recognize again, all because some girl had twisted her energy up.

"And I'm the bitch for wanting Jade to shut you up?" Kristen asked, turning away and sitting back in her seat with the bottle. "Fuck you."

Her voice volleyed up, and it made Anthony sit forward and rest his elbow on his knee. "I ain't raising my voice at you, so don't raise yours at me. Maybe you should chase some healing instead of a marriage proposal."

"Oh, please. You don't know shit about healing. DeeDee was just fighting you in Jade and Jo's driveway. We all saw and heard it."

Venus gulped at the sound of Deeanna's name coming out of somebody else's mouth other than Anthony's.

Kristen said it so smugly that it felt illegal. It was clear she had heard Deeanna's obsessiveness over Anthony, just like Venus had. It was probably what had stirred up her "weirdo shit." Women were funny like that.

After hearing Anthony and Deeanna fight over the phone, Venus couldn't imagine what it must've been like in person. Based on the slant in Kristen's eyes, it must've been that relationship ending argument Anthony told her about and now Kristen was curious about him.

"Watch your mouth," he gritted out. "You don't know nothing about me or her. You just think you do."

"I don't even know why I'm going back and forth with you. You don't know anything about relationships, marriage, or responsibility. All you know is chronic irresponsibility and fightin' and fuckin' your baby mama."

"Hold up," Tash warned, shaking her head. "Not too much on my brother now."

"Okay, y'all..." Jade sat forward, waving her arms. "It's getting nasty. Let's drop it."

It had surpassed nasty, but Jade was young and she had to try to keep the peace on both sides for herself and Josiah.

"He wanted to go there, so I went there." Kristen smiled, shrugging.

Anthony chuckled. "You ain't go nowhere with me. I don't go *nowhere* with a bitch that ain't mine."

He sounded just as smug as she did.

Venus chuckled under her breath and took another sip of her wine, thinking about all the times they'd "went there"—in her classroom...in her car...at his place. She savored this unrefined side of him. It was the side that had waltzed into her classroom and gotten her into the trouble she was in.

"Well, from what I heard, you don't know how to go nowhere with any other chick besides DeeDee, anyway." Kristen rolled her eyes up. "Like I said—chronic irresponsibility and fightin' and fuckin' your baby mama."

Tash gripped his shoulder as he leaned forward. "But you want my chronically irresponsible dick and you mad you can't get it. All this shit is a game to force Zeke to give in to this 'let's settle down and get married' shit so she can keep up with other folks. Don't fall for it, nigga. You ain't ready and she ain't either."

He slapped Zeke's chest, and Zeke didn't even flinch.

Kristen painted another smug smile on her face. "Jade...call his girl and tell her that her nigga is in his feelings. I guess they're still on the outs."

"Call her for what? Shit, she sitting right across from you. That's who you need to be talking to—not me."

The humming from the plane's engine quieted to a soft lull. Nobody seemed to notice but Venus.

Apparently she didn't need to prance across the plane and sit in his lap to signify their situationship—he'd just announced it to everybody without hesitation.

He gave her the same look he'd given her that night at Vaughn's, when their mutual telepathy was still new. It was that "you better tell her" look.

Kristen narrowed her eyes at her as if she'd finally gotten the answer she was looking for since they stepped on the plane.

"Y'all..." Jade started in a pathetic whine. "For the sake of my sanity, *please*—"

"Are you okay?" Venus blurted, looking directly at Kristen.

She was buzzing with Anthony's taste still flowing inside her mouth, so all of her fucks went out the window when he pulled his bottom lip into his mouth and cocked his eyebrow up to give her a nudge.

"Excuse me?" Kristen replied.

"What's with this whole marriage obsession?"

It was so quiet, the cheeky music from Journey's iPad floated to their side of the plane.

"Your lack of a marriage proposal," Venus double downed. "Isn't that what sparked this weird one-sided argument?"

Tash snickered again.

"I wouldn't call it one-sided, but okay." Kristen rolled her eyes up.

"You're arguing with somebody that's told you in several ways they don't want to engage. That's one-sided."

Kristen crossed her arms and stared ahead, avoiding her eyes while the rest of them looked at her.

"You got a lot of big feelings going on right now and they're coming out in some unhealthy ways. Ain't no marriage proposal or relationship gon' fix that—trust me."

"I guess you *would* know."

"Was that supposed to be a dig at my age?"

"Only if you took it that way."

"You're right." Venus nodded, picking up her wine glass. "I took it that way and I'm happy I did. You are *so* right—I would know. I was married for ten years."

"And how did that turn out for you?" Kristen finally looked at her, cocking her head to the side and looking at her empty ring finger.

"Beautifully." She took a sip of wine and glanced down at

Tori, who sucked in a deep breath. "You know, I used to be just like you—young, insecure, and eager to have some man's last name just to keep up with my friends who were on the cusp of marriage."

"That sounds nothing like me."

Venus raised her eyebrows. "Okay."

Everybody's eyes bounced back and forth between them.

"I remember sitting around having this same conversation with my friends. I wanted a lifetime commitment with a man who showed me in so many ways that he didn't see himself spending a lifetime with me—let alone a moment. We'd breakup, and I'd go searching for attention in weird places. We'd make up, and I'd lose sense of my worth and then we got married just like *I* wanted and you know…"

Her voice trailed off and Kristen's folded arms loosened like she wanted her to tell the rest, but that story wasn't meant for the entire plane. It was only meant for the person who basked in her nostalgic sexiness.

"I don't like giving advice, but I *think* you should go where you're wanted and enjoy this lovely outing your best friend invited you on. She didn't have to invite you anywhere, but she did and you're causing havoc. Jealousy doesn't look good on you. You're too pretty for that."

Kristen rolled her eyes and thrust her head back against her seat.

Anthony smiled, eyeing Venus in a way that made her nipples poke against her romper's thin fabric. His eyes raked over her thighs and her arms that were curled around Tori as he sat back against the couch.

Tash went back to rambling in his ear while he gave her another one of those looks—one of those "well played, Mrs. Nunez" looks.

twenty-seven

. . .

"YOU LIKE PLAYING WITH FIRE, HUH?" Dre' asked.

They'd just made it to halftime at Ford Field, and Dre' had finally cornered Anthony. It was bound to happen because his fling with Venus Thibodeaux wasn't supposed to turn into a real thing. It was only supposed to live as Tash's problematic inside joke and nothing more.

They stood off behind the last row of seats in their suite. He caught Venus' reflection in the glass pane next to them. Munch had finally thawed and let Journey show her the game she'd been playing on her iPad, so Venus was free to do adult shit like show Jade and Tash how to mix the perfect margarita at the bar.

"Getting burned feel good sometimes," he replied, shrugging.

"That's a grown ass woman."

Anthony swiped his tongue against his lips, thinking about the way she'd easily read the situation with Kristen, and shut her up with grace. "I know…"

"And that's Munch's teacher, man. That's who you was out with that night, huh? Did you forget what's going on?"

Kind of.

He gulped and his wet palms came back.

See, the thing with Venus was that she made him forget the messy shit in his life. When he was with her, Brian Torres didn't exist and DeeDee had finally cut her ties to his soul but pitied him enough to let him keep his daughter.

Dre' scoffed. "You keep saying shit like you said back on the plane and you gon' have to live up to those grown woman expectations. She ain't DeeDee."

Munch peeled her head from Journey's and pushed up from the floor. She skipped to Venus and grabbed hold of her leg, but Venus didn't let her stay there. She scooped her up, pressing her lips against her cheek while laughing at something Tash said.

Fuck whatever Dre' had to say.

He wanted to bring them back home and watch them in private again. There were so many tiny nuances of motherhood he never knew about—like the way Munch sat between Venus' legs while Venus combed her hair that morning, the way she slathered Vaseline on Munch's face after he gave Munch her bath, and even the way she had laid out Munch's clothes for the day. It was all so different and so good.

"So, what all she know?" Dre' asked.

"The type of shit that can get a nigga caught up."

Dre' whistled. "Oh, you pillow talking like *that*?"

"Overly."

Venus made it easy. All the embarrassing shit he tried to keep between him and DeeDee poured out when she looked at him with those sable colored eyes. All of his skeletons lived within her—his court date, his real job, his fake one, his broken heart.

"What about Toriana?" Dre' asked.

"What about her?"

"Do Venus know about that too?"

"His attorney subpoenaed her to testify before mine could. I didn't even get to explain it to her first."

Dre' grunted, rubbing the back of his neck.

That was never a good sign. He let out that same grunt when Anthony called him from Lola's backyard to tell him the fucked up news about Munch and Brian Torres.

"And how much you paying this lady again?"

"Too goddamn much."

He'd fumbled past the retainer invoice that morning while digging through the junk drawer in his kitchen for a lighter.

He looked away from Venus and Munch's reflections and out onto the field at Josiah, talking with his hands in the team's huddle.

"I don't know about this shit, Nuney."

He expected "Ant" to come out of his mouth because he'd been in Venus' orbit for too long. He didn't have to ask Dre' what he meant because it'd been on Dre's face ever since he stepped onto the plane with Venus.

"Is she the type of woman that'll get on a stand and lie for you if you need her to?" he asked.

Anthony scoffed.

"It won't last past the weekend," he muttered, gripping the seat in front of him. "She know that."

"Oh, that's the lil' lie y'all been telling each other?"

"Ain't no lies, it's life."

Dre' laughed, swiping his head. "You know, the funny thing about life is how much we rely on lies to placate us."

"Ant! Come see!"

Anthony turned around to find Venus while his conscience berated him about how much he looked like a simp.

Shit, at least he was a simp for a woman as righteous as her. She wouldn't fuck his homeboy to satisfy a grudge, air their business out for the world, and she probably wouldn't commit perjury for him. But she loved on his baby and showed him the type of wife he deserved.

She was barefoot and tipsy again and his stomach remembered how much he liked her like that because it fumbled in an excruciatingly pussy way. Fuckin' with Dre' he missed the way she'd probably thrust her hand out to all the staff in the suite and introduced herself as "Venus Thibodeaux" even though she should've said "Venus Nunez."

Damn, Josiah had fucked his head up real bad.

Dre' slapped him on his back. "Go see about her. We'll chop it up later."

He didn't hang around for Dre' to throw out more reasons he and Venus were wrong. Instead, he took long strides toward her.

Tash raised her eyebrows at him goofily as he walked up on them, dancing together to the halftime performance that blasted throughout the stadium. It was some local no-name rapper, but Tash knew the song. She rapped along, twirling Venus around.

Venus giggled. "Look, Ant. Tash says I can help teach one of her classes."

She let go of Tash's hands and danced toward him, pushing her arms around his neck.

He inhaled her as the rest of the suite moved around them—Journey ran by with a cookie, Jade followed behind her with a handful of napkins, Zeke talked to Kristen in the corner with an apologetic look on his face, Dre' had scooped up Munch and pulled Tash away from them, and Venus melted into him during it all.

They swayed back and forth even though the song ain't even call for it.

He pushed his lips against her ear. "Is you tipsy, Mrs. Nunez?"

She tilted her head back and her curls fell away from her face. "I'm *drunk*...on a Sunday when I'm supposed to be in therapy."

"Are you feeling sexy and nostalgic again?"

She nodded, smiling.

"Tell me about the last Sunday you got drunk, then."

"No truth or dare?"

He shook his head. "No truth or dare."

She gurgled up a hiccup that smelled like pineapple and Patrón. "The last Sunday I got drunk, I downed two pitchers of bottomless mimosas at brunch with Ginny. We left early because I felt funny and she had an early flight back to Atlanta. When I got home, I fell in the driveway as soon as I got out of my Uber. After that, I stumbled in my house with bloody knees and found Trey fuckin' our neighbor on our new couch that I saved for."

It came out in a strained whisper while she smiled around the words.

"What you think about that, Mr. Nunez? Is that sexy and nostalgic enough for you?"

The list of people his heart bled for was a short one, but Venus had weaseled her way onto it just like she'd weaseled her way into every other space in his life.

"They got married this summer as soon as our divorce was finalized, and she's gonna have his baby, Ant. My cousin Ginny sent me the screenshots from Facebook. He looked *so* happy."

He scraped his fingers across her waist and pulled her in closer until he felt her wild heart beating against his chest.

As soon as Josiah got home, he needed to hit him up to ask him about the way his words prophesied his future feelings. How could a nigga not wanna watch Venus scribble their last name next to her first name for an eternity?

"Why you do that to me?" he asked, nudging her nose with his.

"Do what?"

"Tell me dangerous shit like that."

"Because it's part of my hist—"

"No. I don't think you understand." He shook his head, palming her ass. "I will kill that nigga."

Her eyes widened until they couldn't get any higher, and then they dropped. She belted out a laugh so loud he felt it in his body.

Her shoulders jumped up and down until she settled and laid her head against his chest.

"Your future Mrs. Nunez, *will not* be a prison wife. You got too much life to live to be talking about killing no good cheating ass niggas." She tsk'd. "My angsty, angsty baby boy—don't talk like that, baby. I'm the feds, remember?"

He smiled, thinking about Lola.

———

"One day when I'm old and grey, I'll tell the staff at my nursing home that I took a PJ to spend five hours in Detroit," Venus muttered, staring up at the television in their suite. "I'll tell them about your young ass friends and their young ass drama and that one annoying lil' girl's obsession with marriage."

They were squished together on a love seat. Anthony massaged her toes while Tori squirmed between them until she got comfortable against his chest and stuck her thumb in her mouth. Venus' stomach fluttered when he pressed his lips against her forehead and pulled her thumb.

"A nursing home?" he muttered, yawning.

"Yes, Ant. That's where us no sibling having childless folks go when we get old and our distant relatives don't wanna take us in."

"You talkin' crazy. Didn't I say you wasn't leaving me?"

"You can't move me into your house with your wife. You know that, right?"

"You got me fucked up."

"Watch your mouth in front of my baby." She giggled around Jade's squealing and the announcer droning about Josiah making a deep pass to the wide receiver.

Anthony raked his fingers against the arch in her foot and pressed deep into it.

The more the day wore on, the more angsty he got, and the more her heart and head got confused. They tugged her back and forth—her heart kept telling her it was okay to swim again and her head kept yelling about how stupid she'd be to let some-body drown her for the second time in her life.

"Touchdown!" Tash yelled, skipping toward them from the seats that faced the field. "It's shot o'clock, V! Wake up!"

Sometimes she was "teacher bae," other times she was "shawty" and now she was "V." She liked "V" the most. It was simple, sexy, and aligned with this new woman she saw every time she looked at herself.

Her eyes widened. She tried to sit up, but her body laughed at her and she fell back against the couch.

Who was she kidding?

She couldn't keep up with them, but Ginny would've applauded her effort. Back when they were sexy coeds, she could go shot for shot with grown men.

"Aht! Aht!" Jade stomped toward her with a solo cup. "Up! We're almost there, sis! There's only four minutes left!"

"Four minutes?" Venus groaned. "In football, that's like forty."

Jade tugged her by the wrist, but Anthony kept his hand on her feet.

"C'mon! Let her go!" Tash laughed. "One more! One more!"

"Give it here," Anthony said, pulling it out of Jade's grasp. "Y'all gon' have her hung over at work tomorrow."

Tash whined. "Okay, *padre*. She can sleep it off on the flight home."

"I'll give it to her." He shooed them away, but Jade was the only one that listened and bounced away to Kristen.

Tash stayed because she was like a little fly that lingered around Anthony's side, buzzing in his ear until she missed Dre'. The alcohol had slowed time down so much so that Venus had time to study them closer.

Tash sat next to him on the arm of the couch, sighing. "I wanna go dancing tonight."

It was a random bit of information, but they were drunk and when folks got drunk, their lips got loose. Tash was no different.

Anthony fingered the forgotten shot and pulled her foot closer before looking over at Tash. "Where at?"

"I don't know. Some Latin club in Buckhead."

"With who?"

"One of the other dancers I met on tour. She lives here too. We were on the same flight back home."

More innocuous information.

Venus rested her chin on her hand, waiting and listening—but mostly listening.

"What you think?" Tash added.

Anthony shook his head and then nodded toward Dre' standing at the bar with Jade.

Tash smacked her lips with another deep sigh, like a petulant younger sister.

"Y'all better bachata y'all asses at home." He snorted, rolling his eyes and then crooking his finger for Venus to come closer.

She sat up, bringing her face closer to his until he caught her chin in his hand.

He stared at her. "Go ask your nigga, Natasha."

"I did."

"Well, it sound like you must've got your answer."

Venus held onto a moan as if he'd been talking to her. It was that unrefined side of him again.

"Whatever." Tash groaned, tugging Tori up from his chest. "I see Zeke ain't the only tender one around here...come on, Munchy-Munch. Let's go eat candy."

"You get her hyped up and you gon' babysit the rest of the day," he said, looking at her over his shoulder.

Tash snickered from behind him before slinking away with a frowning Tori at her side.

Once they were across the suite in front of the dessert table, he smirked and took her shot to the head, pressing his lips against hers afterward.

He pushed his tongue into her mouth. It grazed hers and twirled around it. He kissed her like she hadn't been his for the weekend—sucking her tongue, her breath, and then her lips into his mouth. He tasted like strawberry, expensive tequila, and the joint he and Tash snuck as soon as their plane landed and their feet touched DTW's tarmac. She was swimming again—flailing around in the water with him while he held her to keep her from drowning.

A moan snuck out because she was *that* kind of drunk.

She tried to pull away, but he followed her, gathering her lips back between his and sucking another moan out of her mouth.

There was no more tequila left. He'd fed it to her little by little while she tried to understand how he made it taste so much better.

"Where you going?" he asked huskily, talking into her mouth so only she could hear.

She gurgled out an answer that sounded like gibberish.

"I said you couldn't leave me," he whispered. "Why you not listening to me?"

God, he was so angsty that it made her want to make love to him for an eternity.

Now she was getting blurry eyed, stupid drunk.

She pulled her bottom lip from his mouth and tried to push up from the couch, but he caught her wrist.

"Where you going?"

She eyed the back of Tori's head across the suite and her shoulders tensed. She turned around, blurting out the first thing that came to mind.

"Tacos. I...I want a taco." She swiped her hands down her sides just as a member of the catering staff sat a fresh pan of tortillas on the table next to the bar.

"Okay." He sat forward. "Sit down."

"I can go get it."

He eyed her warily and sat back.

The noise in the suite grew muffled as she turned away from him and walked over to the table. She tried to go for the first tortilla she saw and reached for the tongs, but her hand crashed into somebody else's.

"*Oh.*" She pulled back, looking up. "I'm sor—"

Dre' looked at her with that piercing stare. "You good."

It was the first words he'd said to her all day. He wasn't as warm as Tash, and it shook the confidence she had built before she stepped onto the plane.

He picked up the tongs while her hand hovered above them and then grabbed a plate. "How many you want?"

"I can fix it—"

"I know. How many you want?"

"Just…just one."

He piled the toppings on the taco, even though she hadn't told him what she wanted. He added fajita, vegetables, sour cream, and a dollop of hot sauce.

"The spice will sober you up."

He grabbed a stack of napkins, pushing them and the plate toward her. She eyed the tattoo that swathed his neck and his caramel face, trying to decide what he and Tash had in common that made them fall in love.

"What's wrong?" he asked.

If Anthony were there, he'd remind her of how judgy she was. Of course, a tomboy and a handsome, menacing, green-eyed gangster could fall in love. Anything was possible in Daddy's weird universe.

"You want some water too?"

"No," she replied, grabbing the plate from him. "This is good."

He blinked at her, and she finally saw the softness he hid underneath his aloof attitude. That taco was his peace offering. She couldn't take it and walk away.

She folded the taco and took a bite, eyeing him as she chewed.

"My girl wants to go dancing tonight," he said absent-mindedly.

She nodded, swallowing. "Yeah, I heard."

"What you think about that?"

"Sounds fun." She shrugged.

Tash going dancing had turned into the hot topic of the evening. It even preceded all the talk about the game. Venus seemed to be the only one who understood that Tash was antsy, drunk, and young—*of course,* she wanted to go out dancing.

Tash and Jade screamed again as the four minutes left in the game dwindled to one. She glanced at Dre' out of the corner of her eye as he watched Tash jump up and down.

"Her energy different from mine."

"I can see that. You don't seem like the type of man that likes to go dance bachata. You're...reserved. "

"Something like that." He smirked. "It's been a long time since she went out back at home, though. Before me, she was always out. She even worked at a lounge for a while until I made her stop."

"Mhmm." Venus hummed, licking the sour cream from her lips. "Why'd you do that?"

"Politics."

Where was the conversation even going?

He made her feel drunker than she was and now she had to treat him like she treated Treshawn when he couldn't get to the point during his tangents.

She'd only wandered to the table to shovel a taco in her mouth and mull without getting fussed at—not to listen to more of their *Young and the Restless* drama.

"Is there a specific reason you're brooding so much about bachata dancing?" she asked, hiccuping as the heat from the hot sauce spread across her tongue.

"You might wanna slow down..." He smiled, running his hand across her back and pulling the empty plate from her hands.

A member of the catering staff had been hanging around, and

he caught her elbow, dropping his hand to her wrist. "Can you get my sister some lemons for her hiccups?"

He called her "sister" in the same way he called Jade "sister," even though Venus didn't feel deserving of such a title. They'd only known each other for a few hours, but life with Anthony moved fast.

The girl glanced at his hand and then looked up, smiling.

"I got you." She nodded and walked off on a mission to fulfill his random request.

Venus' chest tightened as one more hiccup rocked it. She sucked in a breath and he stared at her like he'd lost the rest of his words.

"You were brooding about bachata dancing..." she hissed between another hiccup, even though she didn't care anymore.

She wanted to go back to her own problems.

"Right." He nodded. "I was asking what you thought about—"

"I'm drunk, Dre'. I honestly don't think anything about it."

She wanted to scream at the top of her drunken lungs that she was thinking about swimming again—not fuckin' bachata dancing! Every time Anthony pressed his lips against hers, she wanted him to strip them naked and lead them to the ledge so they could jump.

"Yeah..." He shrugged.

The suite erupted, drowning out the awkwardness between them until his voice boomed again. "I know you know a lot, V."

"A lot about what?" she asked in exasperation.

"About DeeDee, about Tori... about us."

His hard tone made her eyes trail his body until they stopped on the bulge at his ankle.

She knew that bulge all too well from the little boys she taught that one summer, and then she remembered a conversation she overheard him and Anthony having on the plane. For some reason, that worrisome PO he had suddenly thought he was a flight risk.

Her cheeks grew warm as she looked back up at him and hiccuped. "Right."

She knew *too damn* much like Anthony mused.

"So like I was saying…" Dre' started again. "If I let her go and something happens, I can't do nothing about it. *I* can't fix nothing right now. You know that, right?"

She looked back down at the bulge underneath his jeans, even though she didn't want to. It was glaring, though.

"So, who fixes your problems, then?"

It was a stupid question that the crowd in the stadium drowned out as they roared.

"Touchdown!" Zeke yelled. "That's game! That's game! Fuck these last few seconds!"

"Don't you *ever* doubt my man again, Nuney!" Jade fussed. "I want half the parlay! No bullshit!"

Anthony's goofy laugh kissed her ears. "I'll give you whatever you want, sis, on God! Just make sure you marry my brother!"

He sounded like her angsty baby boy with the world in his hands, even though everybody kept telling her he wasn't a baby boy at all. He took shit that didn't belong to him in ways she couldn't fathom. He'd hurt men that hurt the people he loved. He'd finessed his way into spaces she'd never experience if she hadn't met him.

"You know he a lover boy, right? He just don't know it," Dre' said, cocking his head to the side.

She didn't even know what a "lover boy" was, but she believed Dre'. She imagined lover boys were boys as angsty as Anthony who worshipped the ground women walked on while playing aloof.

"He young, impulsive, and stupid sometimes…" Dre' trailed off.

He was all of those things, but she'd never met somebody whose bad qualities felt so damn good. He was young, but he made her feel young, too. He was impulsive, but life was too damn short to mull over the silly little things that made it hard. He was stupid, but for all the right reasons.

"He's smart, though—smarter than anybody I know, and loyal. He'll do anything for me, my girl, for our family—because he love us."

There was that stupid, stupid word again.

Love.

She swore when Dre' said it his eyes raked across her face to see her reaction but it could've just been her drunken thoughts.

"He love real hard, V. Even harder than me sometimes."

Anthony pushed up from the couch and took long strides toward Jade. When he got close enough, Jade wrapped her arms around him with a complacent smile until Tash elbowed her way between them with Tori.

"So I gotta be real careful about what I'm out here just agreeing to—even silly shit like bachata dancing that my girl keep crying about. I have to think about all the what ifs, about Tori, about that court date he going crazy over, about Shad's homeboys showing up to put they raggedy hands on my girl—because we both know he too pussy to do it himself. I mean, you met him, right?"

She nodded, even though she knew Anthony hadn't told him that.

Her palms grew sweaty.

"I just figured you'd know what was best, you know? Since you know so much about us."

She swallowed another hiccup, catching his gist. She'd probably never get a chance to have one of these talks with him again.

"Don't," she choked out. "Don't let her go."

The girl walked back up to them with the saucer of lemons.

He grabbed them before Venus could. "'Preciate it."

He thrust the plate toward her, and she grabbed one, even though her hiccups were gone. "V say 'no bachata dancing,' so no bachata dancing then."

He shrugged, leaving her to bite into the sad lemon.

"Dre'?" she called out before he could get out of earshot.

He stopped and looked over his shoulder.

"Would DeeDee have known best?"

He smiled until he chuckled and shrugged. "She turned your man into a lover boy and left him with a baby that ain't his. What you think?"

———

The flight home from away games was always the same.

The flight attendant would dim the lights and lay blankets over whichever kids were there. Tash crashed first because she always got the drunkest. Dre' always wandered into the cockpit to ask the pilot all the technical questions the little boy in him wanted to know. Jade would get an early start on her grading. Kristen and Zeke would find the seat farthest from everybody and lay under each other after fighting all day. This flight home was the same, except now they had Venus and Munch.

As soon as they boarded, Anthony pulled Venus by the hand toward the suite at the very back of the jet before Tash could call dibs on it. Munch bounced on her hip along the way.

She didn't question him about anything anymore and he didn't know if it was because she was still drunk or if it was the excitement of the day.

When they got into the room, she spun around the small space with wide eyes and dilated pupils. He promised himself he'd never get used to that look.

She flopped onto the full sized bed with Munch and then shuffled against it, patting an empty spot next to them. "Come here."

He strolled toward them and reveled in the way she dragged her eyes across his body.

He sat on the edge of the bed to control himself because

Munch was awake. He'd embarrassed her enough for the day with all of his angst.

"So this is what it's like when lots of rich people know you?" She smiled, making him chuckle.

"Nah, this is what it's like when lots of rich people know the rich people that know you. They stop gifting you practical shit like NBA tickets and start giving you shit like this."

Her eyes ballooned. "This was a gift?"

"Yeah, to D."

"For real?"

"Hell yeah. I'd slap that nigga if he ever told me he was buying a jet."

She hunched over, belting out a deep belly laugh. "My mind can't even conceive a gift this big."

"Right. This is what happens when you got ten million dollar NBA rookie contract money—that 'fuck it' money."

"What's 'fuck it' money?" she asked.

"The type of money that'll have you looking at any problem in your life and saying 'fuck it,' 'cause you know you got the world in your hands and you can fix whatever it is."

She giggled, looking at him with that same longing she and Munch looked at each other with.

"What you plan to do when you get your 'fuck it' money?"

He liked when she asked questions like that. She was the only one who believed he'd live long enough to experience something as crazy as "fuck it money."

"I'd buy you a house in the country with a chicken coop and one of those backyard play sets for Munch."

"I wouldn't have to kill any chickens, right?" she muttered, batting her eyes at him.

"Nah, but you still gotta cook my breakfast, so we need the eggs."

"Compromise...I can do that. Compromising is *very* important in a marriage." She wagged her finger with a smile and then laid her hand against her flat stomach.

He hadn't been able to stop staring at it or imagining fake scenarios where they lived happily ever after. Dre' was right. He *was* playing with fire.

He rested on his forearm as Munch tossed her body into Venus' for a random hug.

"Is this supposed to be my lunchtime hug, Bug?" Venus tickled her stomach. "You're late, girl. It's almost dinnertime."

Munch giggled so hard she wheezed.

He shook his head.

She was in love.

It was in her longing stares and the way her mouth opened like she *wanted* to talk to Venus.

"What's a lunchtime hug?" he asked, tugging Venus' foot and dragging them both to him.

They giggled as their bodies slid across the comforter until their laughs melted together and turned into a sweet medley that made him warm.

"All my velcro babies are huggers," Venus replied between laughs. "Treshawn gives me his hug right before recess, Ada gives me hers after breakfast, and Tori's always come as soon as school starts, after lunch, and right before it's time to go home."

She poked Munch's button nose.

Somehow throughout the day, she'd stopped resembling DeeDee and he could almost see himself in her—*almost.*

"Velcro baby? That sounds like it's supposed to be offensive."

She laughed, sitting up on her forearms. "Nah, it means they're special. They *are* the worst kids to have when you don't have any at home, though."

She raked her fingers through Munch's hair and looked at her with that same longing. His stomach did that weird turning again because something was different.

He didn't know when shit had changed *or* what had even changed because it happened so fast. One second she was telling Vaughn about her daddy's chicken coop and the next he was wondering why God hadn't blessed his baby girl with a mama like her. It wasn't right to think—especially when Munch wasn't even his to begin with, but his brain hadn't conceptualized that yet. Lola said it probably never would and only a therapist could help him work through it.

"You want kids?" he blurted in a whisper.

She kept her eyes on Munch, who'd snuggled underneath her breasts.

"Oh, yeah...I always wanted lots of 'em."

"How many?"

"Six."

His eyes bulged. "*Six?*"

She giggled and nodded. "You wouldn't understand the plight of an only child. Playing make believe and dress up with Ginny was cool, but it got lonely when she went back home to be with her own sisters."

He heard that hollowness in her voice that made him angsty. Anytime she talked about life without him and Munch, it made him chase that fire Dre' talked about and stick his hand in it, even when he had no business doing it.

"You didn't wanna have kids with Trey?"

"Of course I did. I wanted everything with him. He was my husband."

He hated to hear that word come out of her mouth when it wasn't tied to him. In his fucked up brain, a husband was for an eternity and he was certain he could live an eternity with Venus.

"Why he ain't give them to you?"

She chuckled, shaking her head. "Give?"

Afterward, she stroked Munch's hair again, brushing the soft curls that had snuck out of her puff throughout the day. She pushed them down and smiled when they sprang back up.

"*I* couldn't give them to him," she murmured.

"What you mean?"

"At my age, men want babies, Ant."

"I know," he muttered back.

"Th...they want legacies and promises of forever. They want

good ass wives whose bodies will cooperate and give them the families society says they deserve."

He scoured her stomach again with a new awareness and thought back to the wetness in her eyes when she confessed her neighbor had been the one to give Trey everything he wanted in a wife.

Her flat stomach folded as she pushed up and ran her fingers across his head. "You'll understand later."

"I promise I won't. It should be illegal to marry a woman and not do right by her, no matter what."

She smiled at him like he was the one who couldn't conceive all the babies he wanted. "Oh, Ant…"

She brushed her finger through his eyebrow.

"Come here…come hold us. You got us together for two more hours. I want you to enjoy us like this before tomorrow."

He'd forgotten about tomorrow just as fast as he'd forgotten about that court date and Lynn's missed calls because life with Venus was such a trip. He'd let her wrap him up in her whimsical teacher world, agree to do shit he said he never would, and she made him tender, just like Tash joked.

He still couldn't understand when shit had changed.

Tomorrow, they'd be back on their respective turfs. She'd squint at him with judgment from behind her desk and he'd accuse her of overstepping her teacher boundaries while signing that evaluation she kept going on about. Then he'd go home and stress over that subpoena. But today those problems didn't exist because they were living.

He reached down and pulled his sneakers off before climbing into the bed with them.

That same familiarity that engulfed him when he watched her in his kitchen came back. It spread through his limbs as he wrapped his arm around her neck and sat his hand on Munch's head. It felt like they'd laid like that before at another time in another universe.

He buried his face in her curls and inhaled. "I'll give you whatever you want—even six other babies."

"Oh yeah?" she muttered back. "You can make a miracle like that happen?"

"Mhmm."

She snickered. "I be forgetting you like black Jesus."

The pilot came over the plane's intercom, mumbling about their itinerary, and Munch lurched in her arms.

"You're a good man, Ant." She yawned, rubbing Munch's head and coaxing her back down. "Never let anybody tell you different."

twenty-eight

• • •

"I KNOW the fuck she didn't..."

Those words pulled Venus out of her sleep in Anthony's front seat. The jet-lag from flying to and from another state in one day made her body heavy—especially her eyes.

She tried to open them, but after so many shots, they wouldn't cooperate.

Leaving was a blur because he'd rushed her and Tori off the plane and ushered them to the car since she'd ruined the possibility of Mikayla covering that one hour of his shift.

She rolled over on her side and peeled her eyes open, belting out a yawn. "What's going on?"

It took a minute for her eyes to adjust to the hazy orange from the setting sun, but when they did, her stomach clenched at his frowning face.

"What's wrong?" she asked again.

He squinted and strained his neck at whatever was ahead of their car. She followed his line of vision, but all she saw were the same cars parked in front of his apartment building from that morning. At least, she thought they were the same.

He bit into his bottom lip and lifted his foot off the gas. The car inched forward at a snail's pace until it came to a complete stop in the middle of the parking lot.

"Ant..."

He stiffened, turning his neck to her but keeping his eyes on the row of cars ahead until one of the car's doors flew open and a girl emerged.

"Don't get out the car," he said.

"Why would I get ou... wait, what's going on?"

"Get out!" the girl yelled, barreling toward them with her jet black hair blowing in the wind. "Get the fuck out!"

Her voice was muffled, but Venus recognized its angelic softness and poise.

This was really her.

This was the girl who wasn't emotionally intelligent at all. The girl who violated him. The girl who used to be his.

This was Deeanna.

Somehow Venus knew it was her. Call it a woman's intuition or the aftermath of being with a man who tried to fuck any woman within ten degrees of her. She could always spot *the one*.

She was there in the flesh with a scowl on her face that didn't even mar her delicate features. It wasn't fair to still look so good, even while angry. She was everything Venus thought Mikayla was—long haired and well dressed in a black formfitting jumpsuit. She had a body to die for and was captivating even while lunging toward Anthony's car.

She banged on the driver's side window.

"Who is that?" she yelped, pointing at Venus.

She didn't even ask for her sleeping baby first.

"You thought I wasn't gon' find out where you moved to, huh?" She laughed. "You lying motherfucka! You think people don't talk?"

Her balled fist crashed into the window. "Open the door!"

"Anthony..." Venus called out, picking up her crossbody from the floorboard and turning to Tori in the backseat.

Tori blinked, pulling herself out of her sleep and looking around with her eyebrows furrowed until she stopped on Deeanna standing outside the car. Her bottom lip poked out and quivered, and then all the big emotions she never expressed at school came pouring out.

She rustled around in her car seat, shaking the seatbelt across her chest. "DADDY!"

It was only the third time Venus heard her voice and the first time she witnessed her correlate that word with Anthony, even though it was always written on her face.

"Daddy!"

Her tone was desperate and Venus saw the other times she probably called out for Anthony in her eyes.

"Gimme my baby!" Deeanna yelped, moving to the back passenger door and yanking the handle.

The car rocked.

"Munch..." Anthony muttered, unbuckling his seatbelt. "Hold on, baby."

Now he was the desperate one, twisting his body and reaching for Tori in her car seat.

That laid back swagger melted right in front of Venus' eyes as he pulled at the straps holding Tori in place. As soon as he got her loose, Tori scrambled out of the car seat, hooking her arms around his neck.

"Don't go, Daddy!" she shrilled. "Don't go!"

Venus lost her breath.

God, Tori could talk.

She could say a lot more than a baby her age should've been responsible for saying.

Now it made sense.

Tori didn't have the luxury of letting out those big emotions for stolen markers in class. Hers were stored for moments like these.

"Don't." Venus reached out, tugging his fingers off Tori's back. "I got her—just...just go make her stop. She's scari—"

"If you touch my baby—I swear to God!"

There was one thing Michole always glossed over in their sessions. She was always so focused on healing and moving forward that she never talked enough about the fine art of living with trauma in a world that would always test you.

That same heat crept up her neck from when she got the first inkling of Trey's affair.

"You hear me! Get out!" Deeanna yelled.

Venus felt the mugginess from that day on her skin, smelled the leather from her Uber's seats, and Deeanna sounded so much like the old her she kept trying to run from.

Her hand fell from Anthony's arm and she looked into his eyes. A storm brewed inside them and she got swept in it even though she wasn't supposed to, just like she was never supposed to swim again. Daddy's weird universe was at work again, or maybe that's what she was telling herself to smooth the rough edges of her and Anthony's messy situationship.

Deeanna rushed over to the passenger side and slammed her open palm against the window.

Tori yelped.

"Get away from my car, DeeDee!" Anthony yelled.

"No! Tell her to get out! This why you ain't been picking up my calls?"

Tori started wailing between their words.

"Tell that *bitch* to get out!"

It was funny how Deeanna's concern for Tori got swept away.

Tori's little sock covered feet dug into Anthony's sides as they held each other in the driver's seat.

"Anthony..." Venus let out a sarcastic laugh, shaking her head. "I just want you to know I hit back. I will *beat* her ass."

He shook his head, pulling the door handle. "No."

"I promise you I wi—"

"I know you will, and I promise you I won't let you. You a

'work in progress,' remember?" he yelled over his shoulder as he pushed out of the car with Tori in his arms.

Deeanna rushed them before he could even close the door and Venus held her breath for her and Tori's dramatic reunion, but it never happened. She should've listened closer when Anthony talked about Deeanna and her cunning ways.

She was so smooth that she juked him and Tori and dove inside the car. She crawled across the driver's seat, spreading her flowery scent.

"You thought his mama wasn't gon' tell me about you? Huh? He'll never leave me!" she shouted, getting closer to Venus with rage in her hazel eyes.

Silly girls like Deeanna placed men on pedestals. Venus *would* know, because she used to be that same silly girl.

"Get the fuck out!" Her nails scraped Venus' arm, breaking the skin.

"Girl, get the fuck off o—" Venus yelped until somebody opened the passenger door and jerked her out of the car.

"He'll never love you!" Deeanna yelled.

There was that word again.

Out of all the insults she could've pelted at Venus. That was the one she chose.

Love.

It was there, fluttering around like a fleeting leaf blowing in the wind as they made a scene outside Anthony's apartment.

Venus smelled him and Tori on her body and felt a warm trickle of blood cascading down her arm. He mushed her face into his chest.

"Let her go, Nuney!" DeeDee huffed. "I just wanna talk to her, that's it. I just wanna know why she feels so comfortable prancing around with *my* man and *my* baby. Carlotta told me everything. This trifling ass hoe supposed to be teaching my kid, but she fuckin' you! You fuck every nigga at that school or just mine? I hate bitches like you!"

Every insult was like a little nick to all the progress Michole had bragged about her making.

She braced her arm against Anthony's stomach to push away because she wanted to *talk*, just like Deeanna did. She was so good at talking that Michole had tried to brainwash that out of her, too.

Anthony mushed her head back into his chest.

"Let...her...go!" Deeanna screamed, clapping. "Just let her go!"

"Hey, man. Y'all got to take that somewhere else before I call the police," a gruff voice called out in the distance.

"Shut your old ass—" Deeanna belted, before Anthony cut in.

"Go get in the car, DeeDee!"

"No—"

"I swear to God if you don't get yo' ass in that car and shut up," Anthony hissed.

"I meant what I said! Y'all keep on and I'm calling the police!"

"We just talking, sir. You don't gotta do that!" Anthony yelled back.

They moved, but Venus couldn't see where. Tori's foot dug into her head, while Anthony kept it locked in a vise grip. He raked his nails against her scalp.

"If that girl keep on with all that nonsense, I will. It's quiet here. We ain't had no foolishness like this since they changed management and kicked the riff-raff out."

They were closer to the voice now, but the gravel crunching made her shoulders tighten back up.

She pushed against him again and Tori whimpered.

"I understand," Anthony replied. "We'll be gone in five minutes—"

"Five? You better make it one. They'll come haul all y'alls butts away for disorderly conduct. I've called before and I won't hesitate—"

"No, no, no. Listen, Unc," Anthony pleaded, letting go of her head.

She pushed up, gasping and blinking until the floaters disappeared from her vision and she saw Tori's face buried in his neck. She whimpered, keeping her eyes closed.

"See, my daughter's mother is here to pick her up from me and she just upset about something silly. That's all. Co-parenting struggles, you know?"

Venus peered around his body to look for Deeanna. As soon as she caught sight of her in his car, he gripped her by the neck and pulled her back into him.

"Is that right?" the man hummed. "And what about this one? Is she alright?"

"Huh?" Anthony replied.

After a beat, he jerked his head down and swiped his hand across her face, scooping up the angry tears she hadn't even felt falling. "Oh...my wife. Yeah, she's okay."

She twisted around, ignoring that vomit inducing fluttering in her stomach at the confident way he'd called her his "wife" to a stranger. It felt too good at the wrong moment.

The man's grey eyebrow raised, and she hooked her hand around the cut on her arm. Anthony rested his hand on her waist.

The man eyed her. "Wife, huh?"

"Yeah."

His eyes roved to their naked ring fingers next. He studied her finger the hardest, glaring at the spot where her solitaire diamond used to sit before she pawned it.

"You got any grandkids that go to Hill?" Anthony added, moving his hand on top of hers and lacing their fingers together. "She teach there."

The man's wrinkled face perked up.

Anthony cleared his throat, squeezing her hip. "Right, V?"

"Yeah," she croaked out. "I—I teach kindergarten there."

"I got a couple grands that go there," he grunted back.

Her body heated at the possibility of her running into him at work. He cradled his flip phone in his hands, squinting in the distance behind them.

"I hope you'll drop by for grandparents' day next month," she said. "It's on the sixteenth."

He nodded, relaxing his eyes. "Yeah, my daughter told me. Got the reminder up on the fridge."

Anthony's tense fingers relaxed as he shoved his flip phone back into his pocket.

He wagged his finger at Anthony. "Get that baby inside and get your house in order, young man. It ain't nothing more I hate then seeing two black women go at it in the street over a man. They always the ones risking their careers and livelihoods over y'all."

He said "y'all" like he wasn't a black man, too. He sounded just like Daddy, and it made the hair on her arms stand.

"Take care of your wife," he added.

When he stepped back inside and pulled the door shut, she expected Anthony to hiss out a smart aleck remark after the begging and conniving he had to do to keep the cops away. Instead, he pulled her by the hand across the parking lot until they got to her car.

Tori still hadn't pulled her head from his neck and she had buried her little voice right back inside of herself.

He nudged Venus against the driver's side door, swiping the blood off her arm. "Stay right here. Don't move."

She'd never seen distress on his face until that moment. He looked like he was turning over every word his neighbor said or it could've been the way Deeanna sat stock still in his car, waiting on him like he was still hers.

"Ant..." she muttered around the ball in her throat.

"I'mma go get your purse and your phone."

He talked to the ground, bouncing Tori up and letting her claw her nails into his neck. The ball moved from her throat to her stomach.

"You're not gonna send Tori with her...are you?" He looked back at Deeanna, who'd gotten out of the car to pace around it.

She folded her arms and leaned against the hood, glaring their way.

"Listen...just stay here and let me go get your stu—"

"You're not answering me, Anthony. I asked if you were sending your baby with her."

His eyes darted everywhere except where they needed to be.

"Wait a minute, you're—you're gonna take her upstairs aren't you—"

"Baby..."

The first time he called her "baby" didn't feel sweet. She couldn't savor it or bask in it. It didn't make her giddy because it came out like an "I'm sorry."

He shook his head and reached out to rake his fingers through her hair. "Stay right here while I go get your stuff."

"Anthony..."

"Stay right here, Venus. I'm serious."

He couldn't look her in the eyes.

Even when he backed away to make sure she stayed put, his eyes veered off to the side.

He didn't turn around until he got close to Deeanna. She trailed him so close that if he stopped, she'd topple over him. Her mouth moved, but Venus couldn't make out the words.

She grabbed ahold of her car's sideview mirror to steady herself.

That was the nasty thing about swimming again. Nobody was ever there to save her from drowning. Trey never offered a life vest or even bothered calling for help while she flailed around, trying to come up for air.

She swore there was a smug expression on Deeanna's face when Anthony handed Tori to her and marched back across the parking lot with her purse and keys dangling from his hand. Leti had looked at her the same way while crawling off Trey's lap with her dress hanging down her arms.

When Anthony was back in front of her, bile climbed up her throat. She reached out and grabbed her purse strap, but he wouldn't let her take it.

"Gimme my purse," she gasped out. "Let go."

"I don't want her, Venus," he replied in a strained voice. "Baby, I swear I don't want her."

"Right, I'm sure that's what you thought all the other times she bullied her way back into your life."

He shook his head like he knew what she meant.

She peered past him at Tori crying in Deeanna's arms.

"Go home and...and relax and I'll call you when—"

"No. Hell no!" She shook her head. "Call me and then what? Call me and tell me y'all gon' work it out for the baby? I ain't stupid."

"No." He shook his head. "Nah, I...I just need a minute to talk to her—to calm her down."

"And how you gon' do that, huh? The same way you calm me down?

"Don't do this shit, Venus...don't do this."

"You know...it's not even her or me. It's *you*. You're the problem," she babbled out. "You love too fuckin' hard and...and me and you are existing in two different universes, but we keep trying to pretend like we're not. We weren't meant to last anyway, so I don't even know why I care so much."

———

Jail didn't change DeeDee for the better, but then again, it never changed anybody Anthony knew—not even himself.

She paced the perimeter of his living room with Munch on her hip, trampling over Munch's toys and peeking behind the vertical blinds.

The energy inside the apartment didn't even feel the same. The shit was tainted now with her flowery perfume and fucked up entitled ass aura.

Venus hadn't even been gone for an hour and he already wanted her back, but she was right. It was him. He was the problem. He always had been. He loved too hard and too much and there wasn't enough left to give—not even to Venus Thibodeaux —and she deserved it the most.

"Who bailed you out?" he asked, sitting on the arm of the couch with a turning stomach.

"Keem told me to get a bail bondsman as soon as I got in there, but I told her 'no, I don't even know how that works. Nuney'll take care of it.' Two months later, I'm on the phone with her again, begging her to explain to me how to get that bail bondsman she told me about because you prancing around town with our baby's teacher. By that time, I figured you couldn't control me anymore if I just did the shit myself. Because that's what you like, huh? You like controlling me. It's how you get back at me." DeeDee glared at him from over her shoulder and walked off into the kitchen, sweeping her eyes over the dishes Venus had washed and put on the dish rack to dry.

He swiped his hands down his shorts, remembering how she'd gotten onto him when he told her to throw the dishes in the dishwasher and be done with them.

"I don't believe in dishwashers. I wash them better. You'll see."

She had him believing that shit, too. There were no streaks or specks of food on them afterward. They were perfect. No wonder Munch thought she was magical.

Munch sniffled to herself with a defeated look on her face as DeeDee swung her to her other hip and wiped the tears from her flushed cheeks.

He'd look that way too if his mama was always carting him from pillow to post. He was the only constant in Munch's life and even he wasn't as constant because DeeDee would never let him be.

DeeDee flung open the door to the laundry room and walked inside.

"What you looking for?" he called out, rubbing the back of his neck and pushing up from the couch.

He trekked through the kitchen and into the laundry room.

Inside, she ran her hand across his black button down Venus had washed and pressed.

He groaned, patting his pockets and yanking his phone out. "Fuck."

He should've been an hour into his shift by now. Mona, Mikayla, and Josiah had texted and called. Mona had sent an SOS, Josiah had wanted to know when he'd started fuckin' Munch's teacher, and Mikayla simply wanted to know if he'd gotten back with DeeDee.

"She already begging for you?" DeeDee uttered, eyeing the rest of the laundry Venus tackled in the short time she was there.

He scoffed, swiping to open Mona's text.

If only she knew that Venus Thibodeaux wasn't a beggar.

"Tell her she can go mind her business now."

> **Mona:**
>
> Where are you? Mikayla called in so we're short. I need you at the front of the house with me.

She wasn't even mad, just so frantic that it made him frantic. It wasn't nothing but the Venus effect. He was caring about shit he would've never cared about in the past.

> **Anthony:**
>
> Family emergency. Give me an hour and I'll be there. Keep—

DeeDee wrapped her hand around the phone before he could reassure her he was coming. She yanked it out of his grasp and threw it down.

It slid across the floor for the second time that day.

"What you keep texting her for, huh?" she growled, frowning. "What you need her for, Anthony? I'm right here."

He looked up at her.

She *was* there, but there wasn't that excitement that used to be there in the past when she finally came home to him.

She wanted him to laugh about her breaking his phone and tell her he'd just buy another one. Afterward, he'd console Munch and tell her, "Mama and Daddy weren't mad at each other." He always promised her they never were, but she never believed him until she saw them kiss. Then, he was supposed to forget about Venus because she wasn't enough for him. DeeDee was supposed to have been everything he needed.

He stared at her bare baby face. Her pupils dilated to hazel discs, and her nostrils flared. Two months in jail *really* hadn't changed a thing.

"Daddy..." Munch croaked, pushing her arms out for him to grab her.

He tried to take her, but DeeDee held her in place until Munch stiff armed her.

"Let go!" Munch huffed. "I want Daddy."

They'd really fucked up, because he wasn't even "Noni" anymore.

"Stop it," DeeDee hissed. "You're hurting Mama's feelings."

"I don't care!" She pushed her body back and forth against DeeDee's. "Go away!"

Ironically, these were the times she looked nothing like DeeDee and the most like Brian. He and Josiah googled the nigga before their first court date. They studied Brian's face so much so the picture became ingrained in Anthony's brain until he waltzed into the courtroom and Anthony saw him in the flesh. Josiah said Munch had his bushy eyebrows, his complexion, and even the same little beauty mark on her cheek.

"Let me go!" she screeched, slapping DeeDee's chest and pushing away.

"Stop!" DeeDee rasped as Munch bent back, kicking her feet back and forth.

She tried to drag her hand across Munch's head, but Munch didn't want that. That was the last thing she wanted, and after five years, DeeDee should've known that.

"Man, give her here." He sighed. "She don't want you to touch her head."

"You don't know what my baby wants!"

"And you do?"

They were regressing again because he didn't have his house in order, just like his neighbor had said. It was embarrassing to have another grown man point out how out of control he'd let his life get.

"I knew enough to feed her without you, I knew enough to get her back and forth to school every day without you, I knew enough to get her new clothes, shoes, and car seats after you lost everything, I knew enough to get a lawyer to fix your fuck up."

"*My* fuck up?" She shook her head, chuckling to herself. "You still in your feelings about what happened?"

She always referred to it as "what," as if it would soften the fact she slept with another man and carried his child while telling anybody that would listen that she loved Anthony. Lola said it was audacious—maybe even embarrassing.

"*She'll get her karma,*" Lola would hiss, shaking her head.

He stared at the sparkling Rolex she still wore, even though she said she was done with Brian the first time she called him from jail.

"I did what you told me to do and asked him to sign his rights away. He said 'no.' I asked for split custody like you told me to. He said 'no.' I did everything you asked me to do and when it didn't go your way you abandoned me in jail! What else you want from me, Anthony? You want me to go back in time with a magic wand and rewrite history? I can't do that! He wants his daughter and I can't do anything about it! *You* decided to risk everything and pay all this money for that expensive ass lawyer with no guarantee. *You* did that when I told you the odds were slim!"

His heart constricted and his tongue grew heavy.

He didn't know what a heart attack was like, but he was sure it felt just the same as hearing DeeDee call Munch 'Brian's daughter.'

"I told you to just enjoy the time you had with her—not run off with her and hire a lawyer!"

Munch gave her arms another slap that didn't land as hard as she wanted, and he didn't give DeeDee time to decide how to handle her again. He reached out and grabbed Munch's hot arms. He pulled her, but DeeDee wouldn't let up and his vision grew blurry.

"Gimme my baby, man," he muttered pathetically. "Let go."

"No, you need to get yourself together. You trippin' again."

"Get myself together?" He howled, digging his fingers underneath hers. "Get *myself* together? You the one that just got out! You layin' your head at your mama's because that nigga kicked you out that penthouse he had you in when his wife decided not to leave him. You ain't know I knew that, did you? Yeah, motherfuckas be telling me stuff, too."

"Oh, you think you better than me now?"

Sometimes he did. Not on no holier than thou shit, but he knew his heart was more solid than hers.

Another salty tear trickled between his lips. He swiped it with his forearm before Munch saw, but it was too late.

She inhaled and gurgled out a—"Daddy?"

"Answer me!" DeeDee yelped. "You think you're better than me, don't you?"

Munch slapped her hands over her ears, widening her eyes. "Stop yelling!"

He tried to grip her again, but DeeDee wouldn't let go. She held her tighter and stared into his face.

"Oh, all of a sudden you don't have nothing to say back?"

She laughed as her face lit up. "It's that teacher, huh? She hasn't figured out you're just like me?"

There she was again, comparing them.

"What you got out of this one, Anthony? Huh? A free step-mama while I was gone? She know I let you sleep with all those ditzy ass girls like her to get all your lil' anger out your system? Seems like she did a nice job. You're all mellow now—crying instead of breaking shit. Kudos to her."

Her tone changed to that light innocent one he fell for when she waltzed up to him in their high school geometry class, pretending not to understand their assignment.

"Maybe I should go up to that school and thank her?" She bounced Munch up and down.

Munch let her hands slip from her ears because she'd been played by that voice, too. DeeDee gripped her cheeks and twisted her face to look at her.

"Should Mama go thank Ms. T for all the dishes and laundry she washed?" she squealed. "Principal Bivins is still there, right? I should go tell him alllll the ways Ms. T took care of you and Daddy while Mama was in trouble."

"If you take yo' motherfuckin' ass—"

She whipped her head around and bugged her eyes at him, hiking her eyebrow up. "Your baby can hear you."

"If you go up there and talk to that man, I swear to God..."

She laughed, looking him up and down and raking her hand across Munch's hair. "Oh, Daddy has a crush on Ms. T, Toriana? That's why he's so different? You knew that and didn't tell Mama? You always tell me everything about Daddy."

She said it flippantly, but her eyes lit like she'd finally found what she'd been searching for.

Her shoulders bounced as she laughed harder.

"A *crush*? Nuney's got a crush. Wait—wait, no, excuse me. Anthony Nunez has a crush. That's who you are now, right? *Anthony*." She mocked Venus' drawl. "You love her, Anthony? That's why you let her play house with my family?"

Their arms brushed each other's as they played tug of war with Munch's soft body.

When Deeanna was angry, it didn't seep out of her pores and make him want to cradle her to his chest. It sat in her head where he imagined it simmered until it exploded with all the conniving plans she'd been conjuring up.

"I know you heard me. Do you love her, Anthony?"

Love?

He swallowed, pulling at Munch again.

DeeDee had never asked him about that word unless it pertained to her. She was always chasing it and waiting on it to come out of his mouth when they made love, when they talked about Munch, or even when they argued.

"Answer me."

His phone buzzed from the floor and he looked at it.

"She doesn't care about you like I do. You know that, right?" she muttered in that hypnotizing voice.

"Look at me." She reached out and twisted his face like she'd done Munch's.

She even swiped those annoying ass tears that wouldn't stop falling. "She wouldn't do any of the shit I've done for you. Tell me what she does for you."

The thing about DeeDee was everything was transactional. Nothing ever came from the heart and somehow, during the years they'd spent going back and forth with each other, she'd turned him into the same type of heartless ass person.

He pulled his face back, but she held it tighter.

"Tell me…" she gritted out.

He shook his head.

He knew better than that and it was impossible to put into words anyhow.

There was no particular *thing* Venus did that made him obsessed with her. She would never do a bid for him. She probably wouldn't get on a stand and lie for him, and she'd already showed him she wouldn't put up with the stupid shit he was always doing to stay ahead. All she did was care and somehow that felt better than the shit DeeDee bragged about doing for him.

"Baby," she whispered, scraping her nails down his face.

His stomach contracted, and he choked on a gag. "I told you to stop calling me that."

"She doesn't care abou—"

He yanked his head out of her hand. "Nah. *You* don't care about me."

His skin burned where her fingers scraped.

"You don't give a damn about me." He shook his head, fighting off the nostalgia she tried to evoke out of him by using *that* word.

That shit didn't even belong to her anymore. It was Venus' word. No other woman said "baby" and meant it like Venus did.

"If you cared about me, we wouldn't be here, but you don't get that—do you?"

"Don't start this shit again, Nuney," she spat.

They probably looked stupid as hell with their arms tangled around Munch, arguing about the shit he just couldn't get over. Maybe he should've taken Lola's advice and talked to that therapist she found last summer, but then again, what could a therapist do? They couldn't implant his DNA into Munch or make him stop hating DeeDee.

"Nuney..." she called out with caution.

His eyes traced her face, and he picked it apart.

What the fuck did he ever see in her?

They weren't meant for forever. She'd thrown that away the moment she let Brian give her the one thing she said she'd only give him.

"We can work this ou—"

"Work what out?" He scoffed. "Ain't nothing between me and you to work out."

"You so damn delusional that you got *me* delusional, you know that? I'm spending thousands of dollars on a family attorney to fight for another man's baby, Deeanna—another nigga's seed. Do you hear how crazy that sound?" he rasped. "And you think I don't deserve better than you? You actually think I still love you? You really think that low of a nigga?"

Afterward, he wanted to stuff those words back in his mouth because her baby face dissolved behind the hot tears that fell down his face.

He and Munch were always the only ones crying in these moments. There were times he wondered if DeeDee was even human until he'd go off and remind her just how little she respected him.

"You don't love me anymore?" she uttered.

"DeeDee..."

As soon as his throbbing fingers relaxed, she yanked Munch's body from them and took off out of the laundry room. That familiar gurgling in his stomach came back as he ran after them while trying to hold it all down.

"Don't leave with my goddamn baby, Deeanna! Stop!" Desperation spilled out of his mouth as he tripped over Munch's backpack and stumbled behind them.

Their feet pounded across the living room floor, out the front door and down the stairs until they got back to the parking lot.

He kept his eyes on the back of her black jumpsuit.

There was a split second where he thought he had her. The black fabric was inches from his fingers, but she faked him like she'd done to get to Venus and he lost his one chance.

She ran up to her car, yanking the driver's side door open and sliding in with Munch in one swift motion. As soon as he got close enough to the car, she slammed the door, missing his fingers by an inch.

She'd left it unlocked and running and he'd been too caught up with Venus to realize it.

He pounded on the window. "Open the door!"

Munch cried again.

Her screams made him claw at the handle and yank it. He

shook it so hard that it flew off the door, leaving pieces of plastic scattered across the concrete.

"Open it!" he screamed. "Don't do this shit to me!"

She hit the gas, and he jumped back as she sped out of the parking lot with Munch wailing in her arms.

He choked on the exhaust while holding onto a chunk of the handle. When he looked up, that same neighbor was back outside his front door, ashing a cigarette on the ground and shaking his head.

He turned to go back inside.

twenty-nine

. . .

ON THURSDAY, Tori's desk was still empty.

Her pink nameplate sat undisturbed with the edges she'd plucked, curling up at the ends.

Venus took a sip of her coffee while fighting her jittering leg that hadn't stopped shaking since she sped out of Anthony's apartment complex without looking back.

When she walked into the front office to check her mailbox, Paula had yelped that she mailed a truancy notice to Tori's house and if Tori didn't come on Friday, she'd have to send another less than friendly one.

She had sucked her teeth, typing on her computer and glancing up at Venus after every other word. *I thought he was one of the good ones.*

Afterward, Venus had asked her if she'd even sent out the truancy notice to the correct address. She hadn't meant to say something so smart-alecky, but living life without Anthony made her testy.

A hot splash of coffee landed on Venus' baby blue blouse, rousing her out of her thoughts.

She hissed as it singed her skin. "Shit."

The brown stain sank into her shirt as she slammed her mug

down and snatched a handful of Kleenex from the box on her desk.

"Okay girl, I said you could *borrow* my Louboutins, not keep them. Desmond says they make my calves look sexy," Logan babbled, waltzing into her classroom. "I need them for next weekend. We're going to some sushi restaurant to celebrate the fact his fish are still alive. You'll never guess where I found twenty koi fi—are you okay?"

Venus looked up at a frowning Logan standing in front of her desk. "Huh?"

"I asked if you were okay."

Venus pat her flat hair and then dabbed at the stain. "Yeah? Why? What's wrong?"

"Your hair's in a bun and you're...you're glowing."

She dabbed at the stain again, running from Logan's intimidating stare.

She'd never had a glow during a fight with Trey, but what was that old saying? There was a first time for everything—for fights with Anthony, for strange dreams where she belonged to him and Tori, for dewy skin and sore muscles from overdue lovemaking.

God, she missed him and he made her delusional enough to believe they were in a fight when they were actually done.

Logan gasped, dropping her hands on her desk. "I know that glow. Who is he?"

"There is no 'he.' I got a new vibrator."

"Bitch," Logan whispered. "That lie might work on Paula's messy ass, but not me. Nope. You never wear your hair up."

"I always wear it up. *You* just never seen me with it up."

Logan shuffled from around the desk and leaned in so close the curly hair from her bohemian braids tickled Venus' nose.

"Girl, what are you doing?"

Logan closed her eyes and took a deep breath.

Venus' stomach caved in, even though there was no way she could smell Anthony on her. She'd scrubbed herself clean of any trace of him that Sunday night after throwing up all the expensive tequila and food he fed her in Detroit. She'd even tried flushing her feelings down the toilet, but they had the nerve to come back up.

"Logan, stop being weir—"

She crinkled her nose. "You been eating strawberry candy?"

Venus held her breath and rolled back in her chair. "I don't know what you talking about. I hate strawberry flavored anything."

"Well, whatever it is, it's coming out of your pores. Sheesh."

He couldn't have been leaking out of her pores. It was impossible, but then again she was still in Daddy's weird universe, where she had the nagging urge to swim again.

She brought her hand to her mouth until a loud tap against her classroom door made her shoulders jump.

"Ladies," Principal Bivins boomed. "Good morning, good morning."

They looked up at him strolling into the classroom in another sad brown suit with his Marines coffee mug. Logan relaxed her wide-eyed expression and leaned against Venus' desk.

"I'm glad I caught you two together." He walked toward an empty desk, hiking his pants leg up and sitting down.

He had the same forlorn expression on his face as when he wanted Venus to forget about Tori's lost voice.

He stroked his mustache. "How's the situation with ole Smiley been since our chat?"

"Good," Venus replied.

Logan turned to her, wrinkling her eyebrows. "You finally got Anthony to change his mind about the eval? I can finally stop bypassing your 'evaluation pending' notes in Parent Connect?"

"I hope not. We already talked about that, Ms. Thibodeaux," he replied, taking a sip of his coffee.

"What do you mean 'you hope not?'" Logan shot back,

crossing her arms. "More than one concerned teacher has approached me."

They burned holes into Venus' face while she tried to find the right words to make sure they didn't have the same thoughts Paula had because Anthony was a damn good daddy.

"She's been sick," she said, holding the tissue over the coffee stain.

Damn, she wasn't even on the stand yet, and she was already lying for him.

Principal Bivins raised his eyebrows. "Sick?"

"Yeah, a nasty stomach bug. I told Ant—Mr. Nunez, he'd need to get a doctor's note, but he's been busy taking care of her, I assume."

"Hmmm." Principal Bivins hummed, taking another slurp of coffee. "A stomach bug? For how many days?"

"Four."

"And what about the subp—"

"Still in my desk drawer," she cut between his words, keeping Anthony and Deeanna's business as close to the vest as she could.

She dabbed the stain harder.

When she looked up from her chest, she caught Logan's mouth drop and her eyes widening with a knowing glint in them. Her expression came and went so fast Venus almost didn't believe it ever changed.

Logan turned back to Principal Bivins afterward. "And now that we've got our wellness check out of the way, can you tell me why Ms. Thibodeaux shouldn't pursue an eval for a non-verbal student?"

Venus cringed inside, remembering the goosebumps that prickled her skin when Tori screamed out for Anthony. She'd tried to bottle up her voice and keep it. It replayed in her head, along with Anthony's smile.

"You don't have the time for another case, Mrs. Simmons, and the SPED department doesn't even have a seat available."

"Make one available just like I'll make the time available."

"Mrs. Simmons…"

"*Mr. Bivins…*"

"Okay, make one available and then what? We don't even have enough paras around here. So I should stretch my already thin staff to accommodate a student just because Mrs. Simmons said so?" He clanked his mug on the desk and sat forward.

"Yes! She's a baby. Today, she's refusing to talk and tomorrow she might not—"

"Even be enrolled here according to her attendance record. My staff are the only folks sounding off about this. Meanwhile, mama and daddy couldn't even be bothered to advocate for their own baby. I'm done with this discussion," Principal Bivins spat before turning to Venus. "I finally got ahold of our lawyer. He says you have to sign the subpoena and testify, Ms. Thibodeux. This situation is above us."

She dropped the tissue and gripped the edge of her desk. Her throat tightened at that impending court date getting closer while she tried to run further away from Anthony.

"Testify?" Logan hissed. "What's going on?"

Their eyes were back on her again.

Principal Bivins sat back as if he were giving her the floor to divulge Anthony's business that his own family friend wasn't even privy to.

"Tori's parents are involved in a custody dispute, Logan. They subpoenaed me to testify in court."

The first bell of the day dinged, signifying the end of breakfast.

"I gotta head up front to help Mrs. Maloney in the cafeteria, but holler if you need anything, Ms. Thibodeaux. I'll forward you the district lawyers' contact information—not sure if he'll be any help, though." He pushed out of the desk with a groan. "And while I understand both of you guys' concerns, my hands are tied. There're simply not enough resources here and not enough push from mama and daddy. They've got to care, too."

He strolled out of the classroom and into the crowd of little bodies marching through the hallways.

As soon as he was out of sight, Logan whipped around with her finger pointed at her and her mouth hanging open.

Venus gripped her desk harder.

She couldn't tell Logan about Brian. It was too messy and felt like betrayal even if she and Anthony weren't anything, but then again, they were *never* anything but a one-night stand.

"You..." Logan whispered. "You...you...slept with him, huh? He got in your head, didn't he? That's why you sitting up here lying for his ass."

"Logan, I didn't mean to. It just happe—"

Logan held her hand up to stop her impending ramble.

She held her breath, waiting for the Logan she knew to bounce with excitement at the thought of new gossip, but Logan just stared at her.

She dropped her hand she'd been holding up and Venus' stomach dropped too because now that there was no excitement, she knew judgment was coming.

How'd she go from hating this man to making love to him in only a few weeks?

"Do you care about him?" she asked. "Because he ain't nothing like what you wrote on that paper in my office, and ain't nothing wrong with that, but just know he's a package deal and the rest of that package is *very* problematic."

"I—"

"And your job, Venus. Does he know how much you love teaching? That conflict of interest policy ain't there for decoration."

"I—"

"You live and breathe for these babies."

The door creaked open. "Ms. T, I found a worm under the swings this morning. Wanna' see?"

Treshawn ran inside, leading the crusade of the rest of her class just as her heart stammered over an answer.

———

The first week without Munch was always the worst.

"Fuck." Josiah gagged. "You know I got a weak stomach."

Anthony heaved up another mouthful of vomit, and a puddle of red froth sank into the lush grass in Josiah's backyard. The muscles in his stomach contracted, making him bend over and clench his knees.

Dre' pressed his hand against his head with his cigarette dangling between his fingers. The fluffy cloud of smoke snuck up Anthony's nose and made him choke out another gag.

"You gotta breathe, gang," Dre' said.

"I can't," Anthony gurgled back. "I told you that."

"Whatever it is ain't real. It's in your head. Just relax."

He heaved up another mouthful of Jade's spaghetti.

"He got it out yet?" Zeke yelled from the enclosed patio.

"Almost!" Dre' replied, yanking him up by his shirt's collar. "Stand up."

That shit was damn near impossible. His knees felt like mounds of jello.

He dangled from Dre's fingers while swiping his hand across his mouth. "What the fuck did Jade put in that shit?"

"Love, nigga," Josiah replied, clapping him on the chest. "You used to living off Happy Meals, that's all that is."

Dre' took another drag of his cigarette and eyed Anthony as he blew a plume of smoke out his nose. His stare made Anthony swipe the wetness from his mouth again.

Dre' flicked his cigarette to the ground. "V be feeding you Happy Meals? She don't look like the fast food type."

She wasn't.

She was the type that would cook him a meal every night if that's what he wanted.

Josiah raised his eyebrows and then shook his head, looking away. A violent spasm rocked Anthony's stomach and made him bend over again. He roared out another mouthful of red.

"Get you some Pepto and a shot of Casa when you get home." Josiah snickered.

"Shut up, nigga," Anthony gargled out.

Josiah held his hands up.

Didn't his stupid ass know that Pepto Bismol and liquor wouldn't fix the void in his stomach?

He needed Munch to check his heartbeat with her Doc McStuffins stethoscope and then kiss him on his forehead because Lola had taught her kisses cured it all—even heartbreak.

"I'm 'rescribing you a kiss and a nap, Noni," she'd declare, patting his head. *"Let's cuddle."*

Another mangled ball of spaghetti shot up his esophagus and out of his throat. Josiah hiked his leg up as it landed next to his slides.

"Come on now." He groaned, examining his shoes' rubber soles. "Ain't no way it's still anything left in you."

That was probably it. He couldn't remember the last time he ate something before Jade's spaghetti. If Venus knew that shit, she'd wag her finger in his face and fuss until he threatened to bite it.

She and Munch just didn't understand how easily DeeDee made his world stop. *Work* didn't happen, Lynn's calls didn't get answered, and food was the last thing on his mind. He had even flown up in bed that morning with his heart pounding, thinking he'd overslept and missed his opportunity to talk to Principal Bivins like he promised Venus, because no matter how much DeeDee shook his world, he could never forget how to be a daddy.

"C'mon," Dre' murmured, pulling him back up and swiping his hand across his head. "Come sit down."

Dre' and Josiah held him up and walked him back to the enclosed porch, where Zeke waited with his feet kicked up on an end table. He shoveled a mouthful of Jade's cheesecake in his mouth while looking at the way they gripped his shoulders.

"You good?" he asked.

"Yeah, yeah." Anthony nodded, swiping his forehead and collapsing on the chaise across from him.

Dre' sat beside him, tossing his arm around his shoulders, and Josiah flopped next to Zeke.

They peered behind Josiah, searching for Jade through the cracked curtains hanging from the dining-room windows. She waltzed through the kitchen in her pajamas with her silk scarf tied around her locs and Journey on her heels. They talked while Jade gave the spotless kitchen a once over.

She paused and looked over her shoulder like she felt their eyes on her. After a beat, she shrugged and flicked the lights off. As soon as darkness coated the kitchen, Zeke tossed his plate and spoon on the end table and dug a blunt out of his pocket.

They all scooted forward.

The still night air lay between them while Zeke put the blunt to his lips and sparked his lighter.

He blew a cloud of smoke out, looking over at Josiah. "So, what's up? What you wanted us to come over for? You know Jade don't really be fuckin' with us unless it's the weekend."

Dre' chuckled, and Anthony mustered up his last bit of strength to smirk.

"For real. I ain't seen my sister and niece on a Thursday night since I lived here." Dre' whistled. "And we got dinner on top of that?"

"The hell going on?" Zeke chortled. "Let me find out y'all got a goddamn bun in the oven, twin."

Josiah held his finger up and then dug inside of his pocket, pulling a black box from his sweats.

He slapped it on the table next to Zeke's foot like they were playing bones. "*That's* what's going on."

Dre' furrowed his eyebrows first, then he reached out with caution and cracked the box open, exposing a fat pear-shaped diamond that sparkled underneath the dim lighting.

"No shit?" Zeke asked in bewilderment.

He pushed the blunt toward Josiah. "Here."

Josiah took it and put it to his lips while Zeke nudged the box like it was an explosive. When he pulled back, Dre' reached for the diamond and then snatched his hand back like it would cut his skin if he dared to even graze it.

The sight of the ring made Anthony's stomach gurgle again. It looked like it already belonged to Jade, and she didn't even know about it yet. It was classy and dainty like she was.

"What you think, Nuney?" Josiah asked, leaning forward to look at him. "Still think I'm a dumbass?"

Dre' and Zeke stared at him, too. He tried to swallow the cotton in his mouth, but it got stuck.

"Nah, JoJo," he croaked, eyeing the ring again. "You was never a dumbass—just a nigga in love, that's all. I'm proud of you."

Light reflected off the white gold band and made him think about Venus' empty ring finger. He should've been thinking about Jade in that moment, but when Venus Thibodeaux was sad, it engulfed every part of his body—especially his brain.

"It's beautiful." Dre' cleared his throat, finally nudging the ring with his knuckle. "So, what you need from us, baby boy?"

Josiah rubbed the back of his neck and sighed, passing the blunt to Anthony. "Tell me what I'm supposed to do next."

Josiah could've asked Dominic, but Dre' always said that some things were only meant for them to experience together. Maybe Josiah felt like this was one of them.

Anthony took a hit and laid back against the chaise, staring at the ceiling fan whirring in circles. He handed the blunt to Zeke without taking his eyes off of it, and they started a rotation like they were fourteen again and ruminating over Audriana being born. Even Dre' took a hit. It felt like their last hurrah, in a way. Josiah was going to be the first one to take that true leap into manhood. He was done playing house.

"Get on one knee," Zeke said, shrugging. "That's what they do in the movies."

Dre' waved his arms. "Nah, he gotta ask her daddy for his permission first."

"I ain't asking that fanned out nigga shit," Josiah grumbled. "He only call Jade when he want something."

"Then you gotta ask Terry," Dre' replied.

They all looked up at the same time with stoic expressions until they burst out in deep side splitting laughs. It was the first laugh Anthony had let out since he woke up to Venus whispering in his ear on the plane ride back home.

"*I think the bathroom is finally free,*" she'd whispered, making him crack his eyes open. "*You know... I ain't never made love thirty thousand feet in the air. That's living, right?*"

He laid his head against the chaise, smiling into the cloud of smoke that settled around them. He almost saw her purple ringlets through the haze.

"Shit, you gotta pray before you ask, Terry. That's a scary ass lady." Zeke sighed.

Josiah snickered. "She call me 'son' now."

"That's a good thing, right?" Dre' asked.

"Hell nah. That means I get it worse than Jade sometimes. I let Jour stay up an extra hour—'you can't do that, son. Kids need structure.' I promise Jour Disney in the off season—'you gotta tell her 'no' sometimes, son. You'll make her ungrateful.' I breathe wrong—'what're you doing, son? If I gotta do CPR on you, I won't be happy about it. Don't you traumatize my daughter and grandbaby.'"

Josiah grabbed his head and fell back. "And you telling me the first thing I need to do is ask for her permission? I gotta smoke a fat one before I make that drive to Athens."

They were gone now—floating somewhere above the haze inside the porch. The weight of Jade's impending proposal wasn't so heavy anymore. Anthony smiled into the haze at Venus hanging out in the clouds with a sad smile painted on her face at the thought of another one of his stupid friends being obsessed with marriage and DeeDee running off with her Bug.

"Nah, the first thing you need to do is think about an eternity," Anthony blurted, poking his finger out to touch her cute face.

"What you talking about?" Josiah asked.

"When you picture forever, what you see?"

He looked away from Venus and eyed Josiah's placid face. A tiny smile made its way onto his lips.

"I don't know," he muttered, licking them and accepting the blunt from Zeke as it made its way back around to him.

"The fuck you mean you don't know?" Anthony asked. "How you don't think about forever and you about to get married?"

"I mean...I see me, Jade, and Jour, but thinking about forever is some scary ass shit. My brain can't handle it."

"Well, getting married is for forever, you know that, right? Marriage ain't just some piece of paper like people like to throw around. She gonna be your *wife*, JoJo—the beginning and end for you, your strength, your backbone..."

"This nigga acting like divorces don't exist." Zeke fanned his hand, rolling his eyes.

Anthony's empty stomach buzzed when he heard that d-word because Venus had ruined it for him. It wasn't some random ass word he had no connection to anymore. She'd *lived* it and as soon as he put his mouth on hers, he'd lived it too. He tasted the ways it changed her—heard the slight crack in her voice when she talked about how Trey ruined love for her and made her believe she wasn't worthy of receiving it again.

He frowned, turning to Josiah. "You marry my sister to divorce her and I'll beat yo' ass. I swear to God."

"Hold up, she was mine before she was ever your sister," Josiah replied.

Zeke belted out an obnoxious cackle, even though there wasn't shit to laugh about. "Since when Nuney understand so much about marriage? V must got that lethal pillow talk."

There she was again—living in his friend's mouths, even

though they'd only spent one day with her. They didn't even deserve to taste her name.

"Ain't no more 'V.' She gone. So stop bringing her up," he spat, biting into his lip and looking back into the haze for her.

Zeke held his hands up. "My bad—thought you was in love, my boy. I figured you'd found life after DeeDee."

He had and DeeDee had snatched it away as soon as he got a taste of it.

"Shut the fuck up talkin' 'bout my business," he replied, closing his eyes.

"So it's true?" Zeke muttered. "That's why you out here looking all sad and throwing up."

Anthony cracked an eye open. "What you talkin' about?"

"I heard DeeDee got out."

It got so quiet around them the only sounds were the crickets chirping in the trees that surrounded Josiah's backyard. Dre' rubbed the back of his neck and looked at the ground.

"That's why it ain't no more V?" Josiah asked.

Anthony ignored them and blinked at the haze, waiting on Venus to materialize again. He tasted her around the remnants of the vomit that coated the insides of his mouth. She was always there, swirling inside of him with that look of betrayal on her face.

"Yeah. When we got back from Detroit, she was at my crib," he rasped.

"And?" Dre' tried to coax the rest out of him, but it hurt to even think about it, let alone say it out loud.

He swallowed Venus' taste again and swiped at his face. "She took her—DeeDee took Munch again and she won't give her back."

He sounded like that sad dumbass Zeke described—like a five-year-old who'd gotten his favorite toy stolen on the playground. But this was his baby—his world.

"She won't even pick up the fuckin' phone for me. None of 'em will—not even her mama or her brother. I been calling for a week. I even pulled up to her mama's, but they wouldn't answer the door even though I saw her mama's car in the driveway."

He'd called their phones so much they'd blocked his number. All of his desperate texts sat on his phone with no response.

A loud croak came from the back of one of their throats, but he couldn't tell whose it came from. He felt that familiar pang in his chest as he tried to fight through the pain DeeDee always conjured up.

"That's good, right?" Zeke asked.

"Zeke..." Dre' warned. "That's his baby. C'mon."

"That *ain't* his baby. We saw the DNA test he had to get for court. It said zero percent probability of paternity. Shit, he need to take advantage this time and go live his life. Let that doctor nigga take care of his responsibility."

"What you mean 'go live my life?'"

"It mean—keep your money and let that doctor deal with your headache. That bitch ain't brought nothing but havoc to your life. You fighting over a baby that ain't yours, every six months. You almost died the other week tryna come up with money for that overpriced ass lawyer. C'mon, Nuney. Be for real right now. Let that shit go, twin." He waved his hand. "I ain't never seen a nigga that want somebody else responsibility so bad."

"What the fuck you just say to me? You ought to be worried about whatever fucked up shit you got going on with Kristen thirsty ass."

"C'mon, y'all..." Josiah groaned, but it was too late. "Don't do this."

They were past the point of being placated.

"Shit, somebody gotta say it. I'm tired of tiptoeing around it." Zeke huffed. "Let that man have his kid. You done missed how many birthdays and Christmases? DeeDee don't want you to be a daddy—*she* don't even wanna be a mama. She just wanna control you."

"You talking too much, Zeke," Josiah warned. "That ain't your place."

"Then who goddamn place is it? Y'all niggas scared because you know he gon' crash out, but I'm tired of seeing him go through this."

The crazy thing about that angst Lola always laughed about was how it crept up on him sometimes. It slithered throughout his body and wrapped its talons around his heart and squeezed it until he saw red.

"Aye, sit down!" Dre' hissed, yanking Anthony's arm so hard it felt like it would come out of the socket.

He didn't even realize he was suspended in the air with Venus. Her face wrinkled with horror as he tried to claw his way out of Dre's grip and wrap his hand around Zeke's throat to suffocate those words that should've never poured out.

When did he even get up?

Zeke frowned at him from his spot on the chaise.

"Jade gon' trip the fuck out if y'all start fighting and y'all niggas really gon' be banned during the week," Josiah said, sliding his burly body between them.

"All I'm sayin' is, you diggin' in new pussy, my boy. Put a baby in V if you want one so bad," Zeke added, shrugging.

Anthony yanked his arm again, but Dre' still wouldn't let up. "Keep her name out your mouth. You gettin' too comfortable."

Somewhere during the melee, somebody dropped the blunt. It burned next to Zeke's foot while they writhed around each other like they were fourteen and fighting about the possibility of Kemah aborting Audriana.

"Let me go." Anthony bobbed to the left, looking around Josiah.

"I can't do that," Dre' replied, squeezing his arm tighter. "I can't let y'all go there."

"He already went there," Anthony murmured through the haze. "He tellin' me to give up my baby that *I* did skin to skin with! He telling me to forget her like he don't see the way she look at me! Fuck him!"

He had cried when DeeDee pushed Munch out—bawled right there in the delivery room while the nurses comforted him and told him what a "sweet daddy" he was. The first time he locked eyes with Munch, he saw forever in them and just like Josiah couldn't conceptualize forever, he couldn't conceive the idea of abandoning fatherhood when he'd already pledged his life to it.

Zeke raised his arms in surrender, but he still wore a smug smirk.

"Man, fix your face," Dre' boomed from behind him. "You fuckin' around like his heart ain't hurting."

It was broken, actually, but he'd be a bitch if he admitted that out loud to somebody other than Venus.

"He always think the world need to hear his fucked up opinions that nobody ever ask for." Anthony breathed out, breaking out of Dre's hold and swinging around Josiah.

His fist landed at the center of Zeke's mouth in a loud crack.

Zeke's head flew back into the chaise as a trickle of blood flowed down his chin. "You motherfuck—"

"Y'all gotta stop," Josiah hissed, pushing Anthony into Dre's chest.

Dre' gripped Anthony's head between the crook of his arm and hoisted him up.

"Stop," he murmured in a soft cadence. "Stop."

"Let me go."

"I can't let you do that. You hurtin' too much right now."

His body responded before he could.

It shook in Dre's arms and he felt that wetness he hated. It coated his cheeks in streaks and blurred Josiah's face.

He needed to get himself together, no matter how much Venus disagreed. In her world, it was okay to hurt, to cry, to be upset, but in the real world—he couldn't do that.

A sad frown coated Josiah's face. He reached behind him and yanked Zeke up while Dre' locked his arms around Anthony.

"You good," Dre' murmured, rocking him back and forth. "You good."

"Take him out there," he called out to Josiah. "I got Nuney. We ain't gon' wake Jade up."

Tears blurred his vision so badly he could only make out their silhouettes as they stumbled outside the porch. He tried to catch his breath, but it was too far out of reach, so his body gave up.

Zeke muttered about wanting to beat his ass from somewhere in the distance while Dre' pat his back.

"It's love—that's all, twin. You just in love with her and...and with Tori, and sometimes that shit hurts because life happens. It's okay to feel them feelings and if anybody ever tell you it's wrong, fuck 'em," Dre' gritted in his ear. "But you gotta stop running from it."

Love?

He pinched his eyes together, trying his damndest to shake that angst off, but it wouldn't leave.

thirty

. . .

"D'YOU GET my voicemail the other night? Lois died—at least I think it was her," Daddy drawled into Venus' ear as she stared at the sizzling egg in her skillet. "Never thought I'd see the day I'd be burying a damn chicken next to the family dog in the backyard."

"Nobody leaves voicemails anymore, Daddy."

"Well, I do. What's wrong with a voicemail?"

"It's perfectly fine to send a text message."

"A text is a bit casual, don't ya' think? Besides, Lois was one of your favorites. I still don't know how you tell 'em apart."

"I told you to look at their combs. Lois had a pea comb. I hope you marked her grave. You forgot to mark Jake's. Sometimes I don't know if I'm leaving libations for him or Mrs. Donald's Pomeranian you buried out there, too."

Pepper rubbed against her leg, purring and burying his face in the UGG slippers she was supposed to have tossed in the trash chute that morning. She'd scooped them up and walked all the way down the hall with them, but when she opened the cover to the chute, her hand stopped working.

She pushed her spatula under the egg and sucked her teeth when it wouldn't budge. "Dammit."

"D'you oil the pan, Jitterbug?"

"Yes, Daddy," she hissed, shoving the spatula underneath until it peeled from the skillet, leaving remnants of egg stuck to its bottom. "I know how to fry an egg. I been frying eggs for twenty years now. I know I'm supposed to oil the freaking pa—"

"Who is he?"

She flipped the egg and nudged Pepper away with her foot. "Who is who?"

"The *man*," he replied in exasperation. "You ain't fried an egg in years, Venus, and you sound...sad."

She did?

She blinked and stepped back from the stove, trying to ground herself like Michole taught her.

She saw the skillet, heard the egg sizzling in it, smelt her coffee brewing, but she couldn't feel anything. The one person she wanted to feel had left her with nothing to show for their short time together except some stupid mutual telepathy that still worked. They were still in sync and they were *really* in a fight. He'd told her so in her dreams the night before.

"How long we gon' fight for, baby?" he'd asked.

He made it seem as if they were in another silly lover's spat.

She swiped an errant tear from her face. "It wasn't real, you know?"

"What wasn't? The man?" Daddy asked. "You still talking to that therapist lady, right?"

"Daddy, yes...I mean, I missed my last couple of appointments...but...but..." She huffed. "He's not imaginary. I just messed up like I always do with men."

He grew quiet and her neck heated like it did when she told him she was going to marry Trey.

"Do I need to come to Atlanta?"

"No...maybe. I don't know." She gripped the counter.

"Which one is it? What did you do? Did this dude hurt you?"

"No!" She shook her head. "Not in the way you're talking about."

The type of hurt he hinted at left her bobbing on the surface of love—too afraid to go under. Anthony's hurt was the type that reignited her passion. She'd flown up out of her sleep the night before with his name on her lips, telling him she was "tired of fighting." She had nothing left to give. She'd accept his strained relationship with Deeanna, accept that Carlotta didn't like her like Rose didn't, she'd be patient while he fought Brian, she'd let him make love to her every night with no regrets, and she'd stop searching for that grown man because she had him. They didn't have to fight any more.

She swiped at another tear while Pepper purred like he heard her delusional thoughts.

"What's going on, Venus?"

Their screen door creaked in the distance and she knew he was headed onto the porch to sit down.

Their porch was where he digested all of her unwarranted confessions like that festering jealousy she had because Ginny had found her forever while hers fell apart.

"Take the damn egg off the stove," he grumbled. "We can't afford a fire *and* a heartbreak."

She stood up and snatched the skillet, moving it to a different burner. She wasn't even hungry. She'd just forgotten how much love fucked with her appetite.

She dry heaved and Daddy groaned. "That's it. I'm calling Gail and telling her to book me a flight."

"Daddy, stop." She whined. "Don't be bothering Aunt Gail."

"Well, explain yourself, dammit! You calling and getting me riled up, knowing I'm in another state. I'm too old for this, Ve—"

"I ... I think I'm falling in love again," she blurted. "But I'm scared."

She curled her toes inside the UGGS like she was teetering at the edge of that rapper's pool, she and Anthony had swum in.

He groaned, and she knew he was rubbing at the wrinkles on his forehead. "Not this again. I told you it's no such thing as being so afraid of falling in love that you forget how to do it. It's made up. It's in your head. It's just like...like riding a bike or swimming. You never forget how to do it."

It wasn't made up, but she didn't want to argue with him about it.

"What's wrong with the dude?" he muttered.

"Everything. God, he's a mess. He's not perfect, but his heart is," she blurted without thinking. "He makes me feel alive—like...like I just turned twenty-one and I have an entire lifetime to figure things out."

She smiled to herself as tears rolled down her face. She ached to squeeze his handsome face and hear his goofy laugh one more time.

"Then what the hell are you freaking out about? Did I miss something?"

"He's young. He's young, and he's so passionate that it makes him dumb sometimes... and...and I shouldn't have gone there with him."

She probably sounded manic. Hell, she probably even looked that way, crying and ranting and raving about a man she had a two-night stand with.

"Why not?"

"Because he's my student's dad."

He groaned to himself again.

"I violated the trust of one of my babies for selfish reasons, Daddy, but even she doesn't see it that way."

"Venus," he hissed. "The baby saw y'all together? What the hell is wrong with you? You must wanna get fired."

She choked on the rest of her and Anthony's story that was feeling as *Young and the Restless* as his friend's romantic drama.

"Oh, God...sometimes I just don't know."

Now he was ranting to himself like he always did when she went off and did something stupid that only a mother could understand.

Her stomach gurgled while she waited for him to finish.

He sighed. "So now what? You've gone and slept with him and started a relationship. Now what?"

"A...a relationship?" she choked out.

"You're crying over him on a random Friday morning before work. What else could you be in?"

"It was a fling—nothing else."

"A fling, huh?" He scoffed. "So how are you gonna handle him for the rest of the school year?"

That nasty sinking feeling came back at the thought of Anthony having the time to rekindle with Deeanna. They'd show up to court together and then to her classroom as a united front as "Tori's parents."

"Huh?" Daddy grunted. "I'm a man and I know how men are. He ain't done with you yet and all it takes is for one person to run their mouth and it's over. There's so many things that can go wrong."

Times like these were when she needed her mama the most because Daddy saw the world in black and white like most men. He didn't think about the grey areas where love bloomed in the oddest ways, but then again, she didn't blame him. Michole told her he was probably just as traumatized from her failed marriage as she was, but Michole didn't want to therapize him, of course.

"You know...Suzette wouldn't judge you," he finally rasped, reading her thoughts. "She was the more open-minded one."

She smiled at the thought of her mama wagging her finger at him in her defense.

"She was older than me, you know that, right?" he asked.

"Yes, Daddy. You tell me at least once a month."

He laughed. "She was established with a career, and *so* damn beautiful. Then here comes this young knuckle-headed boy with nothing but a record and a failing cleaning business who sweeps her off her feet and reminds her of how it feels to love again."

Butterflies fluttered in her stomach for him. He was still in love after all these years.

"We didn't have long together, but we made that time count —we made you."

She felt his smile from eight hundred miles away.

"What about you, Daddy? What's your advice for me...or are you judging me?"

"Well..." He sighed. "I don't have none—not anymore. I think I've given you enough advice over the years. We've survived affairs, reconciliation, and heartbreak."

She closed her eyes.

"I'm not judging you, though. Just know that Daddy will meet you wherever you end up in this weird universe, Venus Thibodeaux—even if it's with some young imperfect cat with a perfect heart. After all the hell you've been through, you ought to know when you're ready to swim again. Just listen to your heart, but do what's right for the baby. The baby matters the most in all this."

———

"Your call has been forwarded to an automatic voice message system—"

Anthony reached out from his seat at Lynn's island and ended the call before it beeped for him to leave a voicemail. He'd already left enough of those and if anybody got ahold of the last one he left DeeDee, he'd really be done.

His and DeeDee's business echoed throughout Lynn's sterile white kitchen because she'd sent an angry voice note, summoning him to her mini mansion in Buckhead.

She stared at his phone from across the island like it would make DeeDee call back. Mikayla looked away as she leaned against the countertop behind her.

"This isn't good." Lynn groaned, burying her face in her hands. "How the hell are you supposed to show up as a united front when half the front took the kid and went AWOL while out on bond? You called *everybody*, right?"

He nodded, raking his fingers across his scalp.

He kept calling DeeDee's mama, her brother, Kemah, and even the number for an ex that he'd stolen from her phone one night after she fell asleep. None of them answered or called him back, and he didn't know why he expected them to.

"This isn't good, this isn't good," Lynn chanted to herself, shaking her head. "I guess we can add her to the list of people that might fuck this up for us."

She'd go right underneath Venus and Shad.

"I still can't believe that bastard subpoenaed the teacher," she muttered, typing on her laptop. "You've got to start answering your phone. We should've been ahead of this, but you went missing for a whole fucking weekend."

Unfortunately, Lynn hadn't gotten the chance to accept the unbelievable news like he had, nor did she get the news straight from the source. She got it in an email and recounted her frustrations on his voicemail while he spent the weekend attached to Venus—the potential enemy who was also his lover.

"They subpoenaed the goddamn teacher. You need to call me back now," she'd hissed on his voicemail. *"I need to know everything she's documented."*

Suddenly, Lynn's fingers stopped moving, and she flung her head up. "You don't think they're conspiring against us, do you?"

"Who?" he replied.

"Deeanna and Brian."

There went more of him and DeeDee's business floating out into the wild.

He avoided Mikayla's gaze and shook his head.

"How can you be so sure? You said yourself you couldn't trust her. You said she'd run off with him before."

He opened his mouth, but closed it when he remembered the wild look in DeeDee's eyes when he told her he didn't love her anymore.

Mikayla cleared her throat, sweeping her eyes back against

her sneakers. "I think I should head out while you guys talk intricate details, Mom. You need anything before I go?"

"Can you find Deeanna Wheeler and deliver her ass to this house?"

"No, Mom."

"Well then, no, Sunshine, there's nothing you can do for me right now."

Mikayla cut her eyes at him. It was the first time he'd seen her because she'd called out of work every day that week.

She hadn't said a word to him since she opened their front door, looking him up and down like he was a stranger.

He didn't blame her. He had the game fucked up. She was supposed to find out he wasn't shit *after* him and DeeDee won custody, but then Venus showed up and shit got messy.

Lynn's phone chimed, cutting into the awkward silence.

"Hold on. I need to make a call." She blew out a breath and pushed away from the island with her head buried in her phone.

She waltzed out in her pantsuit, leaving the two of them behind. As soon as she was out of sight, he dropped his chin against the cool quartz countertop.

"Your face is busted up," Mikayla blurted, making his eyes dart back to her. "And you have bags under your eyes."

It wasn't the cursing out he expected after their last phone call, but then again she was Lynn's "Sunshine" before she was his, whatever she'd been.

"Can't sleep," he replied.

"Is that why you've been closing all week? Mona said she's been having to put you out."

He shrugged. "Ain't got nothing else to do."

Besides obsess over Munch and pine over Venus.

He thought the first week was the worst, but it was actually the second because he had to force his body into a new routine that didn't revolve around his baby and her difficult ass teacher, he took on dates sometimes.

Working at Vaughn's was the only way to suppress all that

pining and obsessing and a tiny delusional part of him was still holding out—hoping DeeDee would finally do right by him and he'd get his house in order for Venus. So, he kept the pretend job, the apartment with Munch's room, and held onto her little Barbie backpack with Venus' bedazzled folder, just in case.

When Vaughn came behind him in the kitchen at work, gripping his shoulders and asking about Venus, Anthony even told him she was "at home waiting for him." Vaughn had laughed in response.

"You know I'll do anything for the woman who cares too much... and her man," he'd said, snorting. *"All her man has to do is ask."*

"What about the bruise on your face?" Mikayla asked.

He waved his hand. "Just some bullshit."

She chuckled, and he already heard her going on about him and his "non-answers," but she didn't say anything and looked back at Lynn's polished hardwood floors.

She flung her head up like Lynn had. "If you and Deeanna are back together, then why'd she take Tori? Was it because of me? Was it because I called you that day when she was there?"

He shook his head and closed his eyes. "Nah, it wasn't because you called."

"So why—"

"We was never back together."

"Then who was tha—*oh.*"

"Yeah."

"So I was just another bitch for you to use?"

"Bitch" sounded abrasive coming out of her mouth. She pronounced each syllable with that vocal fry he still hated.

She huffed, shaking her head and looking down. "Fuck, I'm so stupid."

For a second he thought he heard Venus' country twang intertwined with her suburban accent, but it was all in his head. It was just that love shit Dre' talked about. It really made him tender.

"You not stupid. Don't say that."

"Then what am I?"

"Naïve."

She scoffed. "That's literally the same thing."

"Nah, it ain't."

She didn't even argue back with him like she would've in the past.

"Stupid would be not even recognizing that I played you. Naïve just means you ain't lived enough life to know better to stay away from opportunistic men like me."

Her cheek lifted until she remembered she was supposed to be mad at him, and then it drooped back into a frown.

She was still cute, even when she was mad. For the first time in a while, he remembered what made him push through all the bodies in that suite at the stadium to get to her after their eyes locked. She had a light that made him think about Venus before she'd met Trey—back before she was his, and he had to remind her of how much life she still had to live.

"But now you know better," he added. "So the next time some random nigga looks you up and down and sees all the ways he can use you, you'll be able to look at him right back and read through his bullshit."

There Venus went again—making him care about shit he wouldn't have cared about before he met her because she was "the woman that cared too damn much"—the woman he loved to make love to, the woman who looked at his baby like she'd given birth to her, the woman that taught him it wasn't a scary thing to fall in love again.

Love?

He smirked to himself, riding the waves of flutters in his stomach instead of fighting against them.

"That's easier said than done—especially if these future so-called opportunistic men look anything like you."

They laughed together.

"I would ask if this means we're breaking up, but naïve me

understands we were never actually anything and I can accept that... eventually." She lifted her cheek. "So, who is she?"

He smirked.

"Not even a hint, huh?"

He eyed her while resting his head on his hand. "The lady with the purple twist out—Munch's teacher."

Her eyes ballooned as Lynn came back with her face buried in her phone and an envelope dangling from her hand.

For some stupid reason, he felt another rush of excitement course through his body after admitting out loud that Venus was his. It was just wishful thinking, though. She only lived in his head now.

"Still don't have her, Sunshine?" Lynn asked, tapping at her phone.

"I get it, Mom. I'm leaving," Mikayla murmured, pushing away from the counter and giving him one last sad smile before trekking back to the front of the house.

He didn't have the same ache in his chest that he had when Venus left him. His shoulders only felt a little lighter because there was one less person weighing them down.

Lynn slid the envelope across the island toward him. It pricked his pinky.

"What's this?" he asked.

"My withdrawal letter. Tanisha was gonna give you the heads up before she mailed you a copy, but you hadn't been answering the phone. I figured I'd give it to you myself since you're here."

He picked it up and fingered it. "What's a withdrawal letter?"

"The trust is in the negative, Anthony. We've run through the retainer. We spent ten thousand on discovery alone. Do you know how hard it is to find a millionaire's dirt? Half your money was spent proving he's a lying, cheating, sleazeball with a harem of side-chicks. If you don't refresh the funds, I'm going to have to file a motion to withdraw from your case." She shrugged, still typing on her phone. "Oh, and Mikayla agreed to the USC move, by the way—guess she's not as invested in you as I thought."

Finally, she looked up from her phone and he saw the pity on her face.

"You don't have contingency money, do you?" she asked, sighing. "When we first met about this, I told you these custody cases can climb into the thousands—especially when you're dealing with someone who has money to burn. I've had clients sell their homes for this. This isn't something you can hustle up the money for and then think everything is gravy. You need steady income, structure, and cushion because he can come back after this final hearing with more bullshit. I explained to you the importance of cont—never mind."

She looked down, shaking her head. "So what do you wanna do? I can file the motion and you'll only be twenty-thousand in the hole and we can be done with this. She took the baby, Anthony—the baby that's not even yours. Your ticket to freedom is right *there*."

She pointed at the envelope. "Take the ticket or find the money. The choice is yours."

thirty-one

. . .

LOGAN STARED at Venus from across her desk.

The only noise was the loud "tick tock" from the clock mounted on the wall behind them. They were ten minutes into their lunch break and nobody had uttered a word. Their King's Wings were cold, but they couldn't take a bite of the honey hot wings because it had been another quiet Monday without Tori.

The kids were slowly forgetting her. They'd stopped putting snacks on her desk for her to enjoy when she got better and stopped saving stickers for her on their good behavior days. Eventually Treshawn would stop peeking over at her empty desk. Paula said she was preparing to send a second notice to their home and maybe even a social work referral.

"So when is she gonna come back?" Logan muttered.

Venus shrugged.

"Shouldn't you have all the insight? I mean, she is your step-kid."

"Shouldn't you be minding the business that pays you?"

Logan rolled her eyes. "I'm gon' let your attitude slide because you're clearly going through something."

Actually, she was drowning even though Daddy said it was impossible.

Logan picked up a wing, taking a bite. "Was the dick good at least?"

Venus choked out a raspy giggle that made her stomach feel less empty. "I don't kiss and tell."

"Psh." Logan flung her hand out. "It was obviously once in a lifetime *eccentric* dick. You still glowing."

That damn glow wouldn't leave, no matter how badly her heart hurt or how many scenarios she dreamed about where Anthony, Deeanna, and Tori drove off into the sunset. It was like her body couldn't reject him.

Logan sucked a glob of sauce off of her finger. "What about court?"

"What about it?" Venus picked up a wing.

"What do you plan to say on the stand? I'm not saying her custody outcome falls on your shoulders, but I've heard some teachers and counselors say their testimony was scrutinized in bitter custody cases."

Venus shrugged, even though her thoughts ran wild. "I haven't thought about it."

"Well, you ought to. It's in two weeks."

She raised her eyebrow. "Have you been eavesdropping on me and Principal Bivins again?"

"No." Logan hissed. "I walked in on Paula and Jillian talking about it."

Venus dropped the wing back into her styrofoam container without even taking a bite.

"Don't worry," Logan added. "I didn't hear anything about you and him. Them nosey hoes still trying to figure out why DeeDee wants full custody of Tori when her and Nuney was just up here in the spring registering Tori for school together."

Venus sighed, wiping the sauce from her fingers across the napkin on her lap.

Daddy was right. All it took was one person to run their mouths about her and Anthony just like they were running their mouths about his custody dispute. Ever since their talk, her heart teetered between wanting Anthony back and wanting him to stay away for the sake of her sanity.

"Can I ask you something, though?" Logan asked, interrupting another one of those heart teetering moments.

Venus shrugged. "Go for it."

"Are you gonna answer or play mum?"

"Girl, ask the damn question."

Logan snickered and then rested her head in her hand and stared at her. "Can you at least tell me if he respected you didn't wanna fall in love again?"

Damn.

The question hit her so hard she almost lost her breath.

"No, he didn't respect that at all," she muttered.

Her answer came out in a barely audible choke, but Logan heard it.

"Shit, Venus," she hissed. "So now what?"

"I show up to court and do my best to make sure he doesn't lose his baby, because life doesn't care about my broken heart. Tori takes precedence over us and our messy adult problems. She needs her daddy, and he needs her—he's home for her."

Logan smirked, and Venus held her breath for a snarky response.

"Thank you," she replied instead.

"For?"

"For caring so much."

Venus smiled, thinking about Vaughn and the moniker he'd given her.

"Venus—the girl who cared too damn much."

She *did* care too much and if Anthony was there, he'd tell her it was nothing wrong with that.

"Now, can I show you something?" Logan added.

Venus nodded, reaching back for her wing while Logan flipped her phone over and dragged her sticky finger across the screen.

"You promise you won't chicken out?"

She tapped on it while Venus watched her and bit into the flavorless chicken.

"It depends on what you're up to." She looked at her curiously until Logan shoved her phone in her face, flashing an Instagram profile that almost made the chicken she swallowed come back up.

All those nasty feelings she'd been trying to bury came trudging back at the sight of Deeanna's perfect face.

Now, her body grew hot.

"What're you doing, Logan?"

She shrugged. "Maybe she'll tell me if Tori is coming back to school. I mean, she is her mama."

"Yeah...okay. I'm sure it's that easy." Venus scoffed, pushing her phone out of her face.

Her silly love struck self didn't want to see anything that would make her feel worse than she already did.

Logan batted her eyelashes. "What if she's trying to run off with her before court so Nuney won't take her?"

Her body grew hotter.

She rubbed her neck and shrugged. "That would be pretty stupid of her. I'm sure the courts frown upon that type of thing in custody cases. They'll put a warrant out for her."

Logan tsk'd, shaking her head. "Listen, I warned you that the other part of your package is *very* problematic."

Yeah, she still had the scar on her arm to prove it, but she still couldn't tell Logan about her and Anthony's business.

"Don't you want to know what's going on? Or do you already know and you not saying anything?"

Logan's questions magnified her worries because there was no way Anthony would keep Tori out of school for that long unless Deeanna had done something.

"Fine. You're right." She blew out a breath, tossing her arms up. "I don't know what's going on."

Logan took her answer and ran with it, tapping around on her phone until it trilled throughout her office.

"Wait!" Venus called out, bracing herself against the desk. "You're calling her? I thought you were just gonna DM her?"

"Hell yeah I'm calling. I ain't about to sit around all day while I wait on her to respond like some lame ass fan." Logan rolled her eyes. "You thought I had a grandiose sense of self-importance? Oh, I ain't got nothing on her."

She held the phone by her mouth with a smug expression.

The first call rang and rang until it stopped. The second call did the same. By the time she made the fifth call, Venus had the urge to get out of there and go back to her classroom. All those unanswered calls were telling her they had no business contacting Deeanna through social media.

"Logan, I'm lea—" She sucked in a breath as the phone stopped ringing.

The line grew quiet and Logan's eyes grew to half their size. She sat up straight.

"I don't have anything for you, Logan," Deeanna answered in a bored tone. "Stop playing on my phone. I'm not Mo."

There it was again—that angelic voice Venus had grown to hate.

"Well, hello to you too, bookie," Logan replied, winking at Venus. "I'm so glad you could answer my call."

"You called *five* times. You almost got blocked. What do you want? We haven't talked since that party at JoJo's over the summer."

Venus shook her head, sitting back and listening for any sign that Tori was with her, but she only heard the soft purring of Deeanna's car gliding across the road as she drove.

"I was calling to check on Tori. We haven't seen her at school in a while."

"Okay?"

"I'm sure Nuney told you I'm working at her school now," Logan said. "They moved me from the high school."

"He doesn't even answer my calls half the time, so why

would he bother calling to tell me that useless piece of information?"

Venus felt a little lighter.

Maybe they weren't talking after all?

Logan rolled her eyes up. "Look, Tori's been absent for a week now. I know you've gotten the calls and saw the letters we've been sending in the mail."

"Yup." Deeanna hummed, even though Venus knew otherwise. "What's that got to do with you? The last time I checked, you weren't the truancy officer or the attendance clerk."

"They're gonna make you go to court if you don't send her back to school or, at the very least, communicate with admin about what's going on."

Deeanna let out a bored sigh. "Yeah, that's how it works, Logan. I read the parent handbook. I also read the social media policy in there too. I don't remember reading it was a good idea for staff to engage with parents through social media even if we knew each other prior to you working there. It's inappropriate."

Venus scoffed at this side of Deeanna. It was the side Anthony had warned Carlotta about.

Logan closed her eyes and took a deep breath. "You know what bitc—"

Venus dove across the desk, reaching for the phone, but Logan waved her off.

"What was that?" Deeanna chirped.

Logan rolled back from her desk, keeping a foot of space between them.

So far, her bright idea had been a terrible one because Deeanna was just as a resourceful as the man she claimed she'd die for. It was easy to see why they'd fallen in love and why Anthony couldn't claw his way out of her trap. She'd played the long game and found a way to keep him tied to her for life.

Venus raked her hand across her head at the thought of all the other ways Deeanna had violated him, even though it didn't matter anymore because her heart was teetering again. She didn't know if his love was worth all this.

Deeanna sighed again. "I'm getting bored with this conversation. What was the point of you calling again?"

"To figure out if you were going to allow Tori to come back to school," Logan gritted out.

"Allow?"

"Yes, *allow*. If she's really been sick, then you need to furnish several doctor's notes to get admin off your ass."

"Sick? Who said she's been sick?"

"Her teacher."

Venus groaned to herself while Deeanna huffed out an "oh, really?"

"Yeah, thankfully, Ms. Thibodeaux had the wherewithal to speak up and tell us she's been sick."

"*Really?*"

"Yeah. Now you got the time to get doctor's notes if that's what needs to be done. She could've sat there and not said anything, because covering for you and Nuney ain't part of her job."

Logan's "politically correct" facade slipped by the second.

Her tiny nostrils flared. "I don't know what shiesty shit you got going on, but you still need to be responsible and send your baby to school. You know what Principal Bivins thinks about you and Nuney?"

No answer.

"He thinks y'all don't give a damn. He won't even let us fight for the resources to assist with Tori's speech problem because he don't even know if she'll be enrolled here for the rest of the year."

There was no smart ass comeback this time—just the car's soft purring while Logan's words lingered.

"Speech problem?" Deeanna asked.

"DeeDee, that baby ain't said a word since the school year started."

Rae Lyse

It got so quiet that Logan's eyes skimmed the phone's screen.

Venus hadn't even realized she'd been shaking her head until it stopped.

"You still th—"

"Where's Ms. Thibodeaux?"

Logan's face balled up. "I'm not sure. On her lunch break, maybe?"

Their eyes met and Logan shrugged, but Venus felt the left-over animosity ruminating beneath Deeanna's question.

"Hmm, okay," she replied.

"Why?"

"Oh, nothing that concerns you, Super Counselor." Deeanna mocked. "You can tell Ms. Thibodeaux I'll see her after school today. I wanna pick up Tori's make-up work and talk to her about this speech thing."

"DeeDee, you need to reach out to her and see if she has time for that. Parent-teacher conferences are scheduled in advan—"

"She'll make time for me."

She didn't even give Logan a chance to debate her before she hung up.

Venus dragged her hands down her slacks and looked up at Logan. "What now?"

"She doesn't care about make-up work, doctor's notes, or her baby, and you know that." Logan tossed her phone on her desk and folded her arms. "You need to check that bitch, Venus, because he ain't got nobody else in his life that's gon' do it and do it right."

———

Deeanna played dirty.

"Look, TiTi." She gasped from down the hallway, pointing at Venus with Tori at her side. "It's Ms. T."

Tori untangled her fingers from Deeanna's and took off

406

running down the empty hallway in her blue dress and matching baby Crocs.

Venus squatted next to her classroom door without thinking about how desperate she looked as Tori pitter pattered down the hallway with a smile so big her eyes pinched together. Somehow, she looked like Anthony. His smile was plastered on her face as she galloped toward Venus' outstretched arms. A week without them was too long. Venus felt it in her chest every time she took a breath. She felt empty.

As soon as Tori's little body curled into hers, a lump formed in her throat.

"Bug," she rasped, holding her as tight as she could.

She smelled like heaven and Venus didn't know why she expected her to smell any other way. She wasn't supposed to project her feelings onto Deeanna, even though Logan said she could.

She pulled away and held Tori at arm's length, dragging her eyes up and down her body.

Next, she pressed her hand to her forehead and then her fat cheeks. "I don't think I feel a fever. Do you feel okay?"

Tori nodded, bouncing on the tips of her toes while Deeanna clinked down the hallway in her heels. Venus took the time to drink Tori in while Tori stared at her like she was the best thing that ever happened in her short life.

"You look so pretty," Venus murmured, fixing her white bow that had drooped down on her run.

She didn't look like the daughter of an illustrious MD and his perfect wife. She looked like her Bug and Anthony's little Munchkin—happy, carefree, and ready for whatever random adventure Anthony decided to take them on.

When Deeanna made it to the classroom's doorway, they didn't exchange pleasantries. They just looked each other up and down. Now she understood what Anthony meant when he said the space between them without Tori was neutral. It was the same between her and Deeanna without him.

Venus cleared her throat, holding Tori's hand tighter and standing up. "You look...nice."

She looked better than nice, but Deeanna didn't deserve to hear that.

"I had court."

Venus raised her eyebrows. "Oh."

There wasn't a pore visible underneath her makeup or a curly hair out of place on her head. The pink pantsuit she wore was the perfect shade for her brown skin. She looked perfect—like a black Barbie.

Venus waved her inside the classroom while Tori stayed glued to her side. "Come in. I got her work together and put it in a folder for you."

She pulled Tori to her desk while Deeanna teetered in a circle, staring at the classroom.

Venus looked at her out of her peripheral. "You can sit at our Play-Doh table."

Deeanna's lip curled up as she eyed the round table with the kids' projects lying around it.

"Go show, Mama," Venus said, nudging Tori toward her.

Tori took off to the table with that same grin, like it had been too long since she'd seen a clump of Play-Doh. She ran her fingers across the back of a chair.

Deeanna followed behind her and eased into the chair she fingered. She flung her Chanel bag on the table, narrowly missing Treshawn's one eyed dinosaur.

Venus snorted, rolling her eyes. "Nice bag."

Deeanna glanced at her, looking her up and down again as if she was searching for something to compliment her on in return. Instead of finding a compliment, she let out a little laugh.

Venus grabbed Tori's folder from on top of the subpoena in her desk's drawer and walked over to the table. She sat in the chair across from Deeanna. Tori had followed and sidled up next to her, wrapping her arms around her middle while Deeanna stared.

She was still that same velcro baby, even with her mama there. Her little arms were tense and Venus saw the cautious look on her face as she looked between her and Deeanna.

Venus tapped her arm. "All your classmates left you little trinkets and 'get well soon' cards. I put them in your cubby. Why don't you go look while me and Mama talk?"

Tori nodded, sticking her thumb in her mouth and bouncing off to her cubby.

"Did you need something else? Logan only said you wanted to pick up her make-up work." Venus folded her arms.

Deeanna pursed her lips and narrowed her eyes because she probably still wanted to beat her ass and a tiny unhealed part of Venus wanted to beat hers, too.

"She said you told the staff Tori was sick."

"I did."

"Who told you to say that?"

"I told myself to say it."

Deeanna nodded, crossing her arms in the same way Venus had crossed hers. "You're not her mother."

"I wasn't trying to be. I was being compassionate to a single daddy who doesn't quite have it all figured out yet."

"A single daddy?" Deeanna swiped her nose and looked around the classroom. "I'm not whatever it is he said I was. This was my first time going to jail.'"

He hadn't said enough about the type of woman Deeanna was. In fact, she wasn't a woman at all—just a little girl pretending to be one.

Venus gave her a polite smile. "I don't think I know what you're talking about."

"Oh?" She laughed, flinging her hands up. "I forgot we're at *your* job...where you can get fired for fucking a parent."

Venus nodded with a scoff.

Checkmate.

They hadn't even been in the same space for thirty minutes, but again, Deeanna played dirty.

Venus leaned forward. "Do you give Dr. Torres' wife the same hell you give me?"

That one wasn't a checkmate.

It was a gut punch because Deeanna's pretty brown face turned pale.

"No?" Venus added, picking up Treshawn's dinosaur and fingering its squishy body.

"You don't know what you're talking about. You ought to be concerned with Principal Bivins still hanging around in the front office. I could end all of this with one conversation. You know that?" Deeanna spat back.

"Oh really? Just like you ought to be concerned with why you keep trying to make somebody else's husband yours?"

"You don't know what the fuck you're talking about." Deeanna laughed, lowering her voice.

"Oh, but I do. I bet every time you think you snagged him, his wife throws a wrench in your plans. Wives can be conniving like that." She looked up at Deeanna.

She looked a lot like Leti had looked after being confronted— shamefaced and in love with another woman's man. She used to throw wrenches in Leti's "happily ever after" plans all the time —she beat her ass, dragged Trey to therapy, and changed his phone number on a whim once. None of it mattered.

"You really have no clue what you're talking about," Deeanna replied.

She sounded as if she was trying to convince herself more than Venus, even though the truth was on her face.

"I guarantee you I do." Venus dropped the dinosaur. "Just like I know you had court today for all that swiping you do with other folk's credit cards."

"He told you that?" she muttered breathlessly.

She tried to wipe the shock off her face, but the damage had already been done.

"Of course, he told me. He tells me everything—even all the little embarrassing secrets he convinced you to shut up about—

like how you thought you finally had Brian when you got him to promise to make you and Tori his family and instead of whoopin' your behind like you deserved, Mrs. Torres did you one better. She convinced Brian to do the worst thing a person can do to a woman because none of this is him—it's all her getting back at you."

She'd never forget the torture in Anthony's voice when he belted out his and Deeanna's darkest secrets in the passenger seat of her car.

The room grew so quiet that all she heard was the scraping of paper as Tori flipped through the mementos in her cubby.

Deeanna's nose flared and her hand balled into itself on top of the table. "What else he told you about us?"

"Us?" She belted out the same laugh Deeanna had when she looked her up and down. "Y'all ain't been an 'us' in a long time. It don't matter how many times you get on your knees and beg for his forgiveness."

"You nosey ass bi—" She stopped herself when a staff member shuffled past the door. "You listened to our phone call?"

"Oh, I answered it."

Her head flung back, and the color came back to her face.

"What else you know?"

"I'm not about to go tit for tat with you, Deeanna, and I'm not about to let us act like two fools in front of Anthony's baby again. I respect him way too much for that."

"His baby?" She pushed against the table, shaking the containers of Play-Doh. "Girl, fuc—"

"Ms. T?"

Her heart fluttered.

There it was again.

That little angelic voice that almost didn't sound real.

She turned around, searching for Tori, but she was already halfway across the room on her way to them. She skipped through the desks with a big grin on her face.

"Walk, Bug," she almost squealed.

She wanted to tell her to keep talking—to say something—to say *anything*, but babies were delicate. In Tori's little world, praising her for doing something she knew how to do all along didn't make sense, so Venus followed her lead.

"What you wanna show us?" Venus asked, biting into her lip as her leg shook.

"Me and you," she chirped back, bouncing up to her and leaning into her side again.

Her tiny yellow painted fingernail pointed at the purple blobs Ada had drawn into a handmade card. The only recognizable features on them were Venus' big hair and Tori's pink bow.

"Wow, Bug. We look fabulous." She ran her finger against the paper next to Tori's.

She took the time to steal another whiff of her and touch her juicy curls that dangled from her puff. She felt Deeanna's scorching stare, but she didn't care, because it wasn't fair that God had given her such a beautiful blessing she couldn't see.

There she went, projecting again.

"Why don't you go show Mama? Then you can take some tape off my desk and go hang it outside in our miniature art gallery so the rest of the school can see?"

Tori nodded and walked over to Deeanna.

Venus watched them like the mother hen Tori had turned her into because Shelly hadn't prepared her for her worst velcro kid of all—the one who would make her crave motherhood so much it hurt to exist.

"Look, Mama," she said. "It's me and Ms. T together. Daddy likes us like this."

Deeanna picked her up in one swift motion and Tori smiled bigger when she pressed her glossy lips to her cheek.

They didn't look like mother and daughter. They looked like babies—like sisters. Seeing their faces side by side made Venus' stomach twist into knots.

"Do you wanna add Mama and Daddy to the picture before

you put it outside? I saved the newest purple crayon just for you," Venus said.

She nodded eagerly.

"Go get it off my desk. It's next to the tape."

She pat Deeanna's cheek as if she was prepping her for her time away and then climbed off her lap. It made a lump crawl up Venus' throat.

When Tori got behind her desk, the words came out before Venus had time to stop them.

"What kind of life your baby gon' have with a man who never wanted her, Deeanna? You ever think about that?" she hissed.

There she was—projecting again, but she couldn't help it.

Deeanna's eyes darted over to Tori, who hummed as she scribbled two extra purple blobs to the picture. For the first time she didn't have a smart ass quick-witted response.

"I try not to," she replied in a flat tone. "I try not to think of her with them at all."

Tori stopped humming. "Finished! I'm gonna go hang it up!"

They both looked her way as she snatched the tape off the desk and then took off into the hallway with the picture dangling from her hands.

"Well, in two weeks you not gonna have a choice but to think about it because they're gonna show up together in court and take your baby from you."

"Shut up." She shook her head.

"I'll never shut up about that one." Venus pointed toward the hallway. "And I'll never sugarcoat shit when it comes to her wellbeing."

Deeanna shook her head.

"That lady hates you. Do you actually think she gon' love Tori like Anthony? Like his granny do? Do you think she gon' look at your baby like you look at her? You think that family gon' love on her like we do? You can talk shit about me all day long, but I would *never* try to take your baby away from you.

I've heard you scream for her. I see the way you look at her. I know you love her—even when you use her as a pawn and dangle her between Anthony and Brian. I know you'd never purposely harm her."

Logan might've wanted her to check Deeanna, but sometimes there was no need to. Sometimes Venus had to take heed of what Daddy said and meet folks wherever they were.

Deeanna's eyes welled with tears, but they didn't fall.

She cleared her throat and looked away. "Why do you even care so much? He doesn't want me anymore. He told me he didn't love me. Just tell him to move on. When he's in love, he'll listen to whatever—he'll *do* whatever."

Venus couldn't even gloat about her confession. It didn't feel right.

She scoffed instead. "Yeah...like accept a baby that's not his."

Deeanna huffed.

"I would never ever tell him to move on. Any woman that comes after me that has the nerve to do that doesn't love him. He wouldn't listen anyhow. Tori ain't his, but I know I can't look at her without seeing him. It's not even about paternity or...or physical features. DNA don't matter. It's about who she looks for when her little world is crumbling and it damn sure ain't Brian."

Deeanna stared at the mess on the Play-Doh table instead of looking up.

Venus pushed up and walked over to her desk, snatching up the box of Kleenex.

She carried them back to Deeanna, tapping her on the shoulder. "Here."

No matter how much they hated each other, they were on neutral turf, and neutral turf was its own place with its own unwritten rules.

Deeanna pulled a tissue from the box and dabbed at her eyes as Venus eased onto the table next to her bag. "Do you know this was the most she's ever said in this classroom?"

"Logan said she had a speech problem, but my baby is smart—"

"I know, but these are the things that happen when you're constantly disrupting a child's life. I think first she missed her daddy… and then her mama…and then she shut down. Babies need structure, reassurance, and routine. They can't thrive in chaos, Deeanna." Venus smiled, reaching out to fix the little Chanel brooch she'd pinned onto her pantsuit. "You'll get it together. I believe in you. Now you can tell Anthony to put his claws away. I've heard her talk."

Deeanna chuckled, rolling her eyes. "He swears it's them against the world."

"It is. He'd steal the moon for her." Venus smiled, remembering the euphoric look on his face as he stared up at the moon on their first date.

Their eyes met and for the tiniest second Venus saw the girl Anthony fell in love with—the poised, pretty girl with the brilliant mind.

"Now, after all this, the least you can do is let him have his child—let him have his peace," Venus uttered as Tori rounded the classroom's doorway.

She bounced back up to them, but stopped once she saw Deeanna's wet face.

"What's wrong, Mama?" she asked, tilting her head. "I came right back…and you said you weren't mad at Ms. T anymore 'cause you know she's my favorite."

Venus didn't think she'd ever get used to the novelty of her little voice and all its tiny nuances—like the way she left out some of the consonants in her words or how much she sounded like Deeanna—poised and soft.

Venus held her arms out and Tori ran into them with her eyebrows wrinkled.

She picked her up and pat her back as Deeanna sniffled. "Those ain't nothing but happy tears, Bug. We were just talking about how you have the best mama in the whole wide world. She's so pretty and smart, just like you, Munchkin."

thirty-two

• • •

LOLA HUNG on the side of Anthony's car, blowing out a cloud of cigarette smoke.

She sighed, looking down at her cracked driveway. "You need twenty-thousand more dollars, Anthony? Are you shittin' me?"

He laid his head against his headrest and closed his eyes. "Yeah… make sure you tell Carlotta, since her Publix money so long."

"Don't start. She means well, she just doesn't think sometimes." She groaned. "That lady don't do no type of pro bono work?"

"She one of the most successful family law attorneys in the city. A fucked up nigga with a record that's feuding with his ex-girlfriend's millionaire baby daddy ain't exactly the type of case you offer to take for free."

"You check with any other lawyers to see if they could?"

He snorted, swiping his hand across his bruised cheek. "Come on. Brian got billboards of his face around the city. I got to pay to play."

"Fuck it. Ask JoJo."

"Hell nah. You know how I feel about that. Besides, he tryna get married and …I… I need to make sure his mental is right before he take that jump—not ask him for money."

And Josiah had offered the money so many times he should've been tired of offering—but that was the curse of being the chosen one. He would carry their burdens, regardless.

"What I look like having another grown man pay to help me keep my daughter—*my* responsibility? The baby I said I'd take care of no matter whose DNA she had. The baby I still begged and cried for after her mama told me she wasn't mine. This is for me to do. It'd be real fuckin' entitled of me to ask JoJo to do that."

"Jesus, sometimes I wished you never even got caught up with that girl."

"Yeah…" he drifted off. "Me too, but then I wouldn't have Munch."

He looked at the flickering light on her porch.

"What if we got a loan?" she exclaimed.

"We?"

She huffed. "Well me. What if I go down to the bank and—"

"I'd never let you do no shit like that for me. You did enough already."

She carted Munch around when he couldn't, fed her, bathed her, bought her things, and loved her. She'd even done more than Carlotta.

"Come on, Nuney…" Lola begged. "Or I can…can ask Larry for the money."

"And have his wife sticking her nose in whatever it is y'all still got going on? I can figure it out. Just…just let me think. I can figure it out."

"Think? I heard that before." She slapped the side of the car. "Don't you go out and do nothing stupid. None of this will matter anymore if you ain't even alive to finish fighting the fight."

He closed his eyes again, flinging his head back. "I know that. I'm…I'm not invincible. I know I got a baby to live for."

"Took you ten years to get that through your thick skull, but I guess it's better you realize it now than when you six feet under." She raked her hand across his head like Venus used to and then slapped the side of it.

The fucked up thing about being in love with Venus was how easily she had snuck her way inside of him. People that cared too much almost always got the shitty end of the stick, but Venus said it was the right way to live and she knew best. So there he was—morphing into the man who cared too damn much.

Love.

He was in love with Venus Thibodeaux.

It sounded perfect in his head and when he was alone, it even flowed perfectly out of his mouth. One day they'd exist in the same universe where his life wasn't so fucked up and he could love her the way she deserved. She wouldn't have to worry about fighting DeeDee in parking lots or stressing about him making it home to her and Munch.

One day...

DeShaun cracked the screen door and poked his head outside. "Granny, you still cooking? I'm hungry..."

Lola shooed him back inside with a wave of her hand and he rolled his eyes, slamming the screen door.

Afterward, she sighed. "What if we get the money and she keeps hiding Tori? Then what? Huh? Then he automatically wins, right?"

His stomach ached to even think about that. He leaned forward, gripping the steering wheel.

Lola tugged his shirt and pulled him back against the driver's seat. "Here."

She thrust the cigarette his way, and he took a pull before handing it back to her.

The moon sat in a hazy white circle above her house while the quiet enveloped them. It was the same quiet that swallowed them when he had sped home with DeeDee's earth shattering news.

He'd pushed open Lola's front door, trampling through the living room and into her bedroom. She shot up in bed like he was a ghost.

"I...she...*Tori ain't mine.*" He'd gasped out.

He'd never forget that day. It was ingrained in his head, just like the day Munch was born.

"Don't think about the worst-case scenario," Lola uttered. "Just think about the best possible outcome."

Her words drifted off while he tried to trick his brain like she suggested, but it was impossible because he still felt the bone chilling loneliness that came with life after Munch and Venus. He was *just* holding them thirty thousand feet in the air.

"What about her teacher?" Lola blurted. "What she tell you to do?"

He cut his eyes at her. "Consulting custody cases ain't part of her job. You know that, right?"

"Don't act like you weren't sleeping with her and consulting with her about everything else in your life." Lola threw her hands up. "What the hell did you do?"

That quiet from before swallowed them again while she took pulls of the cigarette and waited on whatever stupid lie he'd come up with. Venus was there again, though—wagging her finger at him and telling him he'd better not lie to his granny.

"I fell in love with her," he croaked out.

"Oh," Lola whispered, dropping her hands at her sides.

"Yeah...*oh.*"

He gripped the sides of his head. "You said she existed. You promised me she was out there...and... I think—no—I *know* I found her, but I don't even have my shit together to keep her."

"She love you back?"

He pinched his eyes shut.

"*You're a good man, Ant. Never let anybody tell you different.*"

He'd been carrying those words with him ever since she left.

When he opened his eyes, Lola was there, resting her face in her hands with a knowing look.

"I don't kno—"

His ringing phone cut into his words. He reached out to press ignore on the steering wheel until Lola squealed, "look! don't do that!"

He whipped his head toward the screen where DeeDee's name had popped up, along with the picture of Munch he'd replaced hers with. He almost didn't believe it until Lola slapped his shoulder.

He pressed the button to answer the call, and DeeDee crunched into the phone's receiver, talking around chews. "Where you at?"

He lurched forward. "Where am I? Where the fuck—"

Lola pressed her hand against his chest and shoved him back into the driver's seat. She pointed her finger in his face, shaking her head.

"I'm...I'm at my granny's."

DeeDee chewed and there was the faintest sound of Munch's giggle in the background.

"Oh." She smacked her lips. "I talked to your girlfriend today."

He frowned. "Venus?"

"Mhmm. You got another one I need to know about?"

He had so many questions he wanted to ask that his head spun, but Lola was right. He needed to play it cool.

Lola flicked the cigarette onto the driveway and leaned back into the window.

"What y'all talk about?" he asked.

"She says we need to send a doctor's note with Tori because she been out of school."

"You ain't been sending my baby to school?" he belted out. "You lost your goddamn mind? What part of this custody shit don't you understand? Everything we do is under a microscope! I'm convinced you want the nigga to take her!"

Lola waved her hand this time to shut him up because DeeDee was *real* fickle.

"Don't yell at me!" she gritted back. "I went up to that fuckin' school and sat in your new bitch's face for an hour and you still aren't happy?"

He raked his hands down his face and took a deep breath. "A'ight, Deeanna. What...what you need me to do for you? Because you want something, right? That's why you called. You need me to fix something, because that's all I'm good for."

She chewed on the phone while Munch's little voice got closer and his palms grew sweaty. "I wanna talk to Daddy."

His baby was *so* close.

"I need to talk to him first, Toriana. Where's your iPad? You said you were on YouTube," DeeDee murmured like a teenager.

"I thought I told you I didn't want her on no iPad anymore?"

"It's the only thing that'll keep her quiet. I'm trying to take care of stuff." She huffed. "Can you call the pediatrician and ask for the note? She likes you, so she'll do it for you, ya' know? And...and I need gas money and I need help paying that bond money back to my mama."

Lola buried her face in her hands.

"Are you fuc—" He stopped himself and pounded his fist into his hand. "A'ight, DeeDee. I do all that and then what? Then you gon' give me my baby back? You gon' show up to court?"

Finally, she stopped chewing. "You know what—I haven't seen her in two months. You ever think about that?"

"It don't feel so good, do it?"

Now she understood the chest aching pain that came from not having access to Munch. Some days it hurt to breathe while his brain came up with wild scenarios where Munch screamed for him, but he couldn't get to her.

"I get it." She scoffed. "I understand you're 'the bestest daddy' and she likes you more than me, because 'Daddy makes everything happen.' He...he finds all the obscure toys, plays hide-and-go-seek, and reads bedtime stories. I get it! But I carried her for nine goddamn months. I breastfed her, I talked to her while she was in my stomach, I tell her I love her even when she's being a brat and crying for you. I...I didn't want any other man to be her daddy but you. It was a *mistake*, Anthony. A mistake I have to live with for the rest of my life. I told you she was yours, regardless of what any test said."

"Dee—"

"She talked at school today. Venus said she been so quiet they thought something was wrong with her. They thought she needed speech therapy. Why didn't you tell me that?"

He sighed at the way she said "Venus" as if Venus had always been in their lives and keeping the peace for the sake of her Bug.

"Because I was gon' take care of it."

"Take care of it, how? By ignoring their recommendations?"

"Don't act like 'mama of the year' now."

"I never claimed to be!"

"I did what I knew best to keep Brian and his lawyer off our asses. You know how unfit we look on paper already!" he yelled, slamming his fist against the steering wheel. "I ain't like you. I ain't about to lay down for that nigga—I don't care how much money he got."

"Hmph." She huffed, breathing into the phone.

Munch's little voice came back again. "Are you finished? I...I gotta tell Daddy about my portrait with Ms. T."

He flung his head back against the headrest, swallowing. "What else Venus tell you?"

"Nothing you need to worry about," she muttered. "Text me that lawyer's phone number. I need to talk to her before court."

She hung up before he could get another word in.

"So now what?" Lola shook her head, gripping the side of the car. "I told you she existed, you found her, and she loves you and all this bullshit you come with. She did *that*. Now, are you really gon' slow down long enough to keep her?"

thirty-three

. . .

VENUS' subconscious was convinced that her and Anthony's energies would sync together at the perfect time. They'd stop existing in two different universes and finally come together in the right one.

She heard his deep voice in her dreams sometimes—laughing, crying, and begging for her because it was possible their mutual telepathy transcended realities.

She groaned, rolling over in her sleep, searching for his arms she'd gotten used to. She pushed against the sofa, but stiffened when she didn't touch his skin.

How was that possible?

His sinewy chest was right *there*. His voice was just there, too, telling her again how tired he was of fighting because he wasn't a fighter.

"V!" he shouted.

She sprang up from her couch, gasping, and looking around her dark living room. Pepper's shiny coat stood out in the darkness as his stomach rose and fell in a soft cadence from his bed.

She gulped in the gust of air from the fan and eased back onto the couch until that same force that had shaken her awake made her spring up again.

"V!"

Loud pounds sounded throughout her apartment. "V! C'mon. Come open the door for me."

It felt like another fever dream with Anthony.

She whisked away the sweat that had pooled onto the back of her neck as she tossed and turned while the banging grew louder.

"V! I know you home. I saw your car in the garage."

"That can't be..." She breathed out, tossing her blanket from over her legs and pushing up.

Pepper mewled from his bed and yawned as she pattered to the door. She stuck her face against the peephole, convinced this dream would end like all the rest.

"Ant?" she muttered to herself.

He paced around her front door. She jumped as he laid his forehead and fist against it.

"Baby." He grunted, turning his head to the side. "I called... and...and I texted you, but you ain't answer. I'm tired of fighting, for real. I ain't even a fighter."

She pulled away from the door, twisting the lock and then the deadbolt. When it swung open, he stepped back like he wanted her to see the torment on his face. His red eyes sagged and his wet lips hung open.

Seeing him in the flesh made her lose sense of herself and she forgot about the truth of them existing in two different phases in their lives. Her hands ached to touch him—to check him for any new cuts, scrapes or heartbreaks since she had her hands on him last.

"Ant..." she uttered, furrowing her brows. "What're you doing here?"

He pushed his hand to his forehead while looking at the ground. "Go get dressed."

"What? Get dressed? I have to work tomorrow."

"We ain't gon' be out long. Just go get dressed."

She shook her head, folding her arms over her hard nipples

as her neighbor cracked his door. His blue eyes dragged across Anthony's body.

She frowned and motioned toward the inside of her apartment with her head. "Come in."

While he followed her inside, she kept space between them so their bodies wouldn't touch because she just didn't trust herself when she was in love.

She gasped to herself as that word floated around her head again. If Michole was there, she'd tell her she was giving too much power to the word, but Michole didn't know Anthony. He embodied that scary ass word, and he didn't give a damn that she was trying to stay away from him.

He sidestepped her, and she turned and locked the door. "Slow down and tell me what's going on. I can't go anywhere tonight. I have to get up at—"

He walked up to her so fast she didn't feel his hand circle her neck until he squeezed it with just enough force that she melted into him.

The darkness inside the apartment heightened her senses. The sweet scent of strawberry clung to his skin and made her legs tremble as he pushed his hot lips to her neck.

"What did you do?" He murmured, pushing his tongue into her skin. "What'd you say to her?"

She opened her mouth to ask, "who?" but a pathetic moan tumbled out instead. He pushed his hand underneath her tank top and thumbed her hard nipples until her forehead fell against the door.

"Talk to me," he whispered hotly. "Tell me what the fuck is going on in your head, Venus."

She closed her eyes and that fleeting leaf came to tease her. It brushed against her skin as he rolled her nipples between his fingers and then yanked her around.

"You don't want me no more?" he asked, staring down at her. "You wanna separate for real?"

She opened her mouth like she did in her dreams, but another groan came out when her fingers pressed against his freckles.

He was there.

He was *really* there.

"Nah." He closed his eyes, shaking his head. "You gotta want me if you convinced her to let me have my baby. You...you got—"

She pressed her lips against his and pushed her tongue into his mouth.

Wanted him?

Didn't he know he made her feel the most alive?

He didn't need to mull over whether she wanted him when she already belonged to him. She was his the first day they locked eyes in her classroom.

He moaned into her mouth as they writhed against the door. His hands fell from underneath her shirt and scraped down her sides until they reached her cotton shorts.

He yanked them down.

The frigid air tickled her bare middle while he dropped to his knees in front of her like nothing had changed between them.

Her hands fell onto his head and her fingers dug into his scalp. He picked her leg up, tossed it over his shoulder, and then parted her lips.

"Fuck it. It don't matter if you want me or not because I love you. You know that, Venus? I'm fuckin' in love with you. You can learn to love me like I love you because I ain't leaving you again. I...I let you go on your lil' rant and let you have your space, but fuck this fightin' shit. We not separating no more." He blinked up at her through his long lashes before he buried his face between her legs.

"Ant!" she squealed.

Tears welled in her eyes as his tongue thrashed right between her folds. That euphoric feeling that always engulfed her when he was around came swooping over her like a warm hug. She reveled in it, biting into her lip until she tasted blood.

He pulled away from her, gasping. "Let it out before you hurt yourself."

Her shoulders drooped at those words and then it all came out like he demanded.

"Baby..." she sobbed, hooking her fingers around his ear. "I don't...I don't want us to fight anymore, either."

It was torture.

He pecked her moist lips. "You for real? You not gon' run from me again?"

She shook her head as if he could see her in the dark. "I won't run again. I swear."

"Mhmm. You not a runner no more. Remember?"

She nodded, clunking her head against the door as he dove back between her legs.

She couldn't believe she'd lived a life without him before—without his richness, wisdom, and pleasure. In fact, she was convinced she'd never known what it was like to fall in love before he came along, because falling in love with Trey wasn't so easy.

She didn't remember rolling over one morning and thinking to herself, "fuck, I can't live without this man," but she'd done it so many times after meeting Anthony that she lost count.

His tongue found its favorite spot between her folds. It curled around it and flicked against it. She was on the cusp of one of those orgasms he'd introduced her to, and he felt it.

He stopped and hovered over her wet mound. "Talk to me. Tell me you'll come with me tonight. Tell me you forgive me. Tell me we're meant to last."

The words were stuck to the roof of her mouth.

"Tell me."

He wrapped his tongue back around her clit and she knocked her head against the door with a loud thud. That terrifyingly good pressure built up in her abdomen and made her clamor against his face.

"Ba—baby…" she hissed. "Wait…wait."

She should've known better.

His muffled voice vibrated against her. "No. You just told me you not a runner no more. So stop running from it. Don't ever run from me again."

"Anthony!" she sobbed.

Her screams rattled the walls of the apartment as the pressure gushed out of her. They reached every nook and cranny of her little entryway and would have her shamefaced when she ran into her neighbors the next day.

Wetness trickled onto the tiled floor and rolled underneath her toes as they curled. His tongue traced the wetness down her leg as tremors tore through her body.

It didn't matter how much time they spent apart—he was still obsessed with all the parts of her no other man had ever touched.

She choked on a hiccup as he kissed his way back up to her stomach. "You satisfied now?"

"Satisfied about what, Ant?" she rasped in a tired groan with her eyes closed.

"Now you know I still worship the ground you walk on, Venus Thibodeaux."

She felt for the light switch. When her fingers hit it, she flicked it up and cracked her eyes open.

She blinked until they got adjusted to the bright light. Once she convinced herself she could handle him, she glanced down at his honey colored face.

He bit into his bottom lip and dug his fingernails into the thigh she still had resting on his shoulder.

She reached down and stroked his cheek, reveling in the man Deeanna was still obsessed with and she got it. She understood why Deeanna would die for him. He made the shit too easy.

That fleeting leaf wasn't so fleeting anymore. It landed right at her feet this time, and she couldn't brush it off anymore. He'd turned her into some new woman who wasn't afraid to swim anymore. She'd jump headfirst in the water for him.

He brushed his lips back against her thigh and she felt like they were right back by that pool during their first night together.

She exhaled. "And now you know I'd do anything for you. I never left you, baby. You know I can't do that."

He closed his eyes.

"You don't need to know what I told Deeanna. That's between me and her. You just need to keep being the man I fell in love with and being the bestest daddy in the world for Tori. I know we don't have all the answers or...or everything neat and put together, but we gon' work it out, Ant."

———

When Venus Thibodeaux was in love, her eyes dilated like she'd taken a hit of some forbidden shit and a dewy glow illuminated off of her skin that made her look ethereal.

She glanced at Anthony in her bathroom mirror with those sable colored eyes he was convinced he couldn't live without.

"Yes, Ant?" she asked, brushing a coat of mascara through her lashes. "What's the problem? Why you keep looking at me?"

She didn't just look into his eyes when she told him she loved him. She pierced them and then jumped into his soul. To a sane man, that type of intensity might've been scary, but to him it was exhilarating because her love wasn't shit like DeeDee's. It didn't have conditions. It was limitless and reminded him he wasn't invincible or DeeDee's savior. He was just a boy in love who was scared of being seen doing the one thing everybody always told him he couldn't do.

He glanced over his shoulder at her empty bedroom for the fifth time as Pepper nudged him on his leg like it wasn't midnight. There were still boxes stacked in corners like she had just left Trey last week and moved into the bare apartment.

He shook his head, looking down at Pepper.

"Why my wife don't got a bed to sleep in, Pepper?" he mumbled, leaning against the bathroom's doorframe.

Pepper meowed back with his big ass mouth and Venus snorted, putting her mascara back in its tube. "Don't be messy. I'm working on it, okay?"

He rolled his eyes and roamed into her closet that was attached to the bathroom to eye all of her clothes hanging up. He took a big whiff, inhaling her, and his shoulders dropped in satisfaction.

"Work on it for what? You want a bed, I'll get you a bed."

"Nuh uh. Save your *resourcefulness* for whatever mission we're going on. I wan—need to buy my own furniture," she yelled from the bathroom.

He chuckled and brushed his hands across a row of blouses. "Mission?"

"Yes. Where the hell we going?"

"To take care of one last thing."

He didn't realize he was waddling in a circle, trying to take in every piece of her until his head got dizzy and he stopped in front of a box of purses.

"And that is?" she asked as he squatted and sifted through the purses.

"I need another twenty-thousand dollars."

"Twenty?" she choked out. "For?"

"Gotta replenish Lynn's retainer or she gon' withdraw from my case."

"Wait a minute...what? What do you mean, another twenty-thousand? What happened to the money you already paid her?"

His hand stopped on a tiny black leather bucket bag that was the perfect size for the "mission" they were going on. Thanks to her, it'd be his last.

He pulled the purse from under a backpack and walked back into the bathroom. "It's gone."

He watched her reflection in the mirror.

"Gone? Gone how?"

Panic took over her eyes. It swallowed the satisfaction that had been there from finally getting him back and getting DeeDee to cooperate. She didn't know yet that nothing came easy with Munch.

"It's a custody case, baby. I'm...I'm not fighting some nigga working at McDonald's that might not even show up to court. He tryna tell me my money ain't long enough to fuck with him, but one thing I never do is count myself out—especially not when it come to my baby."

Her eyes followed him as he opened the purse and dug through it. "But twenty-thousand dollars, Anthony? How the fuck can she just expect you to come up with that money overnight?"

"Everybody's world don't stop for me like yours does. I'm just another client to her." He pulled out a stale stick of gum and a lip-gloss that had seen better days.

"Okay...fine," she said, throwing her arms up in exasperation. "Do whatever it is you do and sell that Benz, then. We...we can figure out another car situation."

"*You* not figuring out nothing." He threw the gum in the bathroom trash bin and stuck the lip-gloss on the acrylic vanity she had next to her sink.

"Bab—"

"No." He walked up to her like he'd done when she let him inside her apartment.

His middle smashed against her back as he buried his face in her neck.

"Ant..."

"I can't..." He shook his head, inhaling her. "I can't keep hustling to patch shit up and expecting it not to fall apart later.

I…I need to fix this permanently. Let me fix it. Let me be a man. I ain't Trey. I don't need you to hold my hand."

Her body was warm and made him wish he could bury his dick inside of her to commemorate their reunion, but there was no time for that.

"Fine." She tossed the mascara down and twisted around in his arms as her purse dangled from his hand. "Why'd you dig that purse out? I ain't carried that in years."

She pressed her hands to his chest and then glanced down at it.

"Because I need you to hold something for me tonight."

Her fingers curled into his shirt. "And that is?"

"Wrong turf."

"You can't scare me away, you know that, right? I live on your turf now and I ain't going anywhere."

He reached up and plucked one of her errant curls before tucking it behind her ear. "I'll explain later—just come with me. If you come, I'll get you a California king."

She laughed and curled her fingers into his shirt like she was fighting herself. He didn't know why. He was hers, after all. She could touch him whenever she wanted. It just hadn't settled in her brain yet.

"That can't even fit in this place. Besides, I told you, that's something I need to do for myself."

"Is that some shit you and your therapist agreed on?" he asked, brushing his hands across her back.

"No…I…I actually haven't talked to her in a while and that's not good."

"Why you ain't been going to therapy?"

"Because my time was occupied by somebody who had me rescheduling appointments."

"Oh yeah? Who was that?"

"Some beautiful crazy ass young dude who's convinced I can keep up with him."

He smiled.

There she went, saying shit nobody had ever said to him. *Beautiful?*

First, his brain was beautiful, and now he was. A nigga like him had never been called beautiful.

"So now what?" she asked, like Lola had while tilting her head.

He shrugged, uncurling her fingers from his shirt and placing the purse strap between them. "Now I take Munch's teacher to work for one last night."

thirty-four

. . .

"A CLUB, ANTHONY?" Venus huffed.

The neon lights on the sign outside Playhouse flickered and music thumped from inside. Security lingered outside the front door, talking, laughing and patting down the men that waited in line.

"It ain't shit but a lounge," he muttered, killing the engine.

It really wasn't even that. It was an after hours spot turned restaurant turned after hours spot again. He'd been there once when it was new and exciting—back before all the old heads started meeting there to blow off steam during the week.

"At my big age, any place with hookah, hoes and loud music is a club and here I am, dressed like I'm going to the movies," she replied.

"Don't act like jeans and a white tee don't get my dick hard," he replied, reaching over her and rummaging through the glove compartment. "We not here to be seen, anyway."

She groaned to herself as his hands brushed the pistol she'd made him put back the first night they spent together.

She watched as he pulled her purse from between her legs and unbuttoned it.

"This isn't a neutral place, is it?" she whispered as he stuck the pistol in the bag and snapped it back closed.

He shook his head and swiped the smear of lip gloss that had snuck under her bottom lip. "It ain't even about the place. It's the person."

"Wai—huh?"

He smashed his lips against hers, stealing one of those kisses he'd never get used to. "Shh. Tighten up."

"Nuh uh." She shook her head. "This ain't one of those 'tighten up' situations. Tell me what you need *that* for. You know how I feel about that."

He smiled at her. "I'm about to go talk to a nigga that I threatened to kill over you. Don't let that nice house or money fool you. He still a dog just like me and we don't forget shit like that. This can go really good or really bad."

He saw the moment she put the pieces together in her head.

"Vaughn?" she asked, frowning. "What you need to talk to him for?"

He leaned back into the driver's seat and looked at the car's roof. "You trust me?"

He glanced at her out of the corner of his eye as she leaned over the console and stared at him. The moonlight illuminated her long lashes and hit the high points on her face.

He didn't know when he'd get used to her staring at him like that, but he didn't even want to. Lola would've said they were just in their honeymoon phase, but there was a ripple deep in his stomach that told him life with Venus *was* a honeymoon. Trey just ain't appreciate that shit.

"Shit, I trust you with my life," she finally muttered.

He nodded, biting into his lip and dropping his hand into hers. "And I trust you with mine, so I'm taking your advice and being resourceful where it matters—now come on."

He let go and pushed out of the car.

This night wasn't like the first one they spent together. There weren't any covert looks or reluctant hand holding. This time, she leaned into his side as soon as she stepped out of the car and he tossed his arm over her shoulders.

The bucket bag dangled off her arm, and he stooped down to brush his lips against her ear. "Will you ever stop being so goddamn sexy?"

She smiled up at him as they walked to the line of people that waited outside the building. "Nope."

He laughed at the newfound confidence in her voice. Even in her jeans and plain t-shirt, she looked better than all the other women there. She didn't need a tight Mugler dress or Louboutins to exude sex appeal—it oozed out of her naturally.

He pulled her to the front of the building where the security guards stood around talking to each other. They paused once they noticed her because niggas would have to be blind to not notice the power she held in her "movie outfit."

The biggest one smirked, squirting a line of spit from the side of his mouth. "You missed the line, playboy."

He pulled his arm off Venus and wrapped it around her waist while the dude stared at her but talked to him.

"Nah." He shook his head. "I seen it, but my Unc say I'm straight."

"Your Unc? Who your Unc?"

"Vaughn."

The dude blew a raspberry and fanned his hand. "Vaughn who?"

"The bald-headed nigga that drive that." He pointed to Vaughn's spotless midnight black Rolls Royce that he parked in front of the restaurant when he popped in for operations meetings or to do random shit like the favor he'd done for Lynn.

"Nigga, you don't know no goddamn Vaughn. Gon' on to the line like everybody else."

Anthony nodded, patting his pockets. "Bet."

He felt Venus eyeing him as he pulled his phone out. He

knew her so well that he heard all of her worrisome teacher questions swirling in her head.

"A nigga tried that same trick last week—called his homeboy and had him pretending to be Dough." Him and the other security guard laughed together.

Venus inched closer to him, resting her head against his chest as he unlocked his phone and found Vaughn's name.

She reached up and pressed the "speaker" button. The phone trilled while the security guards fell into a conversation like they weren't there.

"Neph!" Vaughn yelled above the music playing inside. "What's the word?"

Both of the security guards' heads whipped around.

"You said to pull up anytime, so I pulled up. I'm outside Playhouse right now."

"Oh yeah? Come up to the game room."

"Can't. Niggas out here talking about I don't know you. They say I gotta wait in this long ass line—"

"Nah, nah," the burliest one said, inching close to his phone. "It ain't even like that, Vaughn. We ain't know this was your nephew."

Anthony rolled his eyes. "How, when I just stood here and told you?"

"Let him in," Vaughn replied stoically. "He always with me even when he ain't. Remember that shit."

Anthony hung up, and they avoided his gaze.

They waved him over, brushing their hands down his sides and barely grazing him. Afterward, they opened the club's doors while eyeing Venus' ass and forgetting about her little bucket bag that dangled at her side.

Anthony grabbed her hand and pulled her. They wandered through the entrance, walking past the girl collecting the entry fees.

"Hey!" she called out, leaning over the counter. "There's a cover charge. I know they told you at the door."

"Charge it to the game, shawty!" he yelled over his shoulder, tugging Venus.

Inside, they maneuvered through throngs of sections. Juvenile played while he smirked at all the men doing double-takes as Venus walked past them.

That was the other thing about life with her he'd never get used to. She thought the world was his, but it was really hers. He'd have to remind her the next time they made love.

He pulled her in front of him and circled his arms around her waist, guiding her from behind. They ambled the rest of the way —past both bars and up a set of wrought iron stairs.

When they made it to the top, there was another burly dude at the entrance of the game room. He leaned against the door with a toothpick dangling out of his mouth.

As they got closer, he nodded his head. "You Anthony?"

Anthony eyed him, pulling Venus closer to his chest. "Them two fat niggas at the front was giving me problems. You ain't related to them, huh?"

Venus turned to look at him with wide eyes. "*Anthony.*"

The dude smirked, holding his hands up and belting out a loud guffaw. "I don't want no problems. Vaughn said you was coming up here, youngin'. Gon' on inside. He in there waiting for you."

He pressed his back into the door, letting them pass.

They stepped into the room and Venus sucked in a low gasp at the crowd of dudes standing around a pile of money on an empty pool table. They shot dice while cigar smoke floated around in a haze.

Lights danced across her face and he swiped her chin before pressing his lips to her ear. "You okay?"

She nodded and reached for his hand as one dude turned around, spotting them.

"Vaughn!" he shouted over the music, nodding their way.

The group split away from the table and exposed Vaughn, holding an empty glass with his loose tie dangling from his neck.

He had looked the same way the first night Lynn introduced them. He'd bounded toward them with a knowing look as soon as Lynn opened his office door.

"Neph!" he shouted, holding his arms up. "And my favorite woman who cares too damn much."

He walked up to them with liquor leaking from his pores and a smile on his face as he eyed Venus like the rest of the men there had. His look was different, though. There was history there.

He glanced down at her purse and his eyes hardened, but his smile stayed.

"To what do I owe the pleasure?" he asked, pushing his hand out to her first.

She glanced up at Anthony for approval because Trey was still with her, no matter how far they'd come.

He smirked at her reluctance and nodded.

She placed her hand in Vaughn's and after Vaughn let go, he wrapped Anthony under his arm.

"Two visits in one month?" He whistled over the music. "You gettin' tender?"

"I need to talk to you," Anthony replied.

It wasn't what he wanted to say, but that's how shit was when you were in love with a woman like Venus. She made him lame with her comforting nicknames, and tender over her and everything she perceived as important. How could he do this crazy ass shit without her there to remind him he could do anything he wanted?

Vaughn didn't nod in response. Instead, he gave Anthony that same smirk he'd given him when he realized Anthony had memorized the restaurant's menu after only working there for a week.

"Let's go talk then," he said, leading them to an empty room nestled in the back of the game room.

Inside, he pulled them toward a tufted couch. "I'm glad you came. I just got off a flight from Chicago. I wanna get your opinion on something."

They sank onto the couch and Venus scooted into his side like it was their first date again.

Vaughn leaned forward, looking at her. "You out this late on a school night?"

She snaked her arm through Anthony's and rested her chin on his shoulder, nodding. "Ant asked me to come out with him. So I came."

She shrugged, pushing her lips into his shoulder afterward and sliding her hand up the back of his shirt. She dragged her nails across his skin as if she was reminding him she loved him because DeeDee was still stuck to him, too. He needed the reassurance.

"*Ant...*" Vaughn chuckled. "I like that. Women give the best nicknames."

Anthony grabbed her thigh, pulling her closer even though she already lived inside him. She was the reason he'd rolled out of Lola's driveway in a daze, because God had humbled him just like she predicted.

A waitress popped her head inside the door.

"What y'all want to drink?" Vaughn asked. "You want one of those espresso martinis you fell in love with, Venus?"

"Oh, no. We not drinking tonight. I have to be at work later."

"Spoken like a true wife." He laughed as the waitress walked over to them, handing him another glass filled with brown liquor. "They're good for now, sweetheart. Check back in on us later."

She nodded and disappeared as quick as she came, leaving them in the quiet bright room that felt out of place.

"Vaughn's might be headed to Chicago," Vaughn said, taking a sip of his drink. "I had a meeting with a few investors that went well. They wanna try a soft opening if all the chips fall into place, but I'm confident it will."

"Oh yeah? Three restaurants, huh?" Anthony replied.

"Yeah, *three*. I gotta hire staff for two more places. My grandma probably looking down at me now, calling me a 'goddamn fool.'" He leaned back into the couch, sighing. "I ain't worked it all out yet though, neph. All my best front house folks are at midtown—you, Mona, David, Eduardo and lil' Mikayla, but she'll be off to USC soon. I ain't gon' find no more folks like y'all."

He stared straight ahead, tapping his fingers against the glass.

"So what you wanted my opinion on?" Anthony asked.

"You first. You gotta get Venus home. She can't be her best without the proper rest, can she?"

"I'm fi—" she started.

"You right," Anthony cut her off. "I promised I wouldn't have her out long. I need to get her home and put her back to bed."

He swallowed, looking Vaughn straight in his hard brown eyes.

Vaughn nodded. "Take care of your home."

His words sounded too reminiscent of his neighbor's, and it wasn't a coincidence.

"When Lynn brought me to your office, and I told you to interview me, you asked me a question," Anthony said.

Vaughn smirked like he could recall the day as vividly as Anthony could. "Yeah, I did."

The days leading up to their meeting had been a whirlwind —ducking jail calls from DeeDee and threats from her brother for taking his niece, deciphering the legal jargon from Brian's custody petition, learning how to be a single parent, avoiding the judgmental gazes from his niggas because he had the audacity to fight when any other man would've just laid down.

"You asked me if I was living or if I was surviving."

Vaughn nodded, sitting his glass down on the table in front of them. "Yeah...and then you told me you were living. You said that was what you did best—lived, and I said 'okay, will you live long enough to start on Monday?'"

Vaughn leaned forward, reaching for Venus' purse she'd sat

on the table. She reached for it too, but Anthony grabbed her hand, threading their fingers together.

Vaughn lifted it and let the strap dangle from his fingers. "This a gift for me or a guarantee that I won't step out of line again? Because I heard you loud and clear. I can respect that she's yours—ain't no bad blood—only love."

"I would rather have it on me than not."

"I can respect that, too. I would've done the same—men are unpredictable, but I respect you, Anthony. I disrespected you and your woman and you put me in my place. I can hold myself accountable. That's what real men do." He dropped the straps and slid the bag back to Venus. "So, what can I do for you?"

"I need something and you always telling me you good for it."

"Because I am. Just tell me what you need, neph, and it's yours," he urged while Venus scraped her fingers across his back again. "The world is yours—never forget that."

Now he sounded like Venus, and that wasn't a coincidence either, because they were finally existing in the same universe.

"You want me to tell you how you gon' make three restaurants happen in a year. That's what you want my opinion on, right?"

Vaughn nodded.

"You should promote Mona. Bring her up to Chicago with you and then leave me here to run midtown and Sandy Springs. I'll have Eduardo and Mikayla train the staff we hire at Sandy Springs before you and Mona leave and we'll find another sommelier as good as David," he rasped. "I want it. I want that job you keep asking me about... but I need a signing bonus. Mona said it's not common in our industry but you did it for Chef Torrence. She said you only give 'em if the person is worth it."

Vaughn dragged his fingers across his glass. "A signing bonus, huh?"

"Yeah, I got a few loose ends I need to tie up."

He swore he felt Venus holding her breath beside him until Vaughn looked up and smirked.

He drummed his knuckles against the table and twisted his lips, but Anthony wasn't moved by his hesitation. He understood why Venus was, though. Their life together was just starting, but she still hadn't come to terms with the fact that he wasn't Trey.

Finally, Vaughn chuckled, swiping at his lip. "And if I say 'no,' then what?"

Anthony glanced at Venus and then at him. "You ain't the only nigga with restaurants in Atlanta."

Vaughn howled out a laugh, gripping his knees. "Still that cocky asshole even while negotiating, huh?"

Anthony shrugged, smirking.

"Well...I think—nah, I know—you're worth that bag."

Venus exhaled, scraping her fingers against his back again.

Afterward, Vaughn gave him that look he was always running from, but this time, he didn't have the urge to take off and hide. He wanted to stay there and bask in the fact that a millionaire was infatuated with his beautiful brain like Venus had mused.

"So what changed?" Vaughn asked. "What triggered your blossoming?"

"I...I fell in love and decided I ain't wanna survive no more. I got a family to live for."

———

Anthony shoved the club's back door, and they stumbled out into the brisk morning air.

It didn't seem as if they'd been in there for as long as they had because Venus had been wrapped up in Vaughn and Anthony's back and forth. Who knew listening to Anthony discuss restaurant operations would turn her on so much? He still had that same laid back demeanor as when he talked about plating at Vaughn's dining room table. She'd sighed to herself because *she* was the one who would get to listen to Anthony's fascinating musings about the world—not some made up girl in her head.

The sun's rays warmed her face.

She squinted her eyes, trying to adjust to the brightness. "Damn, what time is it?"

He shrugged, pulling her in closer. "I don't know."

There wasn't any panic in her body like the last time they caught the sunrise together, because she'd adopted his relaxed demeanor even if she had to be at work that same day.

She turned around and thrust her arms around his neck, resting her head against his chest. His heart beat in a calm rhythm.

"This is it, right? We took care of everything," she muttered, inhaling him. "It's over?"

"No," he breathed into her ear.

He grabbed her waist and spun her back around, wrapping his arms around her middle. "Look up."

And she did—squinting her eyes up at the sky.

There was the sunrise he had bragged about after their first night together. It sat in a lazy orange haze that made her body melt into his.

She sighed.

Finally.

Her thoughts weren't full of dread and she wasn't calling out to God like Anthony had admonished her for. She was just there, inhaling him, enjoying the sun kissing her face, and smiling at the thought of Tori coming back to school. She wasn't afraid of swimming anymore. Daddy was right all along.

"So, what you want out of life now, Ant?" she asked breathlessly.

"To be happy with you and Munch while I collect that steady, predictable paycheck you always talking about."

445

She giggled in his arms. "Oh, yeah. That slow money?"

He pressed his lips to her ear. "Ain't nothing wrong with that. Slow motion is always better than no motion, remember?"

She sighed again, leaning against him as they rocked back and forth, staring at the sun. "Ain't nothing wrong with it at all. Us grown folks do it every day, baby."

thirty-five

· · ·

THERE WAS nothing opulent about Dr. Brian Torres. He was as basic as his name. He had a medium build, light brown skin, and low cut hair. The only special thing about him was the navy blue suit he donned. It looked as expensive as the Rolex he bought for Deeanna.

He looked straight ahead at Judge Montgomery while leaning back into his seat with a complacent expression, as if he'd already won.

Venus waited for him to look over at Deeanna, but he never did and Mrs. Torres didn't run into the courtroom flustered and late. She was as absent as Brian had been in Tori's life.

"Do you solemnly swear or affirm that the evidence you shall give to the court and jury in the matter now pending before the court shall be the truth, the whole truth, and nothing but the truth? So help you God?" Judge Montgomery asked her with his wrinkled face settling into a soft expression.

Venus gulped. "I do."

She turned from Judge Montgomery and forced her eyes to stay on Brian's plump white-haired lawyer, Ted Barton, instead of veering toward Anthony for reassurance even though she didn't need it. He'd woken her up that morning with his mouth on hers like he always did because he was the early bird out of the two of them.

"Can you state your name for the court?" Ted asked.

"Venus Thibodeaux."

"Ms. Thibodeaux, who are you to Toriana?"

"I'm her teacher."

"And how long have you been Toriana's teacher?"

"For about two months."

He stepped back, giving her a direct view of Anthony, Lynn, and Deeanna sitting behind their table. "Ms. Thibodeaux, have you met Mr. Nunez and Ms. Wheeler before today?"

"Yes."

"In what capacity have you met them?"

"Well—"

"Objection, Your Honor, that's an ambiguous question," Lynn interrupted from her seat next to Anthony's.

"Overruled," Judge Montgomery replied, nodding at Venus. "Keep going."

"Well...I met them as Tori's parents, if that's what you're asking."

Ted nodded. "When did you meet them?"

"I met Mr. Nunez on the second day of school and Ms. Wheeler around the fourth week or so."

"Was there a particular reason you didn't meet Ms. Wheeler until 'the fourth week or so,' as you said?"

Lynn huffed. "Objection, Your Honor. That's a leading question."

"Overruled. Continue, Ms. Thibodeaux."

"I don't know of a particular reason. I just assumed she worked like most of my other parents. It's not uncommon for me to meet parents throughout the first month of school."

She clamped her mouth shut as soon as she finished her sentences because Lynn Jarrett was just like Vaughn described— *a beast in the courtroom.*

"Only answer what you're asked. Don't say more than what's

needed no matter how much you think it'll make him look better," she'd said, sitting back on Anthony's couch and eyeing his hands on Venus' feet. *"Because it won't. You'll just sound partial."*

She hadn't looked surprised when she showed up at Anthony's apartment and Venus answered the door. In fact, Venus swore she'd seemed relieved.

"You said you 'assumed' Ms. Wheeler worked," Ted said. *"Does* she work?"

Lynn huffed, standing up. "Objection. Lack of personal knowledge."

Judge Montgomery nodded. "Sustained."

Venus fiddled with the loose thread on her pencil skirt Anthony had zipped up that morning with his toothbrush hanging out of his mouth. Afterward, he'd circled his arms around her waist and inhaled her until Tori called from Deeanna's phone chirping a mile a minute and garbling out "daddy" every other word because somehow during her first month of kindergarten she'd finally outgrown "Noni."

Venus always faded into the background while they talked because Daddy was right—they had to do what was best for Tori, so they couldn't exist together until she graduated and moved on to her first grade class, no matter how much Anthony disagreed.

Ted laid his hand on the witness stand and caught her eyes. "On Toriana's first progress report, you remarked she needed improvement in reading and speech. Can you tell us your reason for those remarks?"

She curled her toes in the pumps Anthony had watched her slip on while he told Tori he loved her. She avoided Lynn's gaze from her spot between Deeanna and Anthony because Lynn wasn't just a beast in the courtroom—she was a woman first.

She'd sat back against Anthony's couch, pushing her glasses onto her head and narrowing her eyes at Anthony while talking to Venus. *"They subpoenaed the school records, too. I don't have any advice to give about that. Sometimes you have to do what's needed to take care of home—so do it."*

"During the first week of school Tori had difficulty adjusting, as most students do."

Ted cocked his eyebrow up. "You said 'as most students do.' If that's a normal occurrence, then why did you document the concerns and attempt to obtain an evaluation from the school's special education department?"

She stiffened and waited for Lynn to scream out "objection" but Lynn kept quiet this time.

"Well, the NEA's code of ethics says as an educator, I shouldn't suppress or distort subject matter relevant to any student's progress. I did what I would have done for any other student. I documented my observations and concerns and sent a referral to our counselor as that's always the next step regarding any concerns about speech and vocabulary, regardless of my personal feelings on the matter."

Her eyes grazed Anthony's face by mistake and those resurrected butterflies in her stomach fluttered with fervor as his eyes lit behind his glasses. She wanted to kiss him and crawl into his arms.

They were so domesticated they didn't even talk about what she'd say once she stepped on the stand that morning. Her answers flowed out as easy as his "I love you's." They'd even fussed that morning because he wouldn't be still while she pat foundation on that bruise Dre' told him would still be there.

"Can you tell me what occurred after you sent this referral to the counselor?" Ted asked.

"I had a meeting with the counselor."

"What was the basis of this meeting if you already sent a referral? Shouldn't the referral have been sufficient?"

Her stomach tightened as she waited for Lynn again, but Lynn still kept quiet and scribbled on her notepad.

"I wanted advice as to how to approach Mr. Nunez regarding my concerns again because my first time approaching him didn't go well. I knew he'd really be adamant about not agreeing to the evaluation unless I smoothed things over and better addressed my concerns to him."

"What happened when you first approached him?"

"I asked if Tori had an IEP because she hadn't been talking in class. He was offended by my question and told me 'she talks at home.'"

"Did he provide any evidence of this?"

"No."

"And did you believe him?"

"Yes," she replied, straight-faced and stock-still.

"Why is that?"

"He's her father. He knows her the most intimately, and I had only known her for two days. And aside from not talking, she was a perfect student—well groomed, happy, and independent."

She caught the side of Brian's face behind Ted's. It didn't change even though she'd called Anthony "Tori's father."

He didn't even look like Tori and it could've been her projecting again. In her mind, Tori had always been Anthony's, just like he'd convinced her she'd always been his too.

She tried to blink away the images of their reflections in his mirror where he made her forget Trey ever existed.

"You always been mine," he'd utter, thrusting into her in a painstakingly slow way. *"Even before you knew it. God made me just for you. Look at me and tell me I'm right, baby."*

He absolutely was. There was no question about it. It was the reason she could sleep in his bed undisturbed for hours, cook for them with light shoulders, and do what he said when he yanked her by the hair to look at him.

Ted strummed his fingers against the stand. "On Toriana's subsequent progress reports, you marked the need for improvement and a pending evaluation for four weeks. Can you tell the court why you could not obtain that evaluation for those four weeks?"

"Mr. Nunez refused my requests. Unfortunately, I was unable to better address my concerns to him regarding Tori."

"Did he specify why he refused the requests?"

She kept her eyes on Ted's white hair. "Yes, as I told you, he said Tori talked at home and he was also concerned about Tori receiving services she didn't actually need. He was adamant that her speech language development was fine."

"Did he ever provide evidence of this during those four weeks?"

"Again, no, and I didn't ask. That would've been inappropriate regarding such a delicate matter."

A look of annoyance flashed in Ted's eyes and for a moment, she thought he heard the bias in her tone. Lynn told her it'd come out when she least expected it.

"When we talk about people we love, our bodies react unconsciously. Our eyes dilate, our breathing grows shallow, we speak with more passion," she'd said, staring at Anthony's hand in Venus' hair this time. *"You can't turn off being in love—not even on a witness stand."*

She hadn't even told Lynn she loved Anthony, but maybe her body was reacting in that unconscious way Lynn talked about while they sat in his living room. Maybe Lynn felt the heat radiating between their close bodies and smelled their dinner she'd turned off right before she showed up.

Ted's eyes flashed over to Judge Montgomery and then back to her. "Have you ever had any scheduled one-on-one meetings with either Mr. Nunez or Ms. Wheeler?"

"I've met with both of them at different times."

"Regarding?"

She shrugged. "There was a mix up with Tori's transportation forms in the front office the first week of school, so Mr. Nunez and I met about that. We also met about my request for a SPED evaluation and Ms. Wheeler scheduled a separate meeting with me to pick up make-up work for Tori."

"Can you tell us why Tori needed make-up work?"

"She missed about a week of school last month."

"Do you know why?"

"She was sick."

"Do you know if Mr. Nunez and Ms. Wheeler took her to the doctor while she was sick?"

"Yes. Ms. Wheeler brought a doctor's note upon Tori's return to school."

"Are those the only meetings you've had with Mr. Nunez and Ms. Wheeler?"

"Yes."

She glanced over at Deeanna directly for the first time since she'd walked into the courtroom. It was a fleeting glance, but long enough to notice Deeanna's stiff shoulders.

They weren't girlfriends, no matter the kumbaya moment they had in her classroom. Deeanna was simply Tori's mama, and she was Anthony's girlfriend. They only had each other's phone numbers because Anthony ran a tight ship.

She'd learned that him and his friends held some of those archaic beliefs that Rose did so Venus coordinated Tori's pickups and drop-offs between him and Deeanna and fielded Deeanna's random requests for money because that was what she was supposed to do even though Tori didn't know they were a couple. Tash did it with Kemah and if Josiah had a problematic baby mama, Jade would do the same. Deeanna's access to Anthony had been revoked, and Deeanna was still trying to accept that.

The only girly bonding between them were sporadic text messages from Deeanna asking Venus for advice on things she hadn't quite grasped yet—like how to stop Tori's thumb sucking and curb her bed wetting.

"So, how is Toriana doing now?" Ted asked.

"In what capacity?" she replied, shifting in her seat and listening for Lynn's "objection," but it still never came.

"Well, you documented she spent the first month of the school year non-verbal and then you shared she missed a week of school because of an *illness*. That sounds like cause for concern. So, how is she doing now—"

"Objection," Lynn interrupted. "He's mis-characterizing what the witness previously stated."

"Sustained. Restate your question, counsel," Judge Montgomery droned.

Ted let out a quiet huff. "How is Toriana doing in your class as of today?"

"Tori is my only student that knows all of her sight words. She can tie her shoes. She can write her first and last name. She knows how to share with her peers. She uses the bathroom independently. She is kind to herself and others. She can follow directions. With the help of Mr. Nunez and Ms. Wheeler, she is now confident enough to speak in my classroom. Since the school year started, five of her classmates have also been out sick because germs are a common occurrence in kindergarten classrooms. Does that answer your question?"

It grew so quiet in the courtroom that the loud squeaking from Brian sitting forward in his chair made everybody's eyes veer over to him.

She'd ruined it.

She'd let her feelings cloud her judgment and the entire courtroom could probably see how in love she was on her face.

Her heart beat in a loud pounding rhythm that rang through her ears. She avoided Anthony's eyes because she wouldn't be able to take the defeat in them. She'd watched him go right into working eighty-hour weeks for this, get on his knees and pray for this, and threaten to kill men over this and here she went, ruining it.

"I have no further questions, Your Honor," Ted replied, tapping the witness stand one last time before strolling back over to Brian.

"You may step down, Ms. Thibodeaux," Judge Montgomery nodded.

She pushed out of the witness stand and clunked down the steps with everybody's eyes on her.

On her way out of the courtroom, she looked over at Lynn even though she didn't want the reminder of how she'd tanked Anthony's forty thousand dollars, but somehow the light smirk Lynn had on her lips told Venus she didn't think the same.

It was the same "well done" smirk Anthony gave her when she went prancing around, acting like his wife.

———

Vaughn said Anthony was a "family man" now.

He'd said it casually as he strolled into the backdoor of the restaurant with a handful of boxes the night before.

"Venus got herself a family man, huh?" He'd laughed, stroking his eyes across Anthony eating his lunch an hour before closing.

Venus had packed the meatloaf in a Tupperware container she brought from her place and stuck it in a Publix bag she tied at the top.

Anthony had leaned against one of the empty prep stations and nodded. *"Yeah. Maybe one day you'll find you a good woman that'll cook you breakfast, lunch, and dinner. She ain't gon' look as good as mine, though."*

Vaughn had given him the finger in response, because men couldn't turn off their feelings. There would always be that silent competition between them because Venus still made undeserving men feel special. She asked about Vaughn, gave him compliments when they ran into each other, and she remembered random shit like him needing a wreath for his front door.

Even though Vaughn was being a smart-ass, he was right, in a way. Venus had turned Anthony into that family man he never thought he'd live long enough to be, and she'd done it as effortlessly as she'd testified on that stand.

He sucked in a breath as Brian stared down at him from the witness stand with Tori's brown eyes. Venus had just breezed by smelling like home and Anthony wanted to run after her so she could tell him all the shit she liked to tell him between kisses, like "congratulations, you lived for another day, baby" and "I hope you're as happy as you told me you wanted to be. You should only wanna marry a woman that does her best to make you happy like I do."

He stroked the side of his neck where she'd kissed him that morning before they got in separate cars to drive to the court-house for the day-long event.

"Can you tell us about the day Ms. Wheeler told you Tori was your daughter?" Lynn asked Brian.

She didn't waste time with the mundane shit because his lawyer, Ted, had already done that. Judge Montgomery already knew Brian was a filthy rich doctor with three kids, a bored housewife, and an illegitimate child. What more was there to explore besides his affair that had landed him on that witness stand?

Brian cleared his throat and sat forward, adjusting his tie. "I got a phone call from Ms. Wheeler a week after she gave birth, requesting that I take a paternity test because she didn't think her baby was her boyfriend's."

Anthony let out a quiet snort to himself at the way he described DeeDee as if he'd never known her. He cut his eyes over at her in her baby blue dress with her perfect beach waves, laid baby hair, and crossed arms. She didn't even react to Brian's answer.

"Did you ask why she didn't think the baby was for Mr. Nunez?"

"Yes."

"And what was her response?"

"She said she'd been sleeping with the both of us, but she'd been purposely sleeping with her boyfriend on the days she ovulated to make sure if she became pregnant, it would be his. But she said something wasn't right—she said the baby didn't 'feel like his.'"

His breathing grew shallow in that regretful way he'd grown to associate with DeeDee, even though Lynn had warned him.

"You're gonna hear all the things you were never supposed to hear," she'd said, sinking back into his couch, sighing. *"All the things you'll wish you never heard so brace yourself."*

"Did you respond to her claims?" Lynn asked Brian, swiping a piece of hair from her eye.

"Well, yes. I told her women can get pregnant on days they're not ovulating because it happened to my wife and I asked her why she felt the baby wasn't his."

"Her response?"

"She said she kept staring at them in the hospital together and she could tell by the baby's physical features it wasn't his. I asked if he'd noticed too. She said 'no, he's in love with the baby. He named her and signed the birth certificate.'"

Lola was still right about him not being able to understand Munch wasn't his. His heart constricted as Brian sat on the stand talking about shit he had no business talking about—like how in love he was with his Munch.

Brian sounded like every bit of the stranger he was.

Lynn pursed her lips and fiddled with the pen she'd carried to the witness stand. She took long pauses between her questions as if she was letting Brian's answers sink into Judge Montgomery's head.

"Did you ever get the paternity test Ms. Wheeler requested prior to your petition for full custody?"

"No."

"Why is that?"

Brian's shiesty lawyer didn't interrupt, but Lynn said that was a part of the game. Ted would purposely go quiet while she questioned Brian about him and DeeDee to show Judge Montgomery just how unfit they were as Munch's parents. They were young—too young to understand Munch needed stability. DeeDee was a thieving, deceitful mistress, and he was a lowlife criminal that had gone to jail twice throughout his baby's life.

Rae Lyse

"She...she was paranoid he'd find out, so I asked her to see the baby in person."

"*Did* you see the baby in person?"

"No."

"Exactly when did you see the child in person, Dr. Torres?"

"It wasn't until she turned five years old."

"Why didn't you see the baby before then?"

"Ms. Wheeler would go through severe highs and lows—one day she'd be in love with me and the next day she'd be in love with her boyfriend and she'd tell me I'm not allowed to see his baby because he'd kill us both if he found out she had another man around his child."

"During this time, did Mr. Nunez know the baby wasn't his?"

"Yes, she told him in an argument when he tried to break up with her when the baby was a month old. She called me afterwards."

"And did she tell you what that argument was about?"

"He...he had found out about us."

"What had he found out about you and Ms. Wheeler?"

"That...that we had been sleeping together."

Lynn nodded, looking down at her pumps and then back up at him. "Can you tell us about the day you met Toriana Nunez in person?"

Anthony wanted to burst into tears when Lynn finally said Munch's full name because it cemented her existence and made Brian fidget with his tie.

Yes, his baby was real.

Yes, she had his last name.

And yes, she was loved.

"Ms. Wheeler brought her to my condo and introduced us before she left to have drinks with her friends."

Anthony's arm went limp at his side as his body heated.

"What did you and Toriana do while Ms. Wheeler had drinks with her friends?"

"I tried to play with her and watch The Little Mermaid with her like I do with my other five-year-old, but she cried the whole time."

"What was the reason she cried?"

"Objection," Ted cut in. "That's not relevant."

"Overruled. Answer the question, Dr. Torres."

"I asked her why she was crying and...she...she said she missed her daddy and she asked if I could take her to him because he was probably looking for her. She said he didn't like it when her and Ms. Wheeler left without telling him where they were going."

Now, his legs were limp because Munch wasn't even there, but she'd still made her presence known.

"Did Ms. Wheeler tell you the reason they left Mr. Nunez so hastily?"

His eyes veered over to Ted, but Ted still didn't shoot up from his seat to stop Lynn.

Anthony stared at Brian so hard, Brian had no choice but to look over at him while he stammered out an answer. "She...I...we had rekindled our relationship a month prior to her leaving Mr. Nunez. On the day she introduced Tori and I, they had moved into my condo because I told her she could stay there while I figured out how I was going to tell my wife I was leaving her. Ms. Wheeler told me she had to leave hi—Mr. Nunez when he was gone because if he got any idea she was trying to leave, he'd take the baby from her because he didn't trust her."

"Did you petition for full custody of Toriana because you were planning to start a new life with Ms. Wheeler?"

"No."

"So, what exactly was your reason for petitioning for full custody?"

"Things didn't work out between us because I patched things up with my wife, so I asked Ms. Wheeler to leave my condo. A couple of weeks later, I was notified that she'd gotten arrested because she had my credit card on her person at the time of the arrest. I asked the cop that called who she was with when she was arrested and he said 'her daughter,' so I asked if CPS had taken her. The cop told me her father had picked her up."

"And *that* led you to petition for full custody?" Lynn asked, raising her eyebrows.

"Objection, Your Honor," Ted grunted. "Leading."

"Sustained. Restate your question, counsel," Judge Montgomery said, leaning forward as if he wanted to know the reason too.

"Please tell us exactly what led you to petition for full custody, Dr. Torres."

"Well, Ms. Wheeler had been arrested, and I was already privy to Mr. Nunez's prior criminal history from my conversations with her. I talked to my wife, and she said it didn't seem like the child had a stable home life, so I petitioned for full custody."

"Did you agree with your wife?"

He opened his mouth and closed it, sitting up further in his seat. "I mean...yeah...yeah. I did."

Lynn folded her lips under her teeth and nodded. "I have no further questions, Your Honor."

That should've been it, but Lynn said they had to paint the complete picture for Judge Montgomery no matter how ugly it was. So one by one they marched onto that witness stand raising their right hand to God and promising to tell the whole truth— like how DeeDee had never worked a real job because he never required much of her in their relationship. He always took care of home, so she was as bored as Mrs. Torres. Maybe that's why Brian had seemed so enticing that day she met him at the Louis Vuitton store in Lenox while he was buying a Mother's Day gift for his wife.

DeeDee's eyes didn't light up when she talked about the day they met. For a minute, he even thought he heard regret in her voice.

"Can you tell me about your relationship with Mr. Nunez,

Ms. Wheeler?" Lynn asked her softly, resting her forearm against the witness stand.

DeeDee nodded with a little smile. "I think we have a good relationship."

She spoke in that soft voice he used to love.

"Dr. Torres mentioned he was aware that you and Anthony argued in the past. Is that true?"

DeeDee's eyes veered around the courtroom until she finally nodded. "Yes."

"What did you two usually argue about?"

"Mostly about Tori," she uttered, looking down.

He sighed to himself at the vague answers she gave. She was still that wild card who was in love with him, even after he'd gone off and fallen in love with somebody else when he promised her he'd never do that shit.

Lynn drummed her fingers on the witness stand. "Why did you guys argue about Tori?"

She looked up, glancing between him and Brian. "Well, he— Anthony can be very passionate about the people and things he loves—especially his daughter. He's the more authoritative parent, whereas I'm more lax. He's strict about screen time, bedtime, and keeping routines. Tori is also very passionate about him and I struggle with that at times because I want her to think I'm the best, just like she thinks he's the best."

"Have you two ever argued in front of Toriana?"

"Yes."

"Can you tell us about those arguments you had in front of her?"

"They were usually always about the same thing." She looked back down at her lap.

"And that was?"

"Me wanting to leave with her or me keeping her away from him when I got upset."

Lynn nodded. "What did you get upset about, Ms. Wheeler?"

She looked up at the ceiling. "It was usually when he tried to break up with me and see other women, when I tried to leave him, or when he threatened to stop supporting me financially."

"Do you two still have those types of arguments in front of Tori?"

"No."

"Can you tell me what changed?"

DeeDee shrugged. "He's got a girlfriend now and I've accepted that it's okay for him to move on and…and I work now. I can take care of myself."

His shoulders lightened, even though he didn't need her approval to move on. He didn't need anything from her anymore except the help she'd promised.

One by one, they kept getting on the stand—her mama, Lola, and Carlotta. *He* even had to get up there and explain that some of those times he went to jail weren't just because he was surviving—sometimes he was just that dumbass Miguel had taught to be infinite. He didn't choke or stammer over his answers like Brian did, because Venus had taught him not to run from his history.

"Own it," she'd told him one night in bed, stroking her fingers across that scar on his arm. *"Get up there and own it. Michole says it's how you take your power back."*

She was right, but he never expected her to be wrong. She'd been on Earth longer than he had, and experienced things he hadn't yet, and admitting to Judge Montgomery he had a *real* job felt as satisfying as applying a salve to a fresh burn. It made it easier to take that power back.

"I'm the general manager at two restaurants," he droned out to Ted while staring at Brian.

"And what does that entail?"

"Different things. I prep business plans, interview, hire and train all the staff, do payroll and timekeeping, occasionally I talk to media, and I analyze competitors and project the restaurant's future performance."

It had only been two weeks since he stepped into his new

role, but Vaughn didn't believe in coddling. It was the same as the streets.

"A man learns by doing," he'd said, slapping his chest. *"So do."*

And he did.

He worked, paid bills, made love to Venus, and took care of her and Munch like he was supposed to.

"Earlier, Dr. Torres recounted some disturbing claims made by Ms. Wheeler. She said you'd kill her and Dr. Torres if you found out he'd been around Toriana. Is that true?" Ted asked him.

"Objection." Lynn stood up, resting her hands on their table. "Relevance."

"Overruled. Please answer the question, Mr. Nunez," Judge Montgomery asked, wrinkling his face.

Anthony nodded. "It's true."

An uncomfortable silence settled over the courtroom as if they were waiting for him to explain himself, but what more was left to say?

He stared at Ted, waiting for whatever bullshit question he'd follow up with.

Ted's Adam's apple jumped as he swallowed and pat his tie. "Is there a particular reason you threatened to harm your girl-friend and her child's father?"

Anthony snorted, looking Ted in his green eyes. "Because he's a strange man who would've been treated the same as any other strange man if they were left alone with my daughter and as a mother, Ms. Wheeler should know better."

The rest of the questions after that were a blur because they didn't matter. He'd gotten his point across.

One thing that never changed about court was how slowly it moved no matter the reason, though. It wasn't like TV, where the judge banged his gavel and haughtily announced his decision for the entire court room as soon as the final witness finished their testimony. At the end, they stood with solemn expressions as Judge Montgomery drawled that he'd retire to his chamber to review their mountain of evidence, parenting plans, motions, and everything else that had accumulated during their war for Munch.

In the hour he was gone, they meandered around the hallway outside the courtroom. Brian and Ted stayed contained to their end and he, Lynn, and DeeDee stayed on theirs. He sat on one of the hard wooden benches and stared at Venus' texts she'd shot off as soon as she got in her car.

> **Venus:**
>
> Do you want me to lay Tori's school clothes out for the rest of the week?

He smiled to himself at the way she spoke, as if she knew they'd won.

> **Venus:**
>
> I got the money you sent for groceries. What do you want for dinner? I can get an early start since I'm off today.

The bench rocked, and he looked up from his phone at DeeDee sitting next to him. She crossed her legs and leaned into the side of the bench, staring at the wood paneling on the wall in front of them.

"I figured you would've thrown that outfit out by now," she muttered, glancing at his Louboutin loafers she'd picked out.

He kicked his foot out, twisting it from side to side as they studied the shoe. "Why would I do that?"

"Because that's what you do when you fall out of love with people. You get rid of all the things that remind you of them."

He smirked and glanced up at her. "Is that what you did with my shit—all our pictures and bullshit from when we were together?"

She laughed, tilting her head to the side. "No. I gave everything to Tori because I want her to know it wasn't always like this. We weren't always apart."

He started to ask "why," but the clerk flung the courtroom door open and Lynn nodded her head, beckoning them back inside.

He pushed off the bench.

"I'm sorry," DeeDee called out before he could walk off.

He stopped and turned around.

"I'm sorry, Anthony," she said again. "I really am. You were really good to me."

She sounded like a little girl and looked like one too as she stared into his eyes, waiting for his response.

He folded his lips under his teeth and nodded. "Yeah, me too, DeeDee."

Her apology didn't feel as satisfying as he used to think it would, because it was just another thing he didn't need from her anymore.

Inside the courtroom, Judge Montgomery sighed, shuffling the mountain of papers in front of him. "Out of my thirty years as a judge, this hasn't been the most complicated custody case I've had the honor of presiding over, but it has been one of the most interesting. I've reviewed both parties' testimonies, both custody plans presented, and the discovery, and as you all know, my main concern is not the feelings of the adults in this situation. Today is all about Toriana—about her safety, stability and what's in her best interest as a five-year-old little girl."

He picked up the papers and tapped them on his bench before looking at Brian and sighing. "Dr. Torres, I admire your willingness to step up and play an active role in your daughter's life despite the particulars of her conception. I will always advocate for a parent being involved in a child's life."

Next, he looked at Anthony with his eyes squinted in slits and a bead of sweat trickled down Anthony's back, seeping through his white button down. He'd been on the receiving end of that look too many times before and the outcome was never good.

After a painful beat, Judge Montgomery's eyes relaxed and his mouth curved into a tiny smile. "Mr. Nunez and Ms. Wheeler, I understand you're both young...and you're trying. You both have jobs. You've created a good life for Toriana according to the evidence presented and the testimony from the other adults in her life. There's no doubt in my mind she loves you both equally and that you both love her a lot. I could hear it in your voices when you were on the stand and let me tell you, I've come across some lousy parents in my day, but one thing I'll never do is punish parents who're trying."

He sighed, swinging his head between all of them. "Mr. Nunez and Ms. Wheeler will continue to have sole physical and legal custody of Toriana and Dr. Torres will have supervised visitation rights once a month since he's still a stranger in Toriana's life, as Mr. Nunez stated. This agreement can, of course, be modified in the future, but as of now, that is my ruling."

When Munch was old enough to understand, Anthony decided he'd explain it all to her—not just some of it. He'd tell her about the messy things the adults in her life did because of love, survival, and not knowing any better. He'd sit her down and tell her not many things came easy with her because parenthood was hard. It was the hardest thing he'd ever done in his life, and that was okay. But the one thing that *did* come easy with her was keeping her right where she was supposed to be.

~The End~

epilogue

. . .

Eight months later

"DAMN, HE'S SEXY," Ginny leaned over on her barstool, hissing in Venus' ear. "Now I understand why Victor was a 'hell no.' I can't believe you were hiding this work of art from me. *Jesus...*"

The jazz and laughter from the surrounding tables drowned out her last few words, but Venus knew they were lusty. Adele's was crowded, despite them closing early for a private event.

Anthony stood behind the bar, talking to a server. He pushed the sleeves up on his button down and rested a hand on top of the bar. They gawked at him from the other end, and he didn't even know it.

It had taken her eight months to tell Ginny about their love affair because she had to work through another irrational fear with Michole. She couldn't fathom the fact God had given her what she needed and delivered it in the most unexpected package. Michole said it was still that whole "not believing she deserved better," belief sticking around. It was stubborn.

Ginny didn't believe Anthony was real until they waltzed into Adele's without reservations and he greeted Venus like he always did when he was at work—with a moist peck and light tap on the ass. He'd only got to shake Ginny's hand and laugh at one of her silly jokes before somebody pulled him away.

"You're married," Venus replied, elbowing her. "Don't make me call Chris."

"I ain't blind, though. How old did you say he was again?"

"Twenty-four."

Ginny held her chest and choked.

"Yeah..." Venus sighed, tilting her head at the way he chewed his bottom lip when he talked to his staff. "I know."

It had taken a week for the shock to wear off when she found his ID in his jeans while doing laundry one day. She'd lived in blissful ignorance until then—convincing herself he was at least twenty-eight, but no, Anthony was nothing but a "young buck" like Daddy had said when they met over FaceTime.

She squirmed against the stool as he dragged his hand across the top of his hair. She'd watched Zeke cut it the night before and had done that same squirming in the chair on his patio to take the edge off while him and Zeke smoked and talked as if they'd never had that fight in Josiah's backyard that Anthony told her about after they reconciled. Anthony said that was normal, though.

"*Brothers fight and make up just like me and you fight and make up,*" he'd said, shrugging. "*Makes the relationship stronger.*"

"Do you love him?" Ginny blurted out of the blue.

She'd skipped right past the shallow questions they asked when they had new flings, but maybe she saw it on Venus' face, just like Lynn had.

Love?

Sometimes she couldn't go to sleep until she got that word out of her system—especially on those nights where Vaughn kept him occupied into the early morning hours.

"*I'm leaving now,*" he'd mutter into the phone, with Vaughn in the background apologizing.

"*I'm not calling to nag. I...I... just—*"

"I love you too, baby. I'm gonna go pick up Munch and I'll call you when we get home."

She'd lie awake, staring at the ceiling in the bed she'd begged him to let her buy until she got that phone call.

She sighed. "He rubs my feet, pays my bills, sings me R&B, and he's convinced he has some type of super sperm that can get me pregnant. Oh, and he's also my personal mechanic."

She waited for Ginny to choke on her French 75 while side eyeing her, but she sat it down and tilted her head instead. "Does he love you?"

Venus smirked, shrugging. "He says he does—says he wants to marry me. I've never been proposed to so much in my life."

Ginny laughed hard, falling into her side. "Like them proposals you moan out while making love?"

"No." Venus shook her head. "Like them get on two knees in the middle of the kitchen while I'm trying to cook proposals, them 'let me run your bath water and bathe you while I ask you to marry me' proposals. That boy listens to Jodeci, girl."

"When you gon' marry me, baby?" he'd ask with his face smashed between her legs in his kitchen. *"Huh?"*

She shuddered, thinking about how much of a *lover boy* her man was.

Ginny sputtered out a laugh. "Damn, girl. What kinda magical pussy you got?"

She shook her head, catching his eyes in the mirror behind the bar. "It's not even that."

He winked at her, and her face warmed.

"Then what is it? I had to hint at marriage for three years before Chris caught on."

Venus snickered, taking a sip of her espresso martini. "I just love him the way he deserves to be loved, Gin. The sad part is he don't even require much."

He liked to come home to her barefoot in his kitchen with his dinner on the stove. He couldn't fall asleep unless her head was on his chest or her voice was on his phone and he liked to make love—slow, passionate, headboard-knocking love that made her toes curl because he was on a mission to give her those six babies she always wanted. It was so intense, tears welled in her eyes while he sucked her lips into his mouth and wiped them away.

"Do you even wanna get married again? The last time we had this conversation, you made it seem like you wanted to do anything but *that*."

"I also said I wanted a man without kids, too." She laughed, thinking back to that horrendous night at that random dive bar.

"And now look at ya'," Ginny cackled as her face warmed.

Balancing two different worlds was hard. She was careful not to leave any traces of herself at his place when Tori was with Deeanna, but deep in the pit of her stomach, she knew Tori knew. Her Bug was too perceptive. Venus saw the knowing look in her eyes when they talked at school and she doubted Anthony was as careful with hiding them as she was. He'd been counting down the days until the last day of school because he wanted them—no—*needed* them together. They'd made it to the last day, but she was still being a wuss.

"God, I don't know, Gin," she muttered. "He's so delicate, no matter how hard he seems. He loves for a lifetime—not a moment and I have to remember that shit when he's on his knees in front of me begging."

"Shit, that's intens—"

"This seat taken?" a smooth baritone voice belted beside her.

Venus shook her head, pulling her purse from the barstool and paying a fleeting glance to the burly brown skinned man. "Oh, no. Go 'head."

She hung her purse from the hook underneath the bar.

Ginny nudged her in the side like she used to when they were sexy coeds who trolled bars looking for men.

She glanced at the man out of the corner of her eye this time, looking at his bulky forearms and the fraternity symbol branded on his arm, but nothing happened. There were no butterflies, wet panties, or squirming.

"You ladies come here often?" he asked, leaning over so they could hear him above the music.

His cologne emanated off of him in a nauseating way.

Ginny grinned. "Oh, this is my first time, but Venus comes all the time."

She tapped Venus' arm playfully.

"You a food connoisseur, Venus?" he asked, raising his finger to flag down Nolan, the bartender.

She snorted, sitting her drink down. "Not even in the slightest."

"So, what you searching for at Adele's every weekend then?" he asked. "I'm Keith, by the way."

He thrust his hand out.

She hesitated, swiping the wetness from her drink down her black sundress and then briefly shaking his hand. "Nothing at all —just enjoying the ambiance and the view."

Ginny reached over her and shook his hand next. "Ginny."

Venus looked up for Nolan afterward, but as soon as he was almost to their end of the bar, Anthony strolled up to him and stopped him. Nolan's dimples sank into his deep brown cheeks as Anthony leaned into his side, talking into his ear while they locked hands like they were boys and they probably were because everybody at Adele's loved Anthony. His granny Lola always told her it was a hard feat to find anybody that didn't love his ass.

His moist lips moved as her heart sped up and that moisture he kept between her legs settled in the seat of her panties.

Nolan chuckled to himself, glancing at their end of the bar and then pulling away from Anthony. Just as she thought he was going to come their way, he turned around and walked the opposite way, leaving Anthony to stroll toward them.

"Uht oh," Ginny murmured under her breath. "Somebody's in trouble."

She dug her elbow into Ginny's side.

"I guess I get special service tonight," Keith said.

It was more than special service because Anthony never had time to do menial shit like take drink orders at the bar, but there he was with that little mischievous smirk gliding their way.

Anthony eased into the space in front of Keith and reached over the bar.

They casually slapped hands.

Keith eyed him up and down. "This your place, youngin?"

"Nah..." Anthony shook his head, leaning on his forearm. "I'm just a nigga on payroll. What you drinking tonight, boss?"

Keith glanced down at the drink menu while Anthony stared at the top of the black drop waist dress she wore as if he hadn't bought it.

Ginny snickered beside her because she didn't know this wasn't one of those "Trey situations" she was used to. *This* was an Anthony situation.

"Hmm... I'll take an old fashioned and I wanna try those fried green tomatoes," Keith said, still scouring the menu.

"You just missed the kitchen, but I'll have my boy Nolan get that old fashioned out to you."

"What?" Keith smacked his lips. "I thought y'all didn't close until midnight tonight."

"Normally we do, but we got a private event going on."

"Oh yeah? What's happening?"

"Mr. Everything got the rooftop deck occupied, so we closing up early to give him and his folks some privacy."

"Josiah Joseph?" Keith whistled, nodding. "Oh y'all doing it like *that*? Guess I'll have to come back then."

"For sure. Come back anytime and I'll take care of you."

"Bet that."

Anthony's low red eyes fluttered back to her.

He'd been smoking during his break and she already tasted his tongue. It was that time of the night where he was all cerebral and high and she hated that this side of him was one of her favorites. It made her nostalgic and ready to hop in his front seat.

"Ladies?" Anthony called out, nodding toward them. "Big

man say he taking care of y'all tonight because y'all look so beautiful, so what y'all having?"

Keith's mouth twitched like he wanted to object until he caught sight of her chest in that dress Anthony had picked out for her while they browsed Saks on a lazy Sunday afternoon after a lunch date. She'd never even stepped foot in that store before him, but it was one of those "Deeanna things" he couldn't shake.

"This one, baby," he'd called out to her, fingering it with low eyes. *"I wanna see you in this one."*

"Oh, he is?" Ginny spurted out a surprised giggle. "Uh...I don't know. I guess another French 75?"

Anthony furrowed his brows, shaking his head. "A French 75? Nah, pretty girls like y'all drink añejo. Ain't that right, Big Man?"

Ginny's eyes got big because she hadn't learned Anthony and his mental foreplay yet. Her man played the long game.

Keith swiped the back of his neck, nodding.

"Two shots of Clase Azul and one old fashioned. Nolan'll get y'all right." Anthony crooked his index and thumb. "You closing out or keeping the tab open for the ladies?"

Keith waved his hand, digging out a credit card and thrusting it at Anthony. "Keep it open."

He grabbed it and walked off and she wanted him to take her with him and she wasn't even tipsy yet.

Keith chuckled when he walked off. "We call him a slick talker where I'm from."

Venus laughed. "And where's that?"

"Breaux Bridge."

"Oh! We passed through there before." Ginny hooted. "Remember that time in college..."

She finally faced Keith head on while Ginny babbled about that one time in college they drove through Breaux Bridge to get to New Orleans for Mardi Gras.

He smiled at them with stark white teeth that didn't move

her because she was so used to Anthony's sparkling mouth. His smell didn't even give her goosebumps because her man smelled better—and she knew he tasted better too.

She tilted her head at Keith as Nolan appeared with their drinks.

What the fuck was Deeanna ever curious about?

Ginny took her shot from Nolan and leaned into Venus' side again. "I ain't never had añejo tequila. I can feel it in my spirit—I'm about to be tore up."

Venus belted out a loud cackle as they clinked their shots against Keith's old fashioned.

"Cheers to Breaux Bridge, college nostalgia, and sexy restaurant crawlers," Keith uttered, eyeing her chest again.

Venus threw her shot back and reveled in the liquor's smoothness. It tasted too good, and Ginny was *so* right.

Three shots later, her heavy eyes wandered around the dining room that was just full of folks laughing and bopping to the soft jazz playing. The only people left were the staff members Anthony trusted enough to have around their family. They wandered around, cleaning up and finishing up last-minute tasks.

Ginny laughed at another one of Keith's quips.

"I think ole boy sold me a dream. Ain't no Josiah Joseph coming up in here tonight. They just wanted to go home early."

Venus' nipples poked against her dress' thin fabric as soon as she spotted Anthony walking an older couple to the restaurant's entrance. He pushed the door open for them, waving them off into the night.

"You looking for the bartender?" Keith asked her.

Sometime between their second and third shots, he'd turned to face her with his legs splayed open in an "I'm ready for you," way.

She waved her hand, knowing Anthony had shooed Nolan away to take a break before folks started showing up and running him crazy. "Oh nah. I...I don't think I need another one."

Her tongue was already heavy enough.

"Aw, come on." Ginny whined. "You know Chris'll be blowing me up soon."

Keith chuckled, glancing at her wedding band. "I'm gonna assume Chris is the husband."

"God *yes*," Ginny blubbered out. "Love him to death, but Mama needs a break from Daddy."

Keith snorted, eyeing Venus' bare legs this time. "What about you, Venus? You running from Daddy, too?"

Her tipsy stomach fluttered and she let out a sloppy giggle at the perfect time. Anthony strolled back behind the bar, bumping fists with Keith on the way and watching his "sexy ass nostalgic wife" laugh.

"Oh, you got the ladies laughing, big man?" he asked, swiping up the check a server had left lying next to Ginny. "What I miss?"

Their eyes met for a brief second before Anthony pulled away, but she was tired of playing and pretending to be curious, so she kept staring at the side of his face. She was drunk on a Saturday night after watching him run a whole restaurant.

Shit, she *needed* him.

She gurgled out a hiccup and swiped a purple curl out of her eye as her giggle simmered into a slight smirk. "Keith wants to know if I'm running from you."

Keith's eyes grew at her bold words until she remembered he didn't know she belonged to Anthony or that the drinks and laughter they shared didn't mean anything, because Anthony liked to tease other men with her presence sometimes. He liked to dangle her in their faces in a "you'll never get her" type of way because she was obsessed with him—with his mind, his body, his face, and his dick. Keith was just a plaything. He was something to entertain her and Ginny while Anthony worked.

Anthony reached across the bar, fingering the top of her dress and pulling it up because it'd slipped down throughout the night as she drank and laughed.

Afterward, he looked over at Keith. "She used to run from me. Not no more, though. What's that old saying—spare the rod, spoil the child? Yeah…I don't do no sparing at home."

Ginny sucked in a breath beside her and her middle thumped as if they didn't have the rest of the night to get through.

She could corner him in his office, in the kitchen, or out back when he snuck off to take another breather. There were *so* many possibilities all those shots made her mind conjure up.

He smirked, looking back at her and letting go of her dress. "Your baby outside waiting for you. I saw DeeDee pull up on the cameras. Go get her and bring her upstairs. I'll be up there after I order Ginny's Uber and close Keith's tab."

She gave Ginny an apologetic smile and slid off the barstool. "Sorry, cousin. We're getting cut off."

Ginny scoffed. "Yeah, for a good ass reason. Please go fuck that man like he deserves."

They howled out loud laughs and embraced each other while Keith stared.

She pulled away from Ginny and turned to him. "Than—"

"'Preciate you keeping my lady and her cousin company tonight," Anthony cut in, flipping through the check he'd picked up and then walking off.

The old her would've felt bad for using Keith, but *V* would never feel bad for a man because she was that "fly ass bitch" with the world in her hands, like Anthony always said.

She gave Keith a delicate wave and grabbed her purse off the hook underneath the bar. He smirked instead of waving back, and she saw in his eyes that he had the same belief Anthony did.

She smiled, trekking out of the side door of the restaurant, past the security that ambled outside and into the parking lot where Deeanna waited in her black baby Benz. The light from her phone illuminated her face as she tapped on its screen.

Venus sighed to herself while she glided across the parking

lot in a steady stride, being careful not to let all the tequila she'd drank catch up to her.

When she got closer to the car, Deeanna eyed her from the driver's seat. She didn't bother rolling down the window—she just hit the locks.

Venus walked to the back passenger door and flung it open without hesitation.

"Bug..." she muttered, stooping down to cover Tori in her car seat.

"Ms. T," Tori croaked out in a throaty whisper as she stretched and yawned. "I knew it!"

She was dressed for the occasion in an all-black sundress and little sparkly sandals. She smelled as sweet as she always looked.

Venus chuckled. "You knew what?"

"Daddy said he had a surprise for me. I knew it was you."

Venus stroked her cheek and wiped the little trail of drool from her lip. "Oh yeah? How'd you know it was me?"

She wrapped her arms around Venus' neck like she'd done on the last day of school the week before. "Because I been asking for you and he said he'd see what he could do. That means 'yes.'"

Venus still hadn't gotten used to her little babbling. She and Treshawn were neck and neck for who chatted the most in class.

"Hi, Deeanna," she muttered, kissing Tori's cheek.

"Cute dress," Deeanna replied, tapping on her phone.

"Thanks." Venus unbuckled the seatbelt that held Tori in her booster. "Go give Mama a kiss."

It was the first time she'd been there in the flesh to see her pick up and drop off coordinating through, but it didn't feel that way. It felt just like it had when she and Anthony made love for the first time—like they'd done it a million times before.

Tori crawled out of the seat and over the middle console.

She planted a kiss on Deeanna's cheek. "I'll be back on Monday. Call me on Ms. T's phone when you miss me, okay?"

Deeanna nodded, pushing her face into Tori's. Eight months

later, they still looked like sisters and Tori still treated her like a delicate flower that needed nurturing.

"I love you lots," Tori added.

They had their own language that Venus caught bits and pieces of when she heard them talking in the background of Tori's calls with Anthony.

"I love you more."

Tori pat her cheek and then hurried back into the backseat. She climbed out of the car and wrapped her arms around Venus' middle.

Venus reached out to push the door closed, but stopped when she caught Deeanna's eyes in the sideview mirror.

"Venus?" Deeanna called out.

Her hand hung on the doorframe. "Yeah?"

"Thank you."

Venus nodded and smiled down at Tori. "No problem, *DeeDee*. I'll talk to you later."

———

The city's lights sparkled around Adele's rooftop terrace. Venus talked in hushed whispers to Munch while she twirled her in circles to the soft jazz the band played while they waited.

Vaughn's florist had taken her time throughout the day, exchanging the restaurant's standard flowers and plants with flowers that were more appropriate for the occasion. Anthony had the event staff take all the chairs and tables away and replace them with cozy chaises and a pergola.

It had turned out just like Venus envisioned because she was always doing all the wife and motherly shit she wasn't supposed to do without a ring.

"*It has to be romantic, Ant,*" she'd said. "*We'll all wear black and her and Journey should wear white because they're the guests of honor.*"

Josiah had thrown the suggestion out to her while she listened in on one of their phone calls.

"Can you plan it, sis?" he'd asked Venus in that innocent way women loved. *"Tell Nuney to let me borrow you for a few weeks. I'll give you right back."*

Anthony smiled as she squatted to hug Munch when Logan walked up to them. Logan high-fived Munch and tugged one of Venus' wild curls. They all laughed together. Desmond walked up behind Logan, wrapping his arm around her shoulder and waving at Munch.

Nolan hung out behind the bar, talking to Jade's mama Terry and Josiah's mama Diane. He poured a martini and handed it to Terry. Zeke hung against the wrought iron that encased the patio, letting Kristen brush the back of his black t-shirt.

Everybody had arrived on time for once, but Tash said only because she'd threatened them. She said she'd be damned if anybody ruined her best friend's night. She waltzed around the terrace with Dre' and Audriana, pointing out all the stuff she'd helped Venus pick out.

Josiah sidled up next to Anthony and hooked his arm around his shoulder. "This love shit ain't such a dumbass feeling, huh?"

Anthony elbowed him in his chest. "You ain't gon' let that shit go, huh?"

"Never. I'm gon' be at y'alls wedding talking about that one time yo' ass was scared of falling in love again like a lil' bitch."

Their heads fell together, and they laughed hard.

Josiah's mind had finally accepted forever, just like Anthony's heart had. Anthony wanted nothing more than to watch Venus do the same boring ass shit day in and day out. Who knew watching her sip coffee and talk on the phone to Ginny would make his dick hard, but it did. In fact, he'd decided that his sole purpose was to make sure she only had time to worry about boring ass shit like laundry, cooking, and gossiping on the phone.

Josiah rested his weight on him as Dominic and Clo' walked

over to Logan, Venus, Mo and Munch with their kids in tow. Clo' still looked eighteen with big hair and supple brown skin despite having two kids and Dominic looked the same yet different. Money and life experiences had made him less guarded. He was inching closer and closer to that Drake status Anthony joked about.

"You call and check on my sister and niece?" Anthony asked Josiah.

"Yeah, they leaving the car with the valet now," he replied.

"Then you need to be up there waiting." Anthony pointed toward the archway Venus picked out.

He felt Josiah suck in a deep breath.

It made Anthony reach up and mush the side of his head. "You got this shit, twin. Forever is an amazing feeling when you spend it with the love of your life."

Josiah nodded before making a beeline to the archway with a determined look on his face. When he made it to the middle of it, Anthony hooked his fingers in his mouth, letting out a loud whistle. Everybody immediately understood, and let out their own whoops and claps, giving Josiah their own stamps of approval while he smiled up at the archway.

The florist had intertwined thistle and plume and Venus had laid white candles around it. There were no cheeky signs to hint at the occasion because she thought those were corny.

"Josiah being on one knee is the epitome of romance," she'd said, shoveling a forkful of grits into her mouth in his office. *"Ain't no corny sign gonna top that."*

The weeks leading up to this night were painful for him, but seemed cathartic to her. She told him her therapist said he might've been internalizing her trauma. She called it vicarious trauma.

Maybe that's why he suddenly felt there was a timer attached to their lives. He wanted to hurry and fix all the shit Trey had ruined—like his lackluster proposal to Venus on his hateful mama's porch, their hasty courthouse wedding, and all the years she spent unhappy, but she assured him there was time.

"I'm not going anywhere," she'd promise him when that panicky feeling would make him fall to his knees in front of her. *"Take your time and enjoy me. I don't want you to regret anything. Remember how you taught me to slow down and be grateful for every day? I'm listening and doing that."*

It only quelled his worries temporarily, though.

They caught eyes right as Munch wrapped her arms around her middle like she always did.

He crooked his finger for them to come to him. She sent Munch first, pointing and mouthing in her ear. He could hear her even though he wasn't close by because she said the same words when he'd keep Munch off the bus and pick her up early from school just to see them together.

"There's, Daddy," she'd say, nudging Munch forward.

This time was the same.

Munch took off and ran into his legs, letting out a squeal.

He stooped down, reveling in the kisses she gave his face. "I guessed what my surprise was!"

He chuckled, glancing up at Venus as she smiled at Desmond before backing away and gliding toward them. "Duh. I knew you would. You the smartest, remember?"

She nodded, grinning.

When Venus got to them, he didn't wait for her to reach for him. He grabbed her and pulled her into his arms. They settled in a comfortable stance, with Munch in front of them.

Everybody hung around in groups, talking like normal, until JuJu, the hostess, pushed open the door to the terrace, leading Jade and Journey outside in their white dresses.

Jade's mind was in other places because she waltzed right past Tash with her head buried in her phone as if it was another normal night of meeting Josiah for dinner. Anthony had been the one to convince her to come, promising privacy and time with him because she'd complained she hardly got to see him anymore.

"You got a new job and forgot about us, Nuney." She'd whined. *"Now who's supposed to be my Spades partner on game night? Jo doesn't know our secret signals and Dre' is an honest Abe, ugh."*

Journey was the first to get an inkling that something was off. She caught eyes with Dominic and grinned as he held his finger to his lips to keep her quiet. She nodded, slapping her hands over her mouth and staring around at everybody with big eyes.

Josiah said she'd been waiting on this moment longer than he and Jade had because at her new private school, "everybody's mama and daddy was married." Josiah said he told her she didn't need to worry about what everybody else was doing, but deep down, that shit fucked with his head.

Venus giggled, sinking back into Anthony's chest with her arms on Munch's shoulders.

Josiah was already on one knee with the ring thrust in front of him, like Venus had told him to do.

Jade didn't look up until JuJu led them right to the archway where her forever waited. She yelped and her phone slipped out of her hands.

"Jo..." she garbled out, covering her face. "Baby. Why didn't you say something?"

He smacked his lips. "C'mon. That would've ruined the surprise, Stink."

They all laughed.

Journey ran into his chest like she always did and twirled around in his arms to face Jade like she was asking Jade to say, "yes," too.

"Jade..." Josiah started. "I know th—"

"Shut up," she cut him off, waving her hand. "Yes! Yes! Yes! You don't need to give me a speech to convince me to do *anything*, Jo. Me and your baby will find a freaking spaceship to get to Mars to be with you, and you know that."

They laughed again as Jade flung her long locs out of her face and bounced on her toes like a little girl. Josiah grinned and shot up with Journey dangling from his arms, shoving the ring on her finger.

Venus sniffled, swiping at her eyes.

Anthony pushed his face into her neck, planting kisses on her hot skin and stopping at her ear.

"I passed the objective, right?" he whispered, kissing the shell of her ear and nudging her hand away to wipe her eyes. "I helped Venus Thibodeaux conquer her fear of love."

She smiled up at him, grabbing the back of his head as fireworks shot into the night sky. "Oh, Ant...I stopped being afraid of that the moment I laid eyes on you. It just took my brain some time to catch up."

about the author

Rae Lyse hails from Southeast Texas. Armed with a profound love for social work and romance, she masterfully weaves the two together, crafting captivating love stories that delve into the complexities of everyday people. Her signature style lies in the slow-burning nature of her stories which allows readers to savor the intricate development of the relationships between her characters. To date, she has penned five highly rated black romances which are all available on Amazon and Audible.com.

acknowledgments

My beta tribe (Ayanna, Terra, Allegra, Mie, and Genel): Thank you for your flexibility, honesty and commitment to my growth as an author. I could go on and on, but seriously, thank you for all that you do and the respectful way you do it.

Jenine Corneal: As always, thank you for your flexibility, patience, and hilarious feedback.

Shaun Chadwick: I'm still going.

Husband: Thank you for having such a beautiful brain—I don't wanna do life with nobody else but your crazy ass. YES, I will marry you—over and over and over and over again.

Erica Holland: First, thanks for being such an amazing human being. Second, thanks for being an equally amazing friend. I can't wait to laugh about our "meet cute" when we're old ladies. Thank you for blindly supporting this project and being my writing buddy.

Jade Olivia: Thanks for always being the sweetest! I'm so proud of you. Thank you for allowing me to be your kindred spirit in this weird author world, lol.

Kena: As always, thank you for sharing your time, space and

energy with me. I wouldn't wanna yap on the phone for hours with anybody else. I'm so proud of you too!

Papa: I don't need nothing—just missing your late-night phone calls and fussing with Granny because you're "wondering what Rae Rae's doing." Thank you for always reminding me I'm still your little girl, even at my big ole age, but most importantly, thank you for letting me be there until the end. I told you I'd come back home.

also by rae lyse

the sun series

Saving Sunflower (The Sun Series Book 1)

The Endgame (The Sun Series Book 2)

Bunny (The Sun Series Book 3)

Thirty (A Sun Series Bonus Story)

standalone

At the End of It All

www.ingramcontent.com/pod-product-compliance
Lightning Source LLC
Chambersburg PA
CBHW031025030726
47497CB00004B/1003